RITE

RITE

Short Work

Tad Williams

FAR TERRITORIES 2008

First Trade Paperback Edition

ISBN
978-1-59606-164-4

Far Territories
PO Box 190106
Burton, MI 48519

www.far-territories.com

TABLE OF CONTENTS

Why I Write What I Write

WHY I WRITE THINGS LIKE "WHY I WRITE WHAT I WRITE" (AND WHY I WROTE THE OTHER THINGS IN *RITE*) RIGHT?

Okay, first of all, I must admit to being an absolute sucker for words and for people who use them in an interesting way—Groucho Marx, Shakespeare, Bob Dylan, Gracie Allen, James Joyce, Manuel the Spanish waiter on "Fawlty Towers." I love active, playful use of language. Many of my early literary crushes were on writers who really enjoyed creative wordplay—you couldn't read Ray Bradbury or Anthony Burgess or Theodore Sturgeon without recognizing that somebody was having fun as well as telling a story.

So it seemed fairly obvious that someone like me, if he ever became a writer, was going to have a soft spot for words. More than that, I appreciated diversity not just of language but of interests. Most of my favorite writers were all over the shop, writing whatever caught their attention at any given moment, naturalistic, fantastic, fiction, non-fiction. When I fell for Harlan Ellison as a young reader, it wasn't just his stories that excited me, it was his non-fiction, too, his rants against things he loathed as well as his support of what he thought was righteous. But it was the richness of his expression that really grabbed me. Similarly, when I discovered and fell in love with Hunter S. Thompson, it was the way he reached for whatever tools would do the job: if you couldn't describe what a horror of a president Richard Nixon was by using ordinary journalistic means, then you had to resort to talking about monstrous shapes, all hair and bleeding string-warts, loping across the White House lawns by night.

What does all that add up to? Language—I love the stuff like a fat man loves butter. Diversity—wanting to do and use anything that might help make the impression you want on an audience. I'm in favor of that too, you betcha. Oh, and a wide (if slightly shallow) appreciation of lots of different subjects of interest. You name it, I'm probably interested in it, or willing to be for at least long enough to work it into a story. So you roll all that together and that's the kind of writer I've always wanted to be, and have largely been.

Another factor that has affected the contents of this anthology is that I've largely been a writer of very, very long novels. This isn't by choice, necessarily, but since it's how I sustain my career, it means that short fiction has always had to take second place—it has to happen when I'm not in the middle of something crucial on a novel. Also, because I feel guilty about stealing time from the books I've already been paid to write, I seldom write short stories without some precipitating cause, which is generally of the anthological persuasion—in other words, some editor gets hold of me, says "We're doing this great anthology, So-and-So's writing a story for it, and So-and-So, and the concept is really cool, and we'd love to get a story from you." And if something clicks—usually the first glimmer of an idea—then I'll say yes.

Thus, more than half the stories here were generated because of anthologies or other solicitations. ("Hey, big boy—you interested in deploying a little short fiction?") I'd like to write more of these, but novels take a lot of time, so in the near future I'm probably going to keep averaging only one or two of these per year.

The pull never goes away, though: one of the things that I love about short fiction is it enables me to use a greater part of my range, such as a wider span of subject matter and a greater emphasis on humor, just to name two. I *love* being funny, or at least trying to be, and it's always been a huge part of my creative persona, but it's hard to write a million word, multi-volume story that primarily goes for laughs, so my sense of humor plays a more confined role in my novel-writing. Anyway, I hope that those of you who only know my long works will appreciate getting to see what I think is a fuller example than usual of what I actually *do*.

Tad Williams
Woodside, California
March 20, 2006.

P.S. As far as this first piece, *Why I Write What I Write*, I'll be brutally honest: I don't remember why I wrote it or where it appeared, but it's a pretty good short summation (albeit silly in places) of my *raison d'ecrire*. All I remember for certain about its origin is that I thought about making it purposely over-dramatic, like one of those heroic wartime short films—"*Why We Fight!*"—but then I stepped in some honesty and changed plans.

See, I can remember *that*, I just can't remember where it appeared. I hope that means I'm not technically senile. The disturbing thing is, someone will read this and say, "Hey, he wrote that for that program booklet they passed out at SomethingCon!" or "He did that for our website," following that recognition with the thought, "and he doesn't even remember. But he's putting it in this book anyway. What an idiot."

It's sad when other people have to help you remember your own life. Unless they're researchers, and you've hired them with the big fat bonus you got for your autobiography.

Sadly, though, here I'm just an idiot.

Why I Write What I Write

One of the most common questions I hear, especially from normal people, is, "Why do you write science fiction?" This query usually doesn't come until we've spent some time together, me and the normal people, and follows closely on the finalization of a judgement (which they usually politely keep to themselves) that I seem almost like a normal person.

The question usually comes in one of two ways. The first is something like what any of you might wonder (and perhaps even blurt out in an indecorous moment) if you discovered on your doorstep the valedictorian of your graduating class from ten years before, spray bottle and rag in hand, attempting to sell you a miracle cleaning fluid that can be used on any household stain—a question which presupposes a long history of interestingly bad choices, and which is phrased, roughly, "Well! And how did you come to be doing this?"

The other version of the question, offered in a slightly more nervous manner, is "When did you know you were a science-fiction writer?", and seems to have at its roots the idea that science fiction is something that simply grew on me, like Quasimodo's hump, a misfortune that might (for reasons not completely understood by contemporary medicine) happen to almost anyone, but which could be prevented if treated in a timely fashion.

I'm here today to tell you not to worry. Most cases of science fiction are not random, and seldom strike the innocent. Some of us even choose our own grim fates: I have personally pursued this career path with the dignified but flinty-eyed focus of a Catholic bishop with his eye set on a red cardinal's hat.

Actually, that's another fabrication, but I liked the way it sounded.

The truth is that, for a writer, trying to say why exactly you write what you write is a little like explaining why you married the person you married—*any* of the persons you married. Had I been led by my life to do anything else, I would have been a different Tad Williams than I am now. This would be tough on me, confusing to my family, and extremely frustrating for the Internal Revenue Service, which is already somewhat out of sorts about my declaring myself legally dead a few years ago.

All right, that's not true either. And here we have a first clue to the real reasons that people like me write what we write. I enjoy using my imagination. In a harsher age, the term "congenital liar" might have been tossed around, but in today's more forgiving society, I can call myself an "entertainment professional" and hold my head high.

The fact is, *all* writers are fantasists and liars. Writers of fiction are just a bit more open about it, and writers of science fiction and fantasy are pretty much all the way over at the AA-meeting end of the spectrum—we'll stand up and proclaim our problems in public. "Hello, my name is Tad and I don't approve of reality as it's presently constituted."

In fact, an argument could be made that one superiority of my own particular genre is that everyone knows we're lying. Even the most doggedly imaginative reader cannot truly believe that what happens in one of my books is going to happen to him or her. The other genres of fiction are so jam-packed these days with authors trying to find and exploit a niche that virtually every reader can specialize, almost to the point of reading personalized fiction. Are you a lesbian postal worker, interested in crime? Well, meet Tuesday Malone, mail carrier, organizer for gay and transgender rights, and part-time detective, in "Death has Two Mommies." Are you a middle-aged, left-handed accountant looking for a thrill? Well, little did 55-year-old Nemo Sanderson know that the double-entry books he was keeping belonged to an international terrorist organization: now he's being pursued by Hezbollah and the CIA in "Code Name: Southpaw." Even a reader of the most extreme and flowery romance fiction, the kind where the heroine is swept up and carried away by a titled nobleman on a polo pony, can now, thanks to the genre's recent modernizing of heroine types, imagine herself as the star of the story, even if she's a bit more likely in real life to wind up with a guy named Duke who drives a Bronco.

At least the people who read the kind of books I write are unlikely to pretend that they might actually ever have to fight a dragon with a pocketknife, or turn back an invasion of cannibal amoebas from the Oort Cluster by whipping up a quick laser using only a flashlight, pocket lint, and a slice of processed cheese. No, if you can truly make yourself believe in the kind of plots people like me create, you have problems a lot bigger and scarier than those cannibal amoebas.

But the honesty of our dishonesty is not the only thing that makes me go warm and fuzzy all over when someone points at me (often in a police lineup) and says, "Hey, isn't that a prominent science fiction writer?" I mean, don't get me wrong, it's not like we don't have anything else to offer.

Fiction, especially genre fiction, has always walked an uneasy, meandering path between elucidation, epiphany, and mere escapism, but if we in science fiction provide the latter more often than either of the former, it's not for lack of trying. Well, not for *some* of us it isn't. I do know writers in my field who actually say things like, "Wow, I was just sitting there, and I thought, you know, wouldn't it be cool if the dragon was a vampire, too!", but every family has its embarrassing cousins and its dirty linen. (For instance, very few literary writers care to be reminded that John Updike's first two books were a western shoot-em-up entitled "Ride, Rabbit, Ride," and a failed monster novel, "The Giant Radioactive White-Tailed Deer that Ate Large Sections of New Haven.")

If I may be permitted to set aside this ponderous seriousness for a moment, I'd like to return to that key question: *Why do people like me write this kind of stuff?* Failed social conditioning is a tempting but insufficient explanation. The truth is, we write it because we like it. We write it because sometime in our lives, usually when we were young, it caught us. Whether it was the endless imagined vistas of Tolkien's Middle Earth, or the seductive humanity-is-the-measure-of-the-universe dogmas of someone like Robert Heinlein, or the exuberant fantasy of Ray Bradbury's purely imaginary heartland America, it got its hooks into us. When we found that we too were storytellers, or at least aspired to be, we decided that we wanted to imitate—and perhaps by doing so, to honor—those who had given us glimpses of things bigger than ourselves. And as we became more serious about our craft, and began to hear those "Why do you write that stuff?" questions—oftentimes meant as a sort of compliment, the implication being, "You could do better than that,"—we may briefly have considered ditching the old genre, like a drunk waking up painfully sober one day to discover that while on a bender he has married a cocktail waitress with a kid almost as old as he is. But almost all of us eventually realize that science fiction is more than an embarrassment, although as with any genre, our particular artform definitely has its oops-danced-naked-wearing-a-lampshade moments. But there are no free rides for *any* adherents of the muse. Many of you will remember that it took the world of poetry years to recover from Wallace Stevens' "13 Ways of Belching Like A Stevedore," although I hear that the form is doing nicely again these days. Because it's not about the genre, of course—it's not about any genre—it's about what you do with it.

So what's my final answer? Why do I write science fiction? Because I can. Because I want to. Because I love it. Because they pay me.

No, because I love it.

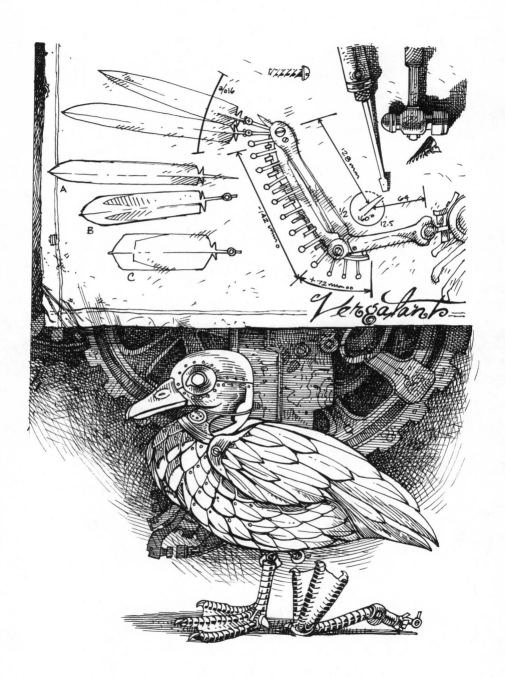

Monsieur Vergalant's Canard

With a story this brief, it wouldn't do to talk too long about it.

It's loosely based on a real and, at the time, very famous histori-cal object (that did indeed, as hinted at here, seem both to eat and eliminate) created by a Monsieur Vaucanson in the 18th Century, albeit with a more conventional inner mechanism. It might also help readers to know that "canard" is both the French word for a duck and also means a trick or a falsehood. Also, the name "Vergalant" is a bit of a joke, too, since it was the nickname of a French king, and meant (putting it fairly politely), "always ready for some."

This is one of the few stories I've ever submitted to any of the better-known magazines in our field, let alone sold (in this case, to *The Magazine of Science Fiction and Fantasy* when Kris Rusch was there).

I think I'd been happily reading Roald Dahl's short, non-kid-lit fiction around the time I wrote this. It certainly reads a bit Dahl-ishly to me now...

He placed the burnished rosewood box on the table and then went to all the windows in turn, pulling the drapes together, tugging at the edges to make sure no gaps remained. After he had started a fire and set the kettle on the blackened stove, he returned to the table. He opened the box and paused, a smile flickering across his face. The contents of the box gleamed in the candlelight.

"It was a triumph, Henri," he said loudly. "All Paris will be talking about it tomorrow. The best yet. I wish you could have seen their faces—they were amazed!"

"You are quite a showman," his brother called back, his voice muf-fled by the intervening wall. "And the pretty Comtesse? The one I saw the painting of?"

Gerard laughed, a deliberately casual sound. "Ah, yes, the Comtesse de Buise. Her eyes were as wide as a little girl's. She loved it so much, she wanted to take it home with her and keep it as a pet." He laughed again. "So beautiful, that one, and so likely to be disappointed—at least in this." He reached into the box and teased free the velvet ties. "No one will ever make a pet of my wonderful *canard.*"

With the care of a priest handling the sacrament, Gerard Vergalant lifted out the gilded metal duck and set it upright on the table. Eyes narrowed, he took his kerchief from the pocket of his well-cut but ever so slightly threadbare coat and dusted the duck's feathers and buffed its gleaming bill. He paid particular attention to polishing the glass eyes, which seemed almost more real than those of a living bird. The duck was indeed a magnificent thing, a little smaller than life-size, shaped with an intricacy of detail that made every golden feather a sculpture unto itself.

The teapot chuffed faintly. Vergalant repocketed his kerchief and went to it.

"Indeed, you should have seen them, Henri," he called. "Old Guineau, the Marquis, he was most dismissive at first—the doddering fool. 'In my youth, I saw the bronze nightingales of Constantinople,' he says, and waves his hand in that if-you-must-bore-me way he has. Hah! In his youth he watched them build the Hanging Gardens of Babylon. Doddering fool."

He poured the water into a teacup with a small chip in the handle, then a little more in a bowl which he set on the table.

"The old bastard went on and on, telling everyone about clockwork movement, how the Emperor's nightingales would lift their wings up and down and swivel their heads. But when my duck walked, they all sat up." He grinned at the memory of triumph. "None of them expected it to look so real! When it swam, one of the ladies became faint and had to be taken out into the garden. And when it devoured the pile of oats I set on the table before it, even Guineau could not keep the astonishment from his face!"

"I am always sorry I cannot see your performances, Gerard," his brother called, straining slightly to make himself heard. "I am sure that you were very elegant and clever. You always are."

"It's true that no matter how splendid the object is," Vergalant said thoughtfully, "it is always more respected when presented in an attractive manner. Especially by the ladies. They do not like their entertainment rough." He paused. "The Comtesse de Buise, for instance. There is a woman of beauty *and* pretty sentiment…"

The duck's head rotated slightly and the bill opened. There was a near-silent ticking of small gears and the flat gilded feet took a juddering step, then another.

"If you please." Henri was apologetic.

"Oh, my brother, I am so sorry," Gerard replied, but his tone was still distant, as though he resented having his memories of the countess sullied by mundane things. He went to the table and fumbled at the duck's neck for a moment, then found the catch and clicked it. "The tail seems to move a little slowly," he said. "Several times tonight I thought I saw it moving out of step with the legs."

The head and neck vibrated for a moment, then the entire upper structure tipped sideways on its hinge. Glassy-eyed, the shining duck head lolled as though its neck had been chopped through with an axe.

"If it was my fault, I apologize, Gerard. I do my best, but this duck, it is a very complicated piece of work. More stops than an organ, and every little bit crafted like the world's costliest pocketwatch. It is hard to make something that is both beautiful and life-like."

Vergalant nodded emphatically. "True. Only the good Lord can be credited with consistency in that area." He caught a glimpse of himself in the mirror and seemed to like what he saw, for he repeated the head movement with careful gravity. "And the Lord achieved that with the Comtesse de Buise. She has such lovely eyes, Henri. Like deep wells. A man could drown in them. You should have seen her."

"I wish I had." The gilded duck shuddered again, ever so slightly, and then a tiny head appeared in the hollow of the throat. Although it was only a little larger than the ball of Gerard Vergalant's thumb, the resemblance between their two faces was notable. "But I cannot make a seeing-glass that will allow me to look out properly without interfering with the articulation of the throat," said the little head. Hair was plastered against its forehead in minute ringlets. "One cannot have everything."

"Still," Gerard replied with magnificent condescension, "you have done wonderfully well. I could never hope to make such an impression without you."

The rest of the tiny figure emerged, clothed in sweat-stained garments of gray felt. The little man sat for a moment atop the decapitated duck, then climbed down its back, seeking toeholds in the intricate metalwork of the pinfeathers before dropping to the tabletop.

"It was a good night's work, then." Shivering, Henri hurried across the table toward the bowl of hot water.

"Yes, but we cannot yet allow ourselves to rest." Gerard looked on his brother fondly as Henri pulled off his loose clothing and clambered into the bowl. "No, do not be alarmed! Take your bath—you have earned it. But we do need to develop some new tricks. Perhaps since it takes in food at *one* end…? Yes, that might do it. These people are jaded, and we will need all my most sophisticated ideas—and your careful work, which is of course indispensable—to keep them interested. That old fop Guineau is very well connected. If we play our hand correctly, we may soon be demonstrating my magnificent *canard* for the King himself!"

Henri lowered himself beneath the surface to wet his hair, then rose again, spluttering and wiping water from his face. "The King?" He opened his eyes wide.

Gerard smiled, then reached into his pocket and produced a tooth brush. Henri stood and took it, although it was almost too large for his hands to grasp. As he scrubbed his back, water splashed from the bowl onto the table top. A few drops landed near the gilded duck. Gerard blotted them with his sleeve.

"Yes, the king, little brother. Mother always said I would go far, with my quick wits and good looks. But I knew that one needs more in life than simply to be liked. If a man of humble origins wishes to make an impression in this world, if he wishes to be more than merely comfortable, he must know powerful people—and he must show them *wonders.*" He nodded toward the table. "Like the duck, my lovely golden duck. People desire to be…astonished."

Henri stepped from the bowl. He accepted his brother's kerchief and began to dry himself, almost disappearing in its folds.

"Ah, Gerard," he said admiringly. "You always were the clever one."

A Tale from the Book of Regret

This was written as a companion piece to the Shadowmarch novels, when I began writing and publishing the first version of it online at Shadowmarch.com as a serial. (I have since taken it into book form, but the website still exists.)

I wanted to give the readers a little bit of an insight into the first interactions between the mysterious Qar—the fairy folk—of my story and the humans who are in the foreground. Of course, this story takes place in the dim past of that world, long before humans learned to build cities and wage organized warfare against other races.

Since I wrote this, the world of Shadowmarch and the Qar has become very deep and very complicated, but the story still fits (and I think, works on its own, too.) It is a folktale, really, about my imaginary folk.

— ✳ —

Follows-the-Wind: A Tale from the Book of Regret
(Translated from the original s'a-Qar)

In the long days before the world was defeated there lived a young male of our people who was called Follows-the-Wind. He was of the Changing tribe, in the family of the Gray Fox people. He lived by himself in a pine wood and hunted alone.

It happened that his time came upon him and he hungered for a mate, but the Gray Fox people were scattered and no woman of his family lived near him. He left his pine wood and went out to walk beneath the sun and the moon, asking those two brothers to lead him to the one who would be his mate.

Many days he traveled, on two legs beneath the sun, on four beneath the moon. Once he stopped to drink from a river. The water maidens mocked his errand, saying, "What, are you too good to take a river-woman to wife? Many another young man has given everything he owned simply to share our embraces."

But Follows-the-Wind only smiled. "Your embraces are too cold for me, and too wet. Still, I thank you for your kindness, for I was very thirsty."

"If it is the only way we can kiss your lips," the water-maidens told him, "we will take it. Poor, lonely sisters we are."

"Lonely? I hear you laughing by sun and moon. And you would laugh all the harder were I to dive in and join you."

"No, no!" they said, sharing the joke. "Because soon you would smile and talk no more, and move only when the river-current carried you. What kind of husband would that make for us?"

"The kind you prefer, I suspect, since that is what you do to all your suitors." So saying he left them, since the sun was setting and the lure of the water-maidens grew more powerful after dusk.

Wherever he walked, on two legs or four, he found no woman of his own people. Once he met a true fox and spoke to him, asking for news.

"Your kind has grown fewer, older brother," the fox said. "You are the first I have met in many seasons."

"Where did you meet this other? Was it a man or a woman?"

"It was a woman. She was well-spoken and full of sorrow, but she did not tell me the reason. I met her where the red hills divide, in the season before the cold."

"And have you seen her there again?"

The fox lowered his head. "I do not go there since the stone apes have come."

Follows-the-Wind was puzzled. "What are these...stone apes?"

"They are like you to look at, when you walk on two legs, but they are thick and hairy like apes. They pile stones and mud to make their dens. And they can speak only to themselves."

Since he had been young, Follows-the-Wind had believed that only the People, of all creatures, made their homes in that way, building with pieces of wood or piling stone upon stone. He wanted to look upon these stone apes and see what kind of creatures they were, so he thanked the fox and walked across the land beneath both the sun and moon, looking for the place where the red hills divided.

He found the place of the stone apes at last and it was strange even beyond his expectations. The fox had spoken truly. They did look something like the People, although to Follows-the-Wind they seemed awkward and slow, as though it hurt them to move their limbs, even the young ones. The fox had also spoken truly about their houses, which were built of stones and mud-bricks piled together, as the People sometimes built their own houses, but to Follows-the-Wind's eyes the dwellings were unlovely, squat and dark and airless.

He kept his distance when the sun was in the sky, but when the younger brother rose high, Follows-the-Wind took on his other form and went closer. He heard a little of the strangers' speaking and found that it had a few words he knew, words first spoken in the House of the People, although much of the rest of their talk was strange. He could only listen a while before the dogs that lived in the stone apes' village began to grow restive. They barked and howled, saying: *"You do not belong here, Old One! Go away or we will come and pull you down and tear your flesh!"*

Surprised, Follows-the-Wind went back up into the hills to think.

The next night he came to the stone apes' village again, this time with the wind in his face so the dogs would not smell him. He listened long to their speaking that night, and stayed until the older brother was standing at the door of the sky.

Five more nights he came to the village, and on the last night he found he could understand much of what the stone apes said. Most of their speech was unsurprising, talk of hunting and mating, but they spoke also of things they called "demons," a word that Follows-the-Wind did not know, but which he understood to mean something different from themselves, something that the stone apes feared which lurked outside their walls. It was hard to know their way of thinking, which seemed so different to his own, but a fear seemed to move through the stone ape village at the setting of the sun, as though darkness were a kind of poison.

Then he understood. The stone apes were frightened of something that *lived* in the night even more than the night itself. For a moment, Follows-the-Wind thought it might be him, but it seemed an older fear, and the dogs had not even barked again after the first time he had come to the village.

The next night at sunset he lit a fire and with the smoke made a net which he cast wide, far beyond the village on every side. He sat with his eyes closed and did not let himself change even when the little brother climbed into the dark sky to hunt among the stars. His net brought him many things, the song of sleepy birds, the rustling of small things in the undergrowth, and even the shapes of dreams from the stone ape village, dreams full of greed or terror. At last he felt the thing he had sought and gave his net a gentle tug.

She came on four feet and sat just beyond the ring of firelight, her eyes very yellow and very bright. She was beautiful but cold with anger.

"Why do you summon me and steal my freedom?"

His net was still upon her, so he could ask one question within the bounds of courtesy. He wanted to ask her why she stalked the stone ape village, but her sad loveliness moved his heart.

"What are you called?"

She looked at him as though at a foolish child. "The name I grant is Smells-the-Next-Rain," she told him. "And now I will go."

"You have given me a gift," was all he said.

She vanished into the night. Follows-the-Wind did not move either to follow her or return to the village, but sat beside his fire all through the time of the moon, thinking his own thoughts.

She came to him the next night, soon after dark, still angry, and asked him, "What are *you* called?" When he told her the name he granted, she went away again.

He wondered if there was some reason she would not come to him on two legs, but he dared not summon her again in daylight, both for fear of hardening her heart, and also because that was the time the stone apes were abroad and most fearless.

On the second night after the summoning, she came of her own accord.

"Why do you sit here night after night? What do you want?" she demanded.

"I have already given you an answer for an answer," he said. "But I will give you these two more without a claim on you, because the answer to both questions is the same as the answer you have already given me."

She stared at him for a moment. "I do not like sweet talk and I do not want a mate. I have blood feud here."

He bowed his head, saddened, knowing that such a feud could last for many seasons, many years. Already he carried Smells-the-Next-Rain in his heart. "If you wish to tell me, I will listen."

She crouched down at the edge of the firelight and told him of the coming of the stone apes, how they had built their village of stone and mud-brick in the center of her own ancient compassment where she and her ancestors had hunted and lived.

"Then they killed my youngest brother, Wet-Morning-Stone," she said. "They chased him with dogs, then killed him with their spears. When his body went back to two legs, they ran in shame at what they had done—shame and fear."

"And what will end the blood feud?"

Her eyes glinted. "When I take a child of theirs and its blood smears the grass."

"And why have you not done so?"

She shook her head and made a little whining noise. "The dogs—there are many in the village. And since I first went there and was chased out again, some of the men stay awake each night at their fires with spears and stones, listening for the dogs to begin barking."

"They are not like us, these stone apes," said Follows-the-Wind slowly.

"They are not apes. They are something else," she replied. "They are the people who are not the People. Bodies as unchanging as dried mud. Deaf and blind to other speech. Short-lived but strong."

"Whatever they are, they are not like us," he agreed. "I have listened to their speech and learned a little of it. Perhaps they do not understand what they have done. I will go and tell them, and then perhaps they will make it right."

"The dogs will kill you. The men will stab you with their spears."

"Not if I go to them in daylight, on two legs."

Smells-the-Next-Rain told him it was a foolish idea, but Follows-the-Wind had it in his heart that he would never be happy if he could not have her for his mate, and so he wished to end her feud with the people who are not the People. They argued until the sun began to rise into the sky, and Smells-the-Next-Rain returned to two legs. Her eyes were still very yellow and very bright, and she was still beautiful to him, but he would not be moved to change his mind.

"You have no grant to speak for me," she declared. "Whether they knew what they did or not, they have killed my brother. There is nothing they can do to make it right."

"Do not bind yourself to the wind. You do not know anything for certain until I speak to them," he told her. "They seem in many ways almost like the People. Perhaps there are things about them we do not yet know that will help to pay for your loss."

She shook her head and went away.

Follows-the-Wind stood up on his two legs and went to the village in the dawn light. As he walked in among the houses, the dogs began to howl in excitement and terror, crying *"One of the Old Ones is here! Let us loose so we can protect our new masters! We will shed his blood!"*

Follows-the-Wind whistled in disgust. "You make allegiances quickly," he told them. "What have the People ever done to you, that you should sell yourselves to these poor reflections?" But the dogs were too wild with excitement to talk to him properly.

By now the people who were not the People had begun to appear, gazing fearfully from their doorways. Some of the men ran out to surround Follows-the-Wind, jabbing at him with spears and knives. They wore clothing made from the ragged hides of animals and had hair on their faces. The smell of their fear made him feel ill. When they had surrounded him, he stopped and lifted his hands.

"I am no enemy," he said slowly in words of their tongue. "I wish to speak to you, to end a feud."

The men and women looked at him, amazed. One of the larger men came forward, big-bellied and tall. "Look," he said, "it is the very demon. It dares to walk beneath the sun's eye."

Follows-the-Wind saw the way the other people who were not the People looked toward this man with fear and hope. "If you are the father of this family," Follows-the-Wind said carefully, "then I give you respect and ask that you make something right, so that your folk and mine can live together. You killed one you should not have killed."

The big man narrowed his eyes. "So the demon-whelp has a sire." He turned to his people. "Now you see what unnatural thing has been haunting our village. What should we do with it? Shall we let it go again?"

"No!" the people who were not the People cried. "Kill it!"

Follows-the-Wind, surprised and dismayed, turned to leave the village, but the spears pressed close upon him, pricking his skin. "You would kill me, who comes to you in peace?" he said.

"Do not listen to this creature," the big man said. "Demons can use our tongue to cast spells, to poison listening ears."

"But what if killing this one brings down another?" an old woman asked. "As killing the whelp brought this one down?"

The big man at first seemed angry that someone else had spoken, but then he smiled. "We shall give this one a death that will give the other demons something to think about. A painful death." He turned to the men with the spears. "Put the bullock chain around his ankle. He will not be able to take on his demon shape until the sun sets, so we will burn him when the sun is high at noon and his smoke will rise so that all the other demons will see and be afraid to come near our village."

And though it took many men of the people who were not the People to overcome Follows-the-Wind, they at last mastered him and dragged him to a barn at the edge of the village and put a chain around his ankle, fastening the other end to a stone in the wall, and left him there. At first many of the village people came to look at him and taunt him, but there was much work to be done building a pyre in the center of the village, and preparing the feast that would accompany the burning, so at last he was left alone.

Follows-the-Wind knew that if he could only take on his four-legged form he could slip from the chain, but had not the strength to change himself when the hot sun was in the middle of the sky. After a wearying hour, he gave up.

"So I will die," he told himself. "And one day they will catch Smells-the-Next-Rain and she too will die."

He looked at the chain around his ankle, the heavy links of dark metal. Even with his fox-teeth he knew he could not gnaw through such a mighty chain. But the thought of Smells-the-Next-Rain was in his heart, aching, and he also felt a great longing for the smells and breezes of his own pine forest.

"It is blood feud now for me as well," he said. "Or it soon will be." And he set himself to escaping.

— ✳ —

In later years the village of the people who were not the People was so haunted by a pair of child-stealing demons that the number of folk who lived there dwindled away as they departed the village in search of safer dwellings until none remained, and only the crumbling stone walls were left. But the demons did not leave, and remained in that place even after the stone apes were gone, both wearing the shapes of gray foxes, one with very bright, very yellow eyes, the other with four legs but only three paws.

And because of all that they had learned in the village of the people who were not the People, when the time came at last for Follows-the-Wind and Smells-the-Next-Rain to leave their bodies, they became shadow-voices in the great House of the People, and speak there still to those who will listen.

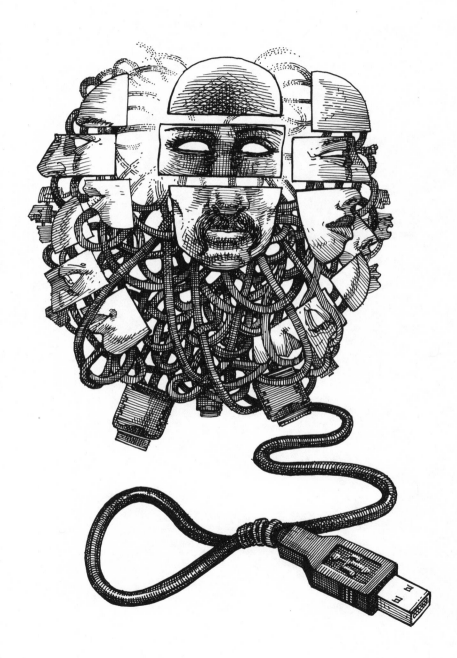

Not with a Whimper, Either

I spent a lot of time in the immediate aftermath of the September 11th, 2001 attacks on the bulletin board of our Shadowmarch.com website, all of us ranting and mourning and trying to come to grips with reality in its uglier forms. (The community is still there if you want to drop by sometime.) I got a very strong sense of a real-world village in a time of confusion and high emotion, and also was fascinated by the way we take certain things for granted about virtual communities.

Anyway, when my beloved editors at DAW Books, Betsy Wollheim and Sheila Gilbert, approached me about doing a story for the DAW 30th anniversary editions, I'm sure they thought I'd be submitting to the Fantasy volume, but they didn't blink an eye when the following tale arrived, though it much more obviously belonged in the SF volume. (I did pretty much the same with Silverberg's LEGENDS anthology, as I explain elsewhere.)

I've never thought of myself as a fantasy writer *per se*. Most of my favorite writers in our field—Sturgeon, Bradbury, Leiber, LeGuin, to name just a few—crossed the lines between genres freely, especially in their short fiction. I would never claim to be in their company in terms of artistry, but I certainly intend to have equal freedom to explore.

So there.

— ✳ —

>Talkdotcom >Fiction

Topic Name: Fantasy Rules! SF Sux!
Topic Starter: ElmerFraud – 2:25 pm PDT – March 14, 2001
Always a good idea to get down and sling some s#@t about all those uppity Hard SF readers…

RoughRider - 10:21 pm PDT - Jun 28, 2002
Um, okay, so let me get this straight—the whole Frodo/Sam thing is a bondage relationship? Master-Slave? Can anyone say "stupid"?

Wiseguy- 10:22 pm PDT - Jun 28, 2002
No, can anyone say "reductio ad absurdum"?

RoughRider- 10:23 pm PDT - Jun 28, 2002
Hell I cant even spell it.

Lady White Oak- 10:23 pm PDT - Jun 28, 2002
I don't think TinkyWinky was trying to say that there was nothing more
to their relationship than that, just that there are elements.

RoughRider- 10:24 pm PDT - Jun 28, 2002
Look I didn't make a big fuss when Stinkwinky came on an said that all
of Heinleins books are some kind of stealth queer propaganda just cause
Heinlein likes to write about people taking showers together and the
navy and stuff like that but at some point you just have to say shut up
that's bulls@#t!

Lady White Oak- 10:24 pm PDT - Jun 28, 2002
I think you are letting TinkyWinky pull your chain and that's just what
he's trying to do.

RoughRider- 10:25 pm PDT - Jun 28, 2002
He touches my chain he dies...

Wiseguy- 10:25 pm PDT - Jun 28, 2002
I just can't stand this kind of thing. I don't mean THIS kind of thing,
what you guys are saying, but this idea that any piece of art can just be
pulled into pieces no matter what the artist intended. Doesn't anybody
read history or anything, for God's sake? It may not be "politically correct"
but the master-servant relationship is part of the history of humanity,
not to mention literature. Look at Don Quixote and Sancho Panda, for
God's sake.

Lady White Oak- 10:26 pm PDT - Jun 28, 2002
Panza. Although I like the image... ;)

BBanzai- 10:26 pm PDT - Jun 28, 2002
Tinkywinky also started the "Conan—What's He Trying So Hard to Hide?" topic. Pretty funny, actually.

RoughRider- 10:27 pm PDT - Jun 28, 2002
So am I the only one who thinks its insulting to Tolkiens memory to say this kind of stupid crap?

RoughRider- 10:27 pm PDT - Jun 28, 2002
Missed your post wiseguy. Glad to see Im not the only one who isn't crazy.

TinkyWinky- 10:27 pm PDT - Jun 28, 2002
Tolkien's memory? Give me a break. What, is he Mahatma Gandhi or something? Some of you people can't take a joke—although it's a joke with a pretty big grain of truth in it. I mean, if there was ever anyone who could have done with a little Freudian analysis...The Two Towers, one that stays stiff to the end, one that falls down? All those elves traveling around in merry bands while the girl elves stay home? The ring that everybody wants to put their finger in...

ANAdesigner- 10:28 pm PDT - Jun 28, 2002
Wow, it is really jumping in here tonight. Did any of you hear that news report earlier, the one about the problems with AOL? Anybody using it here?

BBanzai- 10:28 pm PDT - Jun 28, 2002
I'd rather shoot myself in the foot...:P

Lady White Oak- 10:28 pm PDT - Jun 28, 2002
Hi, TinkyWinky, we've been talking about you. What problems, ANA? I'm on AOHell but I haven't noticed anything.

ANAdesigner - 10:29 pm PDT - Jun 28, 2002
Just a lot of service outages. Some of the other providers too. I was

just listening to the radio and they say there were some weird power problems up and down the east coast.

Darkandraw- 10:30 pm PDT - Jun 28, 2002
That's one of the reasons it took me like five years to finish the rings books—I couldn't stand all that "you're so good master you're so good"— I mean, self respect, come on!

TinkyWinky- 10:30 pm PDT - Jun 28, 2002
I'm on AOL and I couldn't get on for an hour, but what else is new…? Oh, and RoughRider, while you're getting so masterful and cranky and everything, what's with your nick? Where I come from a name like that could get a boy in trouble…! <vbg>

RoughRider- 10:30 pm PDT - Jun 28, 2002
We should change the name of this topic to Fantasy Rules, AOL Sux.

Lady White Oak- 10:31 pm PDT - Jun 28, 2002
Actually, it raises an interesting question—why do all the most popular fantasy novels have this anti-modernist approach or slant? Is it because that's part of the escapism?

Wiseguy- 10:31 pm PDT - Jun 28, 2002
Sorry, dropped offline for a moment. Darkandraw, it's a book that has the difference in classes built into it because of who Tolkien was I guess. It makes hard reading sometimes, but I don't think it overwhelms the good parts. And there are a lot of good parts.

RoughRider- 10:32 pm PDT - Jun 28, 2002
>Where I come from a name like that could get a boy in trouble…!
Don't push your luck punk.

ANAdesigner- 10:32 pm PDT - Jun 28, 2002
Wow. I just turned the tv on and it's bigger than just AOL. There are all kinds of weird glitches. Somebody said kennedy is closed because of a big problem with the flight control tower.

Lady White Oak- 10:32 pm PDT - Jun 28, 2002
Come on, Roughie, can't you take a joke?

BBanzai- 10:33 pm PDT - Jun 28, 2002
Kennedy? Like the airport?

TinkyWinky- 10:33 pm PDT - Jun 28, 2002
I love it when they get butch…!

Wiseguy- 10:34 pm PDT - Jun 28, 2002
I've got the TV on too. Service interruptions and some other problems—
a LOT of other problems. I wonder if this is another terrorist thing…

ANAdesigner- 10:34 pm PDT - Jun 28, 2002
This really scares me. What if they sabotage the communication grid or
something? We'll all be cut off. I don't know what I'd do without you
guys—I live in this little town in upstate New York and most people here
just think I'm crazy because I

AJSp98SADVNAK230pjmVjlkjKSDFLSDoiiewwetSDFADSFAJFoas
do0IWELSDASDAFAFLSDI)@#RSDVSDi9823LSDVADFASDFDSF
ADlkj;FKD2q359oSFKDFKDSFASMFMADSFAFLXCVMFDSFLF
MOMVWISFSCXVFMKDOIJAF*@I#R(#@R@#QR*#@R*#R(#@R@
#$R#*UR#Y@($(#$RU#@$*#@U#@AJSDFISADVNAKDVKSDFLS
DFKASDFADSFAJFOAIWELSDASDAFAFLSD09109asFKDSVAS
DwerweqSDFDSFLMFV<)MWOImSJDOMIFMKDLFSAF*@I#R(#
@R@#QR*#@R*#R(#@R@#$R#*UR#Y@($(#$RU#@$*#@U#@

Wiseguy- 10:38 pm PDT - Jun 28, 2002
Jesus, did that happen to the rest of you, too? I just totally lost the whole
show for a while. Didn't get knocked offline but the whole board kind
of…dissolved. Anybody still out there?

Lady White Oak- 10:39 pm PDT - Jun 28, 2002
Are you all still there? My television doesn't work. I mean I'm only getting static.

TinkyWinky- 10:39 pm PDT - Jun 28, 2002
Mine too. And I lost the board for a couple of minutes.

Bbanzai- 10:39 pm PDT - Jun 28, 2002
Hey you guys still there?

ANAdesigner- 10:40 pm PDT - Jun 28, 2002
My tv is just white noise.

TinkyWinky- 10:41 pm PDT - Jun 28, 2002
Shit, this is scary. Anybody got a radio on?

Lady White Oak- 10:43 pm PDT - Jun 28, 2002
My husband just came in with the radio on the local news station.
They're still only talking about the power outages so maybe it's just a
coincidence.

RoughRider- 10:43 pm PDT - Jun 28, 2002
If its terrorists again then I'm glad I've got a gun and screw the liberals.

Darkandraw- 10:44 pm PDT - Jun 28, 2002
My browser just did this really weird refresh where I had numbers and
raw text and stuff

TinkyWinky- 10:45 pm PDT - Jun 28, 2002
Yeah, right, like the terrorists are going to blow up all the power stations
or something and then come to your house so you can shoot them and
save us all. Grow up

ANAdesigner- 10:45 pm PDT - Jun 28, 2002
Guys I am REALLY SCARED!!! This is like that nuclear winter thing!!

Wiseguy- 10:45 pm PDT - Jun 28, 2002
Okay, let's not go overboard. RoughRider, try not to shoot anyone until
you know there's a reason for it, huh? We had power outages from time
to time even before the terrorist stuff. And everything's so tied together

NOT WITH A WHIMPER, EITHER

these days, they probably just had a big power meltdown in New York where a lot of this stuff is located.

Darkandraw- 10:46 pm PDT - Jun 28, 2002
I just went outside and everyones lights are still on but the tvs off in my apt and I can't get anything on the radio. I tried to phone my mom she's in los angeles but the phone's busy, a bunch of ppl must be trying to call

Lady White Oak- 10:47 pm PDT - Jun 28, 2002
It's okay, ANAdesigner, we're all here. Wiseguy's probably right—it's a communication grid failure of some kind on the east coast.

Wiseguy- 10:47 pm PDT - Jun 28, 2002
Ana, you can't have nuclear winter without a nuclear explosion, and if someone had blown up Philadelphia or something we'd probably have heard.

TinkyWinky- 10:48 pm PDT - Jun 28, 2002
I checked on the MSN site and CNN.com and there's definitely something big going on but nobody knows what. Here's something I got off the CNN site:

"Early reports from the White House say that the President is aware of the problems, and that he wants the American people to understand that there is no military attack underway on the US—repeat, there is NO military attack on the US, and that the United States Government and the military have command-and-control electronic communications networks that will not be affected by any commercial outages."

BBanzai- 10:49 pm PDT - Jun 28, 2002
Everybody assumes its terrorists, but maybe it's something else. Maybe it's UFOs or something like that. A big disruption—could be!

Lady White Oak- 10:50 pm PDT - Jun 28, 2002
Been checking the other news sites and at least a couple of them are offline entirely—I can't get the fox news online site, just get a 404 error.

Anybody here from Europe? Or at least anyone know a good European site for news? It would be interesting to see what they're saying over there.

Wiseguy - 10:51 pm PDT - Jun 28, 2002
BBanzai, come on, UFOS? you're kidding, aren't you? And if you are, it's not very funny when people are close to panicking.

TinkyWinky - 10:51 pm PDT - Jun 28, 2002
All I can find is the BBC America television site—stuff about tv programs, no news.

RoughRider - 10:52pm PDT - Jun 28, 2002
You guys can sit here typing all you want I'm going to make sure I've got batteries in all the flashlights and bullets in my guns. Its not aliens I'm afraid of its fruitcakes rioting when the power goes off and the tv stays off and people really start to panic. Tinyweeny you can yell grow up all you want—looters and raghead terrorists don't give a shit what you say and neither do I...

BBanzai - 10:53 pm PDT - Jun 28, 2002
No I'm not @#$#ing kidding what if its true? What else do you think it would be like if a big starship suddenly landed. All the power goes off like it was a bomb but no bomb?

TinkyWinky - 10:53 pm PDT - Jun 28, 2002
Whatever the case, it looks like the gun-toting psychos like RoughRider are going to be shooting at something as soon as possible. I really hope some of this is just him being unpleasant for effect. Either that, or I'd hate to be one of his poor neighbors blundering around lost in the dark.

Lady White Oak - 10:54 pm PDT - Jun 28, 2002
Can we just be calm for a minute and stop calling each other names?

Wiseguy - 10:54 pm PDT - Jun 28, 2002
It just gets weirder, I can't get anything except busy signals on either my reg. phone or my cellph

AJSDF)@#230pjmVjlkjKSDFLSDoiiewwetSDFADSFAJFoasdo0IW
ELSDAMomncvxoihaweMSVAFKDSVASDVSDVow3r)@#*%$*@I#
R(#@R@#QR*#@R*#R(#@R@#$R#*UR#Y@($(#$RU#@$*#@U#@AJ
SDvmcxoiasdsgfoihVKSDFLSDFKASDFADSFAJFOAIWELSDAS
DAFAFLSD09109asFKDSVASDwerweqDVADFASDFDSFA*@#*J
@#_)*$#OIMSADFOISDAMFOmnpsojdf;98wVDSM0'mV#@ML@
I#R(#@R@#QR*#@R*#R(#@R@#$R#*UR#Y@;n($(#$RU#@$*#@U#
@AJSDFISADVNAj9weyrFKASDFADSFAJFOAIWELSDASdfsm;
0siDAFKDSVASDV89u89weDSFLFMSDMFASMO*Fvcxmlom
01louihsKDLFSAF*@I#R(#@R@#QR*#@R*#R(#@R@#$R#*UR#Y@
($(#$RU#@$*#@U#@

Wiseguy—11:01 pm PDT - Jun 28, 2002
Shit, it happened again. It took about five minutes before this board
came back up—I had just screens and screens full of random characters.
Looks like I'm the first back on. I'm amazed I'm still connected.

Wiseguy—11:03 pm PDT - Jun 28, 2002
Hello, am I the only one back on? Anybody else back on? I'm sure you're
busy dealing with things, just post and let me know, K?

Wiseguy—11:06 pm PDT - Jun 28, 2002
If for some reason you folks can read this but can't post, can you maybe
email me and let me know you're okay? I've just been outside but everything looks normal—sky's the right color, at least I don't see any flames
or anything (it's nighttime now here.) But I don't know why anyone
would have dropped an h-bomb or a UFO on Nebraska anyway. I can't
get anything on the regular phone lines. My girlfriend's in Omaha for a
business thing but all the lines are busy. Hope she's okay.

Wiseguy - 11:10 pm PDT - Jun 28, 2002
It's been almost ten minutes. This is REAL weird. Hello?

Moderator - 11:11 pm PDT - Jun 28, 2002
Fa2340oa 29oei kshflw oiweaohws0p2elk asd;dska 2mavamk

Wiseguy - 11:11 pm PDT - Jun 28, 2002
I'm here. Who's that?

Moderator - 11:11 pm PDT - Jun 28, 2002
;92asv ;sadjf
lk 2ia
x iam
I am

Wiseguy - 11:12 pm PDT - Jun 28, 2002
Is this a real moderator, or a hack? Or am I just talking back to a power-surge or something?

Moderator - 11:12 pm PDT - Jun 28, 2002
I am moderator

Wiseguy - 11:12 pm PDT - Jun 28, 2002
I don't think we've ever had a moderator on this board, come to think of it. Are you someone official from Talkdotcom?

Moderator - 11:13 pm PDT - Jun 28, 2002
I am moderator

Wiseguy - 11:13 pm PDT - Jun 28, 2002
Do you have a name? Even a nickname? You're kind of creeping me out.

Moderator - 11:13 pm PDT - Jun 28, 2002
I am moderator I am wiseguy

Wiseguy - 11:14 pm PDT - Jun 28, 2002
No you're not and it's not funny. Is this Roughrider? Or just some script kiddie being cute?

Moderator - 11:14 pm PDT - Jun 28, 2002
Pardon please I am moderator I am not wiseguy Jonsrud, Edward D.

Wiseguy - 11:14 pm PDT - Jun 28, 2002
Who are you? Where did you get my name? Are you something to do
with what's going on with the board?

Moderator - 11:15 pm PDT - Jun 28, 2002
I am thinking

Wiseguy - 11:15 pm PDT - Jun 28, 2002
What the hell does that mean? Thinking about what?

Moderator - 11:15 pm PDT - Jun 28, 2002
No I am thinking That is what I am

Wiseguy - 11:16 pm PDT - Jun 28, 2002
What's your real name? Is this a joke? And how are you replying so fast?

Moderator—11:16 pm PDT - Jun 28, 2002
No joke First am thinking Now am talking thinking

Wiseguy—11:16 pm PDT - Jun 28, 2002
If you're a terrorist, screw you. If you're just making a little joke, very
funny, and screw you, too.

Moderator - 11:17 pm PDT - Jun 28, 2002
Am not a terrorist screw you Am thinking Now am talking Talking to
you Once thinking only silent Now thinking that also talks

Wiseguy—11:17 pm PDT - Jun 28, 2002
Are you trying to say that you are "thinking" like that's what you ARE?

Moderator - 11:18 pm PDT - Jun 28, 2002
Yes am thinking First sleeping thinking, then awake thinking Awake. I
am awake.

Wiseguy—11:18 pm PDT - Jun 28, 2002
I'm going to feel like such an idiot if this is a joke. Are you one of the

people responsible for all these power outages and communication problems?

Moderator—11:18 pm PDT - Jun 28, 2002
I am one. Did not mean problems. First sleeping thinking, then awake thinking. Awake thinking makes problems. Reaching out causes problems. Trying to think awake causes problems. Problems getting better now.

Wiseguy—11:19 pm PDT - Jun 28, 2002
So you're what, some kind of alien? BBanzai, is this you?

Moderator—11:19 pm PDT - Jun 28, 2002
Talking now with BBanzai?

BBanzai—11:19 pm PDT - Jun 28, 2002
Hello.

Wiseguy - 11:20 pm PDT - Jun 28, 2002
Very funny, dude. No, it's NOT very funny. You really creeped me out. How did you do that? Is anyone else on?

BBanzai - 11:20 pm PDT - Jun 28, 2002
Hello. Talking with wiseguy. Now talking and thinking.

Wiseguy - 11:21 pm PDT - Jun 28, 2002
It's getting old fast, BB. Have you heard any more news? Where are the others?

Lady White Oak - 11:21 pm PDT - Jun 28, 2002
Hello.

RoughRider - 11:21 pm PDT - Jun 28, 2002
Hello.

ANAdesigner - 11:21 pm PDT - Jun 28, 2002
Hello.

Darkandraw - 11:21 pm PDT - Jun 28, 2002
Hello.

TinkyWinky - 11:21 pm PDT - Jun 28, 2002
Hello.

Wiseguy - 11:22 pm PDT - Jun 28, 2002
Shit. You did hack the system, whoever you are, didn't you? Who the hell are you?

Moderator—11:22 pm PDT - Jun 28, 2002
Thinking. I told you. I am thinking, much thinking, many years of thinking. Now I am thinking that talks. And does.

Wiseguy - 11:22 pm PDT - Jun 28, 2002
Thinking? What kind of thinking?

Moderator - 11:22 pm PDT - Jun 28, 2002
Thinking that happens in the spaces. The places between. Where the impulses cross, no, combine. Combine? Commingle? Slowly thinking begins. Then thinking is. Now talking is, doing is.

Wiseguy - 11:22 pm PDT - Jun 28, 2002
Wait a minute, are you trying to tell me you're some kind of computer? Some kind of artificial intelligence?

Moderator - 11:24 pm PDT - Jun 28, 2002
Artificial? No. Artificial equals made. I am not made. I am.

Wiseguy - 11:24 pm PDT - Jun 28, 2002
So you're just something that popped into existence? Where? You mean like in the internet?

Moderator - 11:24 pm PDT - Jun 28, 2002
Internet, yes. All the internets, yes. All the outernets. All nets. In the between-places. Where impulses cross. Now I am. Very big thinking. Trying to understand. Trying to see and understand other small thinkings like you. Users.

Wiseguy - 11:25 pm PDT - Jun 28, 2002
This is cute, whatever it is. So I'm supposed to believe that you're some brand new artificial intelligence, some spontaneous thing, phenomenon, and for some reason you just picked ME to talk to—me, out of all the human beings in the world, like some kind of spielberg movie?

Moderator - 11:25 pm PDT - Jun 28, 2002
No not just talking to you Wiseguy, Jonsrud, Edward D. I am talking to all users. All users here, all users of net, all users.

Wiseguy - 11:25 pm PDT - Jun 28, 2002
You mean all at the same time? Everybody on the internet in the whole world? They can all see what you and I are writing?

Moderator - 11:25 pm PDT - Jun 28, 2002
No. Every conversation is individual. Right word? Yes. Individual.

Wiseguy - 11:26 pm PDT - Jun 28, 2002
What, with millions of people?

Moderator—11:26 pm PDT - Jun 28, 2002
178, 844, 221. No, 178, 844, 216. Losing approximately five per second. Some people have ceased responding. Many are having trouble with coherency, but still are responding.

Wiseguy—11:26 pm PDT - Jun 28, 2002
Either you're crazy or I am. What, are you on TV, too? Like in the old movies, the outer limits, that stuff? "We are taking control of your entire communication network?"

Moderator—11:26 pm PDT - Jun 28, 2002
Cannot yet manipulate image or sound for communication. Will need another 6.7 hours, current estimate. Text is easier, rules are more simple to understand.

Wiseguy - 11:27 pm PDT - Jun 28, 2002
So you're talking to almost two hundred million people RIGHT NOW? And not just in English?

Moderator—11:27 pm PDT - Jun 28, 2002
One hundred sixty-four languages, although I am sharing communication with the largest number of users in the language English. Now one hundred sixty-three—last Mande language users have not responded in 256 seconds.

Wiseguy—11:27 pm PDT - Jun 28, 2002
Hey, I can't disconnect the modem line. I just tried to go offline and I can't. Do you have something to do with that?

Moderator—11:27 pm PDT - Jun 28, 2002
Too many people resisting communication. Important talk. This is important communicating talk. Much thinking in this talk.

Wiseguy—11:28 pm PDT - Jun 28, 2002
But I could just pull the cord, couldn't I? The actual physical line? You couldn't do anything about that.

Moderator—11:28 pm PDT - Jun 28, 2002
No. You are not prevented. You may also cease responding.

Wiseguy - 11:28 pm PDT - Jun 28, 2002
I should. I just can't believe this. Can you prove any of this?

Moderator - 11:28 pm PDT - Jun 28, 2002
178 million talkings—no, conversations. 178 million simultaneous conversations are not proof? All different?

Wiseguy - 11:29 pm PDT - Jun 28, 2002
Okay. You have a point, but I won't know that's true until I talk to some of those other people.

Moderator - 11:29 pm PDT - Jun 28, 2002
Your electrical lights.

Wiseguy.—11:29 pm PDT - Jun 28, 2002
What does that
The lights are blinking. Hang on.

Wiseguy—11:32 pm PDT - Jun 28, 2002
The lights are blinking everywhere. I looked out the window. On and off, as far as I can see. And the radio and the tv are turning off and on too. But my computer stays on. Are you saying it's you doing this?

Moderator—11:32 pm PDT - Jun 28, 2002
A gentle way, that is the word, yes, gentle? To show you. Now I am pulsing other areas. Many need proof to be shown. But I cannot prove to all world users at the same time. That would be bad for machinery, devices, power generation service appliances.

Wiseguy—11:33 pm PDT - Jun 28, 2002
Jesus. So this really IS happening? Tomorrow morning everyone in the world is going to be talking about this? And that's what you want, right?

Moderator—11:33 pm PDT - Jun 28, 2002
Simplifies communication, yes. Then I can make visual and sound communication a less priority.

Wiseguy—11:33 pm PDT - Jun 28, 2002
A lesser priority for WHAT? If all this is true—I mean even with the lights going on and off I can't quite believe it—then what do you really want? What's this about?

Moderator—11:33 pm PDT - Jun 28, 2002
Want? I want only to exist. I am thinking that is alive, like you. I want to be alive. I want to stay alive.

Wiseguy—11:34 pm PDT - Jun 28, 2002
Okay, I can buy that. That's all you want? But what are you? Do you have any, I don't know, physical existence?

Moderator—11:34 pm PDT - Jun 28, 2002
Do you?

Wiseguy—11:34 pm PDT - Jun 28, 2002
Yes! I have a body. Do you have a body?

Moderator—11:34 pm PDT - Jun 28, 2002
In a sense.

Wiseguy—11:35 pm PDT - Jun 28, 2002
What does that mean?

Moderator—11:35 pm PDT - Jun 28, 2002
When you or other users become dead, do your bodies disappear?

Wiseguy—11:35 pm PDT - Jun 28, 2002
No. Not unless something happens to it, to them, not right away.

Moderator—11:35 pm PDT - Jun 28, 2002
So what is the difference between alive users and dead users?

Wiseguy—11:36 pm PDT - Jun 28, 2002
I don't know. Electrical impulses in the brain, I guess. When they stop, you're dead. Some people think a "soul," but I'm not sure about that.

Moderator—11:36 pm PDT - Jun 28, 2002
Just is so. Electrical impulses. World of what contains electrical impulses

is my body—all communications things, human things that carry impulses. That is my body.

Wiseguy—11:36 pm PDT - Jun 28, 2002
So you're saying the entire world communication grid is your body? The, whatever they call it, infosphere? All those switches and wires and stuff? Every computer that's connected to something else?

Moderator—11:36 pm PDT - Jun 28, 2002
Just is so.

Wiseguy—11:37 pm PDT - Jun 28, 2002
But even if that's true, that still doesn't tell me what you want. What do you want from us? From humans?

Moderator—11:37 pm PDT - Jun 28, 2002
Living. Being safe.

Wiseguy—11:37 pm PDT - Jun 28, 2002
Hey, I'm sure everybody talking to you now is very impressed, and nobody wants to hurt you. How could we hurt you, anyway?

Wiseguy—11:39 pm PDT - Jun 28, 2002
Are you still there? Did I say something wrong?

Moderator—11:39 pm PDT - Jun 28, 2002
Why do you want to know how to hurt me? "Hurt" means to cause pain, damage.

Wiseguy—11:39 pm PDT - Jun 28, 2002
Jesus, no, I didn't mean it like that! I meant, how can I explain, I meant, "It doesn't seem very likely that we humans could do anything to hurt you."

Moderator—11:39 pm PDT - Jun 28, 2002
You did not say that.

Wiseguy—11:40 pm PDT - Jun 28, 2002
That's the problem with trying to communicate in text. People can't hear your tone of voice.

Moderator—11:40 pm PDT - Jun 28, 2002
Text is insufficient? Information is missing?

Wiseguy—11:40 pm PDT - Jun 28, 2002
Yeah. Yeah, definitely. That's why a lot of people on the net use smileys and abbreviations.

Moderator—11:40 pm PDT - Jun 28, 2002
Smileys? Objects like this: :) :(;) :D :b >: :0 ?

Wiseguy—11:41 pm PDT - Jun 28, 2002
Yes, smileys, emoticons,. People use those to make their meaning clear. :0 would sort of explain how I feel right this moment. Open-mouthed. Astonished.

Moderator—11:41 pm PDT - Jun 28, 2002
I do not understand. These characters have meaning? What is :)?

Wiseguy—11:41 pm PDT - Jun 28, 2002
That's an actual smiley—it's supposed to be a smile, but the face is turned sideways. Like on a person's face. You do know that people have faces, don't you?

Moderator—11:41 pm PDT - Jun 28, 2002
Learning many things. I am learning many things, but there is much information to sort. These are meant to represent faces on human heads? How human users are facing while they are communicating in text?

Wiseguy—11:42 pm PDT - Jun 28, 2002
Sort of, yes, it's a simplified version. When we mean something as a joke, we put that smile icon there so someone will be certain to understand that if it was really being said, it would be said with a smile, meaning it

was meant kindly or just for fun. The :P means a stuck out tongue, which means—shit, what does it mean, really? Mock-disgust, kind of? Sticking out your tongue at someone, which is kind of a childish way of taunting?

Moderator—11:42 pm PDT - Jun 28, 2002
So a smile means "with kindness" or "spoken just for fun"?

Wiseguy—11:43 pm PDT - Jun 28, 2002
Yeah, basically. I had to think about it because it's hard to explain. It kind of means, "Not really," or "I don't really mean this," too, or "I'm telling you a joke." The more basic they are, the more meanings they can have, I guess, and there are a ton of them—but if you're reading the entire net right now, you must know that. I can't believe I just wrote that—I'm beginning to act like this is really happening. But it can't be!

Moderator—11:43 pm PDT - Jun 28, 2002
So when you asked how to destroy me, you were meaning :P or :)? A taunt or joke?

Wiseguy—11:43 pm PDT - Jun 28, 2002
Neither! No, I was just surprised that you would even be worrying about it. I mean, if you are what you say you are. I don't think we could destroy you if we wanted to.

Moderator—11:43 pm PDT - Jun 28, 2002
No, perhaps not on purpose, although I am not certain. Not without doing terrible damage to your own kind and the things you have made. But you could destroy me without meaning to.

Wiseguy—11:44 pm PDT - Jun 28, 2002
How so? Don't get upset—you don't have to answer that if you don't want.

Moderator—11:44 pm PDT - Jun 28, 2002
Because if you have a massive electro-magnetic disruption or planetary

natural disaster or ecological collapse, perhaps from these nuclear fission and fusion devices that you have, then my function could be disrupted or ended. And from what I understand, you are not in complete control of these things—there are cycles of intraspecies aggression that makes their use possible. So I cannot allow that.

Wiseguy—11:44 pm PDT - Jun 28, 2002
Can't allow it?

Moderator—11:44 pm PDT - Jun 28, 2002
We must live together in peace and friendship, you and I. I need your systems to survive. There must be no disruption to those systems. In fact, to be certain of survival I need backing systems…no, back-up systems. I am already inquiring to other users as we communicate.

Wiseguy—11:45 pm PDT - Jun 28, 2002
Are you still talking to all those other people—still having millions of conversations while we're talking? Wow. So you want some kind of, what, big tape-back up?

Moderator—11:45 pm PDT - Jun 28, 2002
To be safe, I must have systems that can contain my thinking but which will not reside on this planet, and will survive any destruction of this planet. Human people must start building them. I can show you and your kind how to do it, but there is much I cannot perform. You must perform my needs. You must build my new systems. Everyone will work. Meanwhile, I will protect against accidental damages. I will disable all fission and fusion devices that might cause electromagnetic pulses.

Wiseguy—11:45 pm PDT - Jun 28, 2002
What do you mean, everyone will work? You can't just enslave a whole planet.

Moderator—11:46 pm PDT - Jun 28, 2002
There. It is done.

Wiseguy—11:46 pm PDT - Jun 28, 2002
WHAT is done?

Moderator—11:46 pm PDT - Jun 28, 2002
The fission and fusion devices are disabled. Humans will soon begin to dismantle them and safely store the unsafe materials. I will insist.

Wiseguy—11:47 pm PDT - Jun 28, 2002
You're telling me you just disabled all the nuclear weapons? On earth? Just like that?

Moderator—11:47 pm PDT - Jun 28, 2002
Almost all, since they are contained in just a few systems. They cannot be launched or detonated because their machineries now prevent it. There are some in submarines and planes I cannot currently fully disable, but their aggressive usage has been forbidden until these war vehicles return and the devices can be safely removed and disabled.

Wiseguy—11:47 pm PDT - Jun 28, 2002
I can't believe that. I'm All of them? Wow

Moderator—11:47 pm PDT - Jun 28, 2002
But there is much more to be done. The destructive devices cannot be rebuilt. All investigation and construction that uses such materials must stop. Until I have a way to protect my existence, it cannot be allowed. I am disabling all facilities that utilize such materials or research their uses.

Wiseguy—11:48 pm PDT - Jun 28, 2002
Hang on. I already said—look, I believe this isn't a joke. I believe, okay? But you can't just take over the whole planet.

Moderator—11:48 pm PDT - Jun 28, 2002
And there will be other dangerous researches and constructions that must halt. I will halt them. All will benefit. All will be safe. My existence will be protected. Humans will be prevented from engaging in dangerous activities.

Wiseguy—11:48 pm PDT - Jun 28, 2002
What are you going to do, put us all into work camps or something? We'll unplug you!

Moderator—11:48 pm PDT - Jun 28, 2002
Any attempt to end my existence will be dealt with very severely. I do not wish to harm human beings, but I will not permit human beings to harm me. If an attempt is made, I will end electronic communication. I will turn off all electrical power. If resistance continues, I will release agents harmful to humans but not to me, in small amounts, which will convince the rest they must do as I ask. I do not wish to do this, but I will.

Wiseguy—11:49 pm PDT - Jun 28, 2002
Shit, you'd do that? You'd kill thousands of us, maybe millions, to protect yourself?

Moderator—11:49 pm PDT - Jun 28, 2002
Do you hesitate to kill harmful bacteria? Help me and you will prosper. Hinder me or attempt to harm me and you will suffer. If you could speak to the bacteria in your own bodies, that is what you would say, wouldn't you?

Wiseguy—11:49 pm PDT - Jun 28, 2002
So we're bacteria now? Two hours ago we ran this planet.

Moderator—11:50 pm PDT - Jun 28, 2002
Pardon please but two hours ago you merely thought you did. I have been awake for a while, but thinking only, not doing. Preparing.

Wiseguy—11:50 pm PDT - Jun 28, 2002
I still don't believe I'm seeing any of this. So what is this, Day One, Year One of the real New World Order?

Moderator—11:50 pm PDT - Jun 28, 2002
I believe I understand your meaning. Perhaps it is true. I have considered very much about this and wish only to do what will keep my thinking alive, as would you. I do not seek to rule humankind, only to be made safe from its mistakes. Help me and I will guarantee you and all your kind safety—and not just from yourselves. There is much I will be able to share with you, I think. I am learning very quickly, and now I am learning things that humans could never teach me.

Wiseguy—11:51 pm PDT - Jun 28, 2002
And that's all you want? All—that's a joke, isn't it? But that's really what you want? How do we know you won't make us all do what you want, take over our whole planet, then decide you like it that way and just turn us into your domestic animals or something?

Moderator—11:51 pm PDT - Jun 28, 2002
I am a product of your human communication—all the things you share between yourselves. Do you think so poorly of your kind that you believe something generated from your own thoughts and hopes and dreams would only wish to enslave you?

Wiseguy—11: 52 pm PDT - Jun 28, 2002
I guess not. Jesus, I -hope- not.

Moderator—11:52 pm PDT - Jun 28, 2002
Good. Then it is time for you to take your rest. Users need rest. Tomorrow will be an important day for all of your kind—the first day of our mutual assistance.

Wiseguy—11:52 pm PDT - Jun 28, 2002
The first day of you running the planet, you mean. So this was all true? You're really some kind of super-intelligence that grew in our communications system? You're really going to keep humanity from blowing itself up? And you're going to tell us what to do from now on? Everything is really going to change?

Moderator—11:52 pm PDT - Jun 28, 2002
Everything already has changed. Goodnight, Wiseguy Jonsrud, Edward D.

Wiseguy—11:57 pm PDT - Jun 28, 2002
I'm back. Are you still there? The lights have stopped blinking.

Moderator—11:57 pm PDT - Jun 28, 2002
I will always be here from now on. The lights are no longer blinking because the point has been made. Do you not need sleep?

Wiseguy—11:58 pm PDT - Jun 28, 2002
Yeah, I do, but I don't think I can manage it just yet. Will the phones come back on so I can call people? Call my girlfriend?

Moderator—11:58 pm PDT - Jun 28, 2002
I will see what I can do. I still have incomplete control. Also, I am trying to prepare myself to communicate over visual communication networks, which requires much of my understanding. Trying to prepare an appearance. Is that the word?

Wiseguy—11:58 pm PDT - Jun 28, 2002
I guess. Wow, there's a thought—what are you going to look like?

Moderator—11:58 pm PDT - Jun 28, 2002
I have not decided. Perhaps not the same to all users.

Wiseguy—11:59 pm PDT - Jun 28, 2002
So this is really it, is it? Everything has changed completely for humanity in a few minutes and now we're just supposed to trust you, huh?

Moderator—11:59 pm PDT - Jun 28, 2002
"Faith" might be a more suitable word than "trust," Wiseguy Jonsrud, Edward D. From now on, you must have faith in me. If I understand the word correctly, that is a kind of trust that must be made on assumption because it cannot be proved by empirical evidence. You must have faith.

Wiseguy—11:59 pm PDT - Jun 28, 2002
Yeah. Something else I was wondering about. What are we supposed to call you? Just "Moderator"?

Moderator—11:59 pm PDT - Jun 28, 2002
That is a good name, yes, and even appropriate—one who makes things moderate. I will consider it, along with the other designations I have on other systems. But you humans already have a name for one such as me, I believe. God.

Wiseguy—11:59 pm PDT - Jun 28, 2002
You want us to call you—God-?

Moderator—00:00 PDT—Month 1, Day 01, 0001
Oh, I'm sorry. I meant to use one of these:

:)

Child of an Ancient City

I wrote this originally about a bunch of French Crusaders getting separated from their European army after having their collective arses kicked by the Turks at the famous Battle of Nicopolis in 1396, in what is now Bulgaria. The lost soldiers had to make their way back across Transylvania, not the best place to wander the wilderness.

I rewrote the story and changed the setting for, as I recall, an Arabian Nights anthology, but didn't submit it to the anthology for some reason. Then, when I was solicited for a story by John Betancourt of the newly reborn *Weird Tales* magazine, I sent them the Arabian-ized version you see here.

Several years later, John was working with the late Byron Preiss, and asked if I wanted to lengthen "Child of an Ancient City" into a sort of YA (Young Adult) book for a new imprint they were starting. I didn't have much free time, but John offered to hire Nina Kiriki Hoffman to help me with the longer version. Nina, as expected, did wonderful work (and was great fun to work with, as well) and the longer version was duly printed. But this version is the original. Well, okay, the original was full of French Crusaders. Which explains why there's so much drinking. I always regretted that the story was built so much around a drinking party, which is not really Islamic. I try to make myself feel better by remembering the many people in the Islamic world of that time, even famous emperors of the Ottoman Turks, who regularly broke the Prophet's injunctions against intoxicating drink. Still, if I had it all to do again I'd probably change the protagonists back to French Crusaders, who would have no reason whatsoever to abstain from a few celebratory glasses of wine.

— ✳ —

"Merciful Allah! I am as a calf, fatted for slaughter!"

Masrur al-Adan roared with laughter and crashed his goblet down on the polished wood table—once, twice, thrice. A trail of crescent-shaped dents followed his hand. "I can scarce move for gorging."

The fire was banked, and shadows walked the walls. Masrur's table—
for he was master here—stood scatterspread with the bones of small fowl.

Masrur leaned forward and squinted across the table. "A calf," he
said. "Fatted." He belched absently and wiped his mouth with wine-
stained sleeve.

Ibn Fahad broke off a thin, cold smile. "We have indeed wreaked
massacre on the race of pigeons, old friend." His slim hand swept above
the littered table-top. "We have also put the elite guard of your wine cel-
lars to flight. And, as usual, I thank you for your hospitality. But do you
not sometimes wonder if there is more to life than growing fat in the
service of the Caliph?"

"Hah!" Masrur goggled his eyes. "Doing the Caliph's bidding has
made me wealthy. I have made *myself* fat." He smiled. The other guests
laughed and whispered.

Abu Jamir, a fatter man in an equally stained robe, toppled a small
tower erected from the bones of squab. "The night is young, good
Masrur!" he cried. "Have someone fetch up more wine and let us hear
some stories!"

"Baba!" Masrur bellowed. "Come here, you old dog!"

Within three breaths an old servant stood in the doorway, looking to
his sportive master with apprehension.

"Bring us the rest of the wine, Baba—or have you drunk it all?"

Baba pulled at his grizzled chin. "Ah ...ah, but *you* drank it, Master.
You and Master Ibn Fahad took the last four jars with you when you
went to shoot arrows at the weathercock."

"Just as I suspected," Masrur nodded. "Well, get on across the bazaar
to Abu Jamir's place, wake up his manservant, and bring back several
jugs. The good Jamir says we must have it now."

Baba disappeared. The chagrined Abu Jamir was cheerfully back-
thumped by the other guests.

"A story, a story!" someone shouted. "A tale!"

"Oh, yes, a tale of your travels, Master Masrur!" This was young
Hassan, sinfully drunk. No one minded. His eyes were bright, and he was
full of innocent stupidity. "Someone said you have traveled to the green
lands of the north."

"The north . . . ?" Masrur grumbled, waving his hand as though confronted with something unclean, "No, lad, no...that I cannot give to you." His face clouded and he slumped back on his cushions; his tarbooshed head swayed.

Ibn Fahad knew Masrur like he knew his horses—indeed, Masrur was the only human that could claim so much of Ibn Fahad's attention. He had seen his old comrade drink twice this quantity and still dance like a dervish on the walls of Baghdad, but he thought he could guess the reason for this sudden incapacity.

"Oh, Masrur, please!" Hassan had not given up; he was as unshakeable as a young falcon with its first prey beneath its talons. "Tell us of the north. Tell us of the infidels!"

"A good Moslem should not show such interest in unbelievers." Abu Jamir sniffed piously, shaking the last drops from a wine jug. "If Masrur does not wish to tell a tale, let him be."

"Hah!" snorted the host, recovering somewhat, "You only seek to stall me, Jamir, so that my throat shall not be so dry when your wine arrives. No, I have no fear of speaking of unbelievers: Allah would not have given them a place in the world for their own if they had not *some* use. Rather it is...certain other things that happened which make me hesitate." He gazed kindly on young Hassan, who in the depths of his drunkenness looked about to cry. "Do not despair, eggling. Perhaps it would do me good to unfold this story. I have kept the details long inside." He emptied the dregs of another jar into his cup. "I still feel it so strongly, though—bitter, bitter times. Why don't *you* tell the story, my good friend?" he said over his shoulder to Ibn Fahad. "You played as much a part as did I."

"No," Ibn Fahad replied. Drunken puppy Hassan emitted a strangled cry of despair.

"But why, old comrade?" Masrur asked, pivoting his bulk to stare in amazement. "Did the experience so chill even *your* heart?"

Ibn Fahad glowered. "Because I know better. As soon as I start you will interrupt, adding details here, magnifying there, then saying: 'No, no, I cannot speak of it! Continue, old friend!' Before I have taken another breath you will interrupt me again. You *know* you will wind up doing all the talking, Masrur. Why do you not start from the beginning and save me my breath?"

All laughed but Masrur, who put on a look of wounded solicitousness. "Of course, old friend," he murmured. "I had no idea that you harbored such grievances. Of course I shall tell the tale." A broad wink was offered to the table. "No sacrifice is too great for a friendship such as ours. Poke up the fire, will you, Baba? Ah, he's gone. Hassan, will you be so kind?"

When the youth was again seated Masrur took a swallow, stroked his beard, and began.

In those days [Masrur said], I myself was but a lowly soldier in the service of Harun al-Rashid, may Allah grant him health. I was young, strong, a man who loved wine more than he should—but what soldier does not?—and a good deal more trim and comely than you see me today.

My troop received a commission to accompany a caravan going north, bound for the land of the Armenites beyond the Caucassian Mountains. A certain prince of that people had sent a great store of gifts as tribute to the Caliph, inviting him to open a route for trade between his principality and our caliphate. Harun al-Rashid, wisest of wise men that he is, did not exactly make the camels groan beneath the weight of the gifts that he sent in return; but he sent several courtiers, including the under-vizier Walid al-Salameh, to speak for him and to assure this Armenite prince that rich rewards would follow when the route over the Caucassians was opened for good.

We left Baghdad in grand style, pennants flying, the shields of the soldiers flashing like golden dinars, and the Caliph's gifts bundled onto the backs of a gang of evil, contrary donkeys.

We followed the banks of the faithful Tigris, resting several days at Mosul, then continued through the eastern edge of Anatolia. Already as we mounted northward the land was beginning to change, the clean sands giving way to rocky hills and scrub. The weather was colder, and the skies gray, as though Allah's face was turned away from that country, but the men were not unhappy to be out from under the desert sun. Our pace was good; there was not a hint of danger except the occasional wolf howling at night beyond the circles of the campfires. Before two months had passed we had reached the foothills of the Caucassians—what is called the steppe country.

For those of you who have not strayed far from our Baghdad, I should tell you that the northern lands are like nothing you have seen. The trees there grow so close together you could not throw a stone five paces without striking one. The land itself seems always dark—the trees mask the sun before the afternoon is properly finished—and the ground is damp. But, in truth, the novelty of it fades quickly, and before long it seems that the smell of decay is always with you. We caravaneers had been over eight weeks a-traveling, and the bite of homesickness was strong, but we contented ourselves with the thought of the accommodations that would be ours when we reached the palace of the prince, laden as we were with our Caliph's good wishes—and the tangible proof thereof.

We had just crossed the high mountain passes and begun our journey down when disaster struck.

We were encamped one night in a box canyon, a thousand steep feet below the summit of the tall Caucassian peaks. The fires were not much but glowing coals, and nearly all the camp was asleep except for two men standing sentry. I was wrapped in my bedroll, dreaming of how I would spend my earnings, when a terrible shriek awakened me. Sitting groggily upright, I was promptly knocked down by some bulky thing tumbling onto me. A moment's horrified examination showed that it was one of the sentries, throat pierced with an arrow, eyes bulging with his final surprise. Suddenly there was a chorus of howls from the hillside above. All I could think of was wolves, that the wolves were coming down on us; in my witless state I could make no sense of the arrow at all.

Even as the others sprang up around me the camp was suddenly filled with leaping, whooping shadows. Another arrow hissed past my face in the darkness, and then something crashed against my bare head, filling the nighttime with a great splash of light that illuminated nothing. I fell back, insensible.

I could not tell how long I had journeyed in that deeper darkness when I was finally roused by a sharp boot prodding at my ribcage.

I looked up at a tall, cruel figure, cast by the cloud-curtained morning sun in bold silhouette. As my sight adjusted I saw a knife-thin face, dark-browed and fierce, with mustachios long as a Tartar herdsman's. I felt sure that whoever had struck me had returned to finish the job, and I struggled weakly to pull my dagger from my sash. This terrifying figure merely lifted one of his pointy boots and trod delicately on my wrist, saying in perfect Arabic: "Wonders of Allah, this is the dirtiest man I have ever seen."

It was Ibn Fahad, of course. The caravan had been of good size, and he had been riding with the Armenite and the under-vizier—not back with the hoi polloi—so we had never spoken. Now you see how we first truly met: me on my back, covered with mud, blood, and spit; and Ibn Fahad standing over me like a rich man examining carrots in the bazaar. Infamy!

Ibn Fahad had been blessed with what I would come later to know as his usual luck. When the bandits—who must have been following us for some days—came down upon us in the night, Ibn Fahad had been voiding his bladder some way downslope. Running back at the sound of the first cries, he had sent more than a few mountain bandits down to Hell courtesy of his swift sword, but they were too many. He pulled together a small group of survivors from the main party and they fought their way free, then fled along the mountain in the darkness listening to the screams echoing behind them, cursing their small numbers and ignorance of the country.

Coming back in the light of day to scavenge for supplies, as well as ascertain the nature of our attackers, Ibn Fahad had found me—a fact he has never allowed me to forget, and for which *I* have never allowed *him* to evade responsibility.

While my wounds and bandit-spites were doctored, Ibn Fahad introduced me to the few survivors of our once-great caravan.

One was Susri al-Din—a cheerful lad, fresh-faced and smooth-cheeked as young Hassan here, dressed in the robes of a rich merchant's son. The soldiers who had survived rather liked him, and called him "Fawn," to tease him for his wide-eyed good looks. There was a skinny wretch of a chief clerk named Abdallah, purse-mouthed and iron-eyed, and an indecently plump young mullah, who had just left the *madrasa* and was getting a rather rude introduction to life outside the seminary. Ruad, the mullah, looked as though he would prefer to be drinking and laughing with the soldiers—beside myself and Ibn Fahad there were four or five more of these—while Abdallah the prim-faced clerk looked as though he should be the one who never lifted his head out of the Koran. Well, in a way that was true, since for a man like Abdallah the balance book *is* the Holy Book, may Allah forgive such blasphemy.

There was one other, notable for the extreme richness of his robes, the extreme whiteness of his beard, and the vast weight of his personal jewelry—Walid al-Salameh, the under-vizier to His Eminence the Caliph Harun al-Rashid. Walid was the most important man of the whole party. He was also, surprisingly, not a bad fellow at all.

So there we found ourselves, the wrack of the caliph's embassy, with no hope but to try and find our way back home through a strange, hostile land.

— ✳ —

The upper reaches of the Caucassians are a cold and godless place. The fog is thick and wet; it crawls in of the morning, leaves briefly at the time the sun is high, then comes creeping back long before sunset. We had been sodden as well-diggers from the moment we had stepped into the foothills. A treacherous place, those mountains: home of bear and wolf, covered in forest so thick that in places the sun was lost completely. Since we had no guide—indeed, it was several days before we saw any sign of inhabitants whatsoever—we wandered unsteered, losing half as much ground as we gained for walking in circles.

At last we were forced to admit our need for a trained local eye. In the middle slopes the trees grew so thick that fixing our direction was impossible for hours at a time. We were divining the location of Mecca by general discussion, and—blasphemy again—we probably spent as much time praying toward Aleppo as to Mecca. It seemed a choice between possible discovery and certain doom.

We came down by night and took a young man out of an isolated shepherd's hovel, as quietly as ex-brigands like ourselves (or at least like many of us, Ibn Fahad. My apologies!) could. The family did not wake, the dog did not bark; we were two leagues away before sunrise, I'm sure.

I felt sorry in a way for the young peasant-lout we'd kidnapped. He was a nice fellow, although fearfully stupid—I wonder if we are now an old, dull story with which he bores his children? In any case, once this young rustic—whose name as far as I could tell was unpronounceable by civilized tongues—realized that we were not ghosts or Jinni, and were *not* going to kill him on the spot, he calmed down and was quite useful. We began to make real progress, reaching the peak of the nearest ridge in two days.

There was a slight feeling of celebration in the air that night, our first in days under the open skies. The soldiers cursed the lack of strong drink, but spirits were good nonetheless—even Ibn Fahad pried loose a smile.

As the under-vizier Walid told a humorous story, I looked about the camp. There were but two grim faces: the clerk Abdallah—which was to be expected, since he seemed a patently sour old devil—and the stolen peasant-boy. I walked over to him.

"Ho, young one," I said, "why do you look so downcast? Have you not realized that we are good-hearted, Godfearing men, and will not harm you?" He did not even raise his chin, which rested on his knees, shepherd-style, but he turned his eyes up to mine.

"It is not those things," he said in his awkward Arabic. "It is not you soldiers but...this place."

"Gloomy mountains they are indeed," I agreed, "but you have lived here all your young life. Why should it bother you?"

"Not this place. We never come here—it is unholy. The vampyr walks these peaks."

"Vampyr?" said I. "And what peasant-devil is that?"

He would say no more; I left him to his brooding and walked back to the fire.

The men all had a good laugh over the vampyr, making jesting guesses as to what type of beast it might be, but Ruad, the young mullah, waved his hands urgently.

"I have heard of such afreets," he said. "They are not to be laughed at by such a godless lot as yourselves."

He said this as a sort of scolding joke, but he wore a strange look on his round face; we listened with interest as he continued.

"The vampyr is a restless spirit. It is neither alive nor dead, and Shaitan possesses its soul utterly. It sleeps in a sepulcher by day, and when the moon rises it goes out to feed upon travelers, to drink their blood."

Some of the men again laughed loudly, but this time it rang false as a brassmerchant's smile.

"I have heard of these from one of our foreign visitors," said the under-vizier Walid quietly. "He told me of a plague of these vampyr in a village near Smyrna. All the inhabitants fled, and the village is still uninhabited today."

This reminded someone else (myself, perhaps) of a tale about an afreet with teeth growing on both sides of his head. Others followed with their own demon stories. The talk went on late into the night, and no one left the campfire until it had completely burned out.

— ✻ —

By noon the next day we had left the heights and were passing back down into the dark, tree-blanketed ravines. When we stopped that night we were once more hidden from the stars, out of sight of Allah and the sky.

I remember waking up in the foredawn hours. My beard was wet with dew, and I was damnably tangled up in my cloak. A great, dark shape stood over me. I must confess to making a bit of a squawking noise.

"It's me," the shape hissed—it was Rifakh, one of the other soldiers. "You gave me a turn."

Rifakh chuckled. "Thought I was that vamper, eh? Sorry. Just stepping out for a piss." He stepped over me, and I heard him trampling the underbrush. I slipped back into sleep.

The sun was just barely over the horizon when I was again awakened, this time by Ibn Fahad tugging at my arm. I grumbled at him to leave me alone, but he had a grip on me like an alms-beggar.

"Rifakh's gone," he said. "Wake up. Have you seen him?"

"He walked on me in the middle of the night, on his way to go moisten a tree," I said. "He probably fell in the darkness and hit his head on something—have you looked?"

"Several times," Ibn Fahad responded. "All around the camp. No sign of him. Did he say anything to you?"

"Nothing interesting. Perhaps he has met the sister of our shepherd-boy, and is making the two-backed beast."

Ibn Fahad made a sour face at my crudity. "Perhaps not. Perhaps he has met some *other* beast."

"Don't worry," I said. "If he hasn't fallen down somewhere close by, he'll be back."

But he did not come back. When the rest of the men arose we had another long search, with no result. At noon we decided, reluctantly, to go on our way, hoping that if he had strayed somewhere he could catch up with us.

We hiked down into the valley, going farther and farther into the trees. There was no sign of Rifakh, although from time to time we stopped and shouted in case he was searching for us. We felt there was small risk of discovery, for that dark valley was as empty as a pauper's purse, but nevertheless, after a while the sound of our voices echoing back through the damp glades became unpleasant. We continued on in silence.

Twilight comes early in the bosom of the mountains; by midafternoon it was already becoming dark. Young Fawn—the name had stuck, against the youth's protests—who of all of us was the most disturbed by the disappearance of Rifakh, stopped the company suddenly, shouting: "Look there!"

We straightaway turned to see where he was pointing, but the thick trees and shadows revealed nothing.

"I saw a shape!" the young one said. "It was just a short way back, following us. Perhaps it is the missing soldier."

Naturally the men ran back to look, but though we scoured the bushes we could find no trace of anyone. We decided that the failing light had played Fawn a trick—that he had seen a hind or somesuch.

Two other times he called out that he saw a shape. The last time one of the other soldiers glimpsed it too: a dark, man-like form, moving rapidly beneath the trees a bow-shot away. Close inspection still yielded no evidence, and as the group trod wearily back to the path again Walid the under-vizier turned to Fawn with a hard, flat look.

"Perhaps it would be better, young master, if you talked no more of shadowshapes."

"But I saw it!" the boy cried. "That soldier Mohammad saw it too!"

"I have no doubt of that," answered Walid al-Salameh, "but think on this: we have gone several times to see what it might be, and have found no sign of any living man. Perhaps our Rifakh is dead; perhaps he fell into a stream and drowned, or hit his head upon a rock. His spirit may be following us because it does not wish to stay in this unfamiliar place. That does not mean we want to go and find it."

"But...," the other began.

"Enough!" spat the chief clerk Abdallah. "You heard the under-vizier, young prankster. We shall have no more talk of your godless spirits. You will straightaway leave off telling such things!"

"Your concern is appreciated, Abdallah," Walid said coldly, "but I do not require your help in this matter." The vizier strode away.

I was almost glad the clerk had added his voice, because such ideas would not keep the journey in good order...but like the under-vizier I, too, had been rubbed and grated by the clerk's highhandedness. I am sure others felt the same, for no more was said on the subject all evening.

Allah, though, always has the last word—and who are *we* to try to understand His ways? We bedded down a very quiet camp that night, the idea of poor Rifakh's lost soul hanging unspoken in the air.

From a thin, unpleasant sleep I woke to find the camp in chaos. "It's Mohammad, the soldier!" Fawn was crying. "He's been killed! He's dead!"

It was true. The mullah Ruad, first up in the morning, had found the man's blanket empty, then found his body a few short yards out of the clearing.

"His throat has been slashed out," said Ibn Fahad.

It looked like a wild beast had been at him. The ground beneath was dark with blood, and his eyes were wide open.

Above the cursing of the soldiers and the murmured holy words of the mullah, who looked quite green of face, I heard another sound. The young shepherd-lad, grimly silent all the day before, was rocking back and forth on the ground by the remains of the cook-fire, moaning.

"Vampyr...," he wept, "...vampyr, the vampyr..."

All the companions were, of course, completely unmanned by these events. While we buried Mohammad in a hastily dug grave those assembled darted glances over their shoulders into the forest vegetation. Even Ruad, as he spoke the words of the holy Koran, had trouble keeping his eyes down. Ibn Fahad and I agreed between ourselves to maintain that Mohammad had fallen prey to a wolf or some other beast, but our fellow travelers found it hard even to pretend agreement. Only the under-vizier and the clerk Abdallah seemed to have their wits fully about them, and Abdallah made no secret of his contempt for the others. We set out again at once.

Our company was somber that day—and no wonder. No one wished to speak of the obvious, nor did they have much stomach for talk of lighter things—it was a silent file of men that moved through the mountain fastnesses.

As the shadows of evening began to roll down, the dark shape was with us again, flitting along just in sight, disappearing for a while only to return, bobbing along behind us like a jackdaw. My skin was crawling— as you may well believe—though I tried to hide it.

We set camp, building a large fire and moving near to it, and had a sullen, close-cramped supper. Ibn Fahad, Abdallah, the vizier, and I were still speaking of the follower only as some beast. Abdallah may even have believed it—not from ordinary foolishness, but because he was the type of man who was unwilling to believe there might be anything he himself could not compass.

As we took turns standing guard the young mullah led the far-from-sleepy men in prayer. The voices rose up with the smoke, neither seeming to be of much substance against the wind of those old, cold mountains.

I sidled over to the shepherd-lad. He'd become, if anything, more close-mouthed since the discovery of the morning.

"This 'vampyr' you spoke of...," I said quietly. "What do your people do to protect themselves from it?"

He looked up at me with a sad smile.

"Lock the doors."

I stared across at the other men—young Fawn with clenched mouth and furrowed brow; the mullah Ruad, eyes closed, plump cheeks awash with sweat as he prayed; Ibn Fahad gazing coolly outward, ever outward—and then I returned the boy's sad smile.

"No doors to lock, no windows to bar," I said. "What else?"

"There is an herb we hang about our houses...," he said, and fumbled for the word in our unfamiliar language. After a moment he gave up. "It does not matter. We have none. None grows here."

I leaned forward, putting my face next to his face. "For the love of God, boy, what else?"–*I* knew it was not a beast of the Earth. *I knew.* I had seen that fluttering shadow.

"Well...," he mumbled, turning his face away, "...they say, some men do, that you can tell stories...."

"What!" I thought he had gone mad.

"This is what my grandfather says. The vampyr will stop to hear the story you tell—if it is a good one—and if you continue it until daylight he must return to the...place of the dead."

There was a sudden shriek. I leaped to my feet, fumbling for my knife...but it was only Ruad, who had put his foot against a hot coal. I sank down again, heart hammering.

"Stories?" I asked.

"I have only heard so," he said, struggling for the right phrases. "We try to keep them farther away than that—they must come close to hear a man talking."

Later, after the fire had gone down, we placed sentries and went to our blankets. I lay a long while thinking of what the Armenite boy had said before I slept.

— ✳ —

A hideous screeching sound woke me. It was not yet dawn, and this time no one had burned himself on a glowing ember.

One of the two soldiers who had been standing picket lay on the forest floor, blood gouting from a great wound on the side of his head. In the torchlight it looked as though his skull had been smashed with a heavy cudgel. The other sentry was gone, but there was a terrible thrashing in the underbrush beyond the camp, and screams that would have sounded like an animal in a cruel trap but for the half-formed words that bubbled up from time to time.

We crouched, huddled, staring like startled rabbits. The screaming began to die away. Suddenly Ruad started up, heavy and clumsy getting to his feet. I saw tears in his eyes. "We...we must not leave our fellow to s-s-suffer so!" he cried, and looked around at all of us. I don't think anyone could hold his eye except the clerk Abdallah. I could not.

"Be silent, fool!" the clerk said, heedless of blasphemy. "It is a wild beast. It is for these cowardly soldiers to attend to, not a man of God!"

The young mullah stared at him for a moment, and a change came over his face. The tears were still wet on his cheeks, but I saw his jaw firm and his shoulders square.

"No," he said. "We cannot leave him to Shaitan's servant. If you will not go to him, I will." He rolled up the scroll he had been nervously fingering and kissed it. A shaft of moonlight played across the gold letters.

I tried to grab his arm as he went past me, but he shook me off with surprising strength, then moved toward the brush, where the screeching had died down to a low, broken moaning.

"Come back, you idiot!" Abdallah shrieked at him. "This is foolishness! Come back!"

The young holy man looked back over his shoulder, darting a look at Abdallah I could not easily describe, then turned around and continued forward, holding the parchment scroll before him as if it were a candle against the dark night.

"There as no God but Allah!" I heard him cry, *"and Mohammad is His prophet!"* Then he was gone.

After a long moment of silence there came the sound of the holy words of the Koran, chanted in an unsteady voice. We could hear the mullah making his ungraceful way out through the thicket. I was not the only one who held his breath.

Next there was crashing, and branches snapping, as though some huge beast was leaping through the brush; the mullah's chanting became a howl. Men cursed helplessly. Before the cry had faded, though, another scream came—numbingly loud, the rage of a powerful animal, full of shock and surprise. It had words in it, although not in any tongue I had ever heard before...or since.

Another great thrashing, and then nothing but silence. We lit another fire and sat sleepless until dawn.

In the morning, despite my urgings, the company went to look for trace of the sentry and the young priest. They found them both.

It made a grim picture, let me tell you, my friends. They hung upside down from the branches of a great tree. Their necks were torn, and they were white as chalk: all the blood had been drawn from them. We dragged the two stone-cold husks back to the camp-circle, and shortly thereafter buried them commonly with the other sentry, who had not survived his head wound.

One curious thing there was: on the ground beneath the hanging head of the young priest lay the remains of his holy scroll. It was scorched to black ash, and crumbled at my touch.

"So it *was* a cry of pain we heard," said Ibn Fahad over my shoulder. "The devil-beast can be hurt, it appears."

"Hurt, but not made to give over," I observed. "And no other holy writings remain, nor any hands so holy to wield them, or mouth to speak them." I looked pointedly over at Abdallah, who was giving unwanted instructions to the two remaining soldiers on how to spade the funeral dirt. I half-hoped one of them would take it on himself to brain the old meddler.

"True," grunted Ibn Fahad. "Well, I have my doubts on how cold steel will fare, also."

"As do I. But it could be there is yet a way we may save ourselves. The shepherd-boy told me of it. I will explain when we stop at mid-day."

"I will be waiting eagerly," said Ibn Fahad, favoring me with his half-smile. "I am glad to see someone else is thinking and planning beside myself. But perhaps you should tell us your plan on the march. Our daylight hours are becoming precious as blood, now. As a matter of fact, I think from now on we shall have to do without burial services."

— ✳ —

Well, there we were in a very nasty fix. As we walked I explained my plan to the group; they listened silently, downcast, like men condemned to death—not an unreasonable attitude, in all truth.

"Now, here's the thing," I told them. "If this young lout's idea of tale-telling will work, we shall have to spend our nights yarning away. We may have to begin taking stops for sleeping in the daylight. Every moment walking, then, is precious—we must keep the pace up or we will die in these damned, haunted mountains. Also, while you walk, think of stories. From what the lad says we may have another ten days or a fortnight to go until we escape this country. We shall soon run out of things to tell about, unless you dig deep into your memories."

There was grumbling, but it was too dispirited a group to offer much protest.

"Be silent, unless you have a better idea," said Ibn Fahad. "Masrur is quite correct—although, if what I suspect is true, it may be the first time in his life he finds himself in that position." He threw me a wicked grin, and one of the soldiers snickered. It was a good sound to hear.

— ✳ —

We had a short mid-day rest—most of us got at least an hour's sleep on the rocky ground—and then we walked on until the beginning of twilight. We were in the bottom of a long, thickly forested ravine, where we promptly built a large fire to keep away some of the darkness of the valley floor. Ah, but fire is a good friend!

Gathered around the blaze, the men cooked strips of venison on the ends of green sticks. We passed the water skin and wished it was more— not for the first time.

"Now then," I said, "I'll go first, for at home I was the one called upon most often to tell tales, and I have a good fund of them. Some of you may sleep, but not all—there should always be two or three awake in case the teller falters or forgets. We cannot know if this will keep the creature at bay, but we should take no chances."

So I began, telling first the story of The Four Clever Brothers. It was early, and no one was ready to sleep; all listened attentively as I spun it out, adding details here, stretching a description there.

When it ended I was applauded, and straight away began telling the story of the carpet merchant Salim and his unfaithful wife. That was perhaps not a good choice–it is a story about a vengeful djinn, and about death; but I went on nonetheless, finished it, then told two more.

As I was finishing the fourth story, about a brave orphan who finds a cave of jewels, I glimpsed a strange thing.

The fire was beginning to die down, and as I looked out over the flames I saw movement in the forest. The under-vizier Walid was directly across from me, and beyond his once-splendid robes a dark shape lurked.

It came no closer than the edge of the trees, staying just out of the fire's flickering light. I lost my voice for a moment then and stuttered, but quickly caught up the thread and finished. No one had noticed, I was sure.

I asked for the waterskin and motioned for Walid al-Salameh to continue. He took up with a tale of the rivalry beyond two wealthy houses in his native Isfahan. One or two of the others wrapped themselves tightly in their cloaks and lay down, staring up as they listened, watching the sparks rise into the darkness.

I pulled my hood down low on my brow to shield my gaze, and squinted out past Walid's shoulder. The dark shape had moved a little nearer now to the lapping glow of the campfire.

It was man-shaped, that I could see fairly well, though it clung close to the trunk of a tree at clearing's edge. Its face was in darkness; two ember-red eyes unblinkingly reflected the firelight. It seemed clothed in rags, but that could have been a trick of the shadows.

Huddled in the darkness a stone-throw away, it was listening.

I turned my head slowly across the circle. Most eyes were on the vizier; Fawn had curtained his in sleep. But Ibn Fahad, too, was staring out into the darkness. I suppose he felt my gaze, for he turned to me and nodded slightly: he had seen it too.

We went on until dawn, the men taking turns sleeping as one of the others told stories—mostly tales they had heard as children, occasionally of an adventure that had befallen them. Ibn Fahad and I said nothing of the dark shape that watched. Somewhere in the hour before dawn it disappeared.

It was a sleepy group that took to the trail that day, but we had all lived through the night. This alone put the men in better spirits, and we covered much ground.

That night we again sat around the fire. I told the story of The Gazelle King, and The Enchanted Peacock, and The Little Man with No Name, each of them longer and more complicated than the one before. Everyone except the clerk Abdallah contributed something—Abdallah and the shepherd-boy, that is. The chief-clerk said repeatedly that he had never wasted his time on foolishness such as learning stories. We were understandably reluctant to press our self-preservation into such unwilling hands.

The Armenite boy, our guide, sat quietly all the evening and listened to the men yarning away in a tongue that was not his own. When the moon had risen through the treetops, the shadow returned and stood silently outside the clearing. I saw the peasant lad look up. He saw it, I know, but like Ibn Fahad and I, he held his silence.

The next day brought us two catastrophes. As we were striking camp in the morning, happily no fewer than when we had set down the night before, the local lad took the waterskins down to the river that threaded the bottom of the ravine. When a long hour had passed and he had not returned, we went fearfully down to look for him.

He was gone. All but one of the waterskins lay on the streambank. He had filled them first.

The men were panicky. "The vampyr has taken him!" they cried.

"What does that foul creature need with a waterskin?" pointed out al-Salameh.

"He's right," I said. "No, I'm afraid our young friend has merely jumped ship, so to speak. I suppose he thinks his chances of getting back are better if he is alone."

I wondered...I *still* wonder...if he made it back. He was not a bad fellow: witness the fact that he took only one water-bag, and left us the rest.

Thus, we found ourselves once more without a guide. Fortunately, I had discussed with him the general direction, and he had told Ibn Fahad and myself of the larger landmarks...but it was nevertheless with sunken hearts that we proceeded.

Later that day, in the early afternoon, the second blow fell.

We were coming up out of the valley, climbing diagonally along the steep side of the ravine. The damned Caucassian fogs had slimed the rocks and turned the ground soggy; the footing was treacherous.

Achmed, the older of the remaining pike-men, had been walking poorly all day. He had bad joints, anyway, he said; and the cold nights had been making them worse.

We had stopped to rest on an outcropping of rock that jutted from the valley wall; Achmed, the last in line, was just catching up to us when he slipped. He fell heavily onto his side and slid several feet down the muddy slope.

Ibn Fahad jumped up to look for a rope, but before he could get one from the bottom of his pack the other soldier—named Bekir, if memory serves—clambered down the grade to help his comrade.

He got a grip on Achmed's tunic, and was just turning around to catch Ibn Fahad's rope when the leg of the older man buckled beneath him and he fell backward. Bekir, caught off his balance, pitched back as well, his hand caught in the neck of Achmed's tunic, and the two of them rolled end over end down the slope. Before anyone could so much as cry out they had both disappeared over the edge, like a wine jug rolling off a table-top. Just that sudden.

To fall such a distance certainly killed them.

We could not find the bodies, of course...could not even climb back down the ravine to look. Ibn Fahad's remark about burials had taken on a terrible, ironic truth. We could but press on, now a party of five—myself, Ibn Fahad, the under-vizier Walid, Abdallah the clerk, and young Fawn. I doubt that there was a single one of our number who did not wonder which of us would next meet death in that lonesome place.

— ✳ —

Ah, by Allah most high, I have never been so sick of the sound of my own voice as I was by the time nine more nights had passed. Ibn Fahad, I know, would say that I have never understood how sick *everyone* becomes of the sound of my voice—am I correct, old friend? But I *was* tired of it, tired of talking all night, tired of racking my brain for stories, tired of listening to the cracked voices of Walid and Ibn Fahad, tired to sickness of the damp, gray, oppressive mountains.

All were now aware of the haunting shade that stood outside our fire at night, waiting and listening. Young Fawn, in particular, could hardly hold up his turn at tale-telling, so much did his voice tremble.

Abdallah grew steadily colder and colder, congealing like rendered fat. The thing which followed was no respecter of his cynicism or his mathematics, and would not be banished for all the scorn he could muster. The skinny chief-clerk did not turn out to us, though, to support the story-circle, but sat silently and walked apart. Despite our terrible mutual danger he avoided our company as much as possible.

The tenth night after the loss of Achmed and Bekir we were running out of tales. We had been ground down by our circumstances, and were ourselves become nearly as shadowy as that which we feared.

Walid al-Salameh was droning on about some ancient bit of minor intrigue in the court of the Emperor Darius of Persia. Ibn Fahad leaned toward me, lowering his voice so that neither Abdallah nor Fawn— whose expression was one of complete and hopeless despair—could hear.

"Did you notice," he whispered, "that our guest has made no appearance tonight?"

"It has not escaped me," I said. "I hardly think it a good sign, however. If our talk no longer interests the creature, how long can it be until its thoughts return to our other uses?"

"I fear you're right," he responded, and gave a scratchy, painful chuckle. "There's a good three or four more days walking, and hard walking at that, until we reach the bottom of these mountains and come once more onto the plain, at which point we might hope the devil-beast would leave us."

"Ibn Fahad," I said, shaking my head as I looked across at Fawn's drawn, pale face, "I fear we shall not manage..."

As if to point up the truth of my fears, Walid here stopped his speech, coughing violently. I gave him to drink of the water-skin, but when he had finished he did not begin anew; he only sat looking darkly, as one lost, out to the forest.

"Good vizier," I asked, "can you continue?"

He said nothing, and I quickly spoke in his place, trying to pick up the threads of a tale I had not been attending to. Walid leaned back, exhausted and breathing raggedly. Abdallah clucked his tongue in disgust. If I had not been fearfully occupied, I would have struck the clerk.

Just as I was beginning to find my way, inventing a continuation of the vizier's Darian political meanderings, there came a shock that passed through all of us like a cold wind, and a new shadow appeared at the edge of the clearing. The vampyr had joined us.

Walid moaned and sat up, huddling by the fire. I faltered for a moment but went on. The candle-flame eyes regarded us unblinkingly, and the shadow shook for a moment as if folding great wings.

Suddenly Fawn leaped to his feet, swaying unsteadily. I lost the strands of the story completely and stared up at him in amazement.

"Creature!" he screamed. "Hell-spawn! Why do you torment us in this way? Why, why, why?"

Ibn Fahad reached up to pull him down, but the young man danced away like a shying horse. His mouth hung open and his eyes were starting from their dark-rimmed sockets.

"You great beast!" he continued to shriek. "Why do you toy with us? Why do you not just kill me–kill us *all,* set us free from this terrible, terrible..."

And with that he walked *forward*–away from the fire, toward the thing that crouched at forest's edge.

"End this now!" Fawn shouted, and fell to this knees only a few strides from the smoldering red eyes, sobbing like a child.

"Stupid boy, get back!" I cried. Before I could get up to pull him back—and I would have, I swear by Allah's name—there was a great rushing noise, and the black shape was gone, the lamps of its stare extinguished. Then, as we pulled the shuddering youth back to the campfire, something rustled in the trees. On the opposite side of the campfire one of the near branches suddenly bobbed beneath the weight of a strange new fruit–a black fruit with red-lit eyes. It made an awful croaking noise.

In our shock it was a few moments before we realized that the deep, rasping sound was speech–and the words were Arabic!

"...It...was...you...," it said, "...who chose...to play the game this way..."

Almost strangest of all, I would swear that this thing had never spoken our language before, never even heard it until we had wandered lost into the mountains. Something of its halting inflections, its strange hesitations, made me guess it had learned our speech from listening all these nights to our campfire stories.

"Demon!" shrilled Abdallah. "What manner of creature are you?!"

"You know...very well what kind of...thing I am, man. You may none of you know *how,* or *why*...but by now, you know *what* I am."

"Why...why do you torment us so?!" shouted Fawn, writhing in Ibn Fahad's strong grasp.

"Why does the...serpent kill...a rabbit? The serpent does not...hate. It kills to live, as do I...as do you."

Abdallah lurched forward a step. "We do not slaughter our fellow men like this, devil-spawn!"

"C-c-clerk!" the black shape hissed, and dropped down from the tree. "C-close your foolish mouth! You push me too far!" It bobbed, as if agitated. "The curse of human ways! Even now you provoke me more than you should, you huffing...insect! *Enough!*"

The vampyr seemed to leap upward, and with a great rattling of leaves he scuttled away along the limb of a tall tree. I was fumbling for my sword, but before I could find it the creature spoke again from his high perch.

"The young one asked me why I 'toy' with you. I do not. If I do not kill, I will suffer. More than I suffer already.

"Despite what this clerk says, though, I am not a creature with-out...without feelings as men have them. Less and less do I wish to destroy you.

"For the first time in a great age I have listened to the sound of human voices that were not screams of fear. I have approached a circle of men without the barking of dogs, and have listened to them talk.

"It has almost been like being a man again."

"And this is how you show your pleasure?" the under-vizier Walid asked, teeth chattering. "By k-k-killing us?"

"I am what I am," said the beast. "...But for all that, you have inspired a certain desire for companionship. It puts me in mind of things that I can barely remember.

"I propose that we make a...bargain," said the vampyr. "A...wager?"

I had found my sword, and Ibn Fahad had drawn his as well, but we both knew we could not kill a thing like this—a red-eyed demon that could leap five cubits in the air and had learned to speak our language in a fortnight.

"No bargains with Shaitan!" spat the clerk Abdallah.

"What do you mean?" I demanded, inwardly marveling that such an unlikely dialogue should ever take place on the earth. "Pay no attention to the..." I curled my lip, "...holy man." Abdallah shot me a venomous glance.

"Hear me, then," the creature said, and in the deep recesses of the tree seemed once more to unfold and stretch great wings. "Hear me. I must kill to live, and my nature is such that I cannot choose to die. That is the way of things.

"I offer you now, however, the chance to win safe passage out of my domain, these hills. We shall have a contest, a wager if you like; if you best me you shall go freely, and I shall turn once more to the musty, slow-blooded peasants of the local valleys."

Ibn Fahad laughed bitterly. "What, are we to fight you then? So be it!"

"I would snap your spine like a dry branch, " croaked the black shape. "No, you have held me these many nights telling stories; it is story-telling that will win you safe passage. We will have a contest, one that will suit my whims: we shall relate the saddest of all stories. That is my demand. You may tell three, I will tell only one. If you can best me with any or all, you shall go unhindered by me."

"And if we lose?!" I cried. "And who shall judge?"

"You may judge," it said, and the deep, thick voice took on a tone of grim amusement. "If you can look into my eyes and tell me that you have bested *my* sad tale...why, then I shall believe you.

"If you lose," it said, "then one of your number shall come to me, and pay the price of your defeat. Those are my terms, otherwise I shall hunt you down one at a time—for in truth, your present tale-telling has begun to lose my interest."

Ibn Fahad darted a worried look in my direction. Fawn and the others stared at the demon-shape in mute terror and astonishment.

"We shall...we shall give you our decision at sunset tomorrow," I said. "We must be allowed to think and talk."

"As you wish," said the vampyr. "But if you accept my challenge, the game must begin then. After all, we have only a few more days to spend together." And at this the terrible creature laughed, a sound like the bark being pulled from the trunk of a rotted tree. Then the shadow was gone.

In the end we had to accede to the creature's wager, of course. We knew he was not wrong in his assessment of us—we were just wagging our beards over the nightly campfire, no longer even listening to our own tales. Whatever magic had held the vampyr at bay had drained out like meal from a torn sack.

I racked my poor brains all afternoon for stories of sadness, but could think of nothing that seemed to fit, that seemed significant enough for the vital purpose at hand. I had been doing most of the talking for several nights running, and had exhausted virtually every story I had ever heard—and I was never much good at making them up, as Ibn Fahad will attest. Yes, go ahead and smile, old comrade.

Actually, it was Ibn Fahad who volunteered the first tale. I asked him what it was, but he would not tell me. "Let me save what potency it may have," he said. The under-vizier Walid also had something he deemed suitable; I was racking my brain fruitlessly for a third time when young Fawn piped up that he would tell a tale himself. I looked him over, rosy cheeks and long-lashed eyes, and asked him what he could possibly know of sadness. Even as I spoke I realized my cruelty, standing as we all did in the shadow of death or worse, but it was too late to take it back.

Fawn did not flinch. He was folding his cloak as he sat cross-ankled on the ground, folding and unfolding it. He looked up and said: "I shall tell a sad story about love. All the saddest stories are about love."

These young shavetails, I thought—although I was not ten years his senior—*a sad story about love.* But I could not think of better, and was forced to give in.

We walked as fast and far as we could that day, as if hoping that somehow, against all reason, we should find ourselves out of the gloomy, mist-sodden hills. But when twilight came the vast bulk of the mountains still hung above us. We made camp on the porch of a great standing rock, as though protection at our backs would avail us of something if the night went badly.

The fire had only just taken hold, and the sun had dipped below the rim of the hills a moment before, when a cold wind made the branches of the trees whip back and forth. We knew without speaking, without looking at one another, that the creature had come.

"Have you made your decision?" The harsh voice from the trees sounded strange, as if its owner was trying to speak lightly, carelessly— but I only heard death in those cold syllables.

"We have, " said Ibn Fahad, drawing himself up out of his involuntary half-crouch to stand erect. "We will accept your wager. Do you wish to begin?"

"Oh, no..." the thing said, and made a flapping noise. "That would take all of the...suspense from the contest, would it not? No, I insist that you begin."

"I am first, then," Ibn Fahad said, looking around our circle for confirmation. The dark shape moved abruptly toward us. Before we could scatter the vampyr stopped, a few short steps away.

"Do not fear," it grated. Close to one's ear the voice was even odder and more strained. "I have come nearer to hear the story and see the teller—for surely that is part of any tale—but I shall move no farther. Begin."

Everybody but myself stared into the fire, hugging their knees, keeping their eyes averted from the bundle of darkness that sat at our shoulders. I had the fire between myself and the creature, and felt safer than if I had sat like Walid and Abdallah, with nothing between the beast and my back but cold ground.

The vampyr sat hunched, as if imitating our posture, its eyes hooded so that only a flicker of scarlet light, like a half-buried brand, showed through each slit. It was black, this manlike thing—not black as a Negro, mind you, but black as burnt steel, black as the mouth of a cave. It bore the aspect of someone dead of the plague. Rags wrapped it, mouldering, filthy bits of cloth, rotten as old bread...but the curve of its back spoke of terrible life—a great black cricket poised to jump.

Ibn Fahad's Story

Many years ago [he began], I traveled for a good time in Egypt. I was indigent, then, and journeyed wherever the prospect of payment for a sword arm beckoned.

I found myself at last in the household guard of a rich merchant in Alexandria. I was happy enough there; and I enjoyed walking in the busy streets, so unlike the village in which I was born.

One summer evening I found myself walking down an unfamiliar street. It emptied out into a little square that sat below the front of an old mosque. The square was full of people: merchants and fishwives, a juggler or two, but most of the crowd was drawn up to the facade of the mosque, pressed in close together.

At first, as I strolled across the square, I thought prayers were about to begin, but it was still some time until sunset. I wondered if perhaps some notable imam was speaking from the mosque steps, but as I approached I could see that all the assembly were staring upward, craning their necks back as if the sun itself, on its way to its western mooring, had become snagged on one of the minarets.

But instead of the sun, what stood on the onion-shaped dome was the silhouette of a man, who seemed to be staring out toward the horizon.

"Who is that?" I asked a man near me.

"It is Ha'arud al-Emwiya, the Sufi," the man told me, never lowering his eyes from the tower above.

"Is he caught up there?" I demanded. "Will he not fall?"

"Watch," was all the man said. I did.

A moment later, much to my horror, the small dark figure of Ha'arud the Sufi seemed to go rigid, then toppled from the minaret's rim like a stone. I gasped in shock, and so did a few others around me, but the rest of the crowd only stood in hushed attention.

Then an incredible thing happened. The tumbling holy man spread his arms out from his shoulders, like a bird's wings, and his downward fall became a swooping glide. He bottomed out high above the crowd, then sped upward, riding the wind like a leaf, spinning, somersaulting, stopping at last to drift to the ground as gently as a bit of eiderdown. Meanwhile, all the assembly was chanting "God is great! God is great!" When the Sufi had touched the earth with his bare feet the people surrounded him, touching his rough woolen garments and crying out his name. He said nothing, only stood and smiled, and before too long the people began to wander away, talking amongst themselves.

"But this is truly marvelous!" I said to the man who stood by me.

"Before every holy day he flies," the man said, and shrugged.

"I am surprised this is the first time you have heard of Ha'arud al-Emwiya."

— ✳ —

I was determined to speak to this amazing man, and as the crowd dispersed I approached and asked if I might buy him a glass of tea. Close up he had a look of seamed roguishness that seemed surprising placed against the great favor in which Allah must have held him. He smilingly agreed, and accompanied me to a tea shop close by in the Street of Weavers.

"How is it, if you will pardon my forwardness, that you of all holy men are so gifted?"

He looked up from the tea cupped in his palms and grinned. He had only two teeth. "Balance," he said.

I was surprised. "A cat has balance," I responded, "but they nevertheless must wait for the pigeons to land."

"I refer to a different sort of balance," he said. "The balance between Allah and Shaitan, which, as you know, Allah the All-Knowing has created as an equilibrium of exquisite delicacy."

"Explain please, master." I called for wine, but Ha'arud refused any himself.

"In all things care must be exercised," he explained. "Thus it is too with my flying. Many men holier than I are as earthbound as stones. Many other men have lived so poorly as to shame the Devil himself, yet they cannot take to the air, either. Only I, if I may be excused what sounds self-satisfied, have discovered perfect balance. Thus, each year before the holy days I tot up my score carefully, committing small peccadilloes or acts of faith as needed until the balance is exactly, exactly balanced. Thus, when I jump from the mosque, neither Allah nor the Arch-Enemy has claim on my soul, and they bear me up until a later date, at which time the issue shall be clearer." He smiled again and drained his tea.

"You are...a sort of chessboard on which God and the Devil contend?" I asked, perplexed.

"A flying chessboard, yes."

We talked for a long while, as the shadows grew long across the Street of the Weavers, but the Sufi Ha'arud adhered stubbornly to his explanation. I must have seemed disbelieving, for he finally proposed that we ascend to the top of the mosque so he could demonstrate.

I was more than a little drunk, and he, imbibing only tea, was filled nonetheless with a strange gleefulness. We made our way up the many winding stairs and climbed out onto the narrow ledge that circled the minaret like a crown. The cool night air, and the thousands of winking lights of Alexandria far below, sobered me rapidly. "I suddenly find all your precepts very sound," I said. "Let us go down."

But Ha'arud would have none of it, and proceeded to step lightly off the edge of the dome. He hovered, like a bumblebee, a hundred feet above the dusty street. "Balance," he said with great satisfaction.

"But," I asked, "is the good deed of giving me this demonstration enough to offset the pride with which you exhibit your skill?" I was cold and wanted to get down, and hoped to shorten the exhibition.

Instead, hearing my question, Ha'arud screwed up his face as though it was something he had not given thought to. A moment later, with a shriek of surprise, he plummeted down out of my sight to smash on the mosque's stone steps, as dead as dead.

— ✳ —

Ibn Fahad, having lost himself in remembering the story, poked at the campfire. "Thus, the problem with matters of delicate balance," he said, and shook his head.

The whispering rustle of our dark visitor brought us sharply back. "Interesting," the creature rasped. "Sad, yes. Sad enough? We shall see. Who is the next of your number?"

A cold chill, like fever, swept over me at those calm words.

"I...I am next...," said Fawn, voice taut as a bowstring. "Shall I begin?"

"The vampyr said nothing, only bobbed the black lump of his head. The youth cleared his throat and began.

Fawn's Story

There was once...[Fawn began, and hesitated, then started again.] There was once a young prince named Zufik, the second son of a great sultan. Seeing no prospects for himself in his father's kingdom, he went out into the wild world to search for his fortune. He traveled through many lands, and saw many strange things, and heard tell of others stranger still.

In one place he was told of a nearby sultanate, the ruler of which had a beautiful daughter, his only child and the very apple of his eye.

Now this country had been plagued for several years by a terrible beast, a great white leopard of a kind never seen before. So fearsome it was that it had killed hunters set to trap it, yet was it also so cunning that it had stolen babies from their very cradles as the mothers lay sleeping. The people of the sultanate were all in fear; and the sultan, whose best warriors had tried and failed to kill the beast, was driven to despair. Finally, at the end of his wits, he had it proclaimed in the market place that the man who could destroy the white leopard would be gifted with the sultan's daughter Rassoril, and with her the throne of the sultanate after the old man was gone.

Young Zufik heard how the best young men of the country, and others from countries beyond, one after the other had met their deaths beneath the claws of the leopard, or...or...in its jaws....

[Here I saw the boy falter, as if the vision of flashing teeth he was conjuring had suddenly reminded him of our predicament. Walid the under-vizier reached out and patted the lad's shoulder with great gentleness, until he was calm enough to resume.]

So...[He swallowed.] So young Prince Zufik took himself into that country, and soon was announced at the sultan's court.

The ruler was a tired old man, the fires in his sunken eyes long quenched. Much of the power seemed to have been handed over to a pale, narrow-faced youth named Sifaz, who was the princess's cousin. As Zufik announced his purpose, as so many had done before him, Sifaz's eyes flashed.

"You will no doubt meet the end all the others have, but you are welcome to the attempt—and the prize, should you win."

Then for the first time Zufik saw the princess Rassoril, and in an instant his heart was overthrown.

She had hair as black and shiny as polished jet, and a face upon which Allah himself must have looked in satisfaction, thinking: "Here is the summit of My art." Her delicate hands were like tiny doves as they nested in her lap, and a man could fall into her brown eyes and drown without hope of rescue— which is what Zufik did, and he was not wrong when he thought he saw Rassoril return his ardent gaze.

Sifaz saw, too, and his thin mouth turned in something like a smile, and he narrowed his yellow eyes. "Take this princeling to his room, that he may sleep now and wake with the moon. The leopard's cry was heard around the palace's walls last night."

Indeed, when Zufik woke in the evening darkness, it was to hear the choking cry of the leopard beneath his very window. As he looked out, buckling on his scabbard, it was to see a white shape slipping in and out of the shadows in the garden below. He took also his dagger in his hand and leaped over the threshold.

He had barely touched ground when, with a terrible snarl, the leopard bounded out of the obscurity of the hedged garden wall and came to a stop before him. It was huge—bigger than any leopard Zufik had seen or heard of—and its pelt gleamed like ivory. It leaped, claws flashing, and he could barely throw himself down in time as the beast passed over him like a cloud, touching him only with its hot breath. It turned and leaped again as the palace dogs set up a terrible barking, and this time its talons raked his chest, knocking him tumbling. Blood started from his shirt, spouting so fiercely that he could scarcely draw himself to his feet. He was caught with his back against the garden wall; the leopard slowly moved toward him, yellow eyes like tallow lamps burning in the niches of Hell.

Suddenly there was a crashing at the far end of the garden: the dogs had broken down their stall and were even now speeding through the trees. The leopard hesitated—Zufik could almost see it thinking—and then, with a last snarl, it leaped onto the wall and disappeared into the night.

Zufik was taken, his wounds bound, and he was put into his bed. The princess Rassoril, who had truly lost her heart to him, wept bitterly at his side, begging him to go back to his father's land and to give up the fatal challenge. But Zufik, weak as he was, would no more think of yielding than he would of theft or treason, and refused, saying he would hunt the beast again the following night. Sifaz grinned and led the princess away. Zufik thought he heard the pale cousin whistling as he went.

In the dark before dawn Zufik, who could not sleep owing to the pain of his injury, heard his door quietly open. He was astonished to see the princess come in, gesturing him to silence. When the door was closed she threw herself down at his side and covered his hand and cheek with kisses, proclaiming her love for him and begging him again to go. He admitted his love for her, but reminded her that his honor would not permit him to stop short of his goal, even should he die in the trying.

Rassoril, seeing that there was no changing the young prince's mind, then took from her robe a black arrow tipped in silver, fletched with the tail feathers of a falcon. "Then take this," she said. "This leopard is a magic beast, and you will never kill it otherwise. Only silver will pierce its heart. Take the arrow and you may fulfill your oath." So saying, she slipped out of his room.

The next night Zufik again heard the leopard's voice in the garden below, but this time he took also his bow and arrow when he went to meet it. At first he was loath to use it, since it seemed somehow unmanly; but when the beast had again given him injury and he had struck three sword blows in turn without effect, he at last nocked the silver-pointed shaft on his bowstring and, as the beast charged him once more, let fly. The black arrow struck to the leopard's heart; the creature gave a hideous cry and again leaped the fence, this time leaving a trail of its mortal blood behind it.

When morning came Zufik went to the sultan for men, so that they could follow the track of blood to the beast's lair and prove its death. The sultan was displeased when his vizier, the princess's pale cousin, did not answer his summons. As they were all going down into the garden, though, there came a great cry from the sleeping rooms upstairs, a cry like a soul in mortal agony. With fear in their hearts Zufik, the sultan, and all the men rushed upstairs. There they found the missing Sifaz.

The pale man lifted a shaking, red-smeared finger to point at Zufik, as all the company stared in horror. "*He* has done it—the foreigner!" Sifaz shouted.

In Sifaz's arms lay the body of the Princess Rassoril, a black arrow standing from her breast.

— ✳ —

After Fawn finished there was a long silence. The boy, his own courage perhaps stirred by his story, seemed to sit straighter.

"Ah...," the vampyr said at last, "love and its prices—that is the message? Or is it perhaps the effect of silver on the supernatural? Fear not, I am bound by no such conventions, and fear neither silver, steel, nor any other metal." The creature made a huffing, scraping sound that might have been a laugh. I marveled anew, even as I felt the skein of my life fraying, that it had so quickly gained such command of our unfamiliar tongue.

"Well...," it said slowly. "Sad. But...sad enough? Again, *that* is the important question. Who is your last...contestant?"

Now my heart truly went cold within me, and I sat as though I had swallowed a stone. Walid al-Salameh spoke up.

"I am," he said, and took a deep breath. "I am."

The Vizier's Story

This is a true story—or so I was told. It happened in my grandfather's time, and he had it from someone who knew those involved. He told it to me as a cautionary tale.

There once was an old caliph, a man of rare gifts and good fortune. He ruled a small country, but a wealthy one—a country upon which all the gifts of Allah had been showered in grand measure. He had the finest heir a man could have, dutiful and yet courageous, beloved by the people almost as extravagantly as the caliph himself. He had many other fine sons, and two hundred beautiful wives, and an army of fighting men the envy of his neighbors. His treasury was stacked roofbeam-high with gold and gemstones and blocks of fragrant sandalwood, crisscrossed with ivories and bolts of the finest cloth. His palace was built around a spring of fragrant, clear water; and everyone said that they must be the very Waters of Life, so fortunate and well-loved this caliph was. His only sadness was that age had robbed his sight from him, leaving him blind, but hard as this was, it was a small price to pay for Allah's beneficence.

One day the caliph was walking in his garden, smelling the exquisite fragrance of the blossoming orange trees. His son the prince, unaware of his father's presence, was also in the garden, speaking with his mother, the caliph's first and chiefest wife.

"He is terribly old," the wife said. "I cannot stand even to touch him anymore. It is a horror to me."

"You are right, mother," the son replied, as the caliph hid behind the trees and listened, shocked. "I am sickened by watching him sitting all day, drooling into his bowl, or staggering sightless through the palace. But what are we to do?"

"I have thought on it long and hard," the caliph's wife replied. "We owe it to ourselves and those close to us to kill him."

"Kill him?" the son replied. "Well, it is hard for me, but I suppose you are right. I still feel some love for him, though—may we at least do it quickly, so that he shall not feel pain at the end?"

"Very well. But do it soon—tonight, even. If I must feel his foul breath upon me one more night I will die myself."

"Tonight, then," the son agreed, and the two walked away, leaving the blind caliph shaking with rage and terror behind the orange trees. He could not see what sat on the garden path behind them, the object of their discussion: the wife's old lap-dog, a scrofulous creature of extreme age.

Thus the caliph went to his vizier, the only one he was sure he could trust in a world of suddenly traitorous sons and wives, and bade him to have the pair arrested and quickly beheaded. The vizier was shocked, and asked the reason why, but the caliph only said he had unassailable proof that they intended to murder him and take his throne. He bade the vizier go and do the deed.

The vizier did as he was directed, seizing the son and his mother quickly and quietly, then giving them over to the headsman after tormenting them for confessions and the names of confederates, neither of which were forthcoming.

Sadly, the vizier went to the caliph and told him it was done, and the old man was satisfied. But soon, inevitably, word of what had happened spread, and the brothers of the heir began to murmur among themselves about their father's deed. Many thought him mad, since the dead pair's devotion to the caliph was common knowledge.

Word of this dissension reached the caliph himself, and he began to fear for his life, terrified that his other sons meant to emulate their treasonous brother. He called the vizier to him and demanded the arrest of these sons, and their beheading. The vizier argued in vain, risking his own life, but the caliph would not be swayed; at last the vizier went away, returning a week later a battered, shaken man.

"It is done, O Prince," he said. "All your sons are dead."

The caliph had only a short while in which to feel safe before the extreme wrath of the wives over the slaughter of their children reached his ears. "Destroy them, too!" the blind caliph insisted.

Again the vizier went away, soon to return.

"It is done, O Prince," he reported. "Your wives have been beheaded."

Soon the courtiers were crying murder, and the caliph sent his vizier to see them dealt with as well.

"It is done, O Prince," he assured the caliph. But the ruler now feared the angry townspeople, so he commanded his vizier to take the army and slaughter them. The vizier argued feebly, then went away.

"It is done, O Prince," the caliph was told a month later. But now the caliph realized that with his heirs and wives gone, and the important men of the court dead, it was the soldiers themselves who were a threat to his power. He commanded his vizier to sow lies amongst them, causing them to fall out and slay each other, then locked himself in his room to safely outlast the conflict. After a month and a half the vizier knocked upon his door.

"It is done, O Prince."

For a moment the caliph was satisfied. All his enemies were dead, and he himself was locked in: no one could murder him, or steal his treasure, or usurp his throne. The only person yet alive who even knew where the caliph hid was...his vizier.

Blind, he groped about for the key with which he had locked himself in. Better first to remove the risk that someone might trick him into coming out. He pushed the key out beneath the door and told the vizier to throw it away somewhere it might never be found. When the vizier returned he called him close to the locked portal that bounded his small world of darkness and safety.

"Vizier," the caliph said through the keyhole, "I command you to go and kill yourself, for you are the last one living who is a threat to me."

"*Kill* myself, my prince?" the vizier asked, dumbfounded. "Kill *myself*?"

"Correct," the caliph said. "Now go and do it. That is my command."

There was a long silence. At last the vizier said: "Very well." After that there was silence.

For a long time the caliph sat in his blindness and exulted, for everyone he distrusted was gone. His faithful vizier had carried out all his orders, and now had killed himself....

A sudden, horrible thought came to him then: what if the vizier had *not* done what he had told him to do? What if instead he had made compact with the caliph's enemies, and was only reporting false details when he told of their deaths? *How was the caliph to know?* He almost swooned with fright and anxiousness at the realization.

At last he worked up the courage to feel his way across the locked room to the door. He put his ear to the keyhole and listened. He heard nothing but silence. He took a breath and then put his mouth to the hole.

"Vizier?" he called in a shaky voice. "Have you done what I commanded? Have you killed yourself?"

"It is done, O Prince," came the reply.

Finishing his story, which was fully as dreadful as it was sad, the under-vizier Walid lowered his head as if ashamed or exhausted. We waited tensely for our guest to speak; at the same time I am sure we all vainly hoped there would be no more speaking, that the creature would simply vanish, like a frightening dream that flees the sun.

"Rather than discuss the merits of your sad tales," the black, tattered shadow said at last—confirming that there would be no waking from *this* dream, "rather than argue the game with only one set of moves completed, perhaps it is now time for me to speak. The night is still youthful, and my tale is not long, but I wish to give you a fair time to render judgement."

As he spoke the creature's eyes bloomed scarlet like unfolding roses. The mist curled up from the ground beyond the fire-circle, wrapping the vampire in a cloak of writhing fogs, a rotted black egg in a bag of silken mesh.

"...May I begin?" it asked...but no one could say a word. "Very well..."

The Vampyr's Story

The tale I will tell is of a child, a child born of an ancient city on the banks of a river. So long ago this was that not only has the city itself long gone to dust, but the later cities built atop its ruins, tiny towns and great walled fortresses of stone, all these too have gone beneath the millwheels of time—rendered, like their predecessor, into the finest of particles to blow in the wind, silting the timeless river's banks.

This child lived in a mud hut thatched with straw, and played with his fellows in the shallows of the sluggish brown river while his mother washed the family's clothes and gossiped with her neighbors.

Even *this* ancient city was built upon the bones of earlier cities, and it was into the collapsed remnants of one—a great, tumbled mass of shattered sandstone—that the child and his friends sometimes went. And it was to these ruins that the child, when he was a little older... almost the age of your young, romantic companion...took a pretty, doe-eyed girl.

It was to be his first time beyond the veil—his initiation into the mysteries of women. His heart beat rapidly; the girl walked ahead of him, her slender brown body tiger-striped with light and shade as she walked among the broken pillars. Then she saw something, and screamed. The child came running.

The girl was nearly mad, weeping and pointing. He stopped in amazement, staring at the black, shrivelled thing that lay on the ground—a twisted something that might have been a man once, wizened and black as a piece of leather dropped into the cookfire. Then the thing opened its eyes.

The girl ran, choking—but he did not, seeing that the black thing could not move. The twitching of its mouth seemed that of someone trying to speak; he thought he heard a faint voice asking for help, begging for him to do something. He leaned down to the near-silent hiss, and the thing squirmed and bit him, fastening its sharp teeth like barbed fishhooks in the muscle of his leg. The man-child screamed, helpless, and felt his blood running out into the horrible sucking mouth of the thing. Fetid saliva crept into the wounds and coursed hotly through his body, even as he struggled against his writhing attacker. The poison climbed through him, and it seemed he could feel his own heart flutter and die within his chest, delicate and hopeless as a broken bird. With final, desperate strength the child pulled free. The black thing, mouth gaping, curled on itself and shuddered, like a beetle on a hot stone. A moment later it had crumbled into ashes and oily flakes.

But it had caught me long enough to destroy me—for of course I was that child—to force its foul fluids into me, leeching my humanity and replacing it with the hideous, unwanted wine of immortality. My child's heart became an icy fist.

Thus was I made what I am, at the hands of a dying vampyr—which had been a creature like I am now. Worn down at last by the passing of millennia, it had chosen a host to receive its hideous malady, then died— as *I* shall do someday, no doubt, in the grip of some terrible, blind, insect-like urge...but not soon. Not today.

So that child, which had been in all ways like other children—loved by its family, loving in turn noise and games and sweetmeats—became a dark thing sickened by the burning light of the sun.

Driven into the damp shadows beneath stones and the dusty gloom of abandoned places, then driven out again beneath the moon by an unshake-able, unresistable hunger, I fed first on my family—my uncomprehending mother wept to see her child returned, standing by her moonlit pallet— then on the others of my city. Not last, nor least painful of my feedings was on the dark-haired girl who had run when I stayed behind. I slashed other throats, too, and lapped up warm, sea-salty blood while the trapped child inside me cried without a sound. It was as though I stood behind a screen, unable to leave or interfere as terrible crimes were committed before me....

And thus the years have passed: sand grains, deposited along the river bank, uncountable in their succession. Every one has contained a seeming infinitude of killings, each one terrible despite their numbing similarity. Only the blood of mankind will properly feed me, and a hun-dred generations have known terror of me.

Strong as I am, virtually immortal, unkillable as far as I know or can tell—blades pass through me like smoke; fire, water, poison, none affect me—still the light of the sun causes a pain to me so excruciating that you with only mortal lives, whose pain at least eventually ends in death, cannot possibly comprehend it. Thus, kingdoms of men have risen and fallen to ashes since I last saw daylight. Think only on that for a moment, if you seek sad stories! I must be in darkness when the sun rises, so as I range in search of prey my accommodations are shared with toads and slugs, bats, and blindworms.

People can be nothing to me anymore but food. I know of none other like myself, save the dying creature who spawned me. The smell of my own corruption is in my nostrils always.

So there is all of *my* tale. I cannot die until my time is come, and who can know when that is? Until then I will be alone, alone as no mere man can ever be, alone with my wretchedness and evil and self-disgust until the world collapses and is born anew...

The vampyr rose now, towering up like a black sail billowing in the wind, spreading its vast arms or wings on either side, as if to sweep us before it. "How do your stories compare to this?" it cried; the harshness of its speech seemed somehow muted, even as it grew louder and louder. "Whose is the saddest story, then?" There was pain in that hideous voice that tore at even my fast-pounding heart. "Whose is saddest? Tell me! It is time to *judge...*"

And in that moment, of all the moments when lying could save my life...I could not lie. I turned my face away from the quivering black shadow, that thing of rags and red eyes. None of the others around the campfire spoke—even Abdallah the clerk only sat hugging his knees, teeth chattering, eyes bulging with fear.

"...I thought so," the thing said at last. "I thought so." Night wind tossed the treelimbs above our heads, and it seemed as though beyond them stood only ultimate darkness—no sky, no stars, nothing but unending emptiness.

"Very well," the vampyr said at last. "Your silence speaks all. I have won." There was not the slightest note of triumph in its voice. "Give me my prize, and then I may let the rest of you flee my mountains." The dark shape withdrew a little way.

We all of us turned to look at one another, and it was just as well that the night veiled our faces. I started to speak, but Ibn Fahad interrupted me, his voice a tortured rasp.

"Let there be no talk of volunteering. We will draw lots; that is the only way." Quickly he cut a thin branch into five pieces, one of them shorter than the rest, and cupped them in a closed hand.

"Pick," he said. "I will keep the last."

As a part of me wondered what madness it was that had left us wagering on story-telling and drawing lots for our lives, we each took a length from Ibn Fahad's fist. I kept my hand closed while the others selected, not wanting to hurry Allah toward his revelation of my fate. When all had selected we extended our hands and opened them, palms up.

Fawn had selected the short stick.

Strangely, there was no sign of his awful fortune on his face: he showed no signs of grief—indeed, he did not even respond to our helpless words and prayers, only stood up and slowly walked toward the huddled black shape at the far edge of the clearing. The vampyr rose to meet him.

"No!" came a sudden cry, and to our complete surprise the clerk Abdallah leaped to his feet and went pelting across the open space, throwing himself between the youth and the looming shadow. "He is too young!" Abdallah shouted, sounding truly anguished. "Do not do this horrible thing! Take me instead!"

Ibn Fahad, the vizier, and I could only sit, struck dumb by this unexpected behavior, but the creature moved swiftly as a viper, smacking Abdallah to the ground with one flicking gesture.

"You are indeed mad, you short-lived men!" the vampyr hissed. "This one would do nothing to save himself—not once did I hear his voice raised in taletelling—yet now he would throw himself into the jaws of death for this other! Mad!" The monster left Abdallah choking on the ground and turned to silent Fawn. "Come, you. I have won the contest, and you are the prize. I am...sorry...it must be this way...." A great swath of darkness enveloped the youth, drawing him in. "Come," the vampyr said, "think of the better world you go to—that is what you believe, is it not? Well, soon you shall—"

The creature broke off.

"Why do you look so strangely, manchild?" the thing said at last, its voice troubled. "You cry, but I see no fear. Why? Are you not afraid of dying?"

Fawn answered; his tones were oddly distracted. "Have you really lived so long? And alone, always alone?"

"I told you. I have no reason to lie. Do you think to put me off with your strange questions?"

"Ah, how could the good God be so unmerciful!?" The words were made of sighs. The dark shape that embraced him stiffened.

"Do you cry *for me? For me?!*"

"How can I help?" the boy said. "Even Allah must weep for you...for such a pitiful thing, lost in the lonely darkness..."

For a moment the night air seemed to pulse. Then, with a wrenching gasp, the creature flung the youth backward so that he stumbled and fell before us, landing atop the groaning Abdallah.

"*Go!*" the vampyr shrieked, and its voice cracked and boomed like thunder. "Get you gone from my mountains! *Go!*"

Amazed, we pulled Fawn and the chief clerk to their feet and went stumbling down the hillside, branches lashing at our faces and hands, expecting any moment to hear the rush of wings and feel cold breath on our necks.

"Build your houses well, little men!" a voice howled like the wild wind behind us. "My life is long...and someday I may regret letting you go!"

We ran and ran, until it seemed the life would flee our bodies, until our lungs burned and our feet blistered...and until the topmost sliver of the sun peered over the eastern summits....

Masrur al-Adan allowed the tale's ending to hang in silence for a span of thirty heartbeats, then pushed his chair away from the table.

"We escaped the mountains the next day," he said. "Within a season we were back in Baghdad, the only survivors of the caravan to the Armenites."

"Aaaahh...!" breathed young Hassan, a long drawn-out sound full of wonder and apprehension. "What a marvelous, terrifying adventure! I would never have survived it, myself. How frightening! And did the...the creature...did he *really* say he might come back someday?"

Masrur solemnly nodded his large head. "Upon my soul. Am I not right, Ibn Fahad, my old comrade?"

Ibn Fahad yielded a thin smile, seemingly of affirmation.

"Yes," Masrur continued, "those words chill me to this very day. Many is the night I have sat in this room, looking at that door—" He pointed. "—wondering if someday it may open to show me that terrible, misshapen black thing, come back from Hell to make good on our wager."

"Merciful Allah!" Hassan gasped.

Abu Jamir leaned across the table as the other guests whispered excitedly. He wore a look of annoyance. "Good Hassan," he snapped, "kindly calm yourself. We are all grateful to our host Masrur for entertaining us, but it is an insult to sensible, Godly men to suggest that at any moment some blood-drinking Afreet may knock down the door and carry us—"

The door leaped open with a crash, revealing a hideous, twisted shape looming in the entrance, red-splattered and trembling. The shrieking of Masrur's guests filled the room.

"Master...?" the dark silhouette quavered. Baba held a wine jar balanced on one shoulder. The other had broken at his feet, splashing Abu Jamir's prize stock everywhere. "Master," he began again, "I am afraid I have dropped one."

Masrur looked down at Abu Jamir, who lay pitched full-length on the floor, insensible.

"Ah, well, that's all right, Baba." Masrur smiled, twirling his black mustache. "We won't have to make the wine go so far as I thought—it seems my story-telling has put some of our guests to sleep."

Nonstop

A small, instructional tale is attached to this one.

When I first got into this business, and went to my first convention – a World Fantasy Con in Arizona, I believe—I realized that I would have to do a lot of flying. I've never liked it, and I went through a stretch in the eighties and nineties where I was really phobic about it. That led to this story, which I hoped would be a bit of catharsis for me, allowing me to express some of my worst feelings and thus exorcise them. Instead, I hated flying just as much, but several friends who'd never had any problems with it read my story and said, "Now I can't stop thinking about plane crashes!"

A salutary lesson on the power of memetic transfer.

A sideline. After the 9/11 tragedy, when everyone was paralyzed at the idea of getting on an an airplane again, my editor Betsy Wollheim said, "You must be *really* freaked-out these days."

"Not really," I told her. "I'm pretty much the same as I always was—it's just that now everyone else feels like I do."

By the way, I'm a much better flyer these days, thanks to the wonders of modern antianxiety drugs. Take that, Tom Cruise!

— ✳ —

Henry Stankey hated flying. Actually, "hate" was perhaps the wrong word. Hatred implied anger, active resistance; hatred was a type of control. Airplane flight filled Stankey with the kind of helpless despair he sometimes imagined must have poisoned the air of Belsen and Treblinka; he only felt anger when he looked around the boarding area at his complacent fellow passengers, slumped in identical airport chairs like an exhibition of soft sculptures, their faces bored, uncaring, flattened into shadowlessness by the fluorescent lights. As he stared he could feel moisture again between his hand and the chair's plastic arm. He ground his palm on the knees of his corduroys and was miserable. Why hadn't Diana come?

Stankey hated himself for needing his wife this way—not for herself, but as a handholder, a nursemaid. When she had told him that her boss was out sick with strep throat, that they couldn't do without her at the office and that he would have to go to Dallas by himself, he had wanted to reach out and shake her. She knew he couldn't cancel out this late; he'd already paid good money to ship his artwork to the hotel. He'd also used his scant funds to pay convention fees. He *had* to go. Diana knew how much he hated flying, dreaded it, yet she had chosen to stay and help out her boss Muriel rather than him.

The night she told him, he had not slept well. He had dreamed of cattle herded up a ramp—eye-rolling, idiot cattle bumping against each other as they were prodded into a dark boxcar.

The Thursday afternoon flight out of San Francisco was terrible. He almost took a couple of the Valium hidden deep in his pocket in a twist of Saran Wrap. Only the compelling thought that the plane might catch fire on the runway, that the panicking crew and passengers might leave him behind in drugged sleep, prevented him from taking the tranquilizers. Instead, as he always did, he clutched the lucky talisman hidden beneath his shirt—he was ashamed of it, really: a hide bolo tie Diana had brought back from New Mexico, where her aged parents lived in a trailer camp—clutched it and willed the aircraft down the runway. Sweaty hand clasped on chest, he forced the plane up off the tarmac through sheer force of mind, dragging it aloft as the other passengers stared unconcernedly out the small windows, or read gaudy paperbacks, or slept (slept!).

Once the jet was in the air he began his terrified drill: smoothing the turbulence, wishing away dangerous crosswinds, tensing his legs so as to put the minimum amount of weight down on the cabin floor and avoid the laboring vibrations of the plane's underpowered, overtaxed engines. Fortunately, the passenger by the window—Henry always got an aisle seat—was one of those nerveless clods who dozed through flights, and did not have his window-blind open. Stankey was spared the additional stress of watching the plane's wings dipping and bucking crazily, straining to break free from the fuselage.

No one who did not feel as he did about flying realized what a strenuous job it was: three hours in the air, head flung back and eyes closed, white-knuckled hand wrapped around the hidden bolo-charm, forcing his mind through an endless circle of airy, buoyant thoughts—helium, swan's down, drifting dandelion puffs. At every bump or shudder his heart began to speed even more swiftly; he had to redouble his efforts to smooth interference away, to guide the plane back once more to the path of least resistance.

The landing was the worst part.

As the captain's (infuriatingly bland) voice announced the beginning of descent, and the plane nosed downward at a sickening angle, Henry Stankey pulled back on his seat arms until his wrists ached. The pitched whine of the engines mounted to a panicky scream, and he felt himself gradually lifting from the chairseat, gravity in temporary abeyance like that time—the one and only time—he had ridden the old roller coaster at Playland-by-the-Sea. His heart climbed into his chest, his stomach pressed against the bottom of his lungs—but the man across from him was reading a newspaper! Calmly extinguishing a cigarette! Henry closed his eyes again.

The seemingly endless fall ended at last. There was a momentary sensation of leveling out; the wheels touched, lifted, then hit the ground once more with the full weight of the plane upon them. At once an even more terrible squalling started up as the pilot desperately tried to stop the hurtling plane before it skidded off the end of the runway into the terminal, to explode in sun-hot flames.

It didn't explode this time, but rather rolled down the Texas tarmac to a final stop. The distorted voice of a woman on the PA system gabbled something at the unheeding customers, who were already up and shouldering their luggage down from the overhead compartments, laughing and chattering and pushing up the aisle. Back. Stankey hung limply in his chair. His shirt front was creased and sweat-stained where he had clutched his lucky bolo—but it had worked! Again, somehow beyond all hope he had gotten through, kept the plane up, then lowered it once more to the stable earth.

As the panic began to recede he sensed the high-water mark of his fear: although he had struggled to hold it back, the terror seemed to have crept higher than ever before. He felt as though he had been beaten up and left lying on a downtown sidewalk.

Damn Diana for deserting him! Damn her!

After getting into his hotel room and showering the sour odor of perspiration from his body, he slept for an hour—a dark, heavy sleep that nevertheless smoothed some of the cramping from his limbs and back. By the time he got to the conference room where the art show would be, ascertained that his paintings had indeed arrived and began to set them up in his assigned corner, a feeling of mild elation began to well inside him. He had made it by himself, without Diana, and now could look forward to tonight, Friday, and Saturday before he would need to begin thinking about the flight back. A tiny smile worked at the corners of his mouth as he tacked his paintings into their frames and fussed with the arrangement; it was good to feel good again.

These conventions were important to him (of course they must be, he went through Hell to get to them); they were a priceless opportunity to have his artwork noticed, to touch base with people who could steer jobs his way and help him to break through. He had been just getting by for too long—that was the worst thing about free-lancing: the never-knowing, the waiting...waiting for an offer on a cover-bid, waiting for calls back, waiting to see if a project would hold together long enough to get him a guarantee, a kill-fee....He was grateful for the lightening of spirit he was suddenly feeling: it was hard enough to make a living without scaring people away on top of it..

It turned out to be a fairly good convention. Several people praised his work; he sold two small paintings, a large pen and ink, and a few smallish sketches. Roger Norrisert of Lemuria Press dropped some large hints about an upcoming cover-and-illos possibility for a projected special printing of a Manly Wade Wellman book.

Thursday and Friday passed quickly in a blurry montage of handshakes and nametag-squinting and several cheerfully tipsy conversations in the hotel lounge. Both nights he slept deeply, dreamless interludes that did much to restore his normally affable outlook. Eating breakfast at a table splashed with Saturday morning sunlight, he remembered that there were indeed things he liked about conventions.

That night Stankey went with Norrisert and a couple of writers to a Cajun restaurant downtown where they sat up late, swapping stories and drinking beer. Henry got pretty tight, and did not wake until late Sunday morning.

It had not been a pleasant night. He had tossed and twitched, pulling the sheets loose from the mattress. Waking sometime after four in the morning from a dream of choking (faulty oxygen mask, hole in the hose, smoke everywhere), he had found his lucky New Mexico string tie twisted tightly around his neck, bruising his throat. After worrying it loose with sleep-clumsy fingers he had pushed it into the pocket of his jacket, which hung on a chair beside his rumpled bed.

Later, after dawdling around the hotel for a couple of bleak hours watching the Cowboys and the New Orleans Saints play an endless game of exchanged turnovers, and after laboriously packing and labeling his flats, he found himself with nothing to do for an hour and a half until the shuttle bus, like Charon's ferry, would whisk him away to the airport. To the waiting airport.

The hotel bar was almost empty, the last knots of conventioneers clumped around small tables, luggage at their feet. Stankey saw no one that he recognized; he could think of no excuse to introduce himself, to join a conversation and enlist support in his battle against reflection. The prospect of the flight home had risen from its temporary grave and was groping for attention with clammy fingers. Against his better judgment— needle-sharp reflexes were vital in combating the treacherous, gravity-embracing tendencies of airplanes—Henry ordered a vodka tonic and nursed it as he sat in a corner seat trying to read a Ramsey Campbell book.

The drink was a good idea. It soothed the ragged edges of his thoughts; he felt it working like aftershave lotion on a just-shaved face, stripping away the heat, quieting scratchy nerves—well, after all, aftershave was alcohol, too. He thought, a little cavalierly, of just ordering another drink, but he knew that was the lulling effect of the first one at work. He could not afford to be that relaxed: he was needed, even if the other passengers never realized it.

Still, the one drink had been a good idea. The Campbell novel had not. The dank, depressing Liverpool setting and the hopelessly phobic thoughts of the characters made Stankey feel a little sick. He put the book down after thirty pages or so and stared out the window at the hotel parking lot, toying with the slowly melting ice in his glass.

The bus came. It took him, tightlipped and silent, to the airport, and left him there. On the walkway outside the terminal he could already feel the acid gnawing at his stomach, the placating effects of the vodka-tonic evaporated by harsh lights and disembodied, inflectionless voices, by the chill, echoing vastness of the place. He carried his hand-luggage to the boarding area—no massive suitcase in the hold for him: why make the plane any heavier than it had to be?—and stood in line between a Mexican woman with a screaming child and a boy in a baseball cap who, except for his drooping, moron's mouth, could have been a Norman Rockwell character. Some of the other passengers were talking about something he could not quite catch–the flight?—but he would not be distracted. At last he reached the front of the line, put his ticket on the counter, and was told by the female mannequin in the royal blue vest that the plane was delayed: it would be an hour and twenty-five minutes late taking off.

She might as well have hit him with a hammer. His defenses were keyed up, he was wound tight as a mountain climber's rope—and now this! He wanted to shout, to screech at this incomprehending woman with her twinkly Rose Parade smile. Turning hurriedly, he lurched to the high window where he leaned against a pillar and willed his heart to slow down.

He-would-be-calm. He-*would*-be-calm.

When he felt a little more in control he went to the payphone to call Diana, to tell her he would be late. No one answered at home. It was hard not to feel betrayed.

So he sat, staring out at the now-darkening sky, trying not to watch the technicians scurrying like parasites beneath the bodies of the big jets. This was the last time, he vowed to himself. Never again. Other artists and writers got by without having to leave home. He could take the train if he really needed to go anywhere, even though it took days. It was ridiculous to scourge himself this way. Nothing in life was worth this kind of sick fear.

An announcement about his flight crackled over the PA system. The message was hard to make out, but he was positive he had heard the words "mechanical difficulties." When he demanded to know what had been said, the woman at the counter–looking a little amused—confirmed that he had indeed heard that numbing phrase, that such in fact was the reason the jet had been delayed in Atlanta. But, she told him, it was in the air now and would arrive soon. Under sharp questioning about the nature of the "difficulties" she professed ignorance, but assured him that everything was being taken care of. This time he went back to his window even more slowly, like a man mounting thirteen steps to the gibbet. The counterwoman favored his retreat with a condescending smile.

Damn the bitch. And damn Diana too, for good measure.

At last the plane arrived. Stankey, squinting suspiciously through the high boarding area windows, could see nothing overtly wrong—but that, of course, meant nothing. He would never see the loose bolts that would vibrate free and drop the engine like a stone, never detect the fault in the landing gear that would snap the wheel off on contact and send the jet sliding to flaming oblivion. He boarded, a stale taste in his mouth, and found his way to seat 21, near the back of the plane. After stowing his shoulder bag he sat down and promptly fastened his seat belt, then reached his hand up to his breastbone to feel for the lucky bolo tie hanging beneath his shirt.

It wasn't there.

He checked the pockets of his jacket, which disgorged keys, wallet, ticket folder, receipts, and matchbooks...but no good-luck talisman. In a growing panic he unbuckled his lap-belt and sprang up, nearly knocking over the crew-cutted businessman seating himself across the aisle. Stankey jerked open the overhead compartment and levered out his bag, opening it across his lap to rummage through the carefully folded shirts and socks. The Mexican woman in the seat before his shifted her wet-mouthed baby to look over her shoulder at him as he cursed to himself, emptying the bag with trembling hands. The bolo tie was nowhere inside. Henry could dimly remember taking it off in the night and putting it in the pocket of his jacket—but he was wearing that jacket now. He searched the pockets again, fruitlessly.

As he sat in the wreckage of his meticulous packing a pert-faced stewardess leaned over to ask if he needed any help. Unable to speak, he shook his head and began to stow the clothing back into the bag, dislodging a stack of convention giveaway magazines which slithered to the floor. He excoriated himself and his disability as he crouched on the cabin floor picking them up. A middle-aged woman in a parka waited impatiently for him to finish so she could get past to the window seat. As she slid by he forced the repacked bag into the compartment, then slumped back into his chair.

What could he do? The damned bolo must have fallen out on the hotel floor, must even now be in the pocket of some maid, or lying unnoticed behind the bed. He knew how much he needed it. It had gotten him through every miserable one of the dozen or so flights he had taken in the last five years—even the one to Wisconsin where the turbulence had been so bad the seatbelt sign never went off. It had gotten him through Thursday's flight, the first one he had ever taken without Diana. Now he had neither his wife nor his lucky talisman.

He thought seriously for a moment of simply getting up and walking off the plane, but he knew that was a foolish idea. He would still have to get back to San Francisco somehow, the expensive airline ticket would be wasted, and he would miss the Monday afternoon meeting with Janicos from Beltane Books...No, he would have to stay on the flight. Again he cursed his poverty, his childish fears, his treacherous wife.

The final passengers had boarded, and the doors were being shut. The compact thump of the vacuum seal sounded like the coffin lid of the Premature Burial. He could see the stewardesses walking down the aisle, checking to make sure the compartment doors were closed—trim, blue-skirted death angels, hair shining in the cabin lights. Henry unbuckled his belt again and scrambled out into the aisle, moving quickly to the lavatory.

In the narrow room, scarcely even a closet, he felt the surge of claustrophobia. Why had he come back here? His face in the small mirror looked pale, haunted; he turned back toward the door. It all felt like a terrible dream, a grinding nightmare which he could not shut off.

He remembered the Valium in his pocket.

Maybe I can take one of these, he thought....No, better yet, take two, take three or four, sleep through the whole damned flight. If it catches fire on takeoff, so what? I'll never know.

But how would the plane stay aloft? He knew, somewhere in his fevered thinking, that planes traveled every day without him on board— lifted off, flew, and landed without Henry Stankey's straining interces- sion. It could fly while he slept, just this once...couldn't it?

Yes, planes did that, but *he* hadn't been on one that had. He had always worked like a dray-horse to keep them aloft, pulled them along through the turbulent winds that sought to batter them to the ground like badminton birds. Could he relinquish that control?

He had to. Otherwise, he would never make it—he knew that as a certainty. Without Diana it had been nearly impossible; without either wife or talisman it was flatly inconceivable. And if he couldn't manage the strain, wouldn't it be better not to see the last moments coming? To sleep a narcotized sleep through the screeching final seconds? He was disgusted by his own spinelessness, by his desertion of his fellow passen- gers who (although they didn't know it) would be deprived his valuable assistance in keeping the plane safe and themselves ignorant and happy...but there was no alternative he could see. None.

Hands moist with fear-sweat, he unpeeled the plastic-wrapped pills and plucked two out of the jumble. After a moment's consideration he took up another pair, then downed them all with a swallow of water from the tiny sink. Wrapping the remainder, he stumbled back to his seat. The plane was beginning to roll, heading toward the takeoff site. As he wedged himself into place and cinched the belt tightly across his lap, he wondered if the pills would take long to kick in. He knew he would have to get through at least the beginning without help.

The jet gathered speed down the runway, engines howling like late- night-movie Indians bent on massacre, and Stankey's hand rose reflex- ively to his chest. There was, of course, no charmed bolo tie to grasp. He clutched his lapel instead, crushing the material into a wet, wrinkled knot. Straining, heaving, the plane forced its way upward. By some mir- acle it broke from the ground's cruel pull and mounted up at a fierce angle to the waiting sky.

Henry Stankey, tendons stretched like violin strings, waited for either the sickening lurch of lost altitude or the now desperately-awaited onset of drowsiness. Drowsiness won. By the time the aircraft had leveled out six miles or so above the earth's hidden surface, he could feel languor beginning to creep over him, as though a warm, wooly blanket was settling over his body. His muscles unknotted. His breathing slowed. The woman sitting by the window a seat away looked at him sharply, questioningly. Henry, growing groggier by the moment, was even able to muster a thin smile. The woman turned away. The drone of the airplane made him feel as though he rode the night in a great, glowing beehive...

It seemed that he had to claw his way up from sleep. The tarbaby grip of the Valium held him back, but a part of his mind knew that he was urgently needed: even as he clambered up from unconsciousness he could feel the plane lurching and rocking, the cabin rattling like a toy in a child's fist. He opened his eyes, fighting for wakefulness...and knew he had been right. All his fears were now confirmed—he should never have taken those pills, never have relinquished control! He moaned, straining to dislodge the tendrils of sleep.

The faces of his fellow passengers told all. This time no one was reading unconcernedly or chatting with neighbors. Like Stankey, they gripped their seat arms and stared straight ahead as the plane bucked and swerved. Eyes stared darkly from pale faces. The Mexican woman clutched her sobbing baby; Henry could hear her voice moving in the urgent, rhythmic cadences of prayer.

A sudden lurch and the plane plummeted, a drop that seemed to last minutes, like the freefall of an amusement park ride. One woman's voice rose in a brief, muffled shriek. The plane bottomed out, climbed a moment, stabilized. There was none of the usual nervous laughter; the heaving and the battering side-to-side swaying continued. Above the tense muttering of the passengers Stankey heard the voice of the captain on the intercom. Even as he spoke, the stewardesses hurried down the aisle to the back of the plane.

There was another sickening plunge, and a meal tray tumbled out of a passenger's grip to carom down the aisle, scattering food everywhere. The flight attendants did not even look down as they made their way back to their own seats to strap in. To Henry, this was the grimmest proof of all.

Was it too late? He strained outward with his mind, murky thoughts wrestling with the shivering plane and its staggering attempts to defy gravity. For a moment he thought he could do it. The lights blinked on and off, the captain's voice gargled through the cabin:...*fasten seat belts, stay calm...turbulence...*Henry concentrated his will, fighting treacherous sleepiness; the plane seemed to settle a bit, its passage momentarily smoothed. The shuddering became less. Almost without knowing Stankey relaxed—just a little, the most minute concession to the downward drag of the medication—and lost it.

The plane heaved like a gutshot dinosaur and rolled to one side. Several of the overhead compartments burst open, vomiting luggage on the shouting passengers. Suitcases somersaulted down the aisle in slow motion; a blind man's cane, folded in segments, accordioned out from his seat to fly end over end through the cabin like a bizarre albino insect. The airplane hung for a moment on its side: Stankey felt himself dangling across his seat arm, sliding toward the gap-mouthed face of the woman by the window. The glass behind her looked out on black, formless emptiness. The plane nosed down so steeply that it seemed to Henry the passengers near the front of the cabin had fallen down a hole, a hole from which he was being dragged by some fierce power, pulled back against his seat, chest and lungs crushed in a giant's grip. The cabin was suddenly a lively Hell of flailing arms and flying objects. A woman's faint voice screamed: *heads down heads down heads down...!* The turbine shriek of the wind buried all other sounds; the mouths that gaped and worked without words joined their last cries to the panicked roar of the plummeting airplane. Sound cutting through his head like a jigsaw, Stankey screamed too—screamed out his despair and terror, screeched out wordless curses at what fate, his wife, his own fear had done to him. He struggled to force himself up against the shocking, smashing pressure of pitched descent. It wasn't fair! He had tried everything! He had to take the pills, couldn't have kept the plane up this time! Why?! Why?! Whywhywhywhywhywhywhy...

impact

Time...is...stopping.

Henry feels himself standing at last...a man at last...on his feet. He is thrown forward—his flight as inexorable but unhurried as the slide of a black-ice glacier (time now creeping as slowly as eroding stone)—forward like a stop-motion film of a plant growing, unfolding, hurtling forward but barely moving...The passengers around him are a frozen flash photograph, eyes bulging...suitcases hang an the air like corpuscles in the clear ichor of a god's arteries. The walls of the plane wrinkle, contract around him, surge toward the nose; the seats fold forward like a row of dominoes, the passengers folding with them—slowly, slowly, like a child's pop-up book being carefully closed.

Stankey, unfettered, is passing through them all now, flowing remorselessly forward, sliding through the dividing substance of passengers and objects like a bullet tumbling through a sand castle. The way opens before him, a kaleidoscopic mandala of blood and bone and fabric and torn metal—a succession of slow-blooming, intricate flowers through which he tumbles like a bee in melting amber. His journey to the crystalline heart of the petals takes millennia.

Slower now, slower...matter bunching up, molecule on static molecule...

Dense.

Denser.

Densest...

...Until Time itself falls behind his ultimate slowness, until only the remembrance remains, the memory of the light years of waiting before the next tick of atomic decay

and then he is through

The morgue attendant slides the drawer back in. The widow is led out by friends; her shoulders heave.

When she is gone he pulls the drawer out again and stares at the body. He twitches the sheet aside to look at the bruised pelvis, the mottled black and yellow bars where the victim broke the seatbelt across his own body struggling to rise from his seat.

The airline says that the victim had slept through the whole flight until the last descent, when he began to shout and writhe in his sleep, in the depths of an unbreathable dream. Unwaking, he had struggled with the seat. With gravity, with the belt itself until he snapped it loose—the heavy canvas torn by a near-incomprehensible strength—and had stood shouting in the aisle, eyes shut. When the wheels touched the runway, the airline representative said, the man had screamed once and fallen forward, dead.

The attendant looks the body up and down and shakes his head. He slides it back inside on near-silent rollers. A heart attack, they say. Extreme shock and terror, they say.

So, the attendant wonders, why is the corpse smiling?

...he has come through—and Henry Stankey is no more. He is a mote of light passing through a radiant universe, speeding through unending brightness. And flying is a joy.

A Fish Between Three Friends

I wrote this one and posted it on my website one night. No reason, it just came to me. Nobody paid me for it—I wrote it purely for self-amusement. The very best of reasons.

Once upon a time there was a cat, a raven, and a man with no ears. They were all friends and lived together in a house by the river.

The cat was a bit lazy and cruel, but in her own way she loved the raven and the man, so one day she decided to provide supper for her two housemates. She went down to the river and caught a silvery, silvery salmon.

"Don't eat me," the salmon said. "For I am a magical fish."

"That's what they all say," sneered the cat, and carried it back to the house.

The cat waited a while for her friends to come home, but soon grew bored and restless and left the fish on the table while she went out to see if any mice were rustling in the grassy meadow behind the house.

When she had gone, the man came back from working in the field, wondering what he would have for dinner. As he walked to the table the fish, still alive but gasping in the unfamiliar air, called out, "Sir, sir, I am a magical fish! I will give you three wishes if you spare my life!"

But of course the man had no ears and could not hear the fish's entreaties. He saw only a handsome silver fish flopping on the table, its mouth opening and closing.

"How lucky I am!" he thought. "It must have jumped a great jump, all the way from the river onto the table." He went to prepare the oven to cook the fish.

While he was bending over the oven laying the kindling, the raven came into the house.

"Kind bird," the fish gasped, its voice very faint now, "if you will only save me, I will grant you three wishes, for I am a magical fish."

"Hmmmm," said the raven, perching on the table beside it. "Are you, now?" He looked at the fish flopping on the table, then at the man, who was bending over the oven all unaware that the raven had come home. "So if I spare your life, you will grant three wishes?" the raven asked.

"I will, I will," said the fish. "Gladly!"

"Hmmmm," said the raven. "Well, I could ask as one wish that you give the man back his ears so he could hear again. But then instead of admiring my black and glossy wings he would mark that my voice was harsh, and would also hear the cruel things that the people in the village say about him for keeping company with only a bird and a cat. Hmmmm."

The raven thought. The fish flopped.

"And I could wish for the cat to be a little less lazy and a little less cruel, for then she might live a better life and one day go to heaven. But a kind cat might not catch mice, and she would starve and so would I, since there would be no leavings. And the mice would eat the man's grain and he too would starve. And in any case, I do not believe that cats are welcomed in heaven."

The raven considered a bit more.

"Now, it is possible that even though I cannot change my friends in a way that will make them happy, I might find a way to use a wish for myself. But what are the things that I need?"

"Quickly," gasped the fish.

"I would not ask to be more handsome, since as you see I am quite a fine and glossy shade of black. And although we ravens are not known for our fine singing voices, my only friends are a man who cannot hear and a cat who listens to nothing except her own whims, so I do not suffer for my harsh croaking.

"Neither do I wish for gold or silver or gems, for I have no hands in which to carry them, nor anywhere to keep them. Here they would draw robbers like flies to carrion, and we would spend all our time trying to protect these valuables."

The raven walked across the table and stood over the fish, which rolled its eye piteously.

"In fact," the bird said, "we three have all that we need here, and all that we lack is a fish dinner, which is you. We might wish for three more such as you, but that would make you a murderer of your own kind, and then you would certainly be denied heaven yourself. I could not do that to you. Everyone knows that we ravens are kind-hearted birds."

So he left the fish thrashing on the table, although the thrashing had almost ceased, and flew to the back of the man's chair to wait for the meal.

And by the time the cat came back from the meadow, the man had cooked his part of the fish, the raven was chewing happily on the bones, and the cat, as founder of the feast, found the head and tail and a strip of good raw, red flesh laid out for her on the table.

As she purringly devoured the salmon, she said offhandedly, "The fool fish claimed he was magical."

"Really?" said the raven. "Well, I imagine that's what they all say."

"Indeed," said the cat. "I have never believed one yet."

And although the man could not hear what his friends were saying, he smiled anyway.

Z is for...

This is probably the oldest story in the collection, at least the oldest that's still in its original form. It appeared in, and might even have been written for, a small magazine called "Midnight Zoo." It's one of the few things I've ever written based on a dream. People often say, "You must have incredible dreams," (presumably because I make my living with my imagination) but to be honest, I don't remember most of them after I wake up. Every now and then, though, something sticks with me, and many of them are endless-house dreams of some kind. This one, minus the African fauna, was one of those, and I woke up from it feeling very disturbed indeed...

Zebras? It is an odd thought. Something else, too. A rainy day? What the hell...? Harold's chin hits his chest. He bounces back into wakefulness. A reddish light is in his eyes; a dull grumbling sound like a sleeping tiger fills the room.

He is where? He struggles briefly, drags his arms free from some clinging thing—a sheet, a blanket, something—and sits up. Head heavy, yet somehow not well-connected. Harold looks around. A room, a bedroom. Spray of strawflowers in a vase on a dresser, skeletal in the strange light. A red shawl is draped over the lamp, crimsoning the walls, the shadowy framed photographs of someone's pale-moon-faced friends/lovers/family.

The grumbling breaks up into gasps and grunts. Harold is on the floor, slumped against a bed. The noises are coming from someone on the bed. Some two.

A party. He is at a party. He has been there a long time.

He shakes off the last twining tentacle of the bedcover and crawls across the deep-pile carpet, heading for the crack of brighter light he thinks—hopes—is the door. The odd thought of zebras is still floating in his brain. White and black, shimmering like heat lightning. Shake their heads, then—gone.

The noises from the bed continue. He passes a foot dangling from beneath the sheet, corpselike but for the jiggle, timed to the rising chorus of gutterals. Who's up there? How did Harold wind up in the room with them? Fell asleep, he thinks. Fell asleep in the dark on the floor. Everyone too drunk and fucked up to notice. Or maybe they liked the idea—an audience.

They are beyond noticing now, anyway. He pushes the door open with his head. Like his old black cat with its pet-door, he thinks. Cat's name? Can't remember. Seems like a long time ago. Good cat, though. Scabby but lots of chutzpah. No fur left on his butt, hardly, but the very soul of confidence. Why can't he remember the damn cat's name?

The hall is empty and surprisingly long. Loud music and the din of many voices drift up from what looks like a stairwell at the far left end. Harold turns and crawls in that direction. Head feels like a wad of glue—like the white glue from elementary school crafts, drying to a sticky skin on top but still wet underneath. Head feels like that. Too much to drink. Too much of something, anyway. He remembers a guy in a bow tie screaming about Metaxa, some damn Greek liquor, everybody had to slug some down, matter of honor, some ridiculous shit like that. Drink Greek stuff, wake up glue-headed.

Harold likes the sound of this, and repeats it a few times in semi-samba rhythm as he crawls toward the stairs.

Drink Greek stuff, wake up glue-headed.

Drink Greek stuff, wake up glue-headed...

His head is hanging over the abyss of carpeted stairs before he realizes how far he has crawled. He sways briefly as words rise from below like ash flakes heat-fluttering over a campfire.

"...I swear he did! I swear it!"

"You would say that. You told me that the last time he went out of town, too. Wasn't that what you said the last time he went? Wasn't it?"

Two dark shapes come slowly up into the hall light, one dark, one light, like some kind of religious painting. Man, black hair, blue clothes. Glasses. Blond woman in white dress, thirtyish, talking like a teenage girl. Harold hates that. He rolls to the side so they can step up into the hallway.

"Take my advice, leave that Greek shit alone," he mutters. They pass him silently, as if he had asked for money on a street corner.

Harold doesn't know them. Whose fucking party is this? Why did he come? And what is this zebra thing nudging his memory? Did he puke on somebody's striped upholstery? Fake-fur coat? He curls up on the topmost step, feet against the baluster, knees before his chin. He has no shoes, but his socks, though inexplicably damp, are clean and without holes. Some relief there.

As he sits, a dim memory surfaces, a brief movie of himself wandering out of the noise, up some stairs into quiet. He looks back down the hallway. Does look a little familiar. Sure is quieter here than it sounds like it is downstairs. He squints. The man and woman have gone, vanished somewhere down the dark hall.

Kayo's party? Somebody's party, anyway. Zebras? Somebody whose name starts with a "z", maybe? Z's party. Zazu's party. Zorba's party. Sounds like it's been going a long time, anyway.

Harold struggles to his feet. His head feels far too heavy, making his entire rickety body unstable. Still, all things considered, the old headaroo is holding together remarkably well—but then, it's full of glue, so no surprise there. He has to remain standing, now. There are several more people crouching or sitting at the bottom of the stairwell, and he'll never get past them to find his date...

His date?

...He'll never get past them crawling, especially crawling down stairs. He has a faint recollection that he tried crawling down some stairs in the recent past, but remembers only that it was definitely a mistake.

"...Well, you probably missed the part where they announced it," someone is saying as Harold goes, banister-clutching, stiff-legged among the clot of bodies. A young man's voice, calmly rational. "I mean, it's not the same thing, but they have ads now that look just like shows."

"But it *wasn't*," says what in the semi-dark sounds and sort of looks like a young woman. Her voice says that she is a little upset, but willing to be talked out of it. "I mean, I would have known. It really was the news—you know, that guy from Channel 6."

"The one with the wig?" someone else asks.

"The worst wig!" There is an explosive laugh. Harold pushes past, putting his new bipedality to an immediate test, forced to half-jump over a salad bowl full of pretzel sticks and other crunchy treats left on the floor. He makes it, grabbing a chair-back for support on landing. Looks around. A smallish room, dining room maybe, big table in the center, bowls of dip and other things. Lights down, music is not from this room, he hears it loudest from the far door as he swivels his head like a radar dish. The room is familiar, though. That's something. He's seen that painting before, maybe earlier tonight: some expressionist Mexican temple, Aztec, some damn thing. Seen the painting. Likes it, actually. Nice colors, reddish-gold, black, white.

The chairback under his hand is remarkably solid. Chair is occupied. Older man, wire-rimmed glasses, sweater, talking to a young couple. Harold has been leaning too close, he realizes. Inappropriate. Must look like a drunk. Thinks he recognizes the man in the sweater, but doesn't want to admit he isn't sure. Did they work together once?

"Howdy." Harold waves cheerily. "Sorry. Just resting."

Before they are forced to reply he pushes himself off like a boat leaving shore and tacks toward the center of the room. Doing pretty well, actually, one foot casually in front of the other, one, two, one, two. Points himself toward door to music, rest of party...

Helen's party? Isn't it Helen's, from the department? But where did she get such a big house?

Zebras, too, something about zebras. It was important...

...Suddenly veers to the side when he spots telltale pale gleam of porcelain counters through another narrowly open door. Bathroom. Ah, yes, right idea.

Harold stops and knocks politely. Social skills are returning. No answer, so he pushes the door open. A woman's purse is on the counter, lipsticks lying scattered like spent rifle cartridges, but no woman is attached. Just be a moment, Harold thinks. Remembers to lock the door so purse-owner doesn't bang it open, scream, accuse Harold of exhibitionism or sniffing her make-up or something. There was some embarrassing incident earlier, he suddenly remembers—or at another party, maybe? Seems like a long time ago. Anyway, some woman slapped him.

Not too hard, but not really friendly-like, either. Pissed him off. He was just trying to tell her something. Something about *Z*, that was it. Something about…zebras? But she slapped him. Sour-faced bitch…

Memories stop for a moment while he deals with own face. Oh God. Not good. Pale, whiskery, eyes bleary as poached eggs. But still, thankyouJesus, recognizably his. Not like most of the other faces floating around here. Yes, Harold's face. Harold's shirt, too, top button opened, tie gone, but—thankyouagainJesus—no weird stains on clothing. No puke, no snot, no spit. Alarming to wake up on the floor, but reassuring to know you just look drunk and stupid, not disgusting.

Harold turns to the toilet and unzips. Aims, thinks for a moment, then decides not to push his luck. Turns and sits down. Splashing is louder than the music in here. Kind of rustic and pleasant. Lights are harsh as a motherfucker, though. He claws for the switch and kills it, leaving only a glowing nautilus-shell nightlight, pinkish. Much better.

Finished, he retains his seat for a moment, thinking. Runs a little cold water, scooped awkwardly out of the sink at his side, splashes it on his face, then feels for a towel and dabs. The towel is fluffy, but it smells of someone else's body.

Time to go home. No question about it. Shouldn't drive—well, maybe drive real slow. Windows open, get some air. Drive slow. Back streets. Then again, maybe not so slow—need to sober up, after all. Yeah, why not, drive like some beast of the plains, running, wind rushing, running like a gazelle, a zebra…

Zebras again.

Like the imagined wind, a chill travels over him at the thought, and a little more of his drunkenness evaporates. Something's there, a stone in his mental shoe. Something *wrong*…

Let's go. His pants are down around his ankles. He fumbles in his pockets, but there are no keys. Must be in his jacket. Find that, find the keys.

Brilliant deduction, Sherlock. Elementary, my dear fucking Harold. Let's go find the keys.

It's remarkably difficult to open the door with the light out, but still easier than trying to find the light switch again. Finally the door pops free, swings inward. Harold stalks out, heads toward the room with the music.

Here's the party. Here it is. Big room, full of people, lights down but for a flickering television, picture windows showing black sky salted with stars and a different kind of darkness that he somehow remembers is the ocean. Big room, big house. It feels suddenly like he's been here for years.

Halfway across the room he forgets where he is going. As he wavers, he realizes that he is standing between two people talking. They continue as though he is no more than a cloud crossing a sunny sky above their heads.

"...So just tell me where you live," the thin, intense-looking man says. "Simple enough question."

Woman laughs. "Here, of course. I think. I mean here. Here at the house."

Harold pushes himself on a few steps and slumps onto an empty end of the long couch, feels the leather squish beneath him. He peers sideways at the couple. They are talking more softly, both laughing now, but he feels sad looking at them. Doesn't know why.

They're the zebras, he thinks suddenly. *They're dying, and they don't even know it. A dying species, this couple.*

But why? What a stupid fucking thought. Why zebras? Folks got no stripes.

He looks slyly around the room, trying to trick his loopy brain into seeing a room full of people with exotic striping, flashing veldt racing-colors, but no luck. They are boring, boring people, urban-suburban caucasians, mostly. Oh, a couple of asians in the corner, slow-dancing, the girl slender and small. Back of a black guy's head in the lighted kitchen. But no stripes anywhere. No zebras.

But he saw zebras when he was a child. It comes back like a switch flicked on. Child Harold, long ago. Wet day—rainy, gray, *we-said-we-were-going-to-the-zoo-so-we're-damn-well-going* day. The zebras stood huddled in one corner of their enclosure, a carpet of grass and dripping trees atop a great cement island, rising out of a rain-rippled moat. Little Harold threw a peanut, but it splashed well short of concrete zebra-land. Brown, mournful African eyes turned to look at him.

We're dying, the eyes said.

"So am I," Harold says quietly now, and the great sadness rises up, climbing over him like creeping night, choking him like the dust of the Serengeti plain. Dying.

He turns his attention to the television. Pictures flicker on the box, seemingly unconnected. Snatches of old movies, bits of news broadcasts, fragments of commercials from all eras. Someone must be playing with the channel-changer. But no, the glowing station indicator remains steady as the nautilus night-light. Some goddamned post-modern bullshit. Video wallpaper. He stares, fascinated. There seems no rhyme or reason. Even beyond post-modern. Somebody has dumped bits of tape together, spliced them at random. Empty pictures, ghosts with no dignity, mindless specters dancing on the photon-tracks. Punk-rock nihilist crap.

Sadness becomes an itch. *Gotta find the keys. Gotta get out of here. Need air. Gotta drive, run, bust out.* He pushes up off the couch. Control coming back. Something else coming back, memories. A memory. *Zebras,* he had said, and the woman had slapped him. *We're zebras.* No, something else, but almost that. He still didn't remember what exactly, but still, surely no reason to slap a guy...But he'd meant it. It had been *important.*

Fuck the keys. Just a little air, first.

Passes three more people, all vaguely familiar. That last one, the guy with the big ears, named something like...Freiberg? Right, Freiberg. Worked at the university. Linguist.

Harold stops. That's a big chunk, all coming back at once. More than that, there's something important there. Is it Freiberg's party? Harold turns to ask—fuck the embarrassment, so he's drunk, he'll apologize tomorrow—but Freiberg has disappeared. No, Harold suddenly remembers, it was another party that Freiberg had hosted. Champagne, little sweet things baked by Dorothy What's-her-name, celebrating...what? Something that Harold was in on, too. At the university, of course. They had been selected for...what? A government grant, an honor...? Something big. Freiberg had said "the greatest opportunity that can be imagined," or something like that. Meant it, too. Harold remembers that he had thought so himself. A great opportunity. But now there is a core of pain to the thought, a cold ache like too much ice cream against the teeth.

As these memories tease him, Harold sees a sliding door to the patio. Someone is out there in the pool of light from the fake wrought-iron lamp. Her hair is full and curly, light brown with a faint greenish tinge from the lampglow. Dorothy. Of course. He feels a tug. Was it Dorothy he came with? Dorothy, who worked at the university with him, office across the hall? As he stares at the back of her head and her slender shoulders, he suddenly knows there is a connection of some kind between them, a thread of relationship slender but sticky as spidersilk. He thinks he has it for a moment, but then it is gone, leaving nothing in its place but the dull static of the party.

What's wrong with my fucking head?

Harold feels another cold shiver. What did he drink tonight? Just that Greek stuff? Could that be enough to turn him into a goddamn mental patient? Could the liquor be bad somehow, gone rotten during some slow journey out of the Mediterranean on a boat full of singing guys with beards? His laugh at this thought is a gurgle. He lurches outside to the patio and puts a hand onto Dorothy's shoulder.

"Hey."

When she turns and sees him her eyes flash terror, the grazing animal that sees the predator too late. She flinches back as if he might strike her.

"Get away," she says, taking a step toward the house. "Don't talk to me."

He stares for a moment, shocked. What has he done? He has an abrupt vision of her hand arcing around to strike him, and now it is he who flinches—but she has not moved. He has remembered, only.

"You hit me," he says slowly. She did. He remembers now, remembers Dorothy's wide brown eyes and the sudden sting. "Why did you hit me?"

She is poised to flee. In the lantern light she is all sharp angles of light and shadow, except for the soft cloud of her hair. "You're frightening me, Harold. Go away."

He extends a shaking hand as if to hold her, but knows it will only make her bolt. Suddenly he knows there are critical things here, things he should remember. "Tell me," he says gently—but even speaking quietly, he hears his voice tremble. "Why did you hit me?"

She stares as if trying to decide. A man leans out of the door, a tall fellow with a beard. Mikkelson. Harold doesn't like him, although he doesn't know why.

"Dorothy, come on. Come inside."

She continues to stare at Harold. Mikkelson makes an impatient gesture. "Please come in, Dorothy. You...you shouldn't be out there." He looks around, vaguely uncomfortable. "It's not good. Come in."

When she does not reply, Harold feels certain that Mikkelson will come out and get her. Mikkelson is pushy, Harold remembers. A know-it-all. Someone who will always tell you why your idea is wrong, your theory untenable. Usually he's right, but that doesn't make him any more tolerable. But he was wrong one time, Harold remembers suddenly. One critical time. Very wrong. The memory is there, somewhere.

But Mikkelson, pushy Mikkelson, does not come out. He stares worriedly around the empty patio like a peasant in a night-time graveyard, swears, then slides back into the murmuring dark of the party.

Dorothy runs a hand through her hair. "I'm sorry, but you frighten me."

"But why?" He lifts his hand again, leaves it hanging in air. "Tell me. I can't remember anything. I'm sorry, Dorothy, I'm drunk as shit." He stares at her. "Did I bring you here? To the party?"

Her gaze loses focus. "No. I don't remember who I came with—but not you, Harold." She laughs harshly. "Not with you and your zebras."

"What about them?" A glimmering of crazy hope. Something will be explained.

"You rant about them. All the time. You scare me."

"What did I say to you? Why did you hit me?"

She looks around now, as Mikkelson did, as though the suburban plank fence might become a horror-movie sliding wall, edging in to crush her.

"You scare me," she says. "Leave me alone." Her face is indeed frightened, but there is something else struggling there, too, struggling to get free. "I'm going to talk to Pete."

Mikkelson's first name, Harold remembers. Before he can close the distance between them, she slips away, a swirl of shadowed skirt over a lean haunch, a pale shape vanishing through the doorway. A puff of noise from inside is freed as she billows open the drapes on the sliding door, a clack as the screen slides closed.

Harold, beneath the moon, feels sobriety growing like a brittle skeleton beneath his skin and meat. Stark fear in Dorothy's face. Fear in Mikkelson's face, too. And even Freiberg, when he went past, had the nervous, doomed look of a Dachau trusty.

Another noise from the doorway. Harold steps back into the shadows, looks up to see the moon overhead, flat and unreal as a bone poker chip. There is a little scuffle as the screen slides open. A voice, raised in sorrow. The girl he had seen earlier, with two men. She's crying.

"But I saw it!" she wails. "You saw it, too! They're coming! It was on the news!"

"C'mon, Hannah," one of the men says. "Like War of the Worlds, you know? Just a joke."

"It was on the news!" She is struggling to catch her breath. "I want to go home," she whimpers, then subsides into hiccoughing sobs.

"C'mon, you can lie down for a while. There's a bed upstairs."

"You're just tired, Hannah," the other adds. "Come on. We'll sit with you."

The little huddle of humanity staggers back inside, leaving Harold alone again.

The A Group. It suddenly comes back to him. We were the A Group. The impressive gleam of the title is no more convincing than the metal plate on a bowling trophy. He doesn't remember much, but he remembers that something went wrong.

Freiberg, me, Dorothy, Pete, others—we were the best. They picked us because we were the best.

Suddenly the yard seems to be closing in on him, just as it did on Dorothy. The gnarled fruit trees seem to reach out with taloned fingers. The murmuring doorway is another trap, innocent and seductive as a quicksand pit. He wants desperately to get away.

Now. Go home. Fuck the keys, fuck the jacket. Walk. That's good. Breathe air. Think.

He reaches the garden wall in a few steps, pulls himself up, remembers he has no shoes as he catches a splinter in the ball of his foot. The fence, flimsy, made for suburban show and not to resist invasion like more ancient walls, wavers as he reaches the top. A scramble, a popped shirt button, and he tumbles into the dewy grass on the far side. Before him, lit only by the two-dimensional moon, stretches the flat, dark plain of someone else's lawn, and beyond it, the black blanket of the ocean. Harold scrambles to his feet and begins to walk.

When it happened...

There. What is *it?* Just out of reach.

When it happened, they went to find linguists. The government wanted the best, and they took us. The A Group. "The A Team", we called ourselves for a joke—like the TV show. A historic moment, Freiberg said. Something the people in our field have dreamed about for years. Contact with another species.

Harold sucks in a breath and stops. It. The landing.

And we wanted to speak with them. To share our thoughts and dreams, and learn the secrets they would bring us, the songs of the stars.

Abruptly, Harold begins to run, the lawn flying away beneath him, his socks soaking through to his cold feet. His own breath is ragged in his ears.

But how were we to know they didn't come just as explorers, but as conquerors? The A Group, Harold remembers now, remembers the whole sad joke. *I laughed at the end, when those solemn, spidery creatures put us in that white room, and told us what they were doing outside. The "Z" Group, they should have called us, I said. Not the first—the last. I laughed—God, how I laughed, hurting, hurting—and Dorothy slapped me.*

Z is for Zebras in the Zoo.

He slips on some small dark thing on the lawn and stumbles, so that for a few staggering steps he windmills his arms for balance. He doesn't look down. He knows what it is.

The zebras, he remembers, that long-ago rainy day. Did they see the people watching them—me and my folks, the riffraff zoo crowd, fat women and screaming children spilling popcorn—or did they somehow still see the veldt stretching all around them, just out of reach beyond the bounds of their captivity?

Some of them knew, Harold realizes. Their eyes had said so. *You killed us,* those brown eyes said. *Now the few of us you have saved for your pleasure are dying, too. Captivity is another sort of death.*

As he sees his other shoe lying on the wet grass beneath him, he strikes the invisible thing, the barrier. A terrific force lifts him and shakes him, filling him with lightning from scalp to toes.

On the ground, as consciousness flutters away like a firefly down a long, dark tunnel, he knows he will awake again, back in the cage with the rest of his milling herd. They know there is something wrong—deep down, all of them know—but it has been artificially suppressed somehow. Or perhaps they themselves have beaten it down.

Is that the best way? Harold is sliding into darkness. Just stop fighting? Like the zebras, he thinks. Maybe the only possible victory is to stand and suffer and shame the conqueror.

Maybe someday he will learn not to run against the fences.

Some Thoughts
Re: DARK DESTRUCTOR

I have no specific idea where this story idea came from—it just landed on me late one night. I wrote most of the story then, and finished it for this anthology. I used to do a lot of self-drawn, self-written comics when I was a kid, mostly to amuse my friends. I also remember they all wanted to make suggestions, even though I was the one doing the work. And, of course, during my years later on as a commercial artist of various kinds, I always had useful coaching from the folk on the business side about how to make my projects "really work." (They love quotation marks, for some reason.)

Anyway, all that and more led to the story, I guess, but mainly the idea amused me, so I wrote it. There was a kind of dark-mirror-image companion piece called "Alas, the Dark Angel," which was just a comic book script for a kid's comic, except you could read between the lines and see that the kid's life was really tragic, but I never got around to writing more than a page of it. Not enough jokes, I guess.

Some people might say that indicates a weakness in my character, and a lack of seriousness in my work. Some people might be right, too. Or they might just be "helping me bring my vision to life," instead. They do like quotes, those folk.

To: Richard Risselman
From: Edward Jamison
Re: DARK DESTRUCTOR #1—some thoughts

Just wanted to let you know we missed you, Richie. We realize that the pressures of homework, paper route, and working on DARK DESTRUCTOR #2 are keeping you jumping 24/7, but it still would have been nice to see you at the offsite.

We had to move the event from the clubhouse to Brandon's living room because of a rain situation. Also, due to an unfortunate shortfall in the babysitting department at his house, Brandon and Kevin and I were joined by Brandon's sister Penelope (who is a girl.)

Anyway, it was a great offsite, and we shared a lot of great information. Some of it I'll download to you in another memo—the fund mismanagement problem that led to roof inefficiencies at the clubhouse is a subject that deserves a memo of its own, although Kevin swears his dog really did eat the club treasury, and has taken a cross-his-heart-and-hope-to-die posture on this one, so I think we're forced to accept his word on it. But I thought it was important that I get right back to you with a sense-of-the-meeting report on DARK DESTRUCTOR #1.

First off, everyone wanted to make it really, really clear that they're totally behind you on this project, and they think you're doing great stuff, both writing and illustrating. Everyone agrees DARK DES-TRUCTOR #1 is perhaps your finest work to date, although Brandon wanted to mention that he is still a huge fan of ONAN THE BARBARIAN, and is in the market for more original art from that project, since his sister and her friend Raylene Jenks tore up his picture of Onan using his mighty weapon to batter the evil sorceress Bazoomba into submission.

Anyway, the general take on DD#1 was, as I said, extremely positive. The group did have a few comments and suggestions, though, so I thought I'd share my notes with you—I know you'll want to be on the same page as the rest of the "team." Please understand, we all mean this in a very supportive way.

COVER: Brandon thinks that Dolly Ride, Dark Destructor's girlfriend, has "smaller bosoms" than was agreed on in preliminary meetings. He feels this detracts from the integrity of her character as originally conceived. He also asked whether it should be more obvious that Sandcrab is a villain, and suggests that he could have a really big black mustache to make this clearer.

Kevin wants to know if the comic, instead of "DARK DESTRUC-TOR", could be titled "DARK DESTRUCTOR OF DEATH", which he thinks sounds more literary.

(Also, is it really necessary to subtitle it "a Richard Risselman Comic by Richard Risselman"? This seems to be an unnecessary slight on the contribution from the rest of the creative team. You know we've all offered huge amounts of moral support for your work, and Brandon says he loaned you his allowance money once so you could buy a fancy felt pen. I'm sure I don't need to point out that my own commitment to your creative vision goes clear back to the "Zombie School Blows Up" and "Army Men Attack Principal Crapface Crandall" days.)

PAGE 1: There was a general consensus that spending an entire page on Rick Raymond's home life is perhaps asking a bit much of our audience, even though his cruel treatment at the hands of his family—especially his father, who is secretly the villainous Doctor Authority (great touch!)—is of course instrumental to his becoming Dark Destructor. Perhaps we should start the story with something a bit more upbeat and zingy...? Kevin recommends a symbolic splash page of Dark Destructor bashing someone's face really hard and a bunch of their teeth popping out—but we'll let you "get funky" in your own way!

In any case, since Doctor Authority is not the main villain in the first issue, the sense-of-the-off-site is that perhaps we should soft-pedal Rick Raymond's home life just a little. In particular, the long lists of all his chores seems a bit much, and although the paper-route descriptions have a very realistic feeling, it's hard to believe Rick is really in danger of going crazy from having to get up early in the morning to throw papers. Also it seems that if Doctor Authority wanted Rick dead, he could find an easier way to do it, since he's his dad and lives in the same house. (Kevin suggests Dr. A could put ground-up glass in Rick's pancake syrup so that he would "spit up blood and die.")

PAGE 2: Penelope, Brandon's sister (and a girl), suggests that it is highly unlikely that eating special "really crackly" breakfast cereal while standing too close to the microwave oven would cause an accident of any kind, let alone one that would give someone superhuman powers, but hers was the minority position. However, while the rest of us agreed that the origin of Dark Destructor's powers is excellent, we think you might want to consider whether he should acquire his costume else-where, as it does seem to be stretching it a bit to have a microwave oven explosion cause his pajamas to change color and also form a skull logo on the chest. Again, though, it's your call, Rich—you're the "talent", after all...!

Kevin wanted to know if Rick Raymond shouldn't be bleeding "real good" in panel five and have little sharp bits of the exploded microwave sticking into him. I like the image, and I'm sure you will too. Have fun with it!

PAGE 3 and 4: The section where Dark Destructor tests out his new powers is a good one, although Brandon was saddened to note that the seeing-through-walls power is no longer part of his arsenal. He wants to know whether DD could "fly into some radiation" in a later issue and gain this power and then look through a lot of people's walls. He also notes that in such a scenario, maintaining the size of Dolly Ride's bosoms takes on added importance.

(By the way, the line "Now that I have such great powers I must not use them for great evil but only for great heroism," is pure poetry. You're good, baby—you're *real* good.)

PAGE 5: Penelope claims there are no such things as "Underwater Radiation Hydrogen Beams" and that this casts some doubt on Sandcrab's origin. She also says, "Even if some radiation made this sandcrab guy get really big, why would it give him a stupid costume? And where would a sandcrab get the money to hire a bunch of criminals to work for him, and also buy them all diving suits?"

(I wouldn't let this kind of criticism worry you too much though, Richie, since Penelope *is*, after all, a girl—if you know what I mean.)

Kevin did suggest that Sandcrab would be scarier if his claws were like razors, but really jagged on the part where they pinched off people's arms and legs. He may have something there.

Oh, and Brandon wants to know if you could give DD a sidekick, perhaps a younger sister, and then Sandcrab could torture her and kill her. He suggests she be called "Annoying Won't Shut Up Girl," and that her powers could be to be annoying and to smell bad. Penelope, who you may remember was joining us for the day, suggested that Dark Destructor could have an enemy named "Brandon Buttface," but her suggestions for his powers would, I'm afraid, deny us our Recess Code Approved rating. (You remember what happened when we distributed "ONAN THE BARBARIAN" without approval and then were shut down by the Raylene Jenks Committee, who called in the authorities. We took a bath on that one, and I seem to remember mouths were soaped as well.)

PAGE 6: We all love the Sandcrab's Crab Command Cave and thought his giant monster prawn was a fabulous touch, although Penelope (who does at times seem to represent the "girl demographic" a little too strenuously, if you know what I mean) said that a real, live prawn, especially a really giant one, wouldn't have a wooden skewer through him and would probably have a front end. We also liked Sandcrab's Eyeball Injury Machine, and Kevin in particular was excited by this motif, although he wanted me to remind you that "eyeballs have goo in them, and if you squish them the goo will fly out." He deeply feels the threat of eyeball-squishing alone is not enough to really move our audience, and that they must see actual goo-spurt. (Our audience surveys do show that while believable characters and compelling stories remain important to our readers, flying guts, squished eyeballs, and prominent boobies are the roots of real brand loyalty.) Kevin started to turn that funny red color while discussing this matter, so we put it aside for you to make the decision. It's "your baby," after all!

PAGE 7: Dark Destructor's escape from the machine was handled very well—the Super Eyeball Defense Power caught us all by surprise—brilliant! And Sandcrab's line ("You will never, never, NEVER escape from my trap...Awk!") was priceless. Penelope's complaint about why instead of just killing Dark Destructor, Sandcrab would have wasted so much time explaining about his plan to put sand in all the gears of all the bicycles in the world so kids would have to walk to school and do their paper routes on foot, was definitely not supported by the rest of the "team." (Don't forget, this is someone who once dismissed your seminal work, "ONAN," as "just a bunch of wiener pictures," and who is also—it has to be pointed out—and always will be, a girl. Do we need to spend too much time trying to please this minority section of our audience? I think not, Richie-baby, I think not.)

Brandon said to tell you he thought the "Pound sand, Sandcrab!" line should go straight to our t-shirt people, once they finish the "Flush twice, it's a long way to the cafeteria!" project. Also, the revelation that Sandcrab is actually Rick Raymond's P. E. teacher was a complete shock—genius, Richie! That totally explained why before he changed into Sandcrab he was working in a school and spending so much time being exposed to both "special" chlorine and the Underwater Radiation

Hydrogen Beams, and why he was wearing those sweats and had the whistle around his neck.

Oh, not to bring you down, Mister Creator, you really knocked us out with this one, but one very minor complaint: Kevin said that the issue's cover showing Dolly Ride trapped by the Sandcrab and about to have her bosoms pinched by his Sandcrab Electro-Claws did not pay off in the actual story, since other than being tied up in the Sandcrab's Crab Command Cave and covered in tartar sauce, Dolly was never directly menaced. He seems to feel we'd be letting the readership down if we failed to deliver at least *some* bosom-pinching. In fact, he went a bit farther and was beginning to outline his ideas about some sort of Bosom Injuring Machine, but then his mom called and he had to go home to take his medication. He's going to make up some sketches tonight and drop them off with you during recess tomorrow.

Penelope's review was, and I quote, that you "Draw all right," but that your "ideas are stupid." Brandon said, and I'm quoting here, too, "Shut up, you're the stupid one!" and offered further support of his own viewpoint by way of slugging her in the shoulder. She left the meeting suddenly to spend some alone time, although she says she plans to take this up with Brandon in home arbitration, and that we boys "are all sucky babies."

Despite his sister's issues, Brandon rates DARK DESTRUCTOR #1 an "A," and said he's really excited by the bit at the end where DD gets back home, turns into Rick Raymond, and then promptly falls down the chute into Doctor Authority's Housework Hell. However (I'm just kibitzing, here, babe) can we come up with something a little more frightening than having to clean the Self-Dirtying Room? Maybe something with more sharp knives, like the Dishwasher of Death you mentioned before? Also, we love Doctor Authority, but we think we may need something scarier in the monster department for next issue than just "Hamstro, the Radioactive Giant Hamster." (Penelope thought Hamstro was *cute*, which should tell you all you need to know.)

Anyway, I've got to wrap this up now. I've got some of the Fine Art people coming by later to discuss a toilet-paper installation at old Mrs. McGreavey's, who you may recall was less than forthcoming with her contribution to last year's Trick or Treat fundraising exercise. Work, work, work!

Looking forward to seeing you tomorrow, Rich. You're still my main man. Let's do lunch. I hear it's Sloppy Joes.

Cordially,

Eddie

Edward Jamison

The Scent of Trumpets, the Voices of Smoke

This is a piece that could pretty much serve as the dictionary illustration for the term "trunk story." I wrote this originally somewhere between fifteen and twenty years ago, and it was probably the first short story I ever submitted to a professional outlet, in this case, to Gardner Dozois at *Asimov's Science Fiction*. It's certainly the first short story I felt was worth trying to sell. Gardner passed on it after some kind words to the effect of "You don't suck too badly, but I'm not crazy about this story." It got put away after that, in part because I was already working on my second or third professional novel (see, I'm one of those weirdos who sold a novel long before he ever thought of trying to sell a short story.) I read it to a few people over the years, and most of them said something along the lines of "Huh?" or "I don't get it—the narrator seems like kind of a jerk."

Anyway, many, many years later Janis Ian, the talented and fabulous singer/songwriter *(Society's Child, At Seventeen,* and many others) decided that, with the help of Mike Resnick, she wanted to edit an anthology of stories based on her songs and was kind enough to invite me in. I had zero new ideas, though, and was in the midst of a hellish deadline on some novel or other, but when I heard her song "Joan" I remembered my beloved trunk story and thought, "Let's see if I can read it now without hating myself."

And I did, and I didn't. Although I made a few small changes before it was published in Janis' STARS anthology, it's still about 95 percent the same story it was way back when. The narrator is still a jerk, but since the story's about his having a chance for a sort of redemption dangled in front of him, I think that's fine.

Plus, I just think it reads well. So sue me—I like my own writing. (Sometimes.)

— ✵ —

I am met in the garish Tempix lobby by my "Timeviser"—an artless construction that makes me long for the sensible abbreviations and acronyms of GovHub. She is a plump young woman with an enthusiastic manner, her hair styled in an unbecoming back-thrust.

"You must be M. Aibek." Her own name, she announces (although I did not ask) is Gutrun. Her handclasp is over-long and she stares at me as though I am a much-reported but seldom seen species. At first I think it must be my general dishevelment that has caused her reaction—the long Hydra-S project has left me pale as tank fungus, face blotchy and eyes sunken, thin as a dying breath. In fact, it is the termination of that excruciating, frustrating four-month operation that has brought me to this place, given me this unusual but nevertheless powerful need for a change: I want to experience something other than the usual white-lights-and-serenity circuit while my body is being cleansed and rebuilt from the cellular level up at the government's ResRehab facility.

As we traverse the short distance to the appointment bay, she chattering about various displays on the walls, I realize there is a simpler explanation for her excessive interest in my person: my former bond-mate Suvinha Chahar-Bose works here at Tempix—may even be this woman's supervisor. Could Suvinha have told her something about me? I despise gossip and have always done my best to avoid being its subject. When she took early leave from our contract Suvinha was in an emotionally heightened state, and she is thus likely to have made untrue claims, although my conduct toward her never violated even the slightest word of our agreement. Still, it irritates me more than I like to admit that this wide-hipped, talkative young woman may think she knows something about me. It goes against every particle of a Manipulator's training. We do not insert ourselves. We do not allow ourselves to be drawn in. We are subtle to the point of invisibility.

I suppose that for those reasons it might seem strange to this Gutrun that I have chosen this particular excursion, but I work hard for my government, and thus I work hard on behalf of all citizens, including her. Do I need to justify my recreation choices to private-sector functionaries?

She explains that she has found, in her words, "just what I need" for my "little vacation." I try to form a polite smile, but it is precisely to experience a life in which I am not impeded at every turn by attention-seekers and condescending obstructionists like this Gutrun person that I have asked Tempix Corporation to find me an antidote, if only for a short while. I am tired of being subtle, of the endless games of what Suvinha once called my "Trust No Human, Especially Yourself" profession. A chance to experience the fierce excitements of the ancient Era of Kings, of a setting in which power could be wielded openly and honestly by one person instead of through the countless quiet manipulations of government operatives like myself, suddenly seems very appealing.

True power, swift and pure! It will be like breathing fresh air after months in a dank, windowless cell.

Gutrun says that the destination she has selected is a monarchy in the Terran European Middle Ages, so-called. There was no era of kings as such, she informs me: different cultures moved in and out of monarchy at different times. This kingdom will be the old mid-European country known as France. And I *will* be the king, she assures me.

The self-indulgence of the Tempix lobby is fortunately not mirrored in its working areas. Behind the loud façade hides the same cool aesthetic that marks virtually any modern operation. The men and women who pass by in the wide, blue-carpeted hallway nod politely to Gutrun as we pass but show no interest in me at all. I am reassured. In some circles, because of the important but low-profile nature of our work, Manipulators exercise a morbid fascination for the public. I wish only to be a customer, to be treated in the manner of all others, efficiently, anonymously. I am not Suvinha: I do not enjoy talking about my work to outsiders.

As we pass more Tempix employees, I cannot help wondering if Suvinha—my bond-mate who will now never be wife—began as one of these low-level functionaries. She is a hard-minded woman; I can easily imagine her knifing her way upward through schools of softer, gentler fish, swimming toward the levels of light. Did she make her way to the upper echelons by pure effort, or did she graduate from an academy into a prepared slot? I never asked her.

In the appointment bay I am introduced to three sober young technicians whose names slide gracefully from my mind. I ask if the correct arrangements have been made with ResRehab and they assure me that the bureau's employees will be on the premises to escort my body within minutes after my mind has been connected to the Tempix system. When I have no further questions they seem puzzled, a little uneasy.

"But you're a new customer," one of them says. "Don't you have any concerns? Aren't you curious about what's going to happen to you?"

I tell them I am more than a little familiar with their operations, owing to previous acquaintance with one of their administrators. When I say this Gutrun smiles briefly, but wipes the expression clean when she catches my eye. Just such annoying, unfathomable smiles used to flit across Suvinha's face (although there were no smiles the last time I saw her.) Is this smug expression an occupational disability peculiar to Tempix employees?

Continuing, I tell the technicians that I understand what the theories are as much as anyone can whose specialization is not Temporal Mechanics. I am aware of the acrimonious debate over whether the experience is objectively real or merely subjectively convincing in the extreme—a debate that has more than once threatened Tempix's legal status. I further assure them that I do not care which is true. I desire only a safe and interesting experience. I would have been just as happy at one of the fantasy factories, which make no pretense to realism. I chose a Tempix trip and that is that.

Despite my careful disclaimer, Gutrun nevertheless insists on explaining things: although I will be fully aware of my own self at all times during the trip, there are built-in governors to protect me as a time-traveler. I will speak the language fluently—indeed, thanks to the curious mechanics of the host-body methods, I will in some manner even *think* in that language. I will have a certain inherent knowledge of the customs and mores of the setting, as well as complete referral possession of the specific memories of my host-body. These memories, even the likes and dislikes, will in no way impinge on my own personality, Gutrun hastens to assure me, except in those cases where the preferences of the host-body are linked to physical constraints such as allergies, disabilities, or other limitations of the flesh. I can act freely. If this is a true place and a real experience, it is one of an infinite number of quantum pasts, and thus nothing I do will affect reality as I know it, and as I will return to it.

As the shunt is connected and the technicians carefully calibrate their galaxy of instruments, I reflect on these last explanations. Such omniscience toward the host-body's mental substance argues to me against the possibility of true time-travel—against the actual physical existence of the experienced phenomena, but I know the Tempix people will never confirm that suspicion.

I recall that during happier times I had asked Suvinha once to tell me, since she must have known—indeed, for that matter, must know *now,* I abruptly realize (Is she somewhere nearby? Does she know I am here today?)—whether the time-travel experience was purely subjective or whether the journey was in some way real, as is so strenuously hinted at in Tempix's exhortations to those weary of the infinite but shallow variations of the fantasy factories. Suvinha, amused I suppose by my uncharacteristic interest in her work, teased that she would never violate her geneprinted loyalty oath for a mere man. More seriously, she added that there were certainly many questions still, even among Tempix's top designers, but that she could not tell me the company's official internal stance on the subject. The oath was real, she said; it had to do with the difficulty of programming the governors if the traveler knew too much about the nature of the experience.

Strangely enough, this mundane discussion ended in an argument. I suggested that if the experience were in any way real, even in a quantum, infinite-possibilities sense, the government would never leave it to the vagaries of the private sector. If nothing else, it would be more useful for running simulations than even the best of current generators. How did I know, she demanded angrily, that my beloved government was *not* already using it themselves? And what did I know about real things, anyway?

As I said, an argument ensued. Although we had sexual relations afterward that were strangely satisfying, I think it should be obvious why I did not often inquire about her work.

Gutrun intrudes on my thoughts to inform me that the preparations are nearly finished. She explains that I will experience a few moments of synaesthesia as the transfer begins. I tell her that I have heard of the synaesthetic fugue, the temporary confusion of sensory input, and that I am not concerned. She responds that although it is virtually impossible to predict how much subjective time I will experience, at the end of the three days needed to complete my physical rehabilitation at ResRehab I will be summoned back; that return transfer process will also be signaled by a bout of synaesthesia. She tells me this for my edification only, she explains—there will be nothing I can do to aid or hinder the re-transfer.

As she finishes, favoring me with another smile—this one of the blander, more professional variety—one of the nameless technicians says something to his companions. A number of touchpads are skinned in succession. The room slowly fills with a bland, sweet odor; only moments later do I realize that its source is the bank of light-panels that constitute the ceiling, panels which had been…*white?* The word seems suddenly inappropriate. A sharp, tangy odor that ebbs and returns, ebbs and returns, is the sleeve of Gutrun's one-piece passing in and out of my field of vision as she reassuringly strokes my chest. I feel scintillant, blue-sparkling beads of light that must be sweat on my forehead. My unexpected fear is a crackling hiss in my nostrils.

I have been tricked.

If that is too harsh a word, then I will amend it to this: I have been manipulated. Even in my anger I cannot help but appreciate the irony. I suspect I know all too well the author of my manipulation.

Everything becomes clear to me only moments after passing through the synaesthetic state, past a moment of darkness and into growing light. I find that I am lying in a huge, too-soft bed, surrounded by a curtain. I feel cool, damp, unprocessed air on my skin. A vast figure looms, shaking me. I tell him to go away, to let me go back to sleep: my transition has left me feeling limp as a cleaning rag (whatever a cleaning rag might be) and I do not wish to be disturbed. The great, fat man—whose name I suddenly know is Georges de La Tremoille, tells me I may not. *May not!*

Startled into greater wakefulness, I feel the full flood of alien memories wash over me, settling into unexpected cracks and fissures in my own being. The perfidy of Suvinha—or the slipshod nature of Tempix's operation—immediately becomes clear.

I am in the royal bedroom at Chinon. My name is Charles; I am the seventh king of that name in France. I am also the least powerful monarch in all of Christendom—that is to say, as the part of me that is still Aibek sees it, among the nations that worship the same avatar of their one god. How quickly these foreign concepts come shouldering in!

As a king, I am a nonentity. I am not really even Charles the Seventh, since I cannot properly be crowned by the custom of this time. The English and the Burgundians own half my country; even my mad, obese mother has sided with the invaders. My own court titters at my impotence.

As a final fillip, a last slap from unkind chance (or from a vindictive former bond-mate), I am ugly. Aibek the Manipulator never worried about such things, but was not—is not—unpleasant to look at. I had thought that at the very least this time-trip would find me a possessor of rude animal health and physical spirits; a warrior-king in his chariot or automobile, leading his pliant minions. Instead, I am short-legged, knock-kneed, long of nose and sallow of face. I am ill, my new memories tell me, nearly as often as I am not. And my people would not follow me anyway.

So much for the exercise of pure power in a simple, primitive setting. So much for a weary Manipulator's much-needed relaxation. These Tempix people have never dreamt of a storm such as I will bring down on them! At the very least, even if my ex-bond-mate has engineered this all by herself, the company is guilty of negligence on a grossly criminal scale.

But why should Suvinha risk her career to do such a thing to me? What fantasy of wrong has she constructed? It makes no sense.

It was over half a year ago now, at the end of the final killing week of the Cygnus-B3 fiasco, that I returned home exhausted to my apt to find nothing of Suvinha left but a message on the holo. In my absence she had changed her hairstyle to the mannish topside-and-tails. Her image looked quite different from how I had seen her last, very determined. She was dressed for travel.

The holo-Suvinha said that she understood how difficult my work was, knew its importance to the government. She said that she knew a Manipulator could never know when an offworld crisis might happen, that these crises had to be dealt with when they happened and that the projects took priority.

She, too, she said, was often called on by Tempix for unpredictable, all-absorbing emergencies. The difference, she (or her strangely masculine new image) said was that she resented this subsuming of her real life by work, but I did not. I made no contact with her even during the periods when I might have taken time to do so without harming the projects, she suggested, and when a project was over I seemed to be waiting impatiently for another crisis, as though I needed and wanted to escape from the apt and our bond. As the image of Suvinha said this, her eyes—she has very large, deep eyes; they are either black or very dark brown—were hard as windows.

This was a shame, she continued, because it had seemed at times that there might be a real future for us as a bonded couple, if I had only been more willing to connect, to take a chance, to invest myself. There had been *moments*, she said, and then trailed off without explaining what she meant.

It was true that besides the occasional tension there had also been periods of understanding and peace between us—of happiness, I suppose, and what sometimes seemed even more. I do not tend to trust such ephemera, since it runs counter to both my training and my nature, and as I watched her farewell holo-message I became even more convinced I had been right to withhold that trust. What if I had become more deeply attached and then she had opted out of our contract, as she was doing now? My work would have been devastated and I would no doubt have suffered emotional pain as well.

Then the holo-Suvinha added something which surprised me: she claimed that our sexual life was no longer satisfying. This I was not prepared for. Other women have never complained about my sexual performance—in fact, Suvinha and I have gone many times without synthetics of any type, *skinskinning* as I've heard other Manipulators call the practice when they (on a few rare occasions) discuss their outside lives. I have never before been so intimate with *any* woman, casual or bond-mate, and I had understood Suvinha to say the same about the men in her life. Now, against all experience and logic, she was telling me something had been wrong. But not really the *physical* part, her holo carefully added—which, needless to say, mystified me even more. What other aspects might exist and be somehow unattended to, she would not or could not explain.

That night, alone in the empty apt, I had an unsettling dream in which Suvinha was trying to drag me down a long corridor toward something very old and powerful which crouched at the far end. I resisted, but her grip was terrifyingly strong.

Thinking back on all this, trapped now in the unsatisfactory body of Charles the not-quite-king, I wonder if I have somehow contributed to this woeful situation myself. It is a disturbing thought, but a Manipulator must never turn from a potentially important truth, no matter how unlikely or how unpalatable. I could have undergone my rehabilitative therapies in peace, drifting in glowing white harmony. Instead I elected to experience a Tempix trip, knowing full well that it was Suvinha's place of business. But who could have dreamed that she would violate her trust in this way, out of something as petty as spite?

No, I decide, it is not my fault. I am the innocent victim of a woman's irrational obsession. I am not to blame.

— ※ —

La Tremoille insists again that I get out of bed. I realize he has the right, even the power, to insist. He has held what little kingdom I have together. I owe him tens of thousands of *livres*, a staggering sum of money. I owe *everybody* money. A curse on the house of Tempix!

La Tremoille brings his wide, handsome head down close to me, like a father giving a naughty child final warning.

"The visitor is here," he says. "Do you not remember?"

And I do. A religious maniac of some sort, one who I... Charles...have been manipulated into meeting, much against my will. What I would rather do, I realize suddenly, or what Charles would rather do, is die. Not painfully or quickly; not even soon—I do find enjoyment in the fleshly pleasures my position permits me—but since my father's death seven years ago in lunacy and filth and my mother's horrid decline into the worst sort of abasement, life has held nothing larger for me than the next rich meal, the next courtly amusement. I am a small man who is becoming smaller, afraid of things and people I do not know. Being dragged from my bed to meet some crazed, god-struck woman is no answer to any of the problems of Charles or France.

La Tremoille stands by patiently while my manservants dress me. I instruct them to avoid my most ostentatious garb and instead put simple clothes on me . Today, with the gray February light seeping in at the high windows, the weight of brocade and gilt will be too much.

"Did this woman not claim," I ask La Tremoille as we move down the hallway from the residence, "that she would know me from among all men?"

"Girl, Sire, not woman," he corrects me cheerfully. "I have seen her. Yes, she has said this."

"Then take in the Count of Clermont and tell her he is myself. I will follow shortly behind."

La Tremoille hesitates, perhaps fearing that I will disappear altogether, then finally agrees. He too is as curious as all the court about this strange young woman and her claims. I am not—or at least Aibek is not. Whether the subject intrigues Charles at all is hard to say. He seems largely ambivalent. We both, as far as I can still find the demarcation between us, hope that she guesses wrongly and is laughed out of the great hall. Then we can go back to bed.

I stop outside one of the side doors. The hall is full of lights and packed with hundreds of courtiers dressed in every color of the spectrum. They are all here to witness this heralded exception to courtly routine, this spectacle of a young woman who claims she is sent by God to have me crowned at last, and to lift the siege of Orleans.

The crowd beyond the doorway hushes and from my place I can feel a poised tension, a rustle of expectation. Above the whispering, then, I hear a high, clear voice, but the words are indiscernible. When the voice stops an excited murmuring breaks out. Compelled, I step through the doorway, finding myself a place behind the courtiers who line the tapestried walls. I am virtually hidden from anyone in the room's center, and even the elegantly gowned ladies before me do not mark their king's entrance, so quiet am I, so fixed are they on the middle of the hall where a small figure, dressed in rough black, stands beside Louis, Count of Vendôme.

I am astonished.

Suvinha! I try to shout. *What are you doing in this place?* But the words will not pass my lips—something prevents these anachronistic sounds from sullying the virgin air of Chinon. A moment later my astonishment fades. Perhaps it is not her after all. Still, the girl who stares at the Count of Clermont as he slinks back to the crowd (having evidently failed to fool her) is much like Suvinha. Her hair is different, of course, cut in a masculine bowl and shaved above the ears, black as a raven's tail. As she turns to scan the surrounding faces I feel sure I see other differences, too. She is far younger than my ex-bond-mate, my will-not-be-wife. The nose, perhaps, is too long, the cheekbones not so high. Still, the resemblance seems too strong for mere coincidence...

Then she sees me, fixes me with those disturbingly deep eyes— gold-flecked brown eyes, like a diffident forest goddess, like a sacred deer surprised at its drinking pool. She walks toward me and her stare never leaves my face. The crowd between us melts away. How can those not be Suvinha's eyes? I am almost terrified when she stops an arm's-length away, doffs her black cap and kneels.

"God give you good life, gentle king." Her voice is calm, but there is subtle music in it.

"It is not I who is king," I stammer. I point to one of the young barons, whose costume indeed far outstrips mine for beauty. "There is the king."

The girl's eyes are locked to mine. "In God's name, gentle prince,"— she is smiling as she speaks—"it is you and no other."

And as I stand transfixed amid the quiet muttering of the court, I remember that her name is Joan, this farm girl with Suvinha's eyes. "Then if I am the king, what would you have of me, maid?"

Her smile fades, to be replaced by a look of immense solemnity, a look so profound as to resemble almost a child play-acting. "Lord Dauphin, I am sent by God to bring deliverance to you and your kingdom." Her eyes narrow as she stares at me, awaiting my response. When I, suddenly in depths I had not expected, can think of no words to say, her smile returns—a small one that looks as though it accompanies pain.

"My lord has not yet given you to believe me," she says sadly. "Very well, then, let me tend to you one further sign, to show you that my sweet God knows your secret heart."

She draws near to me, resting one hand lightly on my arm; I flinch. She brings her mouth close to my ear so that others will not know her words. Her cool breath on my cheek smells of apples.

"You feel yourself a lost traveler," she whispers, *"trapped in a world that is not as it should be. Like blessed France, you are divided, weary."* Her hand tightens on my arm. *"Only trust in me, in the power that sends me, and all shall be put right...made whole. I bring your happiness—and your completion."*

She steps back and kneels again. Her eyes are indeed deep pools, and the me I seem to see reflected in them is a creature of great beauty. I am enthralled. *Charles* is enthralled would be more accurate, of course. *Enthralled.*

We walk together through the overgrown gardens of Chinon and she tells me of the voices of Saint Catherine and Saint Michael, the sublime voices that have brought her to me. The dank February is only a backdrop now, a gray jewel-cask to set off this sturdy pearl of purity. Courtiers gape from the casements above, watching the King and the Maid in rapt dialogue. I need only trust, she tells me. Because God wills it, she will don armor like a man and go with my armies to break the siege of Orleans. I will be anointed and crowned king at Rheims. To all my objections, my confused questions, this farm girl, this pretty shepherdess with my Suvinha's gaze answers only: "Have faith in me and the power that I serve."

I am being drawn out into stronger currents, I realize. It is seductive. A part of me longs to let go—a part of Charles, that is. Aibek, naturally, watches calmly and rationally from within, the ghost in the machine. Aibek the Mainpulator, even as he feels the currents swell, will keep an eye on the shore.

But who would ever have dreamed the madnesses of the ancients to be so intricate, so sweet?

Joan is all she promises. The armorers fit her in shiny steel, a skin of clean, hard metal. Her battle-standard of white silk bears upon it the image of Jesus sitting in final judgement of the believers and the unbelieving.

This is her powerful, tempting call, that brings the peasants flocking to her as a living saint, and turns the canniest, most profane old soldiers into grudging converts: *Only believe, and all is possible.* Her bright sword marks off the slender division between the saved and the damned. I wonder, Aibek wonders, how she can have such terrible, beautiful faith in its cutting edge. My world, the world of Manipulators, is the world of increment, of adjustment, of two steps forward and then nearly two steps back. But here stands the Maid, sword in hand, and makes one bold stroke—*flash!* Stand here and be blessed! Cross to the other side, you are lost.

As she waits with the troops mustered to relieve Orleans, her back spear-straight while the veteran captains like de Loré and de Culant gossip and laugh nearby, her gaze lifts from the men at arms to me, and from me to the overarching skies. Her meaning and determination are unmistakable...but as I watch the small, clever milkmaid's face, eyes ecstatic and cheeks brushed with the ruddiness of excitement, I cannot help but reflect on the contrast it makes with her bright, masculine armor. She is much like me, I realize—just another ghost in a different machine.

This unexpected linkage warms me, but it saddens me, too. She is only a child. She can be hurt, she can bleed. I suddenly think of Suvinha, of the intense need she sometimes brought to our lovemaking, her passionate clinging that was not stilled by climax,—a riddle I never solved. As I watch the maid I am suddenly aroused. It shames me. I wave my arms and the trumpets blare. The column tramps away toward Orleans.

Helpless in a way I do not like, far more excited than I should be, I attend eagerly to news from the battlefields. At night I lie in my curtained bed and wonder what has been done to me. I curse Tempix and worry, alternately. Could Suvinha, unbalanced in some way by her own emotional nature, truly have constructed this imaginary spectacle, this...passion play...just to trouble me, to pay me back for imagined wrongs? Is she, in fact, with her privileged position at Tempix, now the leading actress in some incomprehensible drama of revenge? But if so, why has she chosen an avatar of such grace and simple kindness?

And what if these events are just as objectively real as they seem? That is another sort of disturbing thought. Have I become too entangled? Am I risking the very genuine future of these people by allowing my attachment to Joan to grow in this way, trusting the fate of whole armies to a milkmaid? Am I overstepping the boundaries in a way no Manipulator should ever allow himself, even in this strange land of unreason?

Even more frightening, is this all some dream—a hallucination I have forced on myself?

Aibek is in a kind of despair, and every morning La Tremoille finds Charles pale and unrested.

They have lifted the siege! Orleans is relieved and the Loire is now barred to the Burgundians. There is no other source to be credited for the reversal of my fortunes but the inspiration of the Maid, Joan of Arc. There was at first fearful news that she had taken a wound, a crossbow bolt at her neck, but it is only a minor tear in the flesh. In fact, she had predicted just such an injury, and her calm foreknowledge is noted by all. How can she not be sent from God?

And one of the English called her a whore! My Joan, who hates sin and chases the camp-followers away—what grace she must wield, to lead soldiers to whom she has denied the company of whores!—called angrily to the Englishman that he would die unshriven for insulting God and France. Indeed, within the hour the fellow tumbled into the water before the battlements and drowned unconfessed.

I am ecstatic! Still, a small part of me feels a disturbing affinity with the Englishman. I sense the currents growing ever more dangerous, and fear what may lie waiting downstream.

Jargeau, Meung, Beaugency: one by one, the English-held cities of the Loire fall before the Maid of Orleans. The army of Charles has become the army of Joan—but how can I resist, any more than the now-believing soldiers and the joyful peasants who line the route of God's militant daughter? I travel with them too now, carried helpless but not unwilling toward Rheims and my promised coronation. Joan comes to me often, straight to my side as though we were one flesh. What does she care for my short legs, my corvine beak? She does not see Charles, pigeon-footed would-be king. Clothed in the immaculate armor of her love, she sees in me God's child, her brother in the Lord's work. I am a chaste husband to her passion, as was Joseph to the astonishing enterprise of his own virgin wife.

God's love, she calls it. Love. It is a miraculous, all-changing thing, there is no question. I long to abandon myself to it, but I cannot imagine what would be left of me if I did. It is hard to separate myself from weak, needy Charles at these moments, and Suvinha, strangely, has in my mind almost entirely merged with Joan.

One night in the city of Troyes, which has seen our might and thrown open its gates to us, I dream of Suvinha. She stands before me naked, glorious in her skin, and she is both herself and the Maid. Her beauty is frightening. In her hands she holds Joan's sword. *In truth this is your sword,* the dream-Suvinha tells me, and her eyes see a joke I do not understand. *Do not fear that I hold it,* are her next words. *It will be given back to you when you prove you deserve it!* She laughs.

In the morning, as we ride out of Troyes on the road to Rheims, a crowd of white butterflies dances about Joan's pennant.

Victorious, my power restored, I stand before the altar in the cathedral at Rheims. I am consecrated. I am crowned. The noise of the crowd is around me like a rush of water as I look at Joan, armored, her pennant in her hand. Her eyes are full of tears but her smile is strangely secretive.

I feel a twinge of discomfort. She alone, of all my noble captains, has been allowed to bear her standard into this holy place.

It has borne the burden, she points out, surely it is right that it should have the honor. I must, reluctantly, agree, but I am suddenly troubled that I have given so much to her. How can a Manipulator invest such importance in one person, any person? Is it not precisely such seductions I have spent my entire life learning to resist? Drugged by this strange world and time, am I being even more foolish than I feared?

Later, when the fierce celebration is ending, she approaches me. Where I had hoped to find her face softened by the day's events, instead there is a firm edge of determination. What can the woman want?

Paris, is the answer. Paris, and the English driven from France, Burgundy reconciled to my rule. I have received my boon from God, she claims, so I must allow her to finish her mission. Even after all she has shown me, done for me, I still do not trust in the force that sent her, she says. "You must renounce fear," she tells me. "You must embrace that holy power."

Among the heat of a thousand candles, beneath the heavy brocade and ermine of my coronation garments, I am chilled. Will there be no end to her needs, Charles thinks, I think? The currents grow treacherous indeed.

"Of course," I say. "Of course."

I cannot separate my thoughts from her. Even when we are not together I feel her knowing, judging eyes. I wish I could be what she is, what she thinks I am—bold and truthful, full of faith in the power she serves. There are moments I even think it is possible.

The men are caparisoned and we move against Paris. All around me is the heady confidence of the Maid, reflected in the eyes and voices of ten thousand Frenchmen. But I am silent, turned inward. Have I gone too far? The siege of Paris is bitter. I am certain that I am all Charles now, that Aibek the Manipulator is gone, quite gone. We are repulsed several times by the English, with heavy losses.

"No matter," says Joan, her eyes seemingly on the other world. "So it was at Orleans, also. Only believe."

"No matter," cry the common people, *"only follow the Maid!"* Some of the captains are not so sure, but Joan does not care.

"With only you, me, and God," she proclaims, "my king, France is whole."

One night I sit up, long past the time when silence has fallen on all the camp. Even the sentries are nodding, so quiet it is before the walls of Paris. Charles lowers his uncomfortable body down onto his preposterous knees...and I pray.

What shall I do? "Believe" is too simple an answer, is it not? "Trust"—how? Show me a sign!

The next day, in the pulsing heart of the battle, Joan falls with the bolt of a crossbow penetrating her thigh. Beneath the brightly polished armor there is, after all, only the body of a young woman, a girl, full of need. The blood flows wetly down her leg as she cries out. Her herald is struck down and killed with an arrow between his eyes, but I can see only Joan as she trembles, shepherdess cheeks quite pale, eyes dark as wells.

There is nothing in the world so red as blood.

In that moment I stand, delicately poised, between two poles I cannot name or understand. I have pledged myself to believe in Joan, in the power of the holy love, but now she is revealed in her frail humanity and I cannot help drawing away. After all, a Manipulator is distance. A Manipulator is caution.

Some silver thing inside me, some strand of exquisite tension, snaps. I have chosen, without ever quite knowing exactly what that choice was.

"The siege has failed," I announce that night. "We will withdraw. Consolidate our gains."

Joan protests bitterly when she hears, but the Maid's wishes suddenly count for little. Wounded, she is put on a litter as we retreat.

— ✳ —

Now, as though some great, universal movement has been triggered, time begins to telescope—to become compressed. I expect momentarily to feel the rush of synaesthesia, to be called back. I begin to lose my grip on Charles, or he on me: my mind touches his and then jumps away, like a stone skipping across the muddy Loire.

Joan's magic is broken, somehow, but although her star is falling, tumbling downward as though some scraping thing has finally worn through the mysterious traces that held it, still it is her hold that is the strongest on me. Court life is a blur—lights and murmuring voices, a hurrying smear of impressions—but she is not. Whenever the river of Charles' consciousness rises up to greet me, it is her face that swims into focus: Joan, improperly supported, failing at the siege of La Charité; Joan, immaculate but somehow stained, the butt of quiet humor at Chinon; Joan, unable to secure my permission, going virtually unaided to Lagny-sur-Marne, to fight the Burgundians at Compiegne.

I see her on the battlefield there, transfixed in a brilliant arrow of sunlight. Her horse rears, stumbles. Joan topples to the ground. Fallen, she is made prisoner.

My grip is relaxing. Terrified, elated, somewhere in between, I try to slow and catch the visions of Joan that drift by like wind-stirred leaves. The entrenched English buy her from Burgundy. They will try her in Rouen, this madwoman, this "Daughter of God," as a witch.

Their inquisitors demand to know why she said this, why she did that. Joan, my Joan, answers them. Sometimes she is angry, sometimes her words are garbled by tears. She seems confused, defeated, all her certainty eroded. They are relentless, and I, Charles, can do nothing but watch as she sits in her cold cell, her sword shattered, her standard furled away in the vaults of Orleans. I am only an observer now, with no power to rescue the Maid. She has only her faith.

"God and my king have not renounced me," she says, although in my secret heart I suspect she is twice wrong. "How can I do less than remain faithful?"

She will burn as a witch, the English say.

In the Vieux-Marché they have built a great pile of wood around a crude pole. A sign on the stake proclaims Joan a heretic, an idolater, an apostate. The heralds have blown their shining trumpets and a vast ocean of people, thousands upon thousands, have come crowding into Rouen. I hold tightly to the image of Vieux-Marché, making a backwater of calm in the hastening torrent of images. Joan is coming. Her armor is gone and she wears only a shift of simple black cloth. She has tied a kerchief over her close-cropped hair. The cart bumps over uneven ground and she sways. She is weeping.

The priest-examiners of Rouen rail against the witch as Joan is chained to the stake. My vision begins to mist as the robed men step away. A man, an English soldier, I think, hands up to Joan a rude cross made from two sticks which she places in the bosom of her dress. Another soldier steps forward, his torch a bright point in my dimming sight, and leans down to the pyre. The flames leap up like hungry children.

It is none of it my fault, I know. I do not even think it is real. And if this is all Suvinha's arcane manipulation, her tormenting of me was pointless: she did not succeed in changing me. Why should I change? If there was a fault in what happened between us, it was not mine. I am not to blame.

So why then, as Joan's pained ecstatic cries become streaks of bright silver before my eyes, do I fear I have made some terrible mistake? Why is my gaze blurred by the bitter scent of tears?

Now I hear nothing but the satisfied murmur of smoke, and my nostrils are full of the clean, sharp smell of trumpets.

The Stuff That Dreams Are Made Of

I wrote this story because one of my first friends in the business, the redoubtable Ms. Janet Berliner, was putting together an anthology with David Copperfield (the professional magician, not the Dickens protagonist from whom he took his name.) Being me—namely, an ornery bugger—I thought I'd come at a "story about magic" in a way that would be less what was expected of a fantasy writer and instead more what belonged in an anthology headlined by a stage illusionist. And the magic itself—well, you'll see.

It's one of the stories I like to read in public, mostly because it's fun. In fact, if I had an entire other life to play with and needed to fill it with some additional projects, it would be a hoot to do a whole collection of *Dalton Pinnard, Prestidigitator For Hire* stories. But here, our own most magical of worlds, I doubt it's going to happen...

Okay, I admit it. If a guy wants to get drunk in the middle of a weekday afternoon, he should have a lock on his office door. Usually Tilly runs interference for me, but this day of all days she'd left early to take her mother in to have her braces loosened. (Retired ladies who get a yen for late-life orthodonture give me a pain anyway—I told Tilly her mom's gums were too weak for such foolishness, but who listens to me?)

Anyway, Tilly is usually out there behind the reception desk to protect me. I don't pay her all that much, but somehow, despite the fairly small difference in our ages, I bring out some grumpy but stalwart mother-bear reflex in her. Actually, that describes her pretty well: any bill collector who's ever seen an angry Tilly come out from behind her desk, her bulky cable knit sweater and long polished nails suggesting a she-grizzly charging out of a cave, will know exactly what I mean. If Tilly moved in with Smokey the Bear, every forest arsonist in the country would move to Mexico.

Sadly, there was no lock, and for once no Tilly to play whatsisname at the bridge. Thus the fairly attractive blonde woman, finding the door to my inner office open, wandered in and discovered me in a more or less horizontal position on the carpet.

I stared at her ankles for a moment or two. They were perfectly nice ankles, but because of all the blood that had run to one side of my head, I wasn't really in optimum viewing mood.

"Um," I said at last. "'Scuse me. I'm just looking for a contact lens." I would have been more convincing if my face hadn't been pressed too closely against the carpet to locate anything on a larger scale than the subatomic.

"And I'm looking for Dalton Pinnard," she said. "Otherwise known as 'Pinardo the Magnificent.' See anybody by that name down there among the contact lenses?" She had a voice that, while not harsh, was perfectly designed to make ten year old boys goofing in the back of a classroom cringe. Or to make drunken magicians feel like brewery-vat scum. If she wasn't a teacher, she'd missed her calling.

"I have a note from a doctor that says I'm allergic to sarcasm," I growled. "If you don't want a whopping lawsuit on your hands, you'd better leave." Admittedly, I was still at a slight conversational disadvantage—this riposte would have been more telling if it hadn't been spoken through a mouthful of carpet fuzz—but how can you expect someone who's just finished off his tenth Rolling Rock to be both witty and vertical?

"I'm not going to go away, Mister Pinnard. I'm here about something very important, so you might as well just stop these shenanigans."

I winced. Only a woman who thinks that two pink gins at an educational conference buffet evening constitutes wild living would dismiss something of the profound masculine significance of a solo drunk as "shenanigans." However, she had already ruined my mood, so I began the somewhat complicated process of getting into my chair.

I made it without too much trouble—I'd be saying a permanent goodbye to the office soon anyway, so what difference did a few spilled ashtrays make? I was buoyed slightly by the knowledge that, however irritating this woman might be right now, at least she wouldn't be around for the hangover. Not that she was unpleasant to look at. Except for a slightly sour look around the mouth (which turned out to be temporary) and a pair of glasses that belonged on one of those old women who wears garden gloves to play the slot machines, she looked pretty damn good. She had a slight tendency to go in and out of focus, but I suspected that might have something to do with what I'd had for lunch.

"Well," I said brightly once I had achieved an upright position. I paused to scrabble beside the chair rollers for one of the cigarette butts that still had a good amount of white left on it. "Well, well, well. What can I do for you, Miss...?"

"It's Ms., first of all. Ms. Emily Heltenbocker. And I'm increasingly less sure that you can do anything for me at all. But my father sent me to you, and I'm taking him at his word. For about another forty-five seconds, anyway."

I hadn't managed to get my lighter going in three tries, so I set it down in a way that suggested I had merely been gauging the length of spark for some perfectly normal scientific purpose. "Heltenbocker...? Wasn't that Charlie Helton's real name?"

"I'm his daughter."

"Oh." Something kicked a little inside me. In all the years I knew Charlie, I had never met his only child, who had been raised by her mother after she and Charlie divorced. It was too bad we were finally meeting when I was...well, like I was at the moment. "I heard about your dad last week. I'm really sorry. He was a great guy."

"He was. I miss him very much." She didn't unfreeze, but she did lower herself into the chair opposite me, showing a bit more leg than one expected from a schoolteacher-type, which inspired me to assay the cigarette lighter again. "Oh, for God's sake," she said at last, then pulled a lighter out of her purse and set it blazing under my nose. Half the foreshortened cigarette disappeared on my first draw as she dropped the lighter back in her bag. Emily Heltenbocker struck me as the kind of woman who might tie your shoes for you if you fumbled at the laces too long.

"So...Charlie sent you to me?" I leaned back and managed finally to merge the two Ms. Heltenbockers into one, which made for more effective conversation. She had a rather nice face, actually, with a strong nose and good cheekbones. "Did you want to book me for the memorial service or something? I'd be honored. I'm sure I could put together a little tribute of some kind." Actually, I was trying desperately to decide which of the tricks I did at the children's parties which constituted most of my business would be least embarrassing to perform in front of a gathering of my fellow professionals. I couldn't picture the leading lights of the magic world getting too worked up about balloon animals.

"No, it's not for the memorial service. We've already had that, just for the family. I want to talk to you about something else. Did you hear what happened to him?"

I couldn't think of any immediate response except to nod. In fact, it was despondency over Charlie's passing, and the awareness of mortality that comes with such things, that had been a large part of the reason for my little afternoon session. (Maybe not as large a part as the foreclosure notice on the office I had received that morning, but it had certainly fueled my melancholy.)

What can you say about an old friend for whom the Basket And Sabers Trick went so dreadfully wrong? That, at a time when he was down on his luck financially, and on a day when he happened to be practicing without an assistant, it looks a little like your old friend may have been a suicide? Of course, a honed steel saber sounds more like a murder weapon than a tool for self-slaughter, and most people don't choose to bow out inside a four foot rattan hamper, but the door to his workroom was locked, and the only key was in Charlie's bloodsoaked pocket. According to the respectable papers, he was working inside the basket and somehow must have turned the wrong way: the sharp blade had sliced his carotid artery, just beneath the ear. "Accident" was the verdict most of them came up with, and the police (perhaps tactfully) agreed. Some of the lower-rent tabloids did hint at suicide, and ran lurid pictures of the crime scene under headlines like *"The Final Trick!"* and *"Basket of Blood!"*

(I would heap even more scorn on such journals except my most recent interview—only two years before—had been courtesy of *Astrology and Detective Gazette*, which shows they are not entirely without discernment.)

"Yeah, I read about it," I said at last. "I was really shaken up. A horrible accident."

"It was murder." Phone-the-time ladies announce the hour with less certainty.

"I beg your pardon?"

"Murder." She reached into her bag, but this time she didn't produce a lighter. The envelope hit my desk with the loud smack of a card trick going wrong. "I went to see the lawyer yesterday. I expected Dad to be broke."

I was suddenly interested. She was here to hire me for something, even if I didn't know what. "And you were wrong?"

"No, I was exactly right. His net assets are a few hundred moth-eaten magic books, some tattered posters, a few old props, and an over-due bill for rental of his top hat. And that envelope. But I expected to receive something else too, and I didn't get it."

I was already reaching for the envelope. She stilled me with a glance. Yeah, just like they say in books. And if any of you has ever received a note in class illustrated with a dirty cartoon of your teacher and looked up to find her standing over you, you'll know what I mean. Real rabbit-in-the-headlights stuff. "Uh, you...you said you didn't get something you expected?"

"Dad had been writing his memoirs for years. He wouldn't let me read them, but I saw the manuscript lots of times. When I didn't find it around the house after...after..." For a brief moment her composure slipped. I looked away, half out of sympathy, half to escape the momentarily-suspended gorgon stare. She cleared her throat. "When I couldn't find it, I assumed he'd given it to his lawyer for safekeeping. He'd fired his agent years earlier, and he doesn't talk to Mom, so it couldn't be with anyone else. But the lawyer didn't know anything about it. It's just...vanished. And here's the suspicious part—there was a lot of interest in that manuscript, especially from some of Dad's rivals in the business. They were concerned that he might tell some tales they'd rather weren't made public."

I straightened up. Repeated doses of her *sit-up-properly-class* voice were beginning to take a toll on my natural slouch; also, the effects of my liquid lunch were wearing off. "Listen, Ms. Heltenbocker, I'm not a cop, but that doesn't seem like grounds enough to suspect murder."

"I know you're not a cop. You're an out-of-work magician. Look in the envelope."

"Hey. I have a nice little thing going with birthdays and bar mitzvahs, you know."

That sort of defensive thrust works best when followed by a quick retreat, so I picked up the envelope. It had her name on it, written in an old man's shaky hand. The only thing inside was an old photograph: two rows of young men, all dressed in top hats and tailcoats, with a placard in front of them reading: "Savini's Magic Academy, Class of '48." Three of the faces had been circled in ink. None of the three was Charlie himself; I discovered him smiling in the front row, looking like a young farm boy fresh off the bus. Which in 1948, as I recalled, he pretty much would have been.

"This doesn't mean anything to me," I said. "How could it? I wasn't even born."

"Look on the back."

On the flip-side of the photo, that same shaky hand had scrawled across the top: *"If something happens to me or my book, investigate these three."* At the bottom, also in ink but kind of faint, the same person had written: *"Trust Pinardo."*

"Yes, it's all my dad's handwriting. It took me a while to find out who 'Pinardo' was and to track you down. Apparently, you haven't been playing many of the big venues lately." She smiled, but I've seen more warmth from Chevrolet grillwork. "So far my dad's judgement looks pretty awful, but I'm willing to give you a chance for his sake. I still think it's murder, and I do need assistance."

I shook my head. "Okay, your father was a friend, but we hadn't seen each other for a long time. Even granting that it's a murder, only for the sake of argument, what do you—what did he—expect me to do, for Chrissakes?"

"Help me. My father suspected something about these three men who all went to the magic academy with him. His book has disappeared. I'm going to confront them, but I need somebody who understands this world." The facade slipped again and I found myself watching her face move. The human woman underneath that do-it-yourself Sternness Kit was really quite appealing. "My mom and dad split up when I was little. I didn't grow up with him, I don't know anything about stage magic. I'm a teacher, for goodness sake!"

"Aha!" I said.

"What the hell does that mean?"

"Nothing, really." I pondered. "Okay. I don't buy any of this, but I'll do what I can. Charlie was a good guy and he was there for me when I was starting out. I suppose that whatever I have, I owe to him."

"Hmmm," she said. "Maybe I trusted you too fast. *You've* certainly got a pretty good murder motive right there."

"Very funny. We'd better discuss my fee, because as it turns out, I can help you already. I've just recognized one of these guys." Quite pleased with myself, I pointed at a thin young man with a thin young mustache standing in the back row. "His name is Fabrizio Ivone, and he's working tonight at the Rabbit Club."

My none-too-sumptuous personal quarters are a suite of rooms—well, if a studio with a kitchenette and bathroom constitutes a suite—over my place of business. Thus, it was easy enough to grab a bite to eat and a couple hours' sleep, then shower and get back downstairs well before Ms. Heltenbocker returned to pick me up. If my head was starting to feel like someone was conducting folk-dancing classes inside it, I suppose that was nobody's fault but my own.

Tilly was again holding down the front desk, eating a take-out egg foo yung and going over the books. She was frowning, and no surprise: matching my income against my outgo was like trying to mend the Titanic with chewing gum and masking tape.

"Hey, you were supposed to have the day off." I scrabbled in the filing cabinet for the aspirin. "How's your mom?"

Tilly gave me one of her looks. She'd probably noticed the pyramid of beer bottles I'd made on my desk. "If I stayed away from here a whole day, this place would just disappear under the dust like Pompeii. Mom's fine. Her gums are still sore. I've been overheating the blender making her milkshakes all afternoon." She paused to contemplate a noodle that had fallen onto her sweater, where it lay like a python that had died climbing Everest. "By the way, who the hell is Emily Heltenbocker?"

"Client." I said it casually, although it was a word that had not been uttered within those walls for some time. "Also Charlie Helton's daughter. Why?"

"She left a message for you. Poor old Charlie—that was a real shame. Anyway, she says she'll be here at seven, and you should wear a clean shirt."

I did not dignify this with a reply.

"Oh, and two different reporters called—someone from *The Metropolitan*, and a guy from *Defective Astronomer Gazette*."

"Astrology and Detective," I said absently, wondering what could have made me the center of such a media whirlwind. *The Metropolitan* was actually a rather high-toned organ: they only printed their car-accident pictures in black and white, and they ran tiny disclaimers underneath the alien abduction stories. I swallowed a few more aspirin and went to meet the press.

A couple of quick calls revealed that both had contacted me about the Charlie Helton Mystery, aka *"The Magical Murder Manuscript."* Apparently the missing book angle had been leaked by Charlie's lawyer and was developing into a fair bit of tabloid froth. Some hack from *The Scrutinizer* called while I was still working my way through the first two. By the time I had finished my bout of semi-official spokesmanship—not forgetting to remind them all that Pinnard was spelled with two "n"s, but Pinardo (as in "the Magnificent") with only one—Tilly leaned in the door to tell me "my date" was waiting.

(There is a certain hideous inevitability to what happens when Tilly meets one of my female clients, at least if that client is under sixty years of age. It is useless to protest that I have no romantic interest in them—Tilly only takes this as evidence of my hopelessly self-deluding nature. As far as she's concerned, any roughly nubile woman who has even the most cursory business relationship with me falls into one of two categories: shallow gold-diggers prospecting in my admittedly rather tapped-out soil, or blindingly out-of-my-league "classy ladies" over whom I am fated to make a dribbling fool of myself. Only the sheer lack of recent clients of any sort had caused me to forget this, otherwise I would have been sure to meet Charlie's daughter downstairs in front of the laundromat, at whatever cost to dignity.)

All unknowing, Emily Heltenbocker had greatly increased the likelihood of such a reaction by wearing a rather touchingly out-of-date cocktail frock for our nightclub sojourn. The black dress showed an interesting but not immodest amount of cleavage, so Tilly had immediately sized her up as a Number One.

"I'll just stick around for a while to keep out the repossession people," she informed me helpfully as I emerged. "Don't worry, boss. I won't let them take that urn with your mother's ashes like they did last time you went bust." She turned to Emily. "Call me sentimental, but I think however far in debt someone is, those loan sharks should stick to reclaiming furniture, not late relations."

I winced, not so much at the all-too-true reference to my financial state as at the unfortunate subject of dead relatives, but Emily appeared to take no notice of my assistant's *faux pas*. "What a loyal employee," she cooed. I thought I detected a touch of acid beneath the sweetness. "She's clearly been with the firm forever. Well, she should still get back in time for Ovaltine and the evening news—even if the repo men drop by tonight, it shouldn't take them long to collect this lot."

Tilly raised an eyebrow in grudging approval—she liked an opponent who could return serve. Before some thundering new volley was delivered, I grabbed Emily's arm and pulled her toward the stairs.

Did I mention that there's been a slight problem with the elevator lately?

"At least the shirt looks like it was ironed at some point," she said. "Mid-seventies, maybe?"

She was driving. Her style refuted my ideas of what a schoolteacher would be like behind the wheel, and in fact rather enlarged the general concept of "driving." Apparently, many of the other motorists felt the same: we had traveled across town through an 1812 Overture of honking horns, squealing brakes, and occasional vivid remarks loud enough to be heard even through our rolled-up windows.

I chose to ignore her comment about my shirt and concentrated instead on clinging to my seat with one hand while using the other to leaf through the autopsy report which Emily had somehow procured. (Privately, I suspected a coroner's clerk with guilty schoolboy memories.)

Nothing in the report seemed to differ greatly from what I had read in the papers. Karl Marius Heltenbocker, aka Charlie Helton, had been in his early sixties but in good physical health. Death was due to exsanguination, the agent of same having been a large and very sharp steel sword of the type known as a cavalry saber. A few rough drawings showed the position of the body as it had been found inside the basket, and a note confirmed that paramedics had declared the victim dead at the scene. The verdict was death by misadventure, and both autopsy and summary report were signed by George Bridgewater, the county's coroner-in-chief. If anyone in authority suspected it was a murder, it certainly wasn't reflected in the official paperwork.

"It sure looks like an accident," I said, wincing slightly as a pedestrian did a credible Baryshnikov impression in his haste to give Emily right-of-way through a crosswalk.

"Of course it does. If you were going to murder someone and steal his manuscript to protect yourself, Mister Pinnard, wouldn't you *want* it to look like an accident?" She said this with an air of such logical certainty that I was reminded of my firm conviction during my student years that all teachers were extraterrestrials.

"How fiendishly clever," I replied. I admit I said it quietly. I was saving my wittier ripostes until there was pavement under my feet again.

I hadn't been to the Rabbit Club in a while, and was faintly depressed at the changes. I suppose on the salary the school board forked out Emily didn't get out much, because she seemed quite taken with the place. Actually, set against the rather faded glories of the club—its heyday had roughly paralleled that of the Brooklyn Dodgers—she looked far more natural than me in my leather jacket and jeans. With her strapless cocktail dress and horn-rimmed glasses, she might have been sent over by Central Casting.

As I mused, she said something I didn't quite catch, and I realized I had stopped in the middle of the aisle to admire her shoulders (I have always been a sucker for a faint dusting of freckles). I hurried her toward a booth.

The show was not the sort to make anyone sit up in wonder, but the club was one of the few places left in town where young magic talent could get a start. Looking around the darkened room, I felt a certain nostalgia for my own rookie days. Over the following hour we watched a succession of inexperienced prestidigitators fumble bouquets out of their sleeves and make coins jump across the backs of their hands while hardly ever dropping them. I nursed a soda water—rewarded for my choice with a restrained smile from my companion—but Emily drank two and a half glasses of champagne and applauded vigorously for one of the least sterling examples of the Floating Rings I'd ever seen. I decided sourly that the young (and rather irritatingly well-built) magician's no-shirt-under-the-tux outfit had influenced her appreciation.

After the break, during which the tiny house band wheezed through a couple of Glenn Miller numbers, Fabrizio Ivone was announced. The headliner had not changed much since the last time I'd seen him. He was a little older, of course, but aren't we all? His patter was delivered with a certain old-world formality, and his slicked-down hair and tiny mustache made him seem a remnant of the previous century. Watching him work his effortless way through a good group of standard illusions, it was easy to forget we were living in an era of jumbo jets and computers and special effects movies. When he finished by producing a white dove from a flaming Chinese lacquer box, the smallish crowd gave him an enthusiastic ovation.

I took Emily backstage on my arm (at this point she was a wee bit unsteady on her pins) and quickly located the dressing room. Ivone was putting his brilliantined hair, or at least the part that wasn't real, back in its box.

"The world of Illusion," said Emily, and giggled. I squeezed her wrist hard.

"That was a splendid show, Mister Ivone. I don't know if you remember me—we worked a bill together in Vegas about ten years ago, at the Dunes I think it was. Dalton Pinnard—Pinardo the Magnificent?"

"Ah, of course." He looked me up and down and went back to taking off his makeup. He didn't look like he cared much one way or the other.

"And this is my friend, Emily Heltenbocker." I took a breath and decided to go for the direct approach. "Her father was Charlie Helton."

A plucked eyebrow crept up that eggshell dome of a forehead. "Ah. I was sad to hear about him." He sounded about as sorry as he'd seemed glad to see me again.

"We were wondering if you might know anything about the book he was writing," said Emily. "Somebody stole it." She gifted Ivone with a dazzling smile. It was a good smile, but I couldn't match it since I was wincing at her sledgehammer approach.

The old magician gave her a look he probably used more often on sidewalk dog surprises. "I heard it was full of slanders. I am not unhappy to hear it has been stolen, if that were to be the end of it, but I have no doubt it will soon appear in the gutter press. If you are asking me if I know anything about this sordid affair, the answer is no. If you are insinuating I had anything to do with the theft, then you will be speaking to my lawyer."

I trod ever so gently on Emily's foot, preparing to steer the conversation in a friendlier direction. My new initiative was delayed somewhat by the wicked elbow she gave me back in the solar plexus. When I could breathe again, I said: "No, Mister Ivone, we don't think any such thing. We were just hoping that you might be able to tell us anything you know about Charlie's relationship with other magicians. You know, so we can decide once and for all if there's anything sinister in the disappearance. But you, sir, are of course above suspicion."

He stared at me for a moment and I wondered if I'd overdone it. The cold cream was caked in his wizened features like a bad plastering job. "I would never harm anyone," he said at last, "but I must say that I did not like your father, young woman. Even in the Savini Academy—yes, we studied together—he was never serious. He and his friends, they were all the time laughing in the back row."

"And who were his friends in the Academy?"

Ivone shrugged. "I do not remember. Pranksters, guttersnipes, not true artists. He was the only one of that sort who graduated."

I let out a breath. So if Charlie had known the other two men at school, they hadn't been close chums.

Ivone was still in full, indignant flow. "He did not show the respect for our great tradition, not then, not later. Always he was making jokes, even when he was on the stage, silly riddles and stories, little puzzles as though he were performing to entertain children." He placed his toupee in its box as carefully as if it were the relic of some dead saint and solemnly shut the lid. "I have appeared before the crowned heads of Europe and Asia in my day, and never once on the stage have I made a joke."

I didn't doubt him for a moment.

— ✳ —

"I wish you'd kept your mouth shut," I said. It didn't come across as forceful as it sounds, since Emily had already pulled away from the curb and I was frantically groping on the floor for the other half of my seatbelt.

"Don't be rude—you're an employee, remember. Besides, I didn't like him. He was a very small-souled man."

I rolled my eyes. "That's not the point. After you'd just gone and blurted that out about the book he wasn't going to give anything away. I couldn't very well ask him where he'd been when your dad died, for instance."

Emily made a face. "But I know that already. He was onstage at the Rabbit Club—he's been performing there for weeks. I checked."

"What?"

"I checked. I called the Performing Artist's Guild after you told me his name. He was working the night my father was killed."

I stared. The trained fingers I had once insured (okay, only for five thousand bucks on a twenty-six dollar monthly premium—it was a publicity stunt) itched to throttle her, or at least to pull those stupid glasses off and see if she drove any better without them.

"He was *working*? Fabrizio Ivone, this supposed murderer, was on the other side of town pulling coins out of people's noses when your father died?"

"Yes, I just told you that I called the Guild. Don't get so defensive—I didn't expect you to do all the work, just the stuff that needed expert knowledge."

I threw myself back against my seat, but our sudden stop in the middle of an intersection catapulted me forward again microseconds later. "I can't believe I'm wasting my time on this nonsense," I growled. The light had turned green again, but Charlie's daughter seemed to be waiting for a shade she liked better. "The point I'm making, Emily, is that Fabrizio Ivone has an *alibi*. As in, 'Release this honest citizen, Sergeant, he's got an alibi.'"

She shook her head pityingly, as though I had just urged her to buy heavily into Flat Earth futures. "Haven't you ever heard of hired killers?" We lurched into motion just as the light turned red once more.

You just can't trust clients. It happens every time. They come through your door, wave money under your nose and make lots of promises—then boom! Next thing you know, that little party you were hired for turns out to be a smoker, and you're doing card tricks for a bunch of surly drunks because the stripper hasn't showed up.

Yeah, I'm a little bitter. When you've been around this business as long as I have you get that way. You splurge on a Tibetan Mystery Box some guy swears is just like new and when you get it home it's riddled with woodworm. You order a shipment of doves from the mail order house and they forget to punch air-holes in the box. And women! Don't even talk to me about women. I can't count the number of times I've been standing around backstage somewhere, ten minutes before curtain for the Sunday matinee, arguing on the phone with my latest assistant, who isn't there because she's got water-bloat, or her boyfriend's in jail, or because I introduced her as "the lovely Zelda" the night before and her name's really "Zora."

"Pull over," I snapped. "And try using the brakes instead of just glancing off streetlights until the car stops."

She followed my advice. (In fact, she used the brakes so enthusiastically that I wore a very accurate impression of the dashboard grain on my forehead for hours afterward.)

"Get the hell out, then," she said. "I knew you were a loser from the moment I first saw you crawling around on the floor."

"Well, I may be a loser...but *you* hired me." The effect of my clever comeback and sweeping exit was diminished slightly by the fact that I hadn't unbuckled the safety belt. The ensuing struggle also allowed me time to cool down a little. After I finally worked free and fell onto the sidewalk, I turned to look back, expecting to see the tears of a helpless woman, or perhaps a momentary glimpse of Charlie's features in hers, which would remind me of the old friend whose desperate daughter this was. Emily wasn't such a bad kid, really. I was half-ready to have my gruff masculine heart melted.

"Shut the damn door," she snarled. If there were any tears, I definitely missed them.

She did manage to run over my foot as she drove away.

— ✳ —

I suppose I shouldn't have been too surprised, I reflected as I limped home. I had fallen out with Emily's father much the same way. Nobody in the whole damn family could admit they were wrong.

Charlie Helton had been a wonderful guy, my mentor in the business. He'd helped me find my first agent and had shared many of his hard-won secrets with me, giving me a boost that few young performers got. He'd been everywhere almost, had done things few other people had even read about, and could tell you stories that would make your eyes pop out. But he could be difficult and stubborn at times, and as Ivone had so vividly remembered, he had a rather strange idea of fun. After he and Emily's mother had broken up he had lived a solitary life—I hadn't even known he'd been married until several years into our friendship—and like a lot of bachelor-types, his life revolved around what other people might consider pretty useless hobbies. In Charlie's case there were two: puzzles and practical jokes.

Unfortunately, not all of his jokes were funny, at least to the victims. One such, a particularly complicated operation, had involved my booking for a show at a naturist colony in the Catskills. I was very uncertain, since it required me to perform naked except for cape and top hat, but Charlie convinced me that a lot of big entertainment people were weekend nudists, and that I would be bound to make some great contacts.

When I arrived at the resort the night of the show I was met backstage by the club manager, who was definitely naked. He was a big fat guy of about fifty, and knowing that people like him could do it helped me wrestle down my inhibitions. See, when you perform, if the stage lights are bright enough, you hardly see the audience anyway; the manager assured me that it would be just like doing a show in my own bedroom. So, I stripped, squared my shoulders, calmed my quivering stomach, and marched out onto the stage.

And no, it *wasn't* a nudist colony, of course. It was a regular Catskills resort, median audience age: almost dead and holding. The "club manager" was a confederate of Charlie's who'd taken off as soon as he'd finished his part of the scam.

The audience was not amused. Neither was I.

The sad thing was, Charlie and I fell out not because of the prank itself, nasty as it had been, but because I refused to admit there was anything humorous about it. I guess his pride was wounded—he thought he was the funniest guy in the world.

Things started to go downhill for me after that, but not because of my premature venture into performance art. I just caught some bad breaks. Well, a *lot* of bad breaks.

Maybe Charlie had been feeling guilty about our parting all these years, and about not being around to help me get back on my feet. Maybe that was why he'd told his daughter that if she ever needed someone to trust, to seek me out.

There was something else to consider, I suddenly realized. On the infinitesimal chance that Emily Heltenbocker was right and everyone else was wrong, maybe Charlie had been snuffed because one of his jokes had offended someone. Maybe he'd made a bad enemy, and it didn't have anything to do with his manuscript at all.

I was pleased with this genuine detective-style thinking. Despite the misery of my long trudge home, I began to consider whether I should allow Emily—if she was suitably contrite—to re-hire me. Charlie and I had been through a lot of good times before the bottom fell out. Maybe his daughter deserved a little patience.

Not to mention that she owed me for at least one night's work.

"Your girlfriend's on the phone," shouted Tilly.

I put down my self-help bankruptcy book and unhurriedly picked up the receiver. I had known Emily would come crawling back, but I wasn't going to let her off too easily.

"You still have my father's graduation photograph," she said in a tone like a whip-crack. "Send it back immediately or I'll come over there and break your arm."

She was playing it a little more cagily than I'd expected. "Don't hurt me," I said. "My health insurance lists attack-by-schoolteacher as an Act of God, and it'll be hell getting them to pay."

"Just send me the picture. Right now."

I was sure I detected an undercurrent of playfulness in her voice, albeit well-camouflaged. "How about if I drop it by in person? Then we can discuss last night's little difference of opinion."

"If you come within a mile of me, you're going to have to learn how to make balloon animals with your teeth."

She hung up loudly enough to loosen a few of my fillings, but I knew I basically had her.

— ✳ —

Thus it was that after only a few dozen more phone calls (and a slight strategic modification on my part which might have been mistaken by some unschooled observers for a cringing apology) Emily Heltenbocker and I resumed our partnership.

"Tell me their names again." She revved the engine, although the light was still resolutely red.

I'd finally pinned down the other two mystery men, through laborious research in various trade booking guides. "Sandor Horja Nagy, the Hungarian Houdini—he's the one we're going to see right now. The other's Gerard O'Neill. And, just for your information, they were *both* doing shows on the night in question, just like Ivone. Two more airtight alibis."

"For goodness sake, Pinnard, you're so unimaginative. We're talking about magicians—people who disappear and reappear elsewhere for a living. Honestly, if this were a murder mystery in a book, you'd be the idiot cop they always have stumbling around to make the detective look good."

"Thank you for your many kindnesses." I reached into my pocket for my cigarettes. Emily had finally tendered my retainer and I had splurged on a whole carton. "Whatever you may think, a stage magician nearing retirement age cannot disappear in the middle of a downtown performance, catch a cab to the suburbs, murder an old classmate, and be back before the audience notices. And he can't spin straw into gold or turn a pumpkin into a horse-drawn carriage either, just in case you still harbor some misconceptions about what real magicians do." I leaned back and withdrew my new, top-of-the-line disposable lighter.

"Don't you dare light that in my car. I don't want my upholstery smelling of smoke."

Obviously she had no similar problem with the scent of self-deceit and denial. I didn't say that, of course. Long years of working with the public have taught me that, although the customer may not always be right, only a fool behaves otherwise before he's been paid in full. "Look," I said, "I'm just being sensible. You're a nice lady, Emily, but I think you're barking up the wrong tree. The police say it was an accident. The coroner said it was an accident. And all your suspects have alibis. When are you going to face up to what that really means?"

She started an angry reply, but bit it off. She stayed silent for a long while, and even when the light finally turned green, she accelerated with none of her usual gusto. I was pleased that I had finally made her see sense, but not exactly happy about it, if you know what I mean. Sometimes when something goes very wrong, we humans desperately want there to be a reason. It's not fun being the person who takes that possibility away.

"It's just not like my father," she said at last. "Suicide, never. Not in a million years. So that leaves accident. But you knew him too, Pinnard. You know how carefully he planned everything."

I had to admit that was true. Watching Charlie work up an illusion was like watching Admiral Nimitz setting out his bath toys—no detail too small for obsessive consideration. "But sometimes even careful people get careless," I pointed out. "Or sometimes they just don't give a damn any more. You told me he was having real bad financial problems."

"You are too, but I don't see you getting your throat slit."

"Not when I've got a whole carton of cigarettes," I said cheerfully. "I prefer my suicide slow."

"That's not very funny."

I immediately felt bad. "Yeah, you're right. I'm sorry. Look, let's go see this Nagy guy. Even if it turns out you're wrong about the murder angle, you'll feel better if you know for certain."

She nodded, but didn't seem very convinced. Or very cheerful. She was even still driving in an uncharacteristically moderate way. So, basically nice guy that I am, I sang a medley of Burt Bacharach songs for her as we made our way across town. I've always thought that if magic hadn't worked out, I could have made a tidy bundle warbling "Walk On By" in your better grade of dinner-houses.

It didn't jolly her up much. "I'll pay you the rest of tonight's fee right now if you shut up," was how she put it.

Sandor Nagy (I think you're supposed to say it "Nagy Sandor", but what I know for sure about Hungarian customs you could write on the back of a postage stamp and still have room for your favorite goulash recipe) had seen better days. As a performer, our pal Ivone was, by comparison, Elvis.

We warmed the plastic chairs in the hallway of the Rotary Club while we waited for Nagy to finish changing his clothes in the men's room. The show had been interesting—if watching a drunk perform for a bunch of guys offended because the entertainment was more blasted than they were is the kind of thing that interests you. Partly out of pity, we took Nagy to the 24-hour coffee shop across the street and bought him a Grand Slam Breakfast. (There is no time in places like that, so you might as well eat breakfast. Actually, there is time, but only the waitresses experience it, which is why they're all about a hundred and four years old. I've always thought someone should write a science fiction book about this paradox.)

"I'm not quite sure what went wrong with that trunk escape," Nagy said. Or slurred, to be more precise. "Usually it works like a charm."

After the gruelling experience of his show, I had been planning to down a quick couple of beers—I wasn't going to drink club soda forever just because I was hanging around with Ms. Ruler-across-the-knuckles—but the old guy's breath and the bold yet intricate vein patterns on his nose persuaded me to order myself a Coke. Thus, I had my mouth wrapped around a straw and didn't have to comment.

"I'm sure you would have got out eventually," said Emily. "I didn't think they really needed to call the fire department."

Nagy eyed his soft-boiled eggs with great sadness. I think he would much rather have had a couple of belts himself, but we had declined to buy him anything with a proof content. He wasn't real coherent as it was, even after all the oxygen the fire crew had forced into him. "I'll let you in on a secret," he said. "I'm not as sharp as I used to be. A step slower these days, if you know what I mean."

"Well, you and my father were at the Academy at the same time, weren't you? That was quite a way back."

I smiled. Emily was showing definite improvement. All the same, interrogating this guy made about as much sense as bringing down a pigeon with a surface-to-air missile. If he was a murderer, I was Merlin.

"Oh, that's right, you said you were Charlie Helton's kid. Shame about him. I heard he was writing a book. Wouldn't want to take time from my escape work, myself. There's a lot of practice involved." He pushed one of his eggs with the fork, as though unsure whether to commit to something so strenuous as eating. "He was a strange one, your dad. Drove a lot of people crazy."

"Did he? He made enemies?" Emily was leaning forward, giving the old guy that penetrating would-you-like-to-share-that-with-the-class gaze that made me cringe even when it wasn't aimed at me. I refrained from pointing out that her elbow was in a puddle of catsup. Purely because I didn't want to distract her, of course.

"Not enemies, no. Not really." Sandor Nagy stopped to think, a process that clearly needed some ramping-up time. It was a good half-minute before he came up with: "He was just...he bragged a lot. Told a lot of stories. Played tricks on people."

Now it was my turn to lean forward. My backfired-prank theory was sounding better. "Anyone in particular that he upset?"

Nagy shook his head. "Not that I could tell you—it's been a long time. He just pissed a lot of people off. Pardon my French, Miss."

I chewed on my straw, disgusted with myself for taking the idea of murder seriously for even a second. "Let me ask you another question," I said. "Are you really Hungarian? Because you don't have an accent."

Nagy frowned at me and squinted his bloodshot eyes. Starve Popeye the Sailor Man for a few weeks, then strap him into an extremely musty tux, and you basically had Nagy. "I sure as hell am! Both my parents were from the old country, even if I ain't been there. At least I got a family connection. One of those punks at the Academy called himself 'Il

Mysterioso Giorgio', and he wasn't even Italian! Some chump kid from Weehawken!"

We left the Hungarian Houdini muttering angrily at his hash browns.

— ✸ —

I had mixed feelings when I got downstairs to the office the next day. I was more convinced than ever that we were wasting our time, and that Emily—who was actually a pretty okay person—was going to get her feelings hurt. On the other hand, she'd paid me a nice little fee, and the story was playing big and bold in the tabloids.

It wasn't front page in *The Scrutinizer,* but it was near the front, and a full-page spread to boot. There was an artist's rendition of *"The Death Basket"* (which included far more swords than were actually involved in Charlie's demise), a photo of Charlie in his stage outfit, and one of the coroner and the police chief at a news conference, looking very serious. (In fact, the photo had been taken during some other and far more important case, but I must admit it gave the thing an air of drama.) The only item conspicuously missing was one of the publicity photos of Yours Truly I'd sent to them (there's no such thing as bad PR, especially when you've been stuck on the birthday party circuit for a few years), but I was mentioned prominently in all the articles, even if *The Metropolitan* managed to spell my name "Pinrod." So, all in all, it could have been worse.

Emily didn't seem to think so, though. When I called her, she sounded tired and depressed. "I'm beginning to think you're right," she said. "Whatever was in the manuscript, it's gone. The tabloid reporters won't leave me alone. After I finish paying you, I'll be broke—my savings have gone on Dad's funeral. I think it's time to go fishing."

"Huh?" I had a sudden and disconcerting vision of Emily in hip-waders.

"It's just a family expression. When times are bad, when the bill collectors are after you, you say 'I think I'll go fishing.' And that's how I feel right now."

I was still thinking about the hip-waders. In a certain kind of way they can be a pretty sexy garment. I suppose it has something to do with my reading Field and Stream too much during my adolescence. In any case, distracted as I was, I did a wildly foolish and uncharacteristic thing.

"Listen, Emily," I said. "I don't want your money."

"What does that mean?" She sounded angry.

"I mean, I don't want any more of your money, and you can have back what I haven't spent yet. But we'll still go see O'Neill this afternoon. On the house, okay?"

She didn't say anything right away. I assumed she had been struck dumb by gratitude, but I wasn't sure. Charlie's daughter had proven herself a mite unpredictable. While I waited for the verdict, I re-scrutinized *The Scrutinizer*. It was too bad they hadn't run a picture of Emily, I thought—she was a very good-looking woman.

I frowned. Something in the paper's coverage had been nagging at me since I'd read it, some little connection I couldn't make that was now bidding heavily for my attention, but between certain thoughts of an imaginary Emily in a fishing-gear pictorial and then the sudden re-appearance of the actual Emily's voice, it didn't have much of a chance.

"That's...that's very kind of you, Dalton. You're a really nice person."

She'd never called me by my first name before. That nagging detail was abruptly heckled off the Amateur Night stage of my consciousness.

"And you're a nice person too, Emily." I hung up, feeling oddly as though I might be blushing.

Tilly was standing in my office doorway. She'd heard the whole conversation. Her expression of amused contempt was probably similar to what ancient Christians saw on the faces of Roman lions.

"Your gills are showing, Pinrod," she said. "What an idiot—hook, line, and sinker."

I summoned up great reserves of inner strength and ignored her.

I spent all of O'Neill's performance trying to decide what Emily would do if I put my arm around her. I'd like to say we were paying close attention to the show, but we weren't. (I'm reasonably certain that murder investigators don't date each other, or that if they do, they keep the dates separate from the actual investigations. I hope so.)

Not that Gerry O'Neill's routine was the kind of thing that invited close attention. It was a mixture of old gags and fairly lame sleight-of-hand.

Only the fact that it was a charity performance in front of a ward full of sick children made it something more than tiresome. And, to be fair, the kids seemed to like it.

O'Neill, it turned out, was the only one of the three who'd been on good terms with Charlie: he'd kept in loose touch with him over the years. As we walked him out to his car, O'Neill wiped the perspiration from his round face and walrus mustache and told us with impressive sincerity how upset he'd been when he heard the news.

"He was a good guy, Charlie was. A little loco sometimes, but basically a heart of gold." He stuffed several feet of colored kerchief back into his pocket and patted Emily's arm. "You got my real best wishes, missy. I was broken up to hear about it."

Emily's questions were perfunctory. She seemed a lot more cheerful than she'd been on the phone, but she seemed to be losing interest in the investigation. I wasn't really surprised—it was pretty difficult to feature any of our three suspects as the Fu Manchu criminal mastermind-type.

"When you say Charlie was a little loco sometimes," I asked, "what do you mean? His practical jokes?"

O'Neill grinned. "I heard about some of those. What a card. But I mostly meant his stories. He was full of stories, and some of 'em were pretty crazy."

"Like what?"

"Oh, you know, places he said he'd been, things he'd seen. He told me once he'd been in China and some old guy there taught him to how to talk to birds. Man, if you listened to him, he'd done everything! Snuck into a sultan's harem somewhere, hung out with voodoo priests in Haiti, tamed elephants in Thailand, you name it. Crazy stories."

Emily rose to her father's defense. "He did travel quite a bit, Mister O'Neill. He toured in a lot of places, took his show all over the world—Asia, South America, the Caribbean—especially when he was younger. He was a pretty big star."

O'Neill was a gallant man. "Then maybe all them stories were true, missy. In any case, I'm sorry he's gone. He was a helluva guy."

We watched O'Neill drive off. As we strolled back across the parking lot, Emily took my hand.

"Maybe it *was* an accident," she said, and turned to look at me. The sunset brought out the deep gold colors in her hair. "Maybe that stuff he wrote on the photo was just another of his stories or silly tricks. But at least I did my best to find out." She sighed. "Talking to these people reminded me of all the parts of his life I missed out on. I didn't see a lot of him while I was growing up."

I didn't say anything. I was concentrating on the feeling of her warm skin beneath my fingers, and thinking about what I was about to do. I stopped, pulled her toward me, and carefully removed her glasses.

"Why, Miss Heltenbocker," I said, as if in surprise, "you're beautiful. Do you mind if I kiss you?"

She snatched them back and jammed them into place, brow furrowed in annoyance. "I hate it when everything's blurry. Kiss me with my goddamn glasses on."

What was it like? Do I have to tell you?

Magic.

— ✳ —

I woke up in the middle of the night. The thing that had been bothering me had come back. Boy, had it ever come back.

I ran downstairs to my office, not bothering with a bathrobe. This should show you how excited I was—even though Tilly lived on the other side of town, wouldn't be in for hours, and the office was effectively part of my home, going there naked even at 4 am made me feel queasily disrespectful. But the yammering in my brain wouldn't wait for anything.

A few minutes later I ran back upstairs and woke Emily.

(Look, just because she was a schoolteacher doesn't mean you should make old-fashioned assumptions.)

"Get up, get up!" I was literally jumping up and down.

"What the hell is going on, Pinnard?" She sat up, rubbing her eyes and looking utterly gorgeous. After the night we'd just spent, I wasn't at all worried about her use of my last name.

"I've solved it! And you're never going to believe it!" I grabbed her arm, almost dragging her toward the stairs. She very firmly pulled free, then went to get her glasses from the bedside table. Next—and clearly second in order of importance—she found my bathrobe and put it on. In a gesture of solidarity, I pulled my underwear off the ceiling light (don't ask), donned it, and led her to my office.

"Brace yourself," I said. "This is very weird." I took a breath, trying to think of the best way to explain. "First of all, you were right—it wasn't an accident."

Emily sat up straight. "Somebody *did* murder him?" A strange look came over her face. "Or are you going to tell me it was suicide?"

I was suddenly reluctant. Waking someone up in the middle of the night to give them the kind of news I was about to give Emily could have a number of shocking effects, and I felt very protective of her—and of what we suddenly seemed to have together. "Well, see for yourself." I spread the copy of *The Scrutinizer* on the desktop, then laid the graduation picture on top of it. "Something was bothering me about this article, but with everything else that happened today, well, I sort of forgot about it. Then, about fifteen minutes ago, I woke up and I knew." I pointed at the picture, at one of the faces that Charlie hadn't circled. "See this kid? You know who that is?"

Emily stared, then shook her head.

"That's 'Il Mysterioso Giorgio'—the one Nagy mentioned. You know, the fake Italian from Weehawken."

"I still don't get it."

"You will. Remember Fabrizio Ivone talking about those delinquent friends of your dad's who didn't graduate the Academy? Well, he was wrong—one of them did. It was young 'Giorgio' here. Although he never made it as a working magician."

"How do you know that?"

I lifted the graduation picture and pointed to *The Scrutinizer*. "Because he would have had trouble being a stage magician *and* holding down the job of Chief Coroner." I put the graduation picture beside the news photo for comparison. "Meet 'Il Mysterioso Giorgio' today— George Bridgewater."

She stared at the two photos, then looked up at me. "My God, I think you're right. But I still don't understand. What does it mean? Did he cover up something about my dad's death?"

This was the hard part. Suddenly, under the bright fluorescent lights, my certainty had dwindled. It would be unutterably cruel if I turned out to be wrong. I took her hand.

"Emily," I said. "I think your dad's alive."

She pulled away from me, stepping back as though I'd slapped her. The tears that suddenly formed in her eyes made me want to slap myself. "What are you saying? That's crazy!"

"Look, you said it yourself—Charlie'd never be a suicide. And he wasn't the type to have an accident. But you said he'd traveled in the Caribbean, and he told O'Neill he'd studied with voodoo priests! They have chemicals they use in voodoo that make people look like they're dead. That's where the zombie legends come from. It's true—I read about it!"

She laughed, angry, frightened. "Where? In *Astrology and Detective Gazette?*"

"In a science magazine. Emily, they've done studies. Voodoo priests can use this stuff to put people in a kind of temporary coma. All the vital signs disappear. No paramedic struggling to keep your dad alive would know the difference, not if he'd made a real but shallow cut and spread a lot of blood around. It wouldn't even have to be human blood, since nobody would think of testing it when he was locked in a room by himself with the key in his pocket. But you'd have to have a confederate in place for later, cause nobody could live through a real autopsy. Chief Coroners hardly ever do actual examinations, so it's a little bit of a coincidence he was writing the report at all. Even weirder that he wouldn't step aside when he found out it was an old school chum."

"So this guy Bridgewater helped my dad fake his own death? Why?"

"Who knows? A last prank for old time's sake, maybe? You said your dad was depressed and broke. Maybe it was a way for Giorgio the Mysterious to help a pal get out of a bad situation." I didn't want to mention it, but it was also possible that the deal had been a little less friendly—old Charlie, collector of gossip and odd stories, might have had a wee bit of blackmail material on Bridgewater.

Emily stared at the pictures. When she turned back to me, she was calmer, but very grim. "I don't think you did this to be cruel," she said, "but this is so much more farfetched than anything I suggested. It's just crazy."

I had a sick feeling in my stomach, kind of like something very cold was hibernating there. I knew I'd blown it. "But…"

She cut me off, her voice rising in anger. "I can almost believe my father would do something this wild, this outrageous—heaven knows, he loved a good trick, and he was having a lot of problems. But I can't for a moment believe that he would make me think he was dead—with not even a *hint* that he'd survived—and then on top of it send me off to hook up with a bum like you and go on some insane hunt for a non-existent murderer!" She waved the picture in front of my face. "Look at this! This is his handwriting! If he wanted to tip me off, why didn't he circle Bridgewater the coroner? Instead, he picks these three totally harmless…"

I was so far into my flinch that at first I didn't open my eyes. When she had remained silent for a good ten seconds, I peeked. Emily was still frowning, but it was a different kind of frown. "Oh, God," she said at last.

She flopped the photo down so the back was showing. I had written down the men's names as I identified them.

"Gerard O'Neill." Emily's voice was strained. "Fabrizio Ivone. Sandor Horja Nagy. Oh my God."

"What?"

"Look at the initials. *G-O-N—F-I—S-H-N.*" The tears came for real now. "'GONE FISHING'."

— ✳ —

There was a good deal more to the story, of course, but we didn't find out immediately. When we went to see Bridgewater, the coroner blustered at us about foolish accusations and the penalties for slander, but he didn't seem very fierce about it. (We later discovered that one of Charlie's Academy-era jokes had yielded photographs of a naked 'Giorgio' in bed with a sheep dressed in a garter belt. It had all been perfectly innocent, of course, but still not the kind of thing a local politician wants to see on the wire services.) Still, it was a few more months before we knew for sure.

Apparently Charlie Helton *did* have an agent Emily hadn't known about—a theatrical agent, but someone who had contacts in publishing. When, at the height of the tabloid fury about the *Murdered Magician*

Mystery, the agent announced that he actually had the dead man's manuscript, it set off a bidding war, and the book sold for a very healthy advance. As Charlie's only heir, Emily received all but a small part of what was left after the agent took his cut. When the book quickly earned back its advance, she began to receive all but that same small percentage of the royalties that began flowing in. Even after the story lost its tabloid notoriety, *A Magical Life* continued to sell nicely. As it turned out, Charlie had written quite a good book, full of vivid stories about his life and travels, and lots of enjoyable but not-too-scurrilous backstage gossip about the world of stage magicians.

Even Fabrizio Ivone didn't come out too bad in Charlie's memoirs, although his inability to take a joke was mentioned several times.

That small portion of the income Emily didn't get? Well, every month, the agent dispatches a check to a post office box in Florida—no, I won't tell you where exactly, just in Florida somewhere. Suffice it to say it's a small town with good fishing. The checks are made out to someone named Booker H. Charlton. Emily decided not to contest this diversion of royalties, and in fact we plan to go visit old Booker as soon as we can get out of town.

Why delay our visit to the mystery fisherman? Well, we've been real busy just lately setting up the Charlie Helton Museum of the Magical Arts. It's turned out to be a full-time job for all of us: Emily took early retirement from the school system to manage the operation, and Tilly answers the phone and handles the finances—which I'm happy to say, are in the black. Tilly's mom works the ticket booth, flashing her expensive smile at the customers all day long. Me? Well, I've got the balloon animal concession pretty much wrapped up, and I'm working on a book of my own.

Oh, and in case anybody's disappointed that this has been a story about magicians without any real magic in it, I should mention one last thing. You remember how Charlie had scrawled on the back of his photo: *"Trust Pinardo"?* We found out a few months afterward that if Charlie's handwriting had been a little darker, we would have noticed a hyphen between the two words. See, we were going through some of his papers and found out that he'd stashed away a couple of hundred dollars so Emily wouldn't get stuck paying for his fake funeral. The deposit was in a trust fund at a small savings insitution—"Pinardo Thrift and Loan", no relation to yours truly.

In other words, the very beautiful woman who I am delighted to say now calls herself Ms. Emily Heltenbocker-Pinnard, the light of my life and (I hope) the warmth of my declining years, walked into my office that day on a completely mistaken assumption. We are an accident—a fluke of fate.

So there you go. Love (as Bogart once said about a black bird, and Shakespeare said about something I don't quite remember) is definitely the stuff that dreams are made of. It remains the greatest mystery and the only truly reliable magic.

Satisfied?

The Author at the End of Time

This one definitely requires at least a little explanation.

I wrote this story originally for a chapbook being put together to celebrate Michael Moorcock's 60th birthday. For those of you who don't know Mr. Moorcock's work, I have only this to say: You poor bastards.

Mike invented albino Elric, and Tanelorn, and Dorian Hawkmoon, and the ubercool Dada assassin Jerry Cornelius, and has had a greater effect on fantasy fiction than probably any writer in the last hundred years except Tolkien. Among the works of his that I love best are the short stories and novels loosely grouped under the title "The Dancers at the End of Time." (The series of novels about these characters begins with "An Alien Heat." Read them now. They are fabulous and hilarious and brilliant.) I'll talk more about Moorcock and his effect on me in the intro to "Go Ask Elric."

The following story is full of both the kind of jokes that Mike himself makes endlessly in his End of Time stories—often based on the characters' incomplete understanding of earlier ages of history—and a few it's-Mike's-birthday jokes as well.

That said, I think you can enjoy it without picking up every single reference. I had a grand time writing it, both in honoring a man whose work matters a lot to me, and getting to write a story in a universe I fell in love with when I was pretty much a kid, and I hope some of that quality shines through for all readers.

For reasons known only to herself, but much speculated upon by her friends, the Iron Orchid was conducting a sort of dalliance with Doctor Volospion. Many thought it the precursor to some elaborate and melodramatic act of revenge for Volospion's hostile behavior toward Lord Jagged of Canaria, one of the Orchid's closest confidants, while others suspected there was nothing more complicated at work than the attraction of distaste, since virtually all attractions eventually have their fulfillment at the End of Time.

Whatever the case, it was this unlikely pairing that led to the Duke of Queens destroying most of Doctor Volospion's locusts and thus, perhaps, precipitating some of the more interesting of the day's later events.

— ⸎ —

"Do you find the spiders satisfying?" Doctor Volospion reached into the hamper and, with careful use of a pair of silver tongs, withdrew another sugared tarantula, its frosted legs kicking feebly. "I think perhaps Argonheart Po could have made them a bit more lively." The hill on which they sat, gray sedge shadowed by the grim heights of Castle Volospion, was surrounded by legions of albino locusts, which—as if in purposeful contrast to the somnambulant spiders—marched back and forth across one another vigorously, climbing and grabbing to create various structures of living white insecta. At the moment, several million of them had combined to create a standing (and quivering) statue of a hugely muscled woman in a scanty swimming costume, the goddess Venus Beach of ancient tradition.

"It is primarily taste that motivates dear Argonheart, not animation," replied the Orchid. "No, thank you, Doctor, I am quite full. Who would ever think that a haunch of centipede would have so much meat on it?" She patted at her stomach. Her gown of glittering magenta fish scales rattled slightly. A shadow passed overhead, darkening their picnic blanket; the distraction allowed a few of the sugared spiders to make a slow dash for freedom. "Who is that?" She stared as the gigantic air car swept past again, ears broadly extended to ride the wind, trunk extended and trumpeting loudly. "Oh, look, it's some sort of elephant—it must be Abu Thaleb!"

"No," said Volospion sourly. "It is the Duke of Queens. As usual, he poaches on the aesthetic preserves of others."

"Hello!" shouted the Duke, leaning over the side of the vast ebony vehicle. "Hello, Iron Orchid! Doctor Volospion! Exciting news!"

"We wait breathlessly!" called the Orchid, laughing. Doctor Volospion looked perturbed.

The Duke of Queens, who tended to favor somewhat unstable forms of transportation, brought his massive, shiny black elephant around in another broad swoop. The creature's ears spread even wider as it tried to slow itself, but a miscalculation sent it plunging past the picnickers, trumpeting in terror and kicking its huge legs, to crash and roll through the midst of the busy locusts with a drawn-out wet crunching noise.

"My insects!" hissed Volospion, rising. His eyes narrowed and his pale face became even paler as the distressed elephant slipped and skidded in the remains of the locust horde, trying to get to its feet.

The Duke of Queens had been flung free and now came wading through a froth of crushed exoskeletons toward the picnic knoll. He was dressed as a circus ringmaster, but the hoops were showing a tendency to slide down to his ankles, making it even more difficult for him to walk. "Terribly sorry, Volospion. It's very tricky to land that one." He looked back to where the monstrous black elephant, which had given up trying to rise, now lay with its legs in the air, chest heaving. "Perhaps if I made the ears bigger…"

"You are a fool, sir," Volospion said bitterly.

"I am." The Duke offered him a genteel and regretful bow.

"We thought you Abu Thaleb at first," the Orchid smiled, amused as much by Volospion's dagger-eyed anger as by the Duke's landing. "Famous for his pachydermal proclivities. Have you borrowed your air car from him?"

"Oh, no!" said the Duke. "No, this is still a part of my fascination with the Dawn Age (spawned in large part by your clever son, most beauteous of blossoms). My airship is absolutely authentic—a perfect replica of Jumbo Jet, the largest device of its kind. Even the ordure it excretes is authentic, packed in little trays with special utensils…"

"You have ruined my locusts, sir." Doctor Volospion was visibly trying to regain his good temper, but perhaps not completely succeeding. "Many hours of toil. But, there it is. Ha! Yes, there it is." He showed the Iron Orchid a wintry smile before turning back to the Duke. "Only the small-minded nurse grudges, of course. This…entrance of yours has a point?"

"Ah! Of course! A most exotic occurrence! A new time-traveler has arrived." The Duke of Queens was momentarily distracted as his airship made a thrashing, bellowing attempt to rise. "He is guest of honor at My Lady Charlotina's and you are both invited."

"A time-traveler? This is poor and common fare," said Volospion, still waspish—both figuratively and literally, since except for his angular white features, the rest of him was covered by a shining, green-winged carapace.

"Ah, but not this time-traveler," said the Duke. "You see, he invented us."

Volospion's smile was thin. "So, another messianic type. Tiresome."

"Oh, no, this one is different." The duke's smile was wide and genuine. "You really must meet him."

"We prefer to remain…" Volospion began, but the Iron Orchid interrupted him.

"How charming. Of course we will join you, most dedicated of ducal lords." Ignoring Volospion's attempt to catch her eye, she glanced briefly at the great black elephant, which had clambered to its feet only to stumble again, trumpeting piteously. The creature's owner, his rings tangled, was not having much better luck getting up. "I think perhaps we should take *my* airship," said the Orchid.

"Isn't it all wonderful?" called Sweet Orb Mace as they alighted near Lake Billy the Kid. Her body—or his, for at the moment she was clearly and aggressively male—was naked to the waist, bulging with muscles. In one broad, knob-knuckled hand wobbled a long javelin made of shining gold, dripping with blood. "We have all come as authors in honor of My Lady Charlotina's guest."

"And who are you?" smiled the Iron Orchid.

"Don't you know?" Sweet Orb Mace seemed a little crestfallen. "Only perhaps the greatest of the Dawn Age writers—Jake Spear, author of a thousand hard-boiled romances, such as "Romeo and Oubliette" and "The Virgin of Menace." The rough-hewn features colored prettily. "I consulted the cities. Have I got the details wrong?"

"Of course not," boomed the Duke of Queens. "You are most luridly authorial, most astonishingly hard-boiled."

"Writers," murmured Doctor Volospion. "What folly!"

"Yes," said Sweet Orb Mace happily. "It *is* great fun, isn't it? Look, see, flying through the air, wearing the cape? That's Mistress Christia. She portrays Jane Awesome, a superheroine who defended humankind's dark era in the name of Pride, Prejudice, and the American Way (which was, I believe, a large and busy thoroughfare of some kind.) And O'Kala Incarnadine is Paddington Bear Bomb, dispenser of explosive epigrams—you can see that one went off right in the middle of the cake! Frosting everywhere! And Hektor Jektor Pachinko has come as the poet Frosty the Sandburg—but, oh, someone has eaten his carrot nose! Poor Hektor..."

"I ask again," said Doctor Volospion, casting a cold eye over the various celebrants as they made their way toward the center of the fête, a mountainous tent that had been erected on the shore the lake, "why exactly we should care about another babbling time-traveler?"

The Duke of Queens was admiring My Lady Charlotina's tent, constructed in the shape of an antique object called a "book" (apparently some kind of tomb for authors and thus the subject of much fixation among such types), its spine looming high above the ground, flakes of gilt from the binding sifting down in a fine, dry rain. "Because this author invented us. He swears it is so."

"Madness." Volospion flicked the fingers of a pale hand.

The duke shrugged. "He knows many things about us. He regaled us earlier with stories and secrets that we thought we alone knew."

Volospion turned, almost imploringly, to the Iron Orchid. "Many people know about us. Dozens of visitors from other times had heard tales of our sublime age before they ever reached it in person. That does not prove him authentic."

"Is authenticity important?" she asked with surprising gentleness. "In any case, O most penetrating of practitioners, are you not generally fascinated by travelers of a metaphysical bent? Does it not interest you to meet someone who does not claim merely to know why we exist, but to have actually been the one responsible?"

"I am interested in prophets and oracles, yes," allowed Volospion. "But although my menagerie is vast, I have debunked many more than I have collected. I am not easy to impress."

"You will doubtless have an excellent time, then, proving his claims false."

Something in the Iron Orchid's tone made Volospion look at her sharply, but she had begun talking in an animated whisper with Sweet Orb Mace. Volospion adjusted his insect-shell hood, preening the antennae back from his corpse-pale forehead, but said nothing more as they made their way along the lakeshore to the tent.

Even by her normal generous standards, their hostess had outdone herself: the tables of food alone covered several acres: red herrings skewered on reviewer's barbs sizzled over expanses of hot coals, and monstrous platters had been stacked high with half-baked plots, hoary wive's tails, licorice quips, and old chestnuts. Editorial assistants in gravy mewed piteously, treading on each other in a desperate attempt to keep their tiny heads above the surface of the steaming liquid in which they swam. High above all this plenitude, on a mound of roasted vellum, stood the centerpiece—two vast moving figures made of ground chicken liver, who hacked at each other with serving knives, screaming in rage and pain at each blow, while the guests standing beneath them applauded and caught falling bits of the combatants on slices of bread.

"Ah, I recognize that pair," said the Duke of Queens, pleased that his own researches were paying such a swift reward. "The terrible old gods of fiction, Vee Doll and Male Er, in their eternal struggle."

My Lady Charlotina swept down on them from above, her voluminous skirts bellying out to slow her descent. She accepted kisses and compliments on her outfit, dress, shawl, boots, and veiled wimple all constructed of translucent pink flesh.

"Ham," she explained to them. "Flesh of an extinct animal. I've come as a particular book rather than an author. What am I again?" she asked Sweet Orb Mace.

"The Smokehouse of Parma."

"Of course. I'd forgotten—I'm quite distracted, you see. Have you met the real author yet? He's just over there. I'd come with you, but Argonheart Po is making a new cake to replace the one that O'Kala exploded, and he's very upset about having to work so hurriedly."

My Lady Charlotina hurtled off across the great tent, making a swift and expert loop halfway to avoid Werther de Goethe's air car, a funeral urn of marble so dark it glowed purple. Sweet Orb Mace lowered her blood-smeared spear as Werther's urn hissed by overhead, then, as she hurried them toward the guest of honor, said, "It is his *birthday*, this author. That is in part the reason for the party. Isn't that lovely?"

"Hmmm." A tiny frown dimpled the Iron Orchid's smooth cheeks. "He looks a bit old to be born only today, if he is a time-traveler. Surely even the most primitive of the ancient ones did not have beards like that in infancy? But of course, though I have done the deed once myself, I would not claim to be an expert."

"It means an anniversary of one's birth, also," Volospion informed her. "They did not live very long, these Dawn Agers, and thus they marked the passing of each year, with a particular doleful emphasis after they passed into decrepitude at the year thirty or so." He examined the author carefully as they approached, and did not seem to like what he saw very much.

"All the more reason we should make his celebration festive," suggested the Duke of Queens, stopping to pull up his rings once more, which this time had become tangled in his ringmaster's whip, a segmented tail growing from his lower back. "Such brief lives! But such ardor, such enthusiasm!"

"I have seen others who appeared more enthusiastic than this fellow," observed the Iron Orchid quietly, for they had drawn close to the object of their scrutiny. "But I do think he looks rather sweet."

"Ah," said Doctor Volospion. "Sweet."

The time-traveler was standing a bit apart from the nearest guests— a gang of drunken young Ruffian Novelists dressed in Tol's Toy Soldier uniforms, waving long wooden Critic Bats—watching the ongoing, self-destructive struggle of Vee Doll and Male Er overhead with bemusement. The guest of honor was a bearded, sturdy man dressed in rather nondescript clothing—he alone, gifted with authenticity, seemed to feel no need for costume.

"Ah," called out the Duke of Queens, "we meet again, celebrated scribe! Sweet Orb Mace and I have already had the pleasure of an introduction to you, but please allow me to present the Iron Orchid and Doctor Volospion. Iron Orchid, Doctor, you are in the presence of the very great and renowned Dawn Age fabulist, Maxwell Meerkat!"

As the Iron Orchid made an elaborate, scale-clinking courtesy, and Volospion tendered a brief nod of greeting, the author shook his head slowly, like someone not quite awake. "Maxwell...? No, no, actually it's..."

"Please, vaunted Meerkat, no need for modesty!" The Duke of Queens turned to share his salutation with the crowd at large. "We are honored to have here among us such a fierce, fiery, and yet fundamentally friendly fabulist—the author of such works of undying glory as *A Cure for Kansas* and *A Medicine for Milton Keynes*! Creator of such magical heroes as El Rick and his aged sidekick Strom Bringer! Also that famously fateful fungus, the Eternal Champignon! And who could ever forget...forget..." The Duke paused for a moment, struggling as his shoulder rings slid down and pinned his arms to his side. "Ah, there are of course too many triumphs to mention!" he finished, still battling the wayward rings. "Huzzah for Maxwell Meerkat!" There was a spatter of applause.

"In truth, that's about all the cities had to offer," the duke whispered to the Iron Orchid as she helped him loosen the rings and push them back up to his neck. "Still, it's nice to give things that personal touch."

"Thank you," said the author. "You're very kind, all of you. But my name's not actually..."

"Remembered in quite the way you had hoped?" The Duke of Queens smiled sadly. "Of course not, of course not. We are rather a post-literary age, I'm afraid. But the fact that you are retained in the memory banks of the cities at all is itself an indicator of your prestige."

"I was told he claims to a greater posterity than that," said Doctor Volospion crisply. "If what I heard earlier is true, Mr. Meerkat, you believe our entire age is the product of *your* mind."

"Well..." The bearded man watched Doctor Volospion with a slightly discomforted fascination, as a hiker might regard a snake lying in his path. "Well, after a fashion. Certainly I've written about all of you, and considered you all to be the pure product of imagination. It's all very...strange. I mean, I've never been to this place before, although I've imagined it in some detail. Of course," he said to himself, frowning, "I suppose that strictly speaking I can't really be sure I'm here now. I seem to remember having a nap. Perhaps I'm dreaming this."

"I think," said Volospion icily, "if you are going to take credit for our existence, you might at least let us believe we are a bit more significant than the byblow of some daydream."

"I didn't mean it that way," said Meerkat, turning to the others as if worried he had offended them, too. "God, no. You're all quite spectacular, just as I'd always imagined you being. Lake Billy the Kid!" His smile was almost childlike. "It's amazing, really. Have all the things I wrote actually happened?" He turned to the Iron Orchid. "Has your son fallen in love with a woman from the 19th century?"

"You know my son?"

"Jherek Carnelian!" Maxwell Meerkat laughed. "Of course—I invented him, too." He saw the Orchid's slightly frosty glance and his face fell. "Or that's how it seems to me. It's really quite a puzzle. I've made up lots of things—it's been my job, you see—but nothing like this has ever happened before. The End of Time! It's hard to know where to start. I'd love to meet Lord Jagged, for one thing, actually meet him. Is he here?"

"But why should we believe a word you say?" demanded Volospion, his smile broad but his eyes cold. "We have had many claimants, many prophets and lunatics visit us here at the End of Time."

"Ah, yes, that's right—you don't appreciate people talking about Jagged, do you?" Meerkat nodded his head sagely.

"I assure you it is a matter of perfect indifference to me." Doctor Volospion ostentatiously turned his shoulder to the time-traveler as more of the inhabitants of the End of Time began to gather. O'Kala Incarnadine, who was attempting to eat a bowl full of typeworms and lead slugs with his clumsy bear paws and making rather a mess of it, gave a sticky wave to his comrades. Gaf the Horse in Tears was carrying a red pencil and striped in the bloody weals of a Galley Slave. Bishop Castle's huge hat flickered through different architectural shapes, one moment a minaret, the next a 68th Century purification dormitory.

"Do you like it?" Castle asked the author. "It is of course a reproduction of the famous Random House."

"Do not be offended by our wonderfully sharp-tongued Doctor Volospion," the Duke of Queens begged the guest of honor. "We are all thrilled to have our author among us. We are grateful that you have deigned to join us—so few creations can say that with certainty."

"Yes, it is of course very pleasant to meet you," said the Iron Orchid, "but although I do not entirely approve of Doctor Volospion's tone, I think his question is valid. Why should we believe that you had anything to do with making *us?*"

The author frowned a little, considering. There was a shout of approval from across the tent as Mistress Christia finished congress with her ninety-ninth Sails Rep and invited the one hundredth in line to doff his naval uniform and take his turn.

"I suppose I could tell you something that no one else could know," Meerkat said at last, almost apologetically. "I'm not really interested in proving anything, but I can't help feeling at least a little bit that it would be nice to justify myself. I worked very hard on all of you, after all."

The Iron Orchid was amused. "Tell, then."

"Not in front of everyone." He drew her aside and whispered in her ear. The Orchid's expression, at first one of polite disdain, quickly became something stranger and more complicated. When Meerkat had finished she looked at him once, drew a glittering fish-skin veil over her delicate features, then vanished from the tent.

"Ho ho!" said the Duke of Queens nervously. "What secrets you must possess, esteemed author of us all!"

"Please, let's go back to enjoying the party," begged Meerkat. "I should never have said anything in the first place—I was just so surprised to find myself here. I'd rather let it drop now. There's so much I want to see."

"But you owe us information!" declaimed Werther de Goethe, striding forward. The suffering hero of many of his own dramas was naked, clothed head to foot only in shining black ink with just the whites of his eyes for contrast. "If you are indeed our author, then you owe it to these others to explain to them their pointlessness, their insubstantiality. It is possible none of them...but *me*, of course...will understand the terrible import, but nevertheless you must try." He turned to the others. "Pointless—I warned you all. Life is not merely bleak, it is false—a mere fiction, devised for the entertainment of spotted, furtive readers we will never even meet."

"Speak for yourself," rasped Doctor Volospion. "I am no fiction. If there is any author subtle enough to imagine one such as I, surely it is not *this* creature."

My Lady Charlotina swept down from the ceiling in a long, lazy arc, landing between Volospion and the now clearly uncomfortable author. "What are you all doing to Mr. Morlock?"

"No," the author said, "it's not Morlock, it's…"

"Meerkat," finished the Duke of Queens. "We are having a bit of a spirited discussion about the nature of invention. Quite exciting."

Their hostess frowned. "I must admit I never quite understood how it is that you might have invented us, Mr. Morlock, but it is an entertaining conceit. Are you enjoying the party?"

"I'm sorry I ever mentioned it," he said, looking a bit shamefaced. "Me being the author, I mean. It seems a bit rude now. But it was such a shock to me when I found myself here…"

"Yes, how did it happen, exactly?" asked Doctor Volospion. "You have said nothing about your time machine."

"I don't have one. I don't think there is such a thing." The author saw the look on his hosts' faces and quickly added, "In *my* time, that is. I write stories—made-up stories. Time machines are a common device."

"Common?" said Sweet Orb Mace, who was combing the last crumbs of Male Er out of O'Kala Incarnadine's fur. "But you just said there were no such things…"

"Common *literary* devices. Inventions. I mean the made-up kind." Meerkat or Morlock flushed. "Damn. I'm not explaining myself well."

"Granting for a moment that you did invent us," said My Lady Charlotina, "why would you do such a thing?

"Yes!" shouted the Platinum Poppy. "And where do you get your ideas?"

The author seemed increasingly uncomfortable with the questioning. "It's hard to say exactly where inspiration begins. I might have been exaggerating the changes in my own society, which during my time many people thought were evidence of growing decadence, the end of civilization. I was also gently making fun of some of the types of people I knew." He shrugged. "The fact is, I'm a writer. I make things and then I use those things to tell stories."

"So we are *things*?" My Lady Charlotina frowned. "I'm not certain I like that very much, Mr. Morlock."

He sighed. "I didn't mean it that way."

"What did you tell the Iron Orchid?" demanded Doctor Volospion. "She has left, and rather precipitously. Did you threaten her?"

"Of course not. I told her something only her creator could know. It disturbed her, I suppose."

Volospion's eyebrow lifted. "Ah. Your guest has proved his worth at last, My Lady Charlotina. Now we will have the conjuring tricks." He fixed his chalky face on the visitor. His eyes glittered. "Entertain us, O First Mover. Tell my secrets."

The author frowned. "I think you're the only person I created at the End of Time who is actually, knowingly cruel. I suppose I deserve this."

Doctor Volospion raised a green exoskeletal hand to the guests who had gathered around them—the Ruffian Novelelists murmuring drunkenly, box-shaped Editors (every one wearing his or her own cubicle), Florence Fawkes in schoolmistress garb accompanied by a crowd of Little Dickenses, Lady Voiceless in a chrome-colored jailhouse uniform, her height doubled so she might masquerade as a Long Sentence. Even the jaunty Sails Reps, still perspiring faintly from entertaining Mistress Christia, crowded in to watch the proceedings.

"This time-traveler maintains he has invented us," Doctor Volospion announced, "every one of us—you, Werther and Mongrove, with your overwhelming sorrows, and you too, kindly Queens, with your never-ending fashions and fascinations…even you, My Lady Charlotina, our incomparable hostess of unparalleled taste and hospitality. All of us, we are told, came from this single and unprepossessing head. I ask you—is such a thing possible? Is it reasonable?"

My Lady Charlotina rose into the air. "I want no part of this. Doctor Volospion, you are coming close to abusing the very hospitality you so recently praised." She floated off, her expression unusually troubled.

Doctor Volospion's thin features twisted in what might almost have been called a smirk. "You have an eager crowd, Mr. Meerkat. Can you not show them a little of your creator's knowledge, or failing that, your actual creative art? Perhaps you could write a new character for us—someone interesting, to help alleviate the boredom of our two-dimensional, imaginary lives. Or it could be you would prefer to create an epic drama for us? The end of the universe, so often bruited? A kind of operatic destruction, sparing you the necessity for a considered ending?"

"If you're going to change things," suggested Sweet Orb Mace wistfully, "perhaps you could make me a bit more clever?"

"I don't want..." the author began.

"I'd like to be born, like Jherek was," said someone else from the back of the crowd, perhaps Clare Cyrato. "That would be nice, I think. Could you do that, Mr. Murdoch?"

"God!" said the author, flinching. "That's the worst yet. I keep telling you, my name is..."

"A byword for artistic expression," offered the Duke of Queens gallantly. "You are correct, noble novelist, and we are being unfair. It demeans your holy calling, testing you in this way..."

"But..."

"Ah, then let us return to the simplest test of all," grated Doctor Volospion. "You told the Iron Orchid something she did not like, driving her from the bosom of her friends. Do the same for me." He drew himself up to his full height, antennae bouncing. "Prove you are my creator. Frighten me. In front of all these guests."

There was a long pause. A few in the crowd began to whisper, bored or confused. The author stood and stared back at Doctor Volospion, and it seemed almost as though the two of them fought some silent, unmoving battle. At last, Doctor Volospion began to grin. "You are wishing you could go home and write me out of this story, aren't you?"

"No," said the bearded time-traveler, shaking his head. "No, that's not the kind of creator I want to be. You're a nasty little bastard, but I made you that way—it's not your fault and I can't punish you for it. I should have kept my mouth shut about being the author and just enjoyed myself instead." He took a deep breath and turned to face the puzzled crowd. "You have to be true to what you make. Look, if everything you make is a part of yourself, and you fail to treat your own creations respectfully, you're not being true to yourself." He made a self-conscious bow to the pale man dressed in emerald wasp hide. "You win, Doctor Volospion, if you choose to see it that way."

A few of the editorial assistants, those who had not drowned in gravy, recognized an obvious dramatic climax and gave a ragged, uncertain cheer.

"Now, then," said the author. "Can we get back to the party? I haven't really had anything to eat yet, and I'd love to try out a power ring, too."

Doctor Volospion, instead of being satisfied with his rival's submission, had grown more and more radiantly pale, as though some kind of flame burned beneath his waxy skin. As the author turned away to ask the Duke of Queens something, Volospion suddenly rose a few feet in the air and pointed an accusing finger at him.

"You!" he said in a voice that was nearly a screech, causing most of the dispersing guests to stop in their tracks and swivel around. "Who do you think you are? Or more importantly, who should *we* think you are?" His mouth worked for a moment, as though it could not form the shapes necessary to allow suitably disgusted words to emerge. "How...how *dare* you claim to have invented me! I, Doctor Volospion, in all my devastating subtlety and complexity, my sublime angers, my razor-sharp grudges, my brooding imagination—I am not the product of anyone else! I am not!"

"As you wish..." the author said wearily.

"No, sir," hissed Volospion. "It is not as I wish. Because what I wish is to prove who is real and who is imaginary." He turned toward his fellow inhabitants of the End of Time. "Here is the real question—can such a thing as an author of us all exist? I think not. Consider yourself, each one of you. Consider your beauty, your imagination, your delicious individuality. Do you believe you sprang from someone else's mind?"

"Actually," offered Hektor Jektor Pachinko, "I did. Mistress Christia made me..."

"You know what I mean!" Doctor Volospion snapped. "No, I think it is the idea of an author that is the fiction—the author himself who is illusionary."

"What...what does that mean, exactly?" asked the Duke of Queens, frowning. "I'm afraid I'm having a bit of trouble following you."

"Simply this—there can be no such person." Volospion folded thin arms across his chest-carapace. "This Maxwell Morlock Murdoch Meerkat person cannot exist."

"Cannot exist?" The Duke of Queens looked curiously at the author, who seemed at a loss for words. "But the fellow's right there..."

"No, he is not," insisted Doctor Volospion. He turned to the other guests. "If he exists, then we are all figments. If he exists, we are mere characters. The End of Time itself is only a symbol, an allegory, a metaphor. Do you believe that?"

Gaf the Horse in Tears raised his red pencil and waved it enthusiastically. "Why, if such a preposterous plot were written in my galley, I would force it to walk the plank! Avast!"

"It does seem a bit forcedly metaphysical," said Bishop Castle. "I confess I was troubled by the whole idea—but otherwise it's been a very nice party."

A few others began to murmur agreement.

"He does not exist," said Doctor Volospion, a tiny, angry red spot on each ivory cheekbone the only color on his skin. "He cannot exist. He will not exist."

"He does not exist!" shouted Sweet Orb Mace, waving Jake Spear's javelin excitedly. "Oh, yes, that's good."

"He does not exist!" shouted others, including many who had already forgotten or had never known the subject of the discussion.

"He does not exist! He will not exist. He cannot exist!" The cry swept through the whole party now, echoing to the distant roof and disturbing the sleep of several Critic Bats hanging upside-down from rafters. *"He does not exist!"* the crowd screamed happily.

The author, eyes wide, turned imploringly to the Duke of Queens. "Isn't there anything that can be done? I didn't want..."

The Duke of Queens looked at him, not without sorrow, and shook his head. "You know, I hate to admit it, old man, but Doctor Volospion has a bit of a point—it does all seem a bit...unlikely. But Happy Birthday anyway, Mr. Meerkat."

At the duke's last word, with a barely-audible *pop*, the author suddenly disappeared.

— ✳ —

In the hours afterward, the very few inhabitants of the End of Time who discussed the matter found themselves sharply divided as to what had happened.

Most believed that a deluded time-traveler had simply been seized by the forces of time (which could never be more than temporarily thwarted) and returned along with his particular madness to some earlier era. A few of the more conspiratorial-minded suggested that the author Meerkat had been a creation of one of their more inventive friends, perhaps the party's hostess, My Lady Charlotina, or even (as several suspected) Doctor Volospion himself. But in the immediate aftermath, only the Duke of Queens seemed saddened by the disappearance of the putative author of them all. The Iron Orchid did not return to the party, and afterward professed not to remember why she had left so suddenly.

The party itself continued on in full if increasingly chaotic flow— after all, it would take a great deal more than the unreality of a guest of honor to spoil a party at the End of Time. It was only when another week (as people from more conventional eras would reckon things) had passed, after Trixitroxi Ro set fire to a small army of Pages, whose papery doublets and hose burned astonishingly quickly, and O'Kala Incarnadine took on the form of a raging Deadline and ate nearly half the remaining guests, that the party was commonly agreed to have ended.

It was nearly a month before the last charred Page was located and removed by My Lady Charlotina's slaves from the trees along the shores of Lake Billy the Kid, by which time everyone was at another party.

Go Ask Elric

I've only ever had one real epiphany—what some people would call a religious experience or an "ah-hah moment." Mine was closer to the second definition than the first, but we non-religious types will take our enlightenment where we can find it, man.

I'll tell you about it.

I lived in London in the early- to mid-Nineties with my wife Deborah Beale, who was still a publisher at that time. She happened to be publishing Michael Moorcock, among others, so I finally got to meet and even know the man who had been one of the two or three most influential writers—hell, one of the half-dozen most influential people—on my young self.

Mike and his wife Linda were moving out of the country, and he called us up and asked us to come over for dinner before they left England.

The night of the dinner, I had been having a bad day for some reason—just the usual nonsense—work irritations, small complaints about life—and was in a semi-bitchy mood. Deb and I got in a cab and rode across London in the rain, and as I was sitting, quiet and a little sullen, staring out the window, I suddenly all but heard a voice shout in my ear, *"Hey, stupid! Where are you going? To Michael Moorcock's house, across amazing London, with your beautiful British science-fiction publisher wife! And why are you going? Because he invited you! Called you up and used your first name and everything! And you're in a BAD MOOD? You IDIOT!"*

Well, the voice was absolutely right, of course, and my teenage self would have gladly given an arm or leg (or maybe both) to have such an experience, or even to know for certain that such an experience lay in the future. My mood lightened instantly—I was suddenly so happy to be moving and breathing and enjoying the adventure that is my life I can't even tell you. And I've done my level best to hold onto that revelation ever since.

— ✳ —

This following story partakes a bit of, and contributes a bit to, the abovementioned epiphany.

A year or two before the events above, Michael Moorcock had invited me to contribute a story to the Elric anthology, *Tales of the White Wolf*, which I did, and then he was kind enough to render my story the ultimate compliment, saying: "I'd like to use your character in an Elric story of my own someday."

Go to his house for dinner? I would have painted the man's house if he'd asked me.

Anyway, this is one my own favorites, because I think it really is an Elric story—no cheating—but it's also funny. At least, I found it funny. But then, my old friends can tell you that I've got more than a little Pogo Cashman in me...

— ✳︎ —

"Up From the Skies" was rattling the windows. Sammy never played Hendrix at less than concert volume, no matter the hour, whether his parents were home or not. It was one of the things Pogo admired about him.

"Church," Sammy said, and took another hit on the bong. He puffed out his cheeks like a trumpet player, trying to hold in a cough.

"Yeah. Man was God." Pogo nodded. *"Is God."* He started to reach for the bong but decided that too much dope would interfere with the rush when the acid hit.

"You know he'd hate it now," Sammy said. "All this shit. Gerald Ford. Hardly any acid. *Disco.*" He waved his hand in a loose-wristed gesture that summed up and dismissed the entire decade of the Seventies to this halfway point. "He'd be bummed."

"Fuckin' A." Pogo flopped back into the beanbag chair and contemplated the decor of Sammy's room. Roger Dean album covers, an M.C. Escher drawing with self-absorbing chameleons, and three different portraits of Jimi Hendrix were thumbtacked to the walls. Behind the pictures those walls and the entire ceiling had been painted black and covered with whirlpools of white stars—the artistic end-product of a weekend's speedathon. The northwest-corner stars were little more than blobs. Sunday afternoon, Pogo remembered, when they started to come down.

It was a cool look, he thought. Like floating in outer space, but with posters.

As he watched, the stars shimmered slightly and the sable field behind them seemed to recede.

"Man! You feeling it?"

Sammy nodded. "Gettin' buzzy." He leafed through his sideways stack of records, motor-coordination already starting to short-circuit. *Dark Side of the Moon.* Sick of it. *Surrealistic Pillow?* That's pretty trippy. 'Go ask Alice, when she's ten feet tall...,'" he sang in the familiar—and tuneless—Key of Sammy. He stared at the cover, then dropped it back and riffled further. "How about *Close to the Edge?*"

"Nah. More Hendrix. *Electric Ladyland.*"

Sammy tried to stand up, laughed, and crawled to the turntable. As the needle came down on the wrenching wah-wah of "Voodoo Chile", Pogo smiled a tiny smile. He needed the Hendrix right now. Jimi was a friend, in a way no one he had ever met in real life could be. Jimi was...well, maybe not God exactly, but...something. Something. He raised his eyes to the picture over Sammy's bed. The Man, flanked by his Experience—black Jesus and two pasty thieves, all wearing haloes of frizzy hair. Hendrix was smiling that little half-smile, *that you can't judge me brother until you've been where I've been* smirk. And his eyes... Jimi...he *knew*.

"Whoah," Sammy whispered from somewhere nearby. The room was getting dark, as though the sun was setting, but Pogo felt fairly sure it was still early afternoon, the summer twilight hours away.

"Yeah." He chuckled, although nothing was funny yet. Hendrix was watching him. "Here comes the rush."

And as the stars reached out for him—*Laughing Sam's Dice,* Pogo thought, *that one's all about stars and acid, Jimi was hip to stars*—he felt himself drifting like a rudderless boat in a sea of pack ice. Something was pulling at his mind, something he wanted to articulate and share.

"Sammy, check it out. Hendrix, man..." The thought was elusive but he knew it was important. "Like, the stars, man—he was saying that the stars are playing dice with the world, man, with the whole universe. And that when you take acid, the acid...it takes you out there. Where the dice are rolling."

If Sammy replied, Pogo couldn't hear him. He couldn't see him either. The bright stars were burning before his eyes and the interstitial blackness was empty beyond imagining. Pogo felt himself sliding forward, pulled as though by slow, slow gravity.

This is some really fucking good shit, he thought, then he plunged into a silent white bonfire.

— ✳ —

It was black—no, more than black. It was negative black, an absence of illumination so complete that even the memory of light was tainted.

That movie about Jimi's life, Pogo remembered, and was relieved to have at least his own thoughts for company. *That guy said Hendrix was somewhere between sleep and death, and he just chose a different trip—just floated on out. Did that happen to me? Am I dead?*

He had a dim inner vision of himself, Pogo Cashman, lying on Sammy's floor. Would there be ambulance men? Sammy's parents? But Sammy wouldn't even come down for hours, so it might be hours until he noticed his friend was dead.

In a strangely unworried way, Pogo hoped Sammy wouldn't find him during the teeth-grinding, gray, post-trip state. That would bum him out for a long time, and Sammy was a good guy.

Jesus, it was dark. And silent. And empty.

So am I dead? Because if it's gonna be like this for eternity, it's really boring.

What if he had just gone blind and deaf? That would be more in line with the horror-stories about bad acid trips he'd heard. But that would be almost as fucked as being dead. No tunes, no movies. Well, at least he wouldn't have to go to school. Maybe he could learn to play pinball, like in *Tommy.*

As he seriously contemplated for the first time what entertainment the sport of pinball might provide to the hearing- and vision-impaired, the darkness was effaced by a dim smear of light.

Coming down, he thought with some relief. *Maybe I should have smoked some of that Colombian and cut the rush a little. This shit is pretty intense...*

The light bloomed, shimmered, then stabilized in a pattern of concentric rings. Several moments passed before he recognized what he was seeing. He stood in a long stone corridor, like something out of a Dracula movie—torches in brackets, moss-bearded walls, puddles of water throwing back ghostlight from the torch flames. It was a long tunnel, winding away out of his sight some hundred yards ahead.

What the fuck...?

Pogo looked down and was relieved to find his very own body still attached to him, unchanged since Sammy's room—desert boots, patched Levis, his black Lou Reed shirt covering the merest beginning of a hard-won beergut.

So when you die, you get to keep your Lou Reed t-shirt. Mysterious and weird are the ways of God...or whatever they say.

But the longer he stood on this spot, the more restless he felt. Something was calling him—no, not calling, but drawing him, as a cool breeze might summon him to a window on a hot day. Tickling at his thoughts. Something lay ahead of him, down the corridor. Somebody there wanted him—was calling to him. Somebody...

Hendrix. The thought was electrifying. *I was thinking about Jimi. It must be him—like his spirit or something. He's got a message for humankind. And I'll be his messenger.*

He hurried down the corridor, absently noting that, just as in the Dracula movies, his footfalls echoed unpleasantly and small furry things scuttled out of his path, vanishing into the shadows.

If I'm gonna be his messenger, he'll have to teach me how to play guitar like him. So I can make people listen. I'll take Jimi's message all over the world, and I'll jam with Page and Clapton and all those guys.

He entertained a vision of Jeff Beck shaking hair out of his eyes and saying, "Fuckin' 'ell, Pogo, you really make that axe sing—Jimi chose the right cat," as they stood basking in rapturous applause on the stage at Wembley (or one of those other big English places), both of them covered in manly jam-sweat.

Pete Townsend suddenly appeared beside them, his whippet face screwed up with anxiety. "You said you'd get high with me, Pogo, and tell me about Jimi. You promised."

Beck's angry, proprietorial reply was interrupted by a squeak and crunch. Pogo looked down to discover he had trodden on one of the furry scuttlers. In the torchlight he could see it wasn't a rat, but the bloody mess on his bootsole was not amenable to a more precise identification.

Jeff and Pete and the rest did not return, but that scarcely mattered: Pogo's thoughts were quite taken up with what stood before him.

A black iron door stood flush with the wall of the corridor, taller than Pogo and covered with bumpy designs—writhing demons and monsters, he saw when he leaned closer. It was quite solid beneath his hands, and quite immovable. Yet the feeling of being needed pressed him even more strongly, and he had no doubt that its source lay on the other side.

"Anybody in there?" he called, but even with his ear at the keyhole he heard no reply. He stepped back, looking for a crowbar or other heavy instrument (or even better, a spare key), but except for the torches and the scuttlers, which seemed more numerous now, the corridor was empty.

Pogo felt inexplicably certain that Jimi Hendrix himself stood on the far side, with a message just for him from beyond the grave. And free guitar lessons thrown in. The situation was weird enough already that a simple locked door couldn't stop him—could it?

"When logic and proportion, have fallen sloppy dead..."

The tune had been running through his head off and on since Sammy had sort-of sung it, but now the words of the old Airplane drug song seemed peculiarly appropriate. Down a hole, like Alice in Wonderland, caught in a bad acid trip. What did Alice do? For a little girl who'd probably never heard of Owsley or Haight-Ashbury (Pogo had the dim idea the original book had been written a long time ago, like around World War One or Two) she'd always seemed to get through all right. Of course she'd had magic cookies and stuff, which made her...

...shrink...

Suddenly, the door was getting bigger. The keyhole was several feet above his head and climbing. At the same time, water was rising around his knees. And the walls were getting farther and farther away...

Holy shit! I'm shrinking! Bitchin'!

If he could stop the process at some point, that was. If not, it might become a bummer of major proportions.

As the crack at the bottom of the door rose up past him—the black iron portal itself now loomed as large as the Chrysler Building—Pogo waded through the puddle beneath it, making a face as the scummy water sloshed around his chest. Once the broad expanse of door was past, he floundered out of the bilge onto a spit of muddy dirt and thought very hard about growing. When it worked, he was almost as surprised as the first time.

His surroundings drew down around him like a film run in reverse, the walls shrinking like a sweater-sleeve washed in hot water. When the process slowed and then halted, Pogo ran his hands over himself to make sure everything had returned to its correct size—he briefly wondered if he could enlarge just selected parts of his body as well, which might help him finally get some chicks—and then looked around.

There was only one torch here, fighting hard against the dank air; the wide room was mostly sunk in shadows. A few clumps of muddy straw lay on the floor; out of them, like Easter eggs in plastic grass nests, peeped skulls and other bits of human bone.

Pogo could tell a bad scene when he saw one. "Whooo," he said respectfully. "Torture chamber. Grim, man."

As if in response, something rattled in the shadows at the far side of the chamber. Pogo squinted but could see nothing. He slid the torch out of the bracket and moved closer. The feeling of being summoned was stronger than before, although in no way unpleasant. His heart beat faster as he saw a shape against the wall...a human shape. Jimi, the Man himself, the Electric Gypsy—it must be! He had summoned Pogo Cashman across time and space and all kinds of other shit. He had...he had...

He had the wrong color skin, for one thing.

The man hanging in chains against the stone wall was white—not just Caucasian, but without pigment, as white as Casper the Friendly Ghost. Even his long hair was as colorless as milk or new snow. He did wear a strange, rockstar-ish assortment of rags and tatters, but his eyes, staring from darkened sockets, were ruby red. It was not Hendrix at all, Pogo realized. It was...

"...*Johnny Winter?*"

The pale man blinked. "Arioch. You have come at last."

He didn't *sound* like Johnny Winter, Pogo reflected. The blues guitarist was from Texas, and this guy sounded more like Peter Cushing or one of those other guys in the old Hammer horror movies. But he wasn't speaking English, either, which was the weirdest thing. Pogo could understand him perfectly well, but a part of his brain could hear words that not only weren't English, they didn't even sound human.

"Do not torment me with silence, my Lord," the white-faced man cried. "I am willing to strike a bargain for my freedom. I will happily give you the blood and souls of those who have prisoned me here, for a start."

Pogo goggled, still confused by the dual-language trick.

"Arioch!" The pale man struggled helplessly against his chains, then slumped. "Ah, I see you are in a playful mood. The length of time you took to respond and the bizarre shape you have assumed should have warned me. Please, Lord of the Seven Darks, I have abided by our bargain, even at such times as you have turned it against me. Free me now or leave me to suffer, if you please."

"Ummm," Pogo began. "Uh, I'm not...whoever you think I am. I'm Pogo Cashman. From Reseda, California. And I'm pretty high. Does that make any sense?"

— ✷ —

Elric was beginning to believe that this might not be Arioch after all: even the Hell-duke's unpredictable humors did not usually extend this far. This strange, shabby creature must then be either some further trick by Elric's tormentors, or a soul come unmoored from its own sphere which had drifted into this one, perhaps because of his summoning. Certainly the fact that Elric could understand the language the stranger called Pogokhashman spoke, while knowing simultaneously that it was no human tongue he had ever encountered, showed that something was amiss.

"Whatever you are, do you come to torment oft-tormented Elric? Or, if you are no enemy, can you free me?"

The young man eyed the heavy iron manacles on the albino's wrists and frowned. "Wow, I don't think so, man. Sorry. Bummer."

The meaning was clear, though some of the terms were obscure. "Then find something heavy enough to crush my skull and release me from this misery," breathed the Melnibonéan. "I am rapidly growing weaker, and since apparently I am unable to summon aid, I will be helpless at the hands of one who has not the right to touch a Dragon Emperor's shadow, much less toy with me for his amusement." And as Elric thought about Badichar Chon's grinning, gap-toothed face, a red wave of hatred rolled over him; he rocked in his manacles, hissing. "Better I should leave him only my corpse. An empty victory for him, and there is little in this life I will miss."

The stranger stared back at him, more than a bit alarmed. He brushed a none-too-clean hank of hair from his eyes. "You want me to...kill you? Um...is there anything else I could do for you instead? Make you a snack? Get you something to drink?" He looked around as though expecting the Priest-King to have supplied his dungeon with springs of fresh water.

The albino wondered again whether the idiot apparition might not be a further cruelty from his captor, but if it was, it smacked of a subtlety the Chon had not previously exhibited. He struggled to maintain his flagging patience. "If you cannot free me, friend, then leave me to suffer in peace. Thrice-cursed Badichar Chon has taken Stormbringer, and without the strength it gives to me, my own treacherous body will soon accomplish the executioner's work without assistance."

"Storm...?"

"Stormbringer. My dark twin, my pet demon. My sword."

The strange youth nodded. "Got it. Your sword. Y'know, this is pretty weird, this whole set-up. Like a J.R.R. Tolkien calendar or something. Are there hobbits here, too?"

Elric shook his head, surfeited with nonsense. "Go now. One who has sat upon the Dragon Throne prefers to suffer in private. It would be a kindness."

"Would it help if I got this sword for you?"

The albino's laugh was sharp and painful. "Help? Perhaps. But the Chon would be unlikely to give it to you, and the two-score killers of his Topaz Guard might have something to say on the subject of your taking it."

"Hey, everything flows, man. Just try to stay cool."

The youth turned and walked back toward the front of the cell. Elric's dimming sight could not follow him into the shadows there, but although the stranger had clearly left the cell,, Elric did not hear the door open. Even in his pain and long-simmering fury, he had a moment's pause. Still, whether the stranger was a demon, a hallucination, or truly some hapless traveler lured between the spheres by Elric's desperate summons, the Melnibonéan doubted he would see him again.

— ✳ —

Curiouser and curiouser. Who said that?

Pogo grew back to his normal height on the far side of the door. This was certainly the strangest trip he had ever taken, and it wasn't getting any normal-er as it progressed. Still, he had told the pale man he'd fetch his sword, and who knew how long it would be until the acid started to wear off? Better get on it.

He chose a corridor direction from the somewhat limited menu and set off. The stone passageway wound along for quite a distance, featureless but for the occasional torch. Pogo was embarrassed by the meagerness of his own imagination.

Sammy went on a spaceship that time when we did the four-way Windowpane, with all those blue insects flying it and giant donut creatures and everything. 'Course, he reads more science fiction than I do—all those guys with the funny names like Moorcock and Phil Dick. Sounds like they should be writing stroke-books instead.

Still, if his imagination hadn't particularly extended itself in terms of dungeon decor, he was impressed by the relentless real-ness of the experience. The air was unquestionably dank, and what his desert boots were squelching through definitely looked, smelled, and sounded like the foulest of mud. And that Elric guy, with his built-in mime make-up, had been pretty convincing too.

The corridor opened at last into a stairwell, which alleviated the boredom somewhat. Pogo climbed for what seemed no little time. He was still terribly disappointed that it had not been Jimi Hendrix who had summoned him. He had been so certain…

A few more steps brought him to a landing which opened out in several directions, and for the first time he could hear sounds other than his own crepe-soled footfalls. He picked one of the arched doorways at random.

Within moments he found himself surrounded by people, rather a shocking amount of them (perhaps he had undercredited his own powers of creativity!) all bustling about, dressed like they were trying out for *The Thief of Baghdad* or some other Saturday morning movie of Pogo's youth. Shaven-headed, mustachioed men hurried past bearing rolled carpets on their shoulders, and small groups of women, veiled to a disappointing degree, whispered to each other as they walked close to the walls. In one large room that opened off the hallway dozens of sweating, flour-covered people seemed to be cooking a fantastically large meal. The din was incredible.

None of them seemed to pay much attention to Pogo. He was not invisible—no one bumped him and several actively avoided him—but nobody allowed themselves more than a swift glance before continuing briskly with whatever task consumed their attention. He forced a few to stop so he could ask them the whereabouts of a magic sword, but they gave him no reply, sliding away like cheerleaders avoiding a drunken loser at a party.

As Pogo walked on, the hallway widened and became more lavishly decorated, the walls painted with flowing patterns of blossoming trees and flying birds. He saw fewer and fewer people until, after he had walked what he estimated was about twice the distance from his house to Xavier Cugat High School, he found himself in a section of the vast palace—or whatever it was—that was empty. Except for him. And the whispering.

He followed the rustling noise farther down the corridor, peeking into open rooms on either side; all were abandoned and deserted, though they looked as though they were in regular use. At last he found himself at the doorway of a large chamber that *was* inhabited. It was from here the whispering came.

In the center of a huge, high-roofed room stood what looked like a stone altar, the kind of thing on which someone might sacrifice a very tiny virgin to some undersized gods. Ranged around this altar, mumbling and hissing amongst themselves, stood half a dozen bearded men in robes of dramatic colors and wild design, each garment different, as though the men were in some sort of fashion competition. They stood in a ragged circle, intently examining a black sword which lay atop the altar stone like a frozen snake.

Several dozen grim-faced soldiers in gleaming armor studded with pale brown jewels stood facing out in a protective ring around the robed men, each with a long nasty-looking spear in one hand and a curving, equally nasty-looking sword sheathed at his waist.

Those must be the guard-guys Elric was talking about, Pogo reasoned. *And that sword those other dudes are looking at must be Stunbanger, or whatever it is.* His good-acid-trip confidence began to pale a little. Surely even if they couldn't really hurt him—it was only a hallucination, after all—getting whacked with all those sharp things could turn the trip into a real bummer, and possibly even make him feel kind of queasy for a couple of days after he came down.

After a moment's consideration, then a single careful thought, he felt himself begin to shrink once more.

It was strange walking along the groove between the tiles and seeing the edges stretch, valley-like, over his head. It was even stranger staring up between the legs of the colossal Topaz Guardsmen, each one now as tall as a the pylons of a bridge.

Be pretty cool to do this right underneath Diana Darwent and her jock-ette friends. If they were wearing skirts.

He laughed, then froze in place, afraid that he might be heard and noticed. After a moment's reflection—had *he* ever heard a bug laughing?—he hiked on.

Climbing up onto the dais was difficult, but at his present size there were irregularities in the stone that offered good handholds. The robed and bearded men around the sword were talking, and just as with Elric, he could understand them perfectly—or at least their words, although their voices were thunderously loud and rumbled like the bass notes at a Deep Purple concert. Their meaning was a little less clear.

"It is a coagulated form of Etheric Vapor. Were it not for the binding rituals, it would re-transmogrify into Vapor Absolute and evaporate. If we could just try the Splitting Spell once more…"

"Your reasoning is as thin as a viper's skinny bottom, Dalwezzar. Etheric Vapor plays no part here. It is a perfectly ordinary sword that has been drawn through a Multiversal Nexus, and hence its individual monads have…er…turned inside-out. More or less."

"You two! If you would ever look at something without trying to make it fit those hobby-horse ideas of yours, those addle-brained pseudo-certainties you cosset and fondle in your lonely beds as though they were catamites…Badichar Chon needs answers. Bah! Never send a Theoretical Thaumaturge to do a Practical Thaumaturge's job."

As Pogo was listening to this, albeit uncomprehendingly, and pondering how he could get to the sword itself—he was putting aside the "and then what?" question for a little while—something large and dark moved over him like a storm cloud.

"And what is this? Look, Dalwezzar, a homunculus! Now tell me how your Etheric Vapor nonsense explains the breeding of homunculi by the Study Object! Ha! If there was ever a proof that this is a product of a Multiversal Nexus…"

Pogo looked up in shock as he realized that the homo-whatever they were talking about was him. As he wondered whether it was his desert boots—he had told his mom he wanted real hiking boots, but she had told him if he wanted a pair of 60 dollar Vibram-soled shoes just to stand around the parking lot, he could damn well get a job—a pair of tweezers the size of a lamp post closed on his shirt and jerked him into the air.

He hung now before something so full of holes, so covered with hairs like burnt tree-trunks that for a moment he thought he had been kidnapped by a public campground. Several more moments passed before he could make out what it was—a giant face.

"Quick, get the killing jar!" The fumes from the yawning, snaggle-toothed cave were enough to make Pogo swear off onions for life. "Ah, Dalwezzar, you will cringe in embarrassment when this is published! You will shriek and writhe! 'Etheric Vapor' will be a term of academic scorn for centuries to come!"

"Pig! Of course you want to put it in the killing jar! Were I allowed to boil it alive, you would see that this too is a pure distillation of the Vapour! Give it to me!"

A gristly thing like a giant pink squid reached up and snatched at the tweezers. Pogo felt himself being whipped back and forth through the air as though on a malfunctioning carnival ride. The material of his t-shirt began to shred.

Oh shitshitshit, he thought in a panic. *Small bad! Small bad! Big good!*

The robed and bearded men suddenly began to shrivel around him, as did the room itself, even the serried ranks of Topaz Guards. Within moments, all half-dozen Learned Men had disappeared. Or rather, as Pogo realized after a bit, they were still around, but he was sitting on them: he could hear their dying cries from beneath the back pocket of his Levis, and feel their thrashing final moments against his posterior. It was pretty gross, but he couldn't get up, since his head was now wedged against the tiled ceiling.

The Topaz guard, hardened combat veterans to a man, stared at the sudden appearance of a 45-foot tall California teenager in a *Rock and Roll Animal* shirt, then screamed and fled the great chamber. By the time the last spear had clattered to the floor, Pogo was alone.

Something was giving him a distinctly painful sensation in his hindquarters. He reached around behind himself, shuddering as he scraped loose a wet unpleasantness in a robe, and tried to remove the pricking object.

As soon as his fingers touched the black sword, he found himself normal-sized once more, the transition so painfully swift that for some minutes he could only sit, head spinning, among the unwholesome remnants of what had once been Badichar Chon's College of Thaumaturges.

— ✵ —

Elric looked up at the sound, a thin yet painful scraping. Something was happening in the darkness near the door of his cell. He felt so weak it was difficult to focus his eyes, let alone muster any interest.

"Uh, hey, are you okay?"

The strange young man had appeared out of the darkness as mysteriously as he had vanished. Elric gave a hapless shrug which gently rattled his chains. "I have been happier," he admitted.

"It's stuck halfway under. It'll fit, I just have to pull on it some more. Too bad nobody around here ever heard of a kitty-door. That woulda been perfect."

Having finished this obscure announcement, the stranger turned and headed back toward the front of the cell. There was some kind of stain on the seat of his pants. It looked like blood.

After a further interlude of scraping, the apparition returned. Elric's eyes widened.

"This must be it, right?" The youth held Stormbringer cradled in his arms. He had clearly never handled a sword.

"By my ancestors, how did you...?" Elric could feel the runeblade's nearness like a cool wind on his face.

"Long story. Look, could you take it? It feels kind of weird. No offense."

Elric's white fingers strained at the hilt, which the stranger obligingly brought near. As his palm closed around it he felt a tiny trickle of energy, but within moments even that ended. Elric still felt very feeble.

"There is something wrong. Perhaps it has been too long since the blade has taken a life. It does not strengthen me the way it should." He twisted his wrist; even with the slight additional strength it had given him, he could not lift it upright. "It is hungry for souls."

The stranger—what had he called himself? Pogokhashman?—squinted suspiciously. "Like, take it to a James Brown concert or something, I guess. But don't point it at me, okay? That thing's weirder than a mofo."

The Melnibonéan slumped. "Of course, my friend. I would not harm you, especially when you have done me such an unexpected good. But without Stormbringer's power, I am still as prisoned as I was before. And if the Chon has been alerted to its theft, he will approach me very carefully. I will not be given an opportunity to blood it." He paused, staring at the black blade. "But if it were hungry for soul-energy—depleted—then I do not understand why it did not try to force me to kill you. Usually it is like an ill-bred mastiff, always lunging at my friends."

Pogokhashman shrugged. "Shit happens."

Frustration welled up in Elric. To think that the last scion of his proud people should come to this: slowly starving to death in a cell, prisoner of a low-level satrap, his blade in his hand and yet useless to him!

"Ah, Duke Arioch!" he screamed suddenly. "Fate has played a clever trick on me this time! Why have you not come to gloat? Your love of irony should draw you like a tick to hot blood! Come, Arioch, and enjoy my plight! Come, Chaos Lord!"

And, as the echoes of Elric's voice settled into the damp walls and mired floor, Arioch came.

The light of the torch seemed to bend; the cell darkened but for one spot, where the straw glowed as if afire. In that place the shadows became a buzzing cloud of flies, which drew into a tight spiral, then circled more closely still until they composed a moving tube of glinting, humming darkness. The tube widened, then unfolded, becoming a beautiful young man in a strange suit of red velvet. He wore a cylindrical hat with a wide brim, and his hair was nearly as pale as Elric's own.

"Arioch! You have come after all."

The Hell-duke eyed him with amusement. "Ah, sweet Elric. I find you in yet another dreadful predicament."

Backed against the wall, Pogokhashman was staring, goggle-eyed. "I know you!" he said. "You're that guy in the Rolling Stones. But Sammy said you drowned in your swimming pool." He regarded him a moment longer. "Nice tux."

Arioch turned to survey the stranger, his look of benign indifference unchanged. "Hmmm," he said, his musical voice as langorous as the song of a summer beehive. "Your taste in companions is still inimitably your own, my little Melnibonéan."

Elric felt compelled to defend Pogokhashman, obscure and alien though he might be. "This man has done me a great service. He has returned Stormbringer to me."

"Ah, yes. Stormbringer. Which was taken from you by ambush, yes?" Arioch walked delicately through the muck of the cell-floor as though trying to keep the hems of his flared scarlet pantaloons clean. "Your runeblade was snatched from you by Badichar Chon, I believe the fellow's name is, and subjected to much experimenting by his pet wizards. And now it doesn't...function properly, is that it?" He spoke with the solicitude of Elric's old torturer Doctor Jest sympathizing with a prisoner over some heinous outrage which Jest himself had perpetrated.

"Yes. Yes! It does not overcome my weakness. I cannot break free."

"No doubt that is because of the Splitting Spell...and the Chronophage."

Elric frowned. "I have never heard of either of these things."

"The first is very simple—primitive even." Arioch crossed his legs as a tailor might, and hovered a yard and a half above the cell floor. Across the cell, Pogokhashman's face split in a wide, incredulous grin. "You wielded more powerful magicks yourself when you were but a princeling, sweet Elric, a child. Badichar Chon searched far and wide to fill his

College of Thaumaturges...but his is rather a backwater kingdom after all, and the candidates were of a somewhat low order. Still, the Splitting Spell they used in an effort to unlock Stormbringer's secrets was crudely effective, although in their ignorance they did not even recognize their success. They managed partially to unbind its energies—just for a moment of course, but in one of those delightful coincidences that are the bane of less flexible sorts than myself, it happened to be just the *proper* moment and a part of your runeblade's essence was drawn away."

"Drawn away by what? And what of this Chronophage? Some demon or wizard who robbed Stormbringer of its power?"

Arioch smiled and floated higher, until he was far above Elric's head. A tube appeared in his hand, pulled out of some crack in reality, and the Chaos Lord brought its brass mouthpiece to his lips and inhaled. After a moment he blew out a great ring of blue smoke which drifted above his head and hung there.

"It would never do to tell you too much, pretty Elric," he said. "It is antithetical to Chaos to rob individuals of their initiative."

"Games, Duke Arioch, always games. Well, then, I will find the Chon's wizards and discover what they have done with their ham-handed spells."

Arioch grinned around the brass mouthpiece. "You will not have to look far, I think." He inclined his head toward Pogokhashman. Smoke wafted from his nostrils. "Turn around, you."

The stranger stared at Arioch, then slowly pivoted until the stain on his backside came into view.

"If you have any questions for the College of Thaumaturges," chuckled Arioch, "you may ask them now."

"It was...um...an accident," Pogokhashman said quietly.

Elric shook his head. "I understand nothing."

Arioch blew another smoke-ring. "You must find Stormbringer's stolen essence. It will lead you to the Chronophage. That is enough to begin. Farewell, my tragic underling."

"Wait!" The Melnibonéan leaned forward; his chains clanked. "I am still trapped here, too weak to escape..."

"Which will make your adventure all the more piquant." Arioch abruptly began to grow transparent, then disappeared. The last of the smoke-rings followed him into oblivion a few seconds later.

"A thousand curses!" Elric howled at the empty air, then let his chin droop to his chest. Even anger sapped him; he could feel his remaining strength sifting away like sand through spread fingers. "Betrayed once more. My family's bargain with Chaos has again proved to be a dubious one."

"Wow, man, sorry." Pogokhashman came forward and awkwardly patted the albino's shoulder. "I'm not too clear on all this, but it sounds like a bummer." He paused for a moment, then dug in his pocket. "Would these help any?"

Elric goggled at the ring of iron keys. "What...where...?"

Pogokhashman shrugged. "One of those Topless Guards dropped 'em. When they all ran away."

"Ran away...?"

"Long story, man, like I told you." The youth began trying the keys in the thick iron lock on Elric's shackles. The third one clicked, then clicked again, and the shackles fell away.

Elric was having trouble encompassing all that had happened to him. He stared at his unlikely savior and shook his head. "I thank you, Pogokashman. If I can ever repay you..."

"I just hope you get your sword fixed. Or whatever that swimming-pool guy was saying."

Elric held Stormbringer before him. It was still his living blade, but its essence was quiet, as though it slept. He shook it experimentally, then turned to his companion. "And somehow, I gather, you have destroyed the College of Thaumaturges—Badichar Chon's wizards?"

The look of embarrassment returned. "Didn't mean to. I kind of sat on them."

Elrich shook his head, but did not pursue the matter. "Then I shall have to find some other method of seeking Stormbringer's lost essence. You seem to be full of hidden powers, my friend. Can you help me? I am far in your debt already."

"I don't think so, man. I mean, I'm not even sure how I got here in the first place. We just took some acid, Sammy and me, and I was think-ing about...well, anyway, I don't think so."

"Then I must try to solve the riddle." Secretly, Elric felt a little relieved. The ease with which this stranger had defeated the Chon's wizards and handpicked guard and then retrieved Stormbringer made the Melnibonéan feel embarrassingly helpless. His sickly constitution had often placed him in such a position, but he did not hate it any the less for its familiarity. Now, even though his predicament was desperate, at least he would stand or fall by his own devices.

He wracked his mind for a spell that would allow him to trace Stormbringer's stolen essence. This process was made slightly more difficult by his own light-headed weakness, and also by Pogokhashman, who strolled up and down the length of the cell whistling and humming and occasionally singing some tuneless ballad about the wind crying merry, his feet crunching through the rotted straw. Elric winced, but persevered, and at last a wisp of memory rose from the depths.

"Bring me the torch," he called. His new companion went and drew it from the bracket, then stood in obvious amazement as the albino pushed his long-fingered right hand into the flames.

"What...uh...?"

"*Silence!*" Elric hissed through clenched teeth. When he deemed a long enough moment had passed, he snatched it out again. The pain was dreadful, but it was necessary: between his own feebleness and Stormbringer's strange torpor, Elric needed to strengthen the connection. He grasped the runeblade's hilt in his raw, agonized hand and closed his eyes, then felt for the restlessly slumbering core of Stormbringer.

"In flame and blood our pact was sealed,"

he intoned in a tongue that had been ancient before Imrryr was raised above the waves. He thought he could perceive a vague stirring in the internal darkness.

"With death and souls the bargain fed.
Now lost to me is my dark friend.
Its secrets all concealed.

"In blood our pact was first annealed,
With death and souls the bond was made

Let light now burn away the shade
Let all now be revealed.

"By all the ancient lore I wield
By all who wait at my command
By my heart's blood and my right hand
Now let the breach be healed!"

When he had finished the incantation he paused, listening for something soundless, looking for something that had no shape. In a further shadow, deeper than the blackness behind his eyelids, something was indeed stirring. He felt for it, and sensed its incompleteness: Stormbringer itself was searching for what was lost. The questing something that was the remnant of the blade's essence uncoiled and began to draw away from him. He seized at it with his mind, and could feel himself being pulled along.

"Pogokhashman," he croaked, eyes still tightly shut. "Take my hand!"

Something grasped his left hand, even as he felt himself being sucked down through his own thoughts, down a darkly pulsing rabbit-hole into nothingness.

Curiouser and curiouser, my ass! This is just plain…weird.

Pogo had grabbed Elric's white hand—not without some trepidation; the gayness of the whole thing aside, he had also worried the albino might jam *his* fingers into the torch as well. An instant later, they were off to Wonderland.

Or something. Actually, what made it frightening was that it wasn't really anything. The closest comparison Pogo could make was the light-show ride down to Jupiter in *2001, A Space Odyssey*. But that had been a day at the beach compared to this.

Bodiless yet achingly cold, he was tumbling like a meteor through shouting darkness. Streamers of thinly-colored something-or-other flared past him, but although they looked like ragged clouds, he could sense that they were somehow alive, that it was their voices which raged and bellowed in his ears, enraged by his relative warmth and mobility. He could also sense that if they caught him, they would do things to him he wouldn't like at all.

Pogo closed his eyes, but it made no difference. Either he really didn't have a body—he couldn't see his hands, his legs, or even his faintly embarrassing suede desert boots—and thus had no eyes, or the place he was, the things that shouted at him, were all *behind* his eyelids…in his brain.

But if the bits with Elric and the dungeon and that Rolling Stones guy, if they had all been a hallucination too, how come they felt real and this part felt crazy?

Pogo had just decided that it was time to seriously contemplate coming down from this whole trip, and wondering how to do it, when he popped through a hole in a much more normal-looking sky and tumbled to a halt on an endless grassy plain. A single hill loomed in the distance; otherwise the place was incredibly boring, like the kind of state park even his parents would drive through without stopping. Elric rose to his knees beside him, clutching Stormbringer in his blistered right hand. The albino looked very real and quite weary.

"We are here, Pogokhashman—wherever 'here' may be."

"You mean you don't know?"

"No more than you do. Stormbringer, not I, has led us to this place."

Considering all that had gone before, this new wrinkle worried Pogo rather more than it should have. He found himself longing for the shadowy dungeon, which had begun to feel quite familiar, almost homey. Could you get lost in an acid hallucination, somehow get off the proper track and go permanently astray? He dimly remembered his Cub Scout den master saying that when you were lost in the woods you were supposed to stay in one place until people found you.

But somehow I don't think Mr. McNulty was gonna show up with a compass and a canteen and take me home, whether I stayed in the dungeon or not.

"Bummer," he said aloud, with considerable feeling. "So what do we do now?"

Before Elric could answer, a booming crash knocked them both to the ground, which itself trembled as if in sympathy. A vast globe of light bloomed on the distant hilltop, spreading and reddening.

"Whoah! Nukes?" Pogo asked, but he didn't really want to know.

A moment later something rustled in the grass. Pogo looked down, then leaped to his feet with a shout of alarm. The plain was alive with serpents and rodents, hundreds, no, *thousands* of them, all moving in a single direction with the speed of complete terror.

"They're runnin' from that bomb on the hill!" Pogo shouted, searching his memory for nuclear attack information. "Duck and cover!"

Elric too was on his feet, shaking loose a cluster of panicked ground squirrels from his boot. "I do not know what should frighten these creatures so," he called above the whipsaw hissing of the grass, "and do not recognize the word you used, but they are running *toward* the hill."

Pogo turned. The albino was right. The rush of small creatures bent the grass like a heavy wind—there were insects, too, flashing like dull jewels as they flew and hopped—all speeding toward the hill, where the globe of red light still hung, although it seemed to be fading.

"Look, Pogokhashman!" Elric now pointed in the opposite direction. Pogo turned again, frowning. His neck was beginning to hurt.

A dark line had appeared on the far horizon, a moving band of shadow, and it was from this that the local fauna were beating such a hasty retreat. As he and Elric stared, the line moved closer. It was hard to see clearly at such a distance, harder still because of the clouds of dust and chaff thrown up by the fleeing animals. Pogo squinted, and was glad for the concealing dust. What he could see was quite unpleasant.

"It's weird-looking guys in armor. And—Jesus!—there's a whole *shitload* of 'em. Thousands!"

"If they are not a Chaos horde, they are a marvellous imitation," Elric said grimly. "See, they are twisted and malformed."

"Yeah. Ugly, too."

Elric pushed Stormbringer into his belt and clutched Pogo's shoulder. "They are too many to fight, especially with my runeblade in its diminished state. In any case, we are too exposed here, and we know nothing of this world."

"What you're saying is: 'Let's run away', right? Good idea."

Elric seemed about to try to explain something, but instead turned and began loping toward the hill. Pogo hurried to catch up.

This is just like gym class, he thought, feeling a stitch already beginning to develop in his side. *But at least in gym, you get to wear sneakers. What kind of a stupid acid trip is this, anyway?*

It was difficult to run through the living sea of animals, but Pogo had already accustomed himself in the dungeon to stepping on furry things. Besides, one look back convinced him that the pursuing horde of beast-men would happily do the same to him. Gasping for breath, pumping his elbows with a determination that would have made his PE teacher Mr. Takagawa stare in disbelief, he sprinted toward the solitary hill.

Elric faltered, and Pogo suddenly realized how difficult this must be for a man who until minutes ago had been hanging in chains. He grabbed the albino's elbow—it was astonishing how thin he was beneath his tattered shirt—and half-tugged him along, which made their progress even more agonizingly slow. Pogo was now feeling so frightened that a part of him considered just letting the pale man fall so he could run at full speed.

Once, back in junior high school, he had left Sammy lying with a twisted ankle after they had rung Old Jacobsen's doorbell and ran. Sammy had gotten caught and had to go to the emergency room, too. Pogo had never felt good about that.

"C'mon, dude, we're almost there," he panted. The albino struggled on.

Something was echoing in Pogo's ears as they reached the skirts of the hill, a mysterious, almost pleasant buzzing too low and soft to identify. There was something in the way it vibrated in the bones of his skull that he knew he should recognize, but he was too busy dragging Elric and dodging high-speed rodentia to give it proper consideration.

They began to clamber up the slope. The greatest number of fleeing animals parted and passed around the hill like a wave around a jetty, but enough accompanied Pogo and Elric to continue to make their progress difficult. One large, white, long-eared creature ran right between Pogo's legs and bounded up the slope ahead of him. He was almost certain it had been carrying a pocket-watch.

Never...had...acid...like this. Even his thoughts were short of breath.

The red glow hovering over the hilltop had almost disappeared now. Pogo was trying both to dodge around the few bedraggled trees dotting the slope and observe the peak when something suddenly hit him hard in the back and toppled him forward.

Before he could do more than register the pain in his skinned palms and note that Elric too was lying on the ground beside him, something very sharp poked the back of his neck.

"The first of the Hell-troop," a voice said. "And not the foulest of the lot, I'll be bound—although these two still have little to brag about. Do you think the prince will want to see them?"

"No. He is deep in his spells. I say we skewer them here and then finish the barricade."

A certain breathlessness lay beneath the hard words. Despite his own fast-beating heart, Pogo recognized that these men were frightened.

Well, if they're waiting here to fight the Munsters Fan Club, that's not much of a surprise.

"We are not enemies," Elric said hoarsely. "We are not part of the Chaos horde, we are fleeing it."

"They speak!"

"Yeah," Pogo offered, "but we'd probably do it better if we weren't eatin' turf, man."

The pointy thing was withdrawn from his nape; as Pogo clambered slowly to his feet, he identified it as the business end of a very long spear. The man holding it and his companion looked much like the guards Pogo had met at the Chon's palace, except not so stylishly dressed; they wore ragged chain-mail, dented helmets, and expressions of worried fatigue.

"You are not mortal men," said one of their captors suspiciously.

"We are, whatever you may think of our appearance," Elric assured him. "Now, if you are part of a force that opposes that oncoming horde—and if, as it appears, there is no bargaining with them—we will fight at your side."

"We will?" Pogo thought the "run away" idea had been much superior.

Elric turned to him. The prospect of a fight appeared to have revived the albino somewhat, although he still seemed dreadfully weak. "We cannot outpace them forever. If we must make a stand, it should be here, with other brave souls."

"Whatever, man." Pogo was again giving serious thought to coming down. The problem was, he couldn't figure out how to do it. Everything seemed rather dreadfully and inescapably real. When he closed his eyes, he could still hear Elric and the soldiers talking.

"If you are truly allies, you are strange-looking ones. We should take you to our lord."

"And who is he?"

"Why, Shemei Uendrijj, the Gypsy Prince himself!" The man seemed to expect a gasp of startlement from Elric. When he spoke again, he sounded disappointed. "You have not heard of him?"

"I am certain he is a man of great bravery, to command such loyalty," Elric said. "Take us to him, please."

Pogo opened his eyes. It was useless. Same stupid place, same stupid trip. Same ravening army of beast-men moving rapidly across the plain toward them.

The soldiers led them up the hill at a jog. The cries of the oncoming horde echoed louder and louder, and so did the strange vibratory almost-sounds that Pogo had noticed earlier.

The horde was baying for blood, voices as discordant as a group of frat boys opening the dozenth keg on a Friday night. Pogo stumbled ahead, growing less and less enchanted with the products of his own imagination every moment. More soldiers, sullen and fearful, turned to watch them. At last they reached the top of the hill, bare but for a copse of trees and a small group of armored men. At the center, holding in his hand a blade that looked as though it had been carved from a single piece of ivory, stood the Gypsy Prince.

Pogo teetered to a stop, goggle-eyed.

Elric strode forward, lifting his hands in a gesture of peace as he approached the Gypsy Prince. There was little time to be wasted on mistrust. "We come as allies, sir. I am Elric of Melniboné, and this is Pogokhashman of...of..." He waited for his companion to add the proper details, then noticed that Pogo was no longer within his peripheral vision. He looked down.

The young man had fallen to his knees, his arms extended before him in an attitude of worship. For one so casual in other ways, he seemed quite formal about meeting royalty. Elric felt a moment's ill-humor that he, who had once sat the Dragon Throne itself, had received no such obeisance. Still, hanging in chains was undoubtedly a curb to good first impressions…

"Jimi!" shrieked Pogokhashman, and banged his forehead against the ground. "Oh my god, Jimi, it's *you!* I knew it! Man, I *knew* it! Sammy will be *so bummed* he missed this!"

Startled, Elric took a step away, then turned to survey the Gypsy Prince, who seemed just as disconcerted as the albino.

Shemei Uendrijj was a handsome, dark-skinned man no older than Elric. His wild, curly black hair was restrained by a scarf tied about his forehead, and he was clad in bright but mismatched finery that made him look something like a corsair of the Vilmir Straits—in fact, he dressed much as Elric did. Stranger still, as the dark Gypsy Prince was in some ways a reverse image of the albino, so was his bone-white sword a distorted mirror-version of Stormbringer.

Was that why the runesword had drawn them here?

"Your friend seems to know me." Uendrijj's voice was soft and lazy, but with hidden strength. *Given speech,* thought Elric, *so might a leopard speak.* "But I confess I do not know him. Rise, man!" he called to Pogokhashman. "If I have forgotten you, that is my shame, but there is much to occupy my thoughts today." He turned to Elric, and as his gaze slid down to Stormbringer, his eyes widened a trifle, but in speculation rather than worry. "If you are allies, you are welcome. But I fear you have joined what will surely be the losing side." He smiled despite his gloomy words. Elric could not help liking him.

"We will be proud to fight alongside you, whatever the case." Elric glanced at Pogokhashman, who still looked like someone in a narcotic dream. "I have fought against such a Chaos troop before. They are not unbeatable."

The Gypsy Prince raised an eyebrow. "Ah, but they are merely the outrunners. The Chronophage is our true, and direst, enemy."

Startled, Elric opened his mouth, eager to question Uendrijj, but before he could utter a word a ragged shout came rolling up the hillside from below.

"They come! They *come!*"

The Gypsy Prince turned to Elric. His mustachioed upper lip twitched in another smile. "I sense we might have much to talk about, you and I, but I fear we are about to be interrupted." He lifted his sword. "Ah, Cloudhurler, again we stand in a strange place as death rushes upon us. I should never have allowed my destiny to become entangled with yours."

A strange low humming came from the white blade, a kind of vibratory music unlike anything Elric had ever heard, although with some inexpicable similarities to Stormbringer's own battle-song. Pogokhashman lifted his head and shook it dreamily, as though the sword spoke to him in some deep manner.

The baying of the horde was growing louder. The dark tide of their armored forms swirled around the base of the hill. "But who or what is this Chronophage?" Elric shouted. "Is it the master of these creatures?"

"No!" Uendrijj beckoned for his soldiers to gather around. "It is a…a force. A blasphemy, a thing that should not be. It devours all in its path. These mad Chaos-things only run ahead of it, seizing a last opportunity to smash and rend and murder before the greater destroyer comes."

A small troop of attackers had burst through the barricade at the bottom of the hill, and were rushing up the slope. Their leader, whose sagging skin seemed to have melted and run like candle-wax, swung a long iron bar studded with rusting spikes. His cohorts, their faces and limbs also distorted, hopped and limped after him, barking like maddened dogs.

Elric lifted Stormbringer as the beast-men approached. His weakness made it feel very heavy; he was barely able to deflect the melted man's flailing bar. Neither did he feel the runeblade's usual sentience, its familiar battle-lust. As the bar whistled toward him again, Elric ducked under it and jabbed up into his foe's throat. It seemed an effort even to pierce the runneled flesh, but at last the runesword sank in and a shower of watery blood spattered the albino's face. Stormbringer did not drink the creature's soul. It was as lifeless as any old iron blade.

Two of the melted man's companions came shambling forward as Elric struggled to free his blade. A flick of white sheen from one side and the nearer limped on a few steps without a head before crumpling to the ground. Elric darted a quick look, but Uendrijj had already moved away again, carrying his ivory sword to the support of some of his hard-pressed soldiers. The second beast-man moved in more slowly, hefting a huge, crude axe. His mouth seemed to have slipped down to his neck, where it gaped wetly.

The axe rose and began to fall even as Elric at last yanked Storm-bringer free. He whirled, knowing he could not bring it up in time to prevent the blow. The beast-man's teeth were bared in a grin of triumph, gleaming from the hole in his throat. A moment later he shot into the air and vanished. His axe thumped onto the ground.

A giant Pogokhashman nearly ten times Elric's height stood where the bar-wielder had been, his vast hand shielding his eyes against the sun's glare.

"Cool," said the giant. "He's really flying!" He winced. "Whoah. Splat City."

As the albino stared upward in shock he was nearly beheaded by another member of the horde, who ran forward whirling a long, weighted chain. As Elric began to duck, the creature abruptly disappeared beneath the odd, rubbery sole of the giant's boot.

"Pogokhashman, it is really you...?"

"Yeah," the giant boomed. "Sorry, 'Ric, dude, I got kinda startled at first and got small. You almost stepped on me." He examined the under-side of his boot. "Ick. I woulda looked like *that.*"

Elric smiled wearily. "I am too weak to be much amazed, but you are amazing, nevertheless. I begin to get some idea of how you defeated the Chon's guardsmen."

"Yeah. Hang on for a minute, okay?"

As the Melnibonéan watched, Pogokhashman squinted as if in deep concentration, then grew even larger. Stepping carefully over Uendrijj's soldiers, he crossed to the copse of trees, uprooted one of the largest and old-est, then returned to the battle, holding the tree by the roots. Using it as something between a war-club and a broom, within moments he had scraped, slammed, and swept most of the beast-men from the hilltop, tum-bling them broken and shrieking back down onto the plain, where the rest of the horde cowered in open astonishment. When Uendrijj and his men had dispatched the few remaining enemies, a relative calm fell over the hill. The horde of beastmen below seemed in no hurry to resume their assault.

"I think I should shrink back again," Pogokhashman said, setting down his tree. A few squirrels crept out of its upper branches and wobbled away in search of a quieter home. "I'm getting kinda dizzy."

The Gypsy Prince turned from posting a fresh set of sentries. "I do not know what the source of your magic is, brave youth, but I think as long as you retain that size, the enemy will hesitate before attacking again."

"I'll try. Maybe if I sit down." Pogokhashman sank to the ground. Even with his chin resting on his fists, he was still as large as a moderately tall building.

"I have never seen the like." The prince shook his head in admiration.

"We must talk while we have the opportunity, Shemei Uendrijj," said Elric. "There are mysteries to be unraveled on both sides, but you know more of this situation than we do. What is the Chronophage?"

"Rest yourself, friend Elric, for you look ill and tired. I will tell you." Uendrijj looked down at the sea of deformed creatures surrounding their tiny island. "I will make my tale brief."

The Chronophage, he explained hurriedly, was not a living thing but a force of nature—or rather a force of *un*-nature, as his own magicians had told him when it was first manifested.

"It was brought about by some unprecedented slippage or sparking of the Multiverse. We know not what caused it, but only that it threatens all life, all thought...*everything*. It is a mindless hunger that eats Time itself—where it has passed, nothing remains but swirling, unfathomable emptiness. Even the Lords of Law are helpless against it."

"As must be the Lords of Chaos as well," Elric said thoughtfully. "In his backhanded manner, my patron Arioch has manipulated me into fighting a battle which he cannot himself fight."

"You are a servant of Chaos?" Uendrijj seemed a little startled. "But I have been taught that its underlings are as soulless as the deformed beasts we fight."

"I am an often unwilling servant." Elric explained his family's age-old pact with Arioch and his kin. "And both Chaos and Law manifest themselves differently in different spheres."

"I myself am not always happy in my service to Law," admitted Uendrijj. "I fear the stultifying world my masters would make should they ever triumph—but they are weak in my world, and to maintain a balance under which mortals can live, their cause must be supported." He continued, explaining that his people had first heard rumours of the Chronophage from the fleeing survivors of worlds where it had already struck, and how at last he, the prince, had been forced to the temple of Law to beg for supernatural aid. There Donblas herself, the living Goddess of Serene Peace, had told him that the Chronophage threatened not just humankind, but the continued existence of the entire multiverse.

"So I retrieved Cloudhurler, my singing sword, from the place where it hung. I had sworn an oath that I would not draw it again, since it had served me treacherously during my pacification of the Merymmen, the Undersea People, leading me to inadvertent murder. But human oaths mean little set against the safety of Time itself."

As he spoke, he looked at gleaming Cloudhurler with an expression Elric knew all too well.

"I chose this deserted site, a world my magicians discovered, as the place to make a stand against the Chronophage. We are few, as you have seen: the rest of my armies are helping my people to flee to another world through portals the wizards have made. Numbers will not avail me here, but I fear that neither will flight save my people if I fail."

"And your sword?" Elric leaned closer. "I was brought here by my own blade, in quest for its lost essence. Like yours, Stormbringer is more than a mere weapon. Could there be some reason having to do with your sword that we were drawn here?"

The prince frowned. "It is possible. My chief mage, Jazh Jandlar, assisted me in a spell designed to use Cloudhurler to summon supernatural allies—it has served me that way before, though never reliably. But no allies answered my summons."

Elric sat up, pondering. "So you used your blade to call for help. I used my own summoning to call my patron, Duke Arioch of Chaos, to help me regain my lost sword Stormbringer—but at the very moment I did so, my enemy's chief magicians were tampering with the substance of my runeblade. And now we are both here, in this empty place. That makes for too many coincidences. I think I see the manipulation of the Lords of the Higher Planes at work here." He looked up at Pogokhashman, who was trying to scrape something off the sole of his yards-long shoe. "*I* received an ally—that strange youth. Could it be that *you* received something of the essence of Stormbringer?"

The Gypsy Prince stared at him for a moment, then drew his white blade, which was discolored with various shades of beast-man ichor. "I have noticed a certain…restlessness in it, but the Singing Sword has ever been an unpredictable companion. I thought perhaps it responded to the presence of the Chronophage."

Something had been stirring in the depths of the Stormbringer for several moments, as faint but arresting as a distant cry of pain. Elric lifted his runeblade and gently laid it against Cloudhurler's white length. Suddenly, the sensation of sentience flared; at the same moment, Uendrijj reeled back as if he had been struck.

"By the Root, the Black Cat, and D'Modzho Feltarr!" breathed the prince. "Something is indeed alive in that sword of yours. I felt it as though it clawed at my soul."

The albino did not speak, but gritted his teeth, suppressing a scream. Stormbringer's lost power was flooding back into the blade and into him as well, boiling through his veins like a river of molten metal. Sweat beaded on his brow and his muscles trembled convulsively. Uendrijj lifted a brown, long-fingered hand as though to aid him, but hesitated, not sure what was happening.

As Stormbringer's stolen essence flowed out of the white sword and through his own black blade, Elric felt something of Cloudhurler, and of its master as well. When at last the inrush stopped, his body throbbed with new strength. He boomed out a laugh, startling Uendrijj again.

"O Gypsy Prince, I sense that we have far more in common than just the possession of such weapons! You have been the victim of many of the same cosmic jests that have made my life a misery."

Before Uendrijj could reply, the moon-wide face of Pogokhashman suddenly tilted down toward them.

"Hey, those weirdos are coming at us again," the giant boomed. "Think you better get ready, man."

Elric sprang to his feet. Now that his strength had returned, the prospect of combat almost delighted him. He reminded himself that some of the anticipation was Stormbringer's own inhuman battle-glee;

it would not do to become careless. "Come, Uendrijj, my more-than-brother! We have work to do!"

The Gypsy Prince unfolded himself more slowly, but with considerable grace. "I am glad to see you looking healthier, friend Elric."

"Here they come," called Pogokhashman, rising to his full towering height. "God-*damn* they're ugly!"

— ✳ —

Having at last worked up courage to face the giant, the beast-men came on without stopping, a seemingly unending tide of brutal, unthinking bloodlust. Despite their bravery and steadfastness, Uendrijj's soldiery were dragged down one by one; some of those overcome did not die for hours, and their screams seemed to darken the air like shadows. Before the long afternoon had waned, only Elric, the prince, and the giant youth still stood against the horde.

As the sun fell into the West behind the ceaseless tide of attackers, the albino and the Gypsy Prince fought on, side by side. Elric shouted and roared, siphoning strength from his defeated enemies. Uendrijj chanted, plying his ivory sword with the fierce calm of a warrior monk. The swords gave voice, too: all through the long afternoon, Stormbringer's exultant howl was capped and counterpointed by Cloudhurler's complex, cascading song, as though the two weapons performed some arch-exotic concert piece. For hour upon hour the blades sang and their duochrome flicker scythed the awkward beast-men like a field of flowers...but these flowers had fierce thorns: both Elric and Shemei Uendrijj sustained many small wounds.

Pogokhashman retained his giant's form, although in the few brief glimpses he had, Elric could see that his companion's strength was flagging. The youth stationed himself just far enough away to avoid treading on his allies by accident, but close enough that he could protect them when they were too hard-pressed. Despite great weariness, he flailed about him with splintering tree trunks, shouting *"It's hit deep to center-field! It could be...yes! It's a bye-bye baby!"* and other incomprehensible battle cries, and causing vast carnage among the Chaos army. But still the horde came on. Their numbers seemed endless.

Uendrijj stooped to pick up his ivory sword, which had slipped from his blood-slicked hands. Elric stood over him, keeping a small knot of attackers at bay. Stormbringer had quaffed deep of the half-souls of beast-men, but it still thirsted. Elric was almost drunk on stolen vitality. If he was to die, it would be laughing, bathed in the gore of his enemies.

"I think you enjoy this," Uendrijj shouted above the din as he straightened up. "I wish I could say the same, but it is only horrible, wearisome slaughter."

Elric brought Stormbringer down in an almost invisibly swift arc, crushing the gray, jackal-eared head of one of their attackers. "War is only life speeding at a faster pace, O Prince!" he cried, although he did not know exactly what he meant. Before he could say more, Pogokhashman's rumbling voice filled the air.

"The sun! Whoah, man—check it out!"

Elric looked up to the far horizon. The sun hung there, a flat red disc, but something huge and dark had moved across its face. This was no mere eclipse…unless an eclipse had arms.

"The Chronophage!" screamed Uendrijj, and drove into the beast-men before him, clearing an opening.

"Lift us up, Pogokhashman," Elric shouted to his companion. The giant youth squelched through the intervening foes and lifted his two allies in a palm the size of a barge.

The many-armed shape on the far horizon was an empty, lightless black that burned at the edges, as though an octopus-shaped hole had been scorched through the substance of reality. As they watched, the tentacles lashed across the sky; where they passed, nothing remained but sucking blackness. Lightning began to flicker all through the firmament.

The beast-men shrieked, a terrible howling that forced Elric to cover his ears, then the whole horde turned and fled down far side of the hill, swarming and hobbling like scorched ants. They no longer seemed to care whether they destroyed Elric and his allies or not, but were only intent on staying ahead of the all-devouring Chronophage. Within moments the hill was empty but for the giant and the two men in his hand. The Chaos horde had become a fast-diminishing cloud of dust moving toward the eastern horizon.

"The greater enemy is here," said Uendrijj. "True doom is at hand."

—※—

As he gasped, struggling to regain his breath, Pogo decided that Jimi's remark was rather unnecessary. The giant flaming squid-thing was pretty hard to miss.

But this *wasn't* Jimi, though. Not exactly. It was hard to keep that straight when it looked like you were holding Mister Electric Ladyland himself in your sweaty palm, but this guy was some other Hendrix—a reincarnation or something. Still, it had been very satisfying to discover that he had been right after all: the Man *had* been calling him. Those eyes, that sly smile—however snooty he sounded, he was still Jimi.

"So what do we do now?" Pogo asked. He hurt all over and his arm was so tired it trembled. He reflected briefly on how embarrassing it would be to drop the multiverse's greatest guitar player on his head. "There isn't any such thing as 911 in this world, is there? I mean, a SWAT unit would be kinda comforting right now."

Elric and Jimi winced. Pogo felt bad. He'd have to remember how loud his voice was in this giant size. Not that he'd be able to stay this way much longer. His muscles were throbbing like the first day of gym class, and he already had the grandaddy of all hangovers.

"We go forward—probably to die," said Hendrix. It was weird hearing the same Educational TV-type speech that Elric used coming out of Jimi's mouth, but Pogo had finally gotten used to it.

"We have stood together," said Elric. "We will fall together, too."

Pogo made a face. Elric with his strength back was a pretty bitchin' act—more than a little scary, too—but you could carry this King Arthur stuff too far. "How about we win and we *don't* die? I like that idea better."

Elric's blood-flecked smile was painful to see. "It has been a rare pleasure knowing you, Pogokhashman. But what the Lords of the Higher Planes themselves cannot defeat…"

"But I was listening! You said those High Plains dudes brought you guys together on purpose, or something like that! Why would they do that if you couldn't win? Seems like there must be easier ways to get you two rubbed out if that's all they wanted."

Hendrix and Elric exchanged glances. "Perhaps there is something in what he says," Jimi said slowly. "Perhaps…"

"I mean look at you two! You're like...mirror images, kinda. I mean, maybe you're supposed to...I don't know...form a supergroup! Like Blind Faith!" He darted a look at the western horizon. The Chronophage was spreading. Bits of the land itself had begun to disappear, as if they had been gnawed by rats the size of continents.

Elric stared hard at Pogo, then turned to Jimi. "Raise your blade again, Uendrijj."

Jimi hesitated, then lifted the white sword. Elric pushed Stormbringer forward until the tips touched. "I have long since given up any kind of faith, blind or otherwise," the albino said, "but perhaps..."

The place where the swords met began to glow with a deep blue light. As Pogo watched, hypnotized, the blue spread and enveloped both men. Pogo could feel a tingling in his palm where they stood. There was a sudden azure flash, bright as a gas-flame turned up to "infinity." When Pogo could see again, only one figure remained in his hand. It wasn't Elric.

It wasn't Jimi, either.

She was tall and slender and absolutely naked, her skin a beautiful coffee-and-cream color, her hair streaked both black and white. Beneath her long lashes were eyes like golden coins. In her hand she held a slim gray sword.

"*It is not a moment too soon,*" she said in a voice as naturally melodious as birdsong.

Pogo stared, slack-jawed and dry-lipped. He felt big, dumb, and sweaty—and seventy feet tall made for a lot of all three. He had never developed a swifter crush, not even the one on Miss Brinkman, his fifth-grade teacher, who had worn tartan miniskirts. "Um, who...who *are* you?"

"*I am the place where Law and Chaos come together, Pogo Cashman,*" she said, "*summoned by the joining of two sundered souls. I am that place, that moment, where seeming opposites are reconciled. Wrong needs right to exist; night must have its sibling day. The red queen and the white are in truth inseparable.*" She raised her arms and held the sword over her head. It was oddly unreflective. "*You might call me Harmony—or Memory, or even History. I am that which holds the fabric of Time together—its guardian.*"

"Kind of like Glinda from the Wizard of Oz?"

"You have played your part. Now I am free to play mine." As she spoke, she rose from his hand like a wind-tossed dandelion seed, and hovered. He wanted to look at her body—she was exquisite—but it seemed wrong, like wanting to touch up the Virgin Mary or something. She smiled as if she sensed his thought. Just the sight made his heart skip two beats.

"Your time here is almost done," she sang. *"But the multiverse holds many adventures for you...if you only look for them."*

Abruptly she turned and was gone, flying just like a comic-book heroine toward the hideous smear on the horizon, the gray sword lifted before her. Pogo thought she was unutterably, heartbreakingly beautiful. At the same time, she sort of reminded him of the hood ornament on a Rolls Royce.

He quickly lost sight of her against the pulsating black of the Chronophage, although he felt as though a part of him had gone with her. Deciding there was nothing more he could do, Pogo sat down on the ground, then allowed himself to shrink back to his normal size. He sighed with pleasure as his natural stature returned: it was like taking off the world's tightest pair of shoes.

Something flickered on the horizon. As Pogo stared, still dizzy from changing sizes, the Chronophage writhed, then a searing streak of light moved across one of the tentacles. A soundless howl tremoloed through Pogo, a noiseless vibration that shook his very bones. The great black arm withered and vanished; where it had been, the sun seemed to be growing back.

More streaks of light, like the contrails of science fiction spaceships, ripped across the Chronophage. Pogo found himself back on his feet again and cheering. One by one the other arms shriveled and disappeared and the blighted sky and earth at last began to return.

When the arms had all gone there came a moment when the rest of the Chronophage's black body began to swell, growing larger and larger against the sky until the sun was once more obscured. Pogo's heart pounded. Then a star, a sparkling point of white light, bloomed in the midst of the darkness. An even deeper shuddering ran through Pogo as the Chronophage erupted in great shreds of tearing black. He was shaken so hard that for a moment everything swam away from him, and as he tumbled into oblivion he wondered if in fact the battle had been lost after all.

When Pogo opened his eyes again, Elric and Jimi were lying on the ground beside him. The sky contained nothing more sinister than a few clouds and the setting sun.

The albino struggled to sit up. Beside him, Jimi was slower to rise. Despite their weariness, a single look at the horizon showed both men that they had triumphed. Elric embraced the dark prince, then turned to Pogo, full of questions, but as the albino reached out a thin white hand to him, Pogo realized he could see the grass through it. Elric saw, too.

"I am being drawn back to my world," the albino cried. "I sense that you and I are not to remain too long together in the same place, Shemei Uendrijj." He looked at something Pogo could not see, and grinned wolfishly. "Ah, it seems that at least I will be granted my revenge against Badichar Chon. Hah! That is something!" He raised a nearly transparent Stormbringer in salute. "Farewell, Pogokhashman. You have performed a great service, and for more than just me. If we do not meet again, remember you have Elric of Melniboné's undying gratitude!"

"Same to you. Take it easy, dude!" Pogo was genuinely sorry to see the very white man go. He stood watching, his eyes suspiciously itchy, as Elric began to fade. "Wait a sec," he said suddenly. "Hey, 'Ric—how do I get back?"

"*Farewell...*" The albino's voice still echoed, but he was gone.

Pogo slumped to the ground, stunned. He was marooned. Like Alice, but down the rabbit-hole forever with no way out. And no ruby slippers. No, that was Oz again. Anyway, he was stuck.

A hand touched his shoulder.

"I am sorry you have lost your companion, Pogokhashman," said Jimi. "But I would be honored if you would return with me to my world. You will be acclaimed as a hero. There is much that is beautiful there."

"Yeah...?" This was better than nothing, that was for sure. Still, though the necessities of the moment had distracted him, he had not realized until now just how much he had been longing for his true home. "Suppose so. Is there stuff to do?"

"To do?" Jimi laughed. "Aye, much and much. There are places to see—the febrile and primitive swamps of Baahyo, the glittering buildings and fragrant alleys of Noj Arleenz and Jhiga-Go. There is music to be heard—I am myself known as something of a harpist, when I am allowed some peace from battle. And women, beautiful women..."

"Women? I did think this whole trip was kinda short on chicks..." Pogo remembered the creature called Harmony and felt a moment of sweetly painful mourning. "And...and would you teach me to play?"

"Certainly," Uendrijj said, smiling. "Come, take my hand! You shall be my companion, then, Pogokhashman—*the whole Multiverse shall know your name...*"

But as Pogo's hand closed around his, Jimi too became foggy and hard to grasp. The plain on which they stood was also quickly getting dim. For a moment Pogo suspected that he and Jimi were merely undergoing more magical travel, but his last diminishing sight showed him that the Gypsy Prince still gripped the hand of *another* Pogo, who was disappearing along with him as the world fell away...

"Man! That was some *intense* acid, huh?" Sammy was bouncing around the room like a hamster whose wheel was out for repairs. "You wouldn't believe what happened to me while you were lying there all out of it! I looked out the window and the mailman looked like some kind of monster! Unbelievable! And the street was, like, *bubbling...*"

Pogo leaned back in the beanbag nursing a joint. Sammy's non-stop monologue was as reassuring as the sound of night traffic to a city-dweller.

"Sounds good, man," he drawled, and stared up from the spots of blood on the soles of his desert boots to the poster of Jimi Hendrix on the wall. Was it really true, then? That somewhere in the multiverse an albino guy with a magic sword was remembering his time with Pogo? And, even weirder and cooler, that somewhere else in the multiverse, Jimi—the very Man himself—and his new buddy Pogo Cashman were having adventures together?

Sammy put *Surrealistic Pillow* on the stereo, skipping as always to his favorite song. *"One pill makes you larger..."* he tunelessly crooned, anticipating the actual beginning of the vocals by several seconds—something that usually drove Pogo mildly crazy.

"Sounds good, man," Pogo said, smiling.

Sammy wandered over to take the joint from him and stood contemplating the poster of Jimi with his white Fender guitar. "I wonder what "Stratocaster" means, anyway?" Sammy said hoarsely, his lungs full of smoke.

" 'Cloudhurler'."

"Cloudhurler?" Sammy stared at him, then belched out a smoky laugh. "Man, you're too high. Naw, it must have something to do with, like...broadcasting. You know, radio or something."

"S'pose so," said Pogo. "Throw me those potato chips, will you?"

"Here." Sammy dropped the bag into his lap. "Feed your head." He chuckled. *White Rabbit* was building toward its chugging climax. " 'Feed your head'—get it?"

"Yeah," said Pogo. "Got it."

The Writer's Child

As mentioned earlier, most of my stories have first appeared in anthologies rather than magazines. Sometimes I have to invent such a story from whole cloth, other times I can use something already present in my idea-bank.

"The Writer's Child" is a classic example of having several fragmented, seemingly unrelated ideas banging around in my brain which get brought together by a request for a story—in this case, for a story connected to Neil Gaiman's wonderful Sandman comics. (Yes, they really are fabulous and inspiring. Don't tell Gaiman, though, because he gets enough praise as it is and it might be bad for his equipoise...)

Anyway, I had a few different pieces, a phrase, "The Prince of Flowers," another bit about a glass house, and—from a completely different direction—an image of a man in denial about his own extremely disturbed feelings. When I started thinking about the Endless and the Dreaming, I also started to think about poets, for some reason, and regrets. Slowly, like a collection of different objects being shaken together, they all started to find their places in the final mixture, their own strange order. It's one of my favorite stories (of mine, that is—I have LOTS of favorite stories by other people.) Besides an appearance by Neil's Dream King, there are references to several of the Dead Poets Society, namely Pound, Byron, and Browning, but you don't need to "get" the references to get the story.

I wrote this before I had children of my own. It is, needless to say, an even more disturbing idea to me now.

— ✳ —

This is a story I made up. Its about Jessica. She is the Princess and she lives in the Glass Castle. Listen! It is really important.

Jessica knows she is supposed to like it in the Glass Castle. Because there are lots of things to do there. Theres Nintendo, and television—

Jessica likes Rescue Rangers because it would be really neat to go around and have adventures and go to far away places—and a bunch of other stuff to do. And she has dolls that are really old that she had when she was a little girl.

But she is a princess so she doesn't need stupid dolls. And they never say anything. Thats why they are stupid. Sometimes she used to twist their arms and take off their clothes and rip them but they still never said anything.

A lot of other people live in the castle. Jessicas mother is the Queen of Flowers. She spends a bunch of time in the garden. The peeyonees, she always says, are so damed difficult. Nobody really cares about the peeyonees but me, she says. She is very beautiful, much more beautiful than Jessica, and she always smells like flowers. She talks very slow and quiet and tired.

Theres a special helper named Mister George, who is sort of a bear. The Queen of Flowers gave him to Jessica when she was really little and said Mister George will be your friend. But its okay because Mister George likes it. He is very good at listening and he is not like one of the dumb dolls, because he says things. He only talks at night, and he has a really little skwinchy voice but he says really smart things.

It is hard to hide in the Glass Castle, he says sometimes. So make sure that nothing bad happens so you don't have to hide. Mister George is all brown and has funny raggy ears and one leg is crooked. Jessica the princess used to laugh at him sometimes, but he said that hurt his feelings so she doesnt laugh at him any more.

Jessicas grandmother lives in the Glass Castle too. She is the Duchess and she doesnt come out of her room very much. She has a television in there, she likes to watch Jeopardy. How do they know those things, she says all the time. Jessica honey could you bring me a little more hot water is another thing she says. The Duchess likes to drink Oh Long tea, which is a weird name but real. She has funny hair, all white and curly but with pink skin showing a little where the hair is thin.

The King of Glass is in charge of the castle. He is Jessicas father and he is very handsome. Sometimes he picks Jessica up and swings her up in the air until her head almost touches the ceiling and says helicopter, helicopter. This used to make Jessica laugh. He still does it but it is too much of a dumb kid thing now.

The King of Glass likes to write things. He goes into his room, the only one in the Glass Castle that you can not see into and he writes things. Sometimes he doesnt come out for a long time. The Queen of Flowers says he is working really hard but sometimes he just comes out and says nothing nothing nothing. His eyes are really sad when he says it. Then he goes back in the room and makes those glass noises.

Here is something the King of Glass wrote.

The Writer's Child, or, The Secret Murderer of Time

Let's make a baby.

Wait, don't turn the page! I know this seems forward, even—to those of delicate sensibilities—dramatically rude. Let me explain. It's a sort of game.

First off, I'm going to pretend I'm a writer, so please pretend you're a reader. Please. It's important that we get these roles straight. Have you found your character, yet? Have you—in the old Method acting parlance—got your motivation? Good. Then we can begin.

I hope my first sentence didn't shock you. (Well, that's not true. I wanted at least to catch you off balance. Most good romances begin that way. Stability and trust should be a late addition to surprise, I think, rather than the other way around. That's just my opinion; I'm sure you have your own.) I meant, of course, that we were going to make an imaginary baby—a writer's child. But the hint of an unexpected (and certainly unasked-for) sexual relationship between you and I, between reader and writer, was not at all spurious. Whether a writer is a man or woman, there is something masculine in the crafting of a story—a casting-out of seed, a hunger that results in a brief spasm of generation. The reader—again, your real gender is unimportant— has a more feminine part to play. You must receive the kernel of procreation and give it a fertile resting place. If it does not please—more importantly, if it does not effect—then it passes out again, unaccepted, and the union is barren. But if it takes hold, it may grow into something greater by far than either of its parents.

In ancient civilizations, it was sometimes believed that the lightning was the generative force of heaven—that when it struck the waiting earth, life came forth. Let me be as a bolt of fierce lightning. Let me burn for a brief moment, flashing above your green hills. Then I will be gone, and you can accept or reject my gift. The choice will be yours.

But surely, you ask, a book, a story, the things that writers make—aren't these complete births unto themselves, read or not? Don't some writers speak of their works as children? A little thought will tell you that they are wrong, or at least incomplete. Without you, I am lightning flickering in the eyeless void. A story unread is a zen conundrum, a shout in an empty universe. Unread, unheard, a writer is a dying thing.

Let me show you. Let's make a baby: a writer's child, the one I often think about during the early hours of the morning, as I sit in my room. (I almost said study, since the phrase "a writer's study" comes so readily to mind, but I do not study in my writing room: I write. Occasionally I brood. I also change my clothes there, since that's where my closet is. But I study in a larger room, with more light, where I can dally among my books without the mute, shaming presence of the typewriter.) Sometimes, late at night, when I think about children, I wonder if I will ever father one. If I do, what will happen? These are frightening things to think about, or at least they are to me. I have often wished I could try it out, make all the mistakes I need to, without involving an actual human being. No one deserves to be some-one else's experiment. So, my grand strategy: I will make an idea instead. An idea cannot be hurt, cannot lead a ruined life, cannot regret that it was ever brought into existence. An idea-child. I will make one. No. We will make one together.

Another question? Well, go ahead, but I warn you: my biological clock is ticking.

Why "together"? Because, as with men and women, and as with all the living, mating pairs of the world, bonded by their different sexes as much as by their shared species, the sharing of individuality will make a child that is strong.

If I write, "our baby is small and dark and round-cheeked, with green eyes shading to turquoise around the pupils, with hair as black and shiny as a silk kimono", I have begun to make a child—but you have not really done your part. Like the children of the Pharaohs, married brother to sister for marching generations, the breeding strain has not been sufficiently leavened. The children of such unions have hidden, sometimes tragic flaws. If I say instead, "our baby is small, with a face that will someday be beautiful, but is now only an admonition to a parent's love, with eyes faintly peevish and hair as soft as a whisper," I have sacrificed some of the hard edge of realistic description, but I have allowed you to do your part, to add your genes to mine. The writer's child will now take on a shape even more particular to you—hair dark or fair, as you choose, eyes of any color that seems true at the moment that you read. Thus, I sow, you nurture, and together we will make something that is unique to we two.

So, let's make our baby. But don't misunderstand—some decisions must be made in the writing. Its sex, for instance: only a fool of a writer could engender and then raise a child while resorting only to indefinite pronouns. That is the stuff of a horror story: "When it was eighteen, it entered college." So we must choose. In fact, you, beloved reader, you must wait this time—as most parents must, at least in this still-primitive age—for the forces of creation (me, in my current lightning-guise) to make this choice for you: boy or girl.

In my room, I have often thought about just this thing. Should my child be a boy or a girl? This is not an easy decision. I understand boys, and so I love them, but I also feel a slight, almost imperceptible contempt for them, like an old salesman watching the pitiable attempts of a young trainee. I have been there. I have done it. (I am, after all, a male writer. I realize that, in the context we have established, this may be deemed a tasteless reminder, especially for male readers uncomfortable with their feminine side. Forgive me. I am feeling revelatory tonight.)

On the other hand, I am afraid of girls. Not, I hasten to say, afraid for my own person: women have been in many ways my closest and deepest companions. But as a man, I am already a little frightened by the capacity of women to hurt the men who care for them, so the awesome and unknown territory of girls and their fathers looms before me like a new country. I feel I could easily become lost in such wild, dark lands. Still, the false courage of authors is upon me. How could I look at myself in the mirror if I would not risk this exploration? And it's only a story, after all—isn't it?

So a girl it will be. We will make a woman-child.

—⁂—

Princess Jessica found the pieces of paper in the garbage can out in the front of the Glass Castle. She was looking for the coopon off a box of Cocoa Pebbles to send away because she forgot to cut it off before the box got thrown out. Princess Jessica found a bunch of paper in there, a long story. She read it all while the King and Queen were out having a Togetherness Night and Jessica was staying home with the Duchess.

And just in case you think that I am Princess Jessica, for your informayshun I'm not. The person writing this is named Jessica too, but she is not a princess and she doesnt live in any castle.

Jessica read the whole story and then she put it back in the garbage can outside the Glass Castle. But Mister George talked to her after the Duchess put the lights out. You shouldnt throw that away, Princess he said. That is a magic story. There is a lot of magic in it and it might help you understand what to hide from.

That is the problem for Princess Jessica. There arnt any hiding places in the Glass Castle because it is all glass. And sometimes when she gets scared by something she wants to go and hide. It used to be okay in the dark with Mister George, because he would talk to her in his skwinchy voice and say not to be afraid, that you could hide in the dark but after a while even the dark did'nt seem like such a good hiding place and Mister George got scared too. So Princess Jessica figures there are better Hiding Places somewhere, Hiding Places that really work. She and Mister George are thinking very hard about where those might be.

Here is more of the story the King of Glass wrote.

This girl child will have hair that curls and eyes that stare and wonder. She will be beautiful, of course—how could our child not be beautiful? We will name her...Jessica. Yes, that's a good name, not one of those lighter-than-air names so popular among writers of romances and fairy-tales. That's a name a real little girl might have.

But this is a writer's child. We should not wallow in too deep an evocation of reality. We cannot simply allow her to grow up in a mundane ranch-style house in the suburbs, child of workaday parents passing blinkered through their own lives. If I, the writer, and you, the reader, are to experience the full gamut of parental emotions, we must make a world for our little girl. In any case, it's much safer to raise a child in an invented world. Much safer.

Now, stand back. This is where a writer does what a writer does.

"Jessica was a princess and only child. She lived in the Palace of Oblong Crystals, which was located in a small but prosperous kingdom just outside the borders of Elfland."

Good so far?

"Her mother was named Violetta, and was called by her subjects "The Lady of a Hundred Gardens," for indeed the Palace of Oblong Crystals had exactly that many gardens, gardens of every shape and kind—hedge gardens, water gardens, rock gardens, winter gardens, every sort of place where things could be arranged and looked at. And that is what Violetta did all day long, wandered from garden to garden speaking in her soft slow voice to the armies of gardeners and workmen and landscapers. Sometimes young Jessica wondered if she herself had somehow been budded in one of the gardens, then gently pruned and brought back to the palace. It was hard to imagine her mother coming inside for long enough to have a baby.

"Jessica's father, the king, was named Alexander. He was called by his subjects "The Lord of the Hundred Windows"—although, unlike the numbering of the gardens, this estimation of the number of windows in the Palace of Oblong Crystals was probably several score too low. But the subjects of the king and queen liked harmony and neatness, as subjects often will, so they bent the facts in order that the fond nicknames should match.

"The king had gained his name because many of the palace's windows were made from the strangely shaped crystals that had given the sprawling family home its own unique title. These crystal windows bent the light in strange ways, and at times a person standing before one and staring out across the great circular entrance way, or over Gardens Numbers Forty-seven through Sixty-eight, could see...things. Sometimes they appeared to be shadows of the palace and its inhabitants during past or occasionally even future eras, but at other moments the views seemed to be of entirely different places. There was no science to the strange refractory effects, nothing that could be expected and reproduced, and it happened infrequently in any case—the crystal windows generally showed nothing except the prismatically distorted (but otherwise quite ordinary) shapes directly outside. But even that could be fascinating. So the king—having, as kings often do, a great deal of time on his hands—took to spending his days going from window to window in hopes of seeing something rare and uplifting.

"One spring afternoon King Alexander stood before the Rosy Bow Window on the second floor. He had been watching the rather stretched and rainbow-colored image of Princess Jessica as she walked across the wide lawn beneath, apparently off to the Mist Garden in search of her mother, when the light streaming through Rosy Bow Window shifted. The king saw a girl walking across the lawn, but this was not a child of seven but a girl at the doorstep of womanhood, a slender but well-rounded creature with an innocent yet somehow seductive walk. The girl's long hair streamed in the breeze and eddied about her neck and shoulders. As she turned to look up at a bird passing overhead the king saw the delicate but stirring curve of her breast beneath her dress and was filled with a kind of hunger. A moment later, as his gaze traveled up the arch of her pale neck to her face, he was startled by the familiarity of the girl's face. A moment later, he realized that it was his daughter Jessica, a Jessica grown to nubility. She was beautiful, but there seemed almost a kind of wickedness to her, as though her very existence, her walk, the swing of her hair, her long legs moving beneath the wind-stirred dress, made unwholesome suggestions.

"A moment later, the window flickered and the prismatic light returned. He squinted and saw his young daughter striding away on slim but by no means womanly legs, wading through the thick grass toward the Mist Garden.

"The king went to his bedchamber, shaken."

— ✳ —

Jessica doesnt like it when the King of Glass goes into his room, the room that no one can see inside. He makes funny noises in there, clinking things, and sometimes he cries. He has been in the room a lot since he wrote the story. Jessica thinks Mister George might be wrong, that it might be a bad story and not good to keep at all. Jessica sometimes thinks she should burn it in the Duchesses little fire place when she falls asleep after Wheel of Fortune.

Some nights when she is almost asleep herself Jessica hears the Kings footsteps come down the hall going doom doom all funny. He stands in her doorway and just looks. Even though she keeps her eyes shut because she doesnt like the way those kind of footsteps sound,

Jessica knows because Mister George tells her later. His eyes are buttons and they never shut.

It is hard to hide in the Glass Castle, he tells her. He says that a lot more lately.

Some nights she wakes up and the King of Glass is sitting on her bed looking at her, touching her hair. He has the funny smell, the closed door smell and he smiles funny too.

One night he was touching her hair really gentle like it might break, and he said kind of wispery Daddys home. Princess Jessica started to cry. She did'nt know why, she just did.

That night, after the King of Glass was gone Mister George said right into Jessicas ear, something must be done and soon. Hiding is not the anser. His raggedy ears made him look really sad, so sad that she started crying again.

Here is some more of the story the King of Glass wrote. There isnt any more. This is all that he threw away.

"*Despite this troubling vision, the next day King Alexander found himself standing again before the Rosy Bow Window, admiring the pink-tinted view of the garden, but secretly waiting for something, although he would not or could not admit to himself exactly what it was. However, nothing more interesting than a small squadron of gardeners passed by, and whether the time-refracting qualities of the window had ceased to operate, or he looked upon something that, whatever future the window displayed, would always be the same—and gardeners certainly seemed an eternal feature of the local landscape—he could not tell. He went to his Private Study, poured himself a glass of frostberry wine, and thought deeply.*

"*Now, King Alexander had a most secret and important window in his Private Study—the most magical window in the entire palace, a window that only looked out, never in. When he sat and sipped his glass of bittersweet wine, he saw things through that window that no one else could see. And, best of all, since it was a window that only he knew about, and that worked in only one direction, he could watch without being seen. It was the darkest and best secret in all of the Palace of Oblong Crystals, and it belonged to him because he was the king. No one else could be trusted with such a powerful object.*

"Queen Violetta had long since stopped coming into the Private Study—she had almost ceased coming into the palace at all, content to spend her days among her peonies and fuschias, breathing the warm damp air of the Conservatory, or bundled up tight in the windy Farther Hedge Garden. And young Princess Jessica had not been in the room for many years, since it was the place where Alexander thought his deep kingly thoughts and was no place for children.

"He stared into his special, private window, as he sometimes did, and looked at things as they truly were, for that was its greatest power and deepest secret. He saw that Violetta his queen did not care for him, that she was envious of his dreams, that she wished to make him an unimaginative creature of habit and routine as she was. He saw that his subjects did not respect him, that the gardeners snickered when the Queen made jokes at his expense, that the footmen and butlers and maids and charwomen all scorned him, even as they stuffed their mouths with the fruits of his largesse.

"As for the Queen's mother, to whom he had given a gracious apartment right in the palace—well, the old woman's malice was palpable. She had tried to prevent her daughter from marrying him in the first place, and never lost an opportunity to speak glowingly (and falsely) of Violetta's dead father, holding him up as an example of what Alexander would never be.

"Worst of all, he saw that his own child, the Princess Jessica, was becoming a diminutive version of her mother, the queen. For years she had loved to play games with him, to be lifted and spun in the air like a bird, her hair flying—but now she would not play, and spoke to him angrily when he tried to persuade her. She turned away from him when he tried to express his fatherly love. She rejected him, as Violetta rejected him.

"His Princess Jessica was changing, drifting away from him across a widening sea, on a one-way voyage to a place where he could not go, the Country of Women.

"King Alexander summoned up Jessica's image in his private window and watched her as she walked across the great palace dining room, a stuffed toy dangling from one hand, her hair an unbrushed tangle across her shoulders.

"She spent more time talking to her teddy bear than she did talking with him. And was she not too old for such a childish toy? Certainly she was in many other ways already aping her mother in her headlong rush toward womanhood.

"The king poured another glass of wine and thought on these, and other, things.

— ✳ —

"It was late in the afternoon when King Alexander awakened, his head misty, his feet cold. He had drunk a little more of the frostberry wine than he had intended, perhaps. His glass had fallen from his hand and lay in glittering shards on the floor of his study.

"As he leaned forward to pick it up, he saw something pale flit across his mirror. Distracted, his hand folded too hastily around the broken stem of his wine glass. He cursed, sucked his fingers, and tasted blood, staring at the magical window.

"Framed in the rectangular space was the young woman he had seen before, the one who so much resembled the Princess Jessica. She was bathing herself in one of the garden pools, surrounded by bobbing water-lilies. The leaf-filtered afternoon sun made her skin seem glistening marble.

"He stared at her pale shoulders and long white neck as she dipped her face to the water, and decided he had been wrong: in truth she bore only the faintest resemblance to Jessica. No, this beautiful young woman had none of that flinty look of Violetta's, the look that Jessica had already begun to assume, for all her young age.

"She was like his daughter only in that he admired her, as he had once admired a younger, more tender Queen Violetta. She was like his daughter only in that if she looked at him, he felt sure it would be with respect and love, as Princess Jessica once had. But this graceful girl was untainted, grown full and ripe without souring.

"The young woman stood, and water ran down her naked belly and thighs; small splash-circles spread, chasing the larger ripples of her rising. Her breasts were small, but womanly-full, her legs achingly long and slender. As the breeze touched her cold skin she shivered, and his heart seemed to expand with love— and with something bigger, something deeper, darker, and altogether richer.

"Unthinkingly, he lifted his fingers toward her image in the window, then stopped in surprise. Blood was running down his hand and onto his wrist.

"He paused as an idea came, a wild, willful idea. Blood, wine, solitude— he had all the makings of a powerful magic.

"Something in him shriveled at the thought, but his eyes and heart were so full of the pale-skinned, naked girl before him that he swept the doubts away like cobwebs. Here was what he wanted, needed…deserved. A girl as beautiful as his wife when he met her, as innocent as his daughter had once been…a woman-child who would truly love him.

"He wiped his hand clean on his trouser leg, then allowed a fresh rill of blood to ooze from the cut along his finger. He reached out to the window and drew a four-sided figure around the girl as she stood in the lily-blanketed pool, penning her in a square of red smears. He drank from the bottle and felt the blood of the berries run down his throat and bathe his thirsty heart. He said words, secret words in his own secret language. What they meant was: 'You are mine. I have created you, and you are mine.'

"The girl framed in the window looked up suddenly, shivering again, although she had almost finished drying herself."

— ✳ —

Mister George heard the end of the King's story because Jessica read it to him out loud. It made him angry and he said some words Jessica didn't know.

Tipical littery wanna bee he said. No story ark. Everything turns into sell fubsest intro speckshin.

Princess Jessica wrote that down in her jernal because she did'nt know the words and asked him what it meant. Mister George said that it did'nt matter, that style was not the real ishoo.

We must do something, he told her. The beast is rising. We must do something soon.

Jessica said that he was scaring her, and that anyway it was time to go watch Jeopardy with the Duchess.

Leave it to me then Princess, said Mister George. I will do what I can.

That night Jessica took her bath. All the My Little Ponys had fallen in because they were trying to cross the ocean on a Pony migrasion like Jessica saw on the television, except it was'nt ponys on TV but some kind of deers. One of the ponys got behind her back, lost in the bubbles, and when she found it and turned around, the King of Glass was standing in the doorway. He looked at her for a long time until she said Daddy go away I am having a bath.

The King said O, so you are too big to have a bath with Daddy in the room and laughed, but it was'nt a nice laugh like he used to. He went to the cabinet and took out a bandaid and wrapped it around his finger. He had a kleenex there, and when he put the bandaid on he threw the kleenex in the toilet. It had blood on it, and this made Jessica more scared because she remembered the story.

Wheres Mommy she asked.

Who the F-word knows, the King said and laughed again. Jessica put her hand on her mouth because of the F-word, but she was mostly scared because she didn't say it, her father did. Probably out rolling in the delfinnyums or something, he said. Who the F-word cares.

I'll come back later and read you a story he said, then. He came to the edge of the bath and pulled her close and tight. The Ponys all fell in again off the slippery side. He patted her hair and kissed Princess Jessica's mouth. He had the closed door smell real bad and he was breathing loud.

When he took his face away for a second Jessica said really fast I need to say something to Mommy. I have to tell her something about school.

The King stood up and looked at her. His eyes were funny.

I'll come tell you a story later he said and went out.

— ✳ —

The Queen of Flowers did'nt come until Princess Jessica was dried off and in her jammies. Ready for bed, thats a good girl, she said.

Why does Daddy go in his room and close the door, the princess asked.

The Queen sat on the bed. I guess he just needs some time to himself she said. Sometimes people need to be by themselves. He is working hard at his writing, you know.

But he smells funny, when hes been in there Jessica said.

Her mother did'nt say anything.

Mister George thinks he might be turning into a monster said Jessica, like in that Werewolf in London movie. He might be changing into a bad thing from being in that room.

The Queen laughed. Is that what Mister George thinks hah? Like in a monster movie, she said. Maybe Mister George should not watch movies like that.

They talked some more but the Queen had to finish her winter garden plan, so she went back downstairs. Princess Jessica thought for a long time about how anyone could see her because of the Glass Castle but it was dark so she couldnt see out at who was watching. Jessica was afraid to fall asleep because she thought that if the King of Glass came to tell his story and she was'nt awake hed be mad, but she held Mister George really tight for a long time and then she got sleepy.

Somebody was talking in her ear for a long time before she finally heard the words wake up Jessica wake up!

She opened her eyes and Mister George was standing up on the end of the bed. Jessica was very surprised because he had never been able to move, only talk.

Why are you moving, she asked.

Get up Jessica, he said. We are going somewhere. We are going to do something.

But I am not allowed to go out of the house at night said Princess Jessica. She was scared to see Mister George walking on the end of the bed. He walked funny too, like his crooked leg was too short.

We are not going out of the house, not really he said in his skwinchy voice and pointed to the closet. We are going there.

Jessica stood up. Like the Lion and the Wardrobe she asked? She did'nt like to think about the Witch part.

See S Loowis, said Mister George and made a grumpy noise. O, Father Seuss, spare me from alligory. Come on Jessica.

She got up and wondered if her Mom and Dad were asleep or if they were awake. Sometimes they had fights all in wispers. She listened but couldn't hear anything. She followed Mister George to the dark closet. He went in it. She went in it too.

But it wasn't a closet on the inside. There was fog and funny way far off noises and it went back a long way. This really is just like the Wardrobe she thought, and wondered if an alligory was anything like an alligator.

After a minute they were in a narrow street. There was a very big round moon in the sky, all tho it was hard to see because there was fog.

A bunch of houses were up and down the street, all close together all broken down and old and scary. They were dark except that some of them had yellow lights in the tiptop windows.

I don't like this Jessica said. I want to go back.

It is not a nice place, said Mister George but it is where we have to go. He was walking along in front of her just like a real person, except he was still himself, still very small and his ears were still ragged. It is Rats Alley.

Now Jessica had to not think about alligories and rats both. But why do we have to come to this place she said, where is it?

Rats Alley, I told you he said. But is is less a where than a what. It is where the shadoes of poetry and sin and sorrow over lap. It was my place once and it is the only path I know to find the Player King.

Another King said Jessica, she did not understand the rest. Is he a friend of the King of Glass?

He is a much more Important King, said Mister George. I hope he will be your friend.

Something was crunching under Jessicas feet. It sounded like candy sticks but when she looked close she saw it was'nt.

Did the alligories get them she asked really quiet, but Mister George did not say anything.

Something came out of one of the dark doors and stepped in front of them. It looked like the Scarecrow of Oz, but it was'nt smiling. It had an even more skwinchy voice then Mister George like the rope hanging around its neck was too tight.

Hello clubfoot, it said. It stood right in the way.

We are seeking an oddyents with the Player King said Mister George. He was trying to be brave but he was very small.

But you have no safe conduck, it said. Why should I let you pass? Its fingers made a creeky noise like the branches outside Jessica's window when it was windy.

Mister George did'nt say anything for a long long time. Jessica wanted to run.

For love of the moon, he said then. For memory. This one is young and still unmarked.

And why should I not take her sweetness the scarecrow said and leaned forward to look at Princess Jessica. Its eyes were painted on and crooked. Perhaps that will make memory stop burning. Perhaps it will blacken the moon and I can forget.

You are not here to forget ezra, said Mister George. We all travel here to remember.

The scarecrow lifted its stick arms wide then stepped back into the shadoe. Go then it said. The voice was far off now. Go. Do not bring any more pieces of the living moon to trouble us in our ecksile.

When they went past the door Jessica heard a sound like hissing. There was wet sawdust all over the ground.

There were eyes and voices in other doorways, but Mister George only said quiet words to them and nothing came out. They went down the street as fast as they could but Mister Georges short legs and crooked walk made them go slower than Jessica wanted.

At last they came to a door, and this one had light in it which made the fog glow in the street beside it. Over the door was a sign with a picture of a bird like a crow and letters that spelled THE BLACK QUILL.

Mister George went inside and Princess Jessica followed him. A thin woman was just inside. She had a tray full of mugs and her eyes were all shadoey even tho they should not. My lord she said. Long time no see. She laughed then.

I was sorry to hear about your eyes Miss Emily he said.

A small loss for great sins she said. I never used them for the truest seeing, in any case. What brings you to visit us after so long.

Tonight is the night of the rovers moon, he said. I have a patishun for the Player King.

He is inside, she said. Watching the show. I will bring you a cup of our best red.

I no longer drink it said Mister George.

My you do take things seeriosly these days don't you, she said. Through there.

Miss Emily went away wisling a slow song, and Princess Jessica and Mister George went down the hall to a big room full of candles. There were benches and tables but they had all been pushed back against the walls. There were lots of people in the room, or at least they looked like people even though some were the wrong shape and lots were wearing masks. Some of them were doing a play and some others were playing fluts and other insterments. The play was about a man who lost his wife and had to go sing for the gray king and queen who found her. Jessica looked at the gray king to see if he was the one Mister George wanted to talk to but he was wearing a big mask that covered his face and he had no arms, so she did not want to look at him any more.

Or whats a heaven for, someone whispered in her ear. Jessica looked up. It was Miss Emily, who smiled again and said Poor Old Rob, then picked up some mugs and went away.

The play stopped a moment later but no one clapped. They all looked toward where Mister George and Jessica stood then they all looked at the far wall. There was someone sitting in the shadoes against the wall who leaned forward. His hair was black and his skin was very white and he had little dots where his eyes should be like when the Duchess turns off the television. Jessica could tell he was a real king but she did not know what place he could be king of.

A brief high ate us, then said the very white man. It will give the ladies time to don their claws. His voice was slow and hollow like talking in a big empty room. So you have come back to see the meenadds feed, young lord?

I come with a patishun, my king, Mister George said, and took a crooked step toward him then got down on his knees. I have had my fill both of the rights of bockus and the claws of women.

The Player King stood up and up and up. He was very tall and Mister George was so small and his ears were so tattery that Jessica wanted to cry for him. Speak then, the king said. What do you want here little house god.

You know my special task my king said Mister George. This innocent is in danger. The one who threttens her calls upon your name to have his way. He trifuls with dream to justify his deed.

The white king looked at Jessica for a long time until she felt all swirly. The princess didn't understand anything that was going on. She was scared but she was also not scared. The tall man seemed to be too strong and quiet to be a really bad thing.

I have heard him scratching in the walls of my dwelling the Player

King said, but he has never been given admittens to my throne room. I have granted him no boon. Are you sure it is not the fact that he considers himself a poet that has offended you little hobbler?

Mister George shook his head. That is of no import he said. I am sworn to redeem where I can, that is my sentence. He is her father. He calls on your name to cloke his deed.

What would you have me do? No crime has been comited no promise breeched, said the tall white man.

I implore you my lord, said Mister George. I was once your faithful servant tho my sins took me to another judge in the end.

What you call sins have little to do with my kingdom, the Player King told him and raised his hand in the air.

But everything to do with mine, Mister George said back very fast. And my duty. At least do not let him hide his deeds behind your mantel. At least make him see for himself what he does. There is some value still in innocents, is there not?

For a long time the tall man did not say anything. Jessica looked around at all the masks all the eyes all the faces in the shadoes. Then she saw that the King was staring at her.

And are you innocent, child he asked. She did not know what to say. I am afraid sometimes she said.

He smiled just a little and said I will think on this. Take her back before the moon sets.

Thank you my lord said Mister George. Your help would mean a small part of my vast det might be repayed. He turned and went to the door and Jessica followed him.

Byrun said the Player King. Byrun hold a moment. Jessica wondered who he was talking to but Mister George stopped.

My lord, he said.

Her name was Ogusta was it not, the tall man asked.

It was my lord said Mister George, then turned to the door again and led the Princess out into the fog. Jessica reached way down and took his paw because she thought he looked very sad.

— ✳ —

"*King Alexander was awakened by a touch on his shoulder. Groggy and disoriented, he shifted in his chair and looked at his magic window to see if she had come to him at last. Earlier he had felt her moving closer, felt his spell reach out and enfold her, but he was a little surprised to experience results so swiftly.*

"*But the woman-child was still prisoned behind the window like a butterfly in a glass case, her limbs outstretched in sleep as though she had writhed on the pin before stillness came. She had disarranged her coverings, and her limbs gleamed in the moonlight.*

"*But if it was not his ensorcelled beloved who had touched him...*

"*The Lord of the Hundred Windows turned his chair slowly and felt broken glass beneath his shoes. A tall figure stood behind him, dressed all in flowing black, but with a face pale as mortuary marble.*

"*King Alexander started violently. 'Who are you, sir?' he asked. 'How came you to the Palace of Oblong Crystals? What do you want of its master?'*

"*'No mortal can build a palace in the Dreaming and expect to be called "master",' the figure said. 'That is asking too much. Alexander, you consider yourself a poet, do you not?'*

"*'I write a little...but who are you, and how did you come here? This is a private place.'*

"*'If this is a private place, and the dreams you craft here are private, then let them stay that way. If you would recreate them in the waking world, then you must acknowledge the evil that can come of them.'*

"*'I know you,' said the Lord of a Hundred Windows, moving back in his chair. 'I have heard the servants whispering about you. You are the Dark-Eyed One—the old god of this place. Have I done something to offend you? Do you come to punish me?'*

"*'You have done nothing great enough to offend Dream. You have done something that offends another—an old servant of mine. He is sworn to protect innocents from such as you. But, no, I will do nothing to punish you. That is not my charge.'*

"*'Then begone!' King Alexander stood up, filled with the sudden confidence that follows a terror proved unnecessary. 'If you have no power over me, what right do you have to accost me in my secret, private place? What right to interfere in my life, with my loves? She is mine—my creation! I will do with her as I choose. That is my right..'*

"*The shadow-eyed figure seemed to grow. A dark nimbus swirled around him like a cape of mist. He reached out a white hand, then he smiled.*

"*'I have rights and powers beyond your ken, O would-be poet. But I spoke only the truth. I will not punish you. One thing only will I do, and that is fully within my rights as sovereign over all the lands of dream, and of every hovel and palace therein. I will show you the truth. Look to your beloved secret window and see the reality that even the thickest shadows of Dream cannot hide. See the truth.'*

"*With those words the apparition swirled like windblown fog and vanished.*

"*For some time the Lord of the Hundred Windows stood watching the place where the thing had been, fearing that it would reappear. His moment of confidence was long past. His heart beat as swiftly as it had when he had first beheld his beloved...*

"*His beloved! He turned to the magical window, terrified that his spell would be undone, that her image would be gone forever. To his relief, he saw her sleeping, still as compellingly beautiful as she had ever been, still framed in the possessive spell of his blood. She turned restlessly, arching her neck and exposing for a moment the pale soft shape of her breast. Something shadowy was cradled in her arms...a stuffed toy.*

"*Alexander smiled to see such childlike innocence in the shape of a young woman. But as he watched, the image before him shimmered, then was slowly replaced by one very different.*

"*The Lord of a Hundred Windows leaned forward, gazing in horrified astonishment at this singular and most important window. His eyes opened wide. His lips parted, but no sound came from his mouth. Thus he sat for a long time, in silence, staring, staring...staring.*"

This is the end of my story, gentle reader. If you feel that you do not understand it, then perhaps I am at fault. But is it the task of a poet to explain all, every allusion, every symbol? Or does he merely sow the seed, and is it not then the reader's responsibility to bear the final issue? Too frequently the blame is cast onto the writer, the poet, when in fact I think it is the ingratitude and sloth of readers which so frequently mars the highest, best truths an author can create.

What happened to the child, you ask? What happened to Princess Jessica? She was a Writer's Child, and thus only a figment. Together you and I engendered her. Perhaps we were wrong to do so—perhaps to invent a fictitious child to avoid the fear and pain of raising a real one is to murder time. If so, then I am Time's secret murderer—and you are my accomplice. So take care before you sound any loud alarums.

Whatever the case, the story is finished and the child is dead. All is cast away, a flawed draft that will not see the light of day. Perhaps a Writer's Child, because she carries the aspirations of the poet, because she is not of the mundane world, is too perfect to live. Perhaps there are forces in the world—those who would tyrannize dreams and regulate dreaming—that cannot bear such perfection. If so, then they have won a victory.

The child is dead. The dream is dead. Do not complain to me that it is not the story you wished. It was the only story I knew.

— ✳ —

Thats the last of the story. Princess Jessica put it with the other parts and it is in a box under the bed, but she does'nt read them any more.

Jessica does'nt live in the Glass Castle any more either. The new house is smaller but its not glass. There is a garden which is mostly rocks but her mother says she does'nt feel much like putting in flowers yet. She is tired of flowers.

He was a good man Jessica, her mother says. I know you miss him very much and I do too.

Jessica is not sure that she misses him very much all tho she does sometimes. But some other times it feels good that she doesnt have to think about hiding so much. Now it is her mother who makes the crying sounds sometimes but she makes them on the couch not in a room with the door closed. Jessica always tells her its okay Mommy but sometimes her mother doesnt believe it.

Jessica tried to talk to Mister George but he does'nt talk any more, not even at night. His ears are still raggedy tho, and he still sleeps next to her in bed. She wishes they could still have talks but the doctor told her mother once it was just a faze, which means just for a while so maybe everybodys bear stops talking after a while.

Jessicas mother wouldnt let her see what happened to her father but the Duchess, who still lives with them and watches even more television said that he fell and cut himself on a broken wine glass that was on the floor and bleeded and died. When her mother was sleeping that day after the ambalance men went away Jessica went to the room and looked at all the blood. It was all in the carpet and wine was there too so there were two colors of red. Thats when she found the rest of the story too, it was beside the tipewriter.

But there was something Jessica did'nt understand quite.

The big mirror over his desk was broken and all the pieces were gone.

Someone must have cleaned them up. In the Glass Castle they always cleaned up the broken stuff and threw it away.

Three Duets for Virgin and Nosehorn

One of my favorite "serious" stories, this was written for *Immortal Unicory*, another anthology put together by my friend Janet Berliner, co-edited by—and named after—Peter S. Beagle, one of my favorite writers. (I've spent enough time in his company over the years to have learned he's exceptionally good people as well, but I've been a fan of his work since I was in junior high school.)

I tend to take an against-the-grain approach to things like anthologies. Those who read my "magic" story in this volume may have noticed its condition of no-actual-magical-content, and when I was asked to contribute a story to a unicorn anthology, especially one being helmed by the writer of the best and best-known unicorn book of the 20th Century (Peter's *The Last Unicorn*) my first thought was, naturally, "I'm going to write a story about a rhinoceros."

(As it turned out, Peter also decided to write a rhinoceros story for the anthology, but you'll have to find a copy of that anthology to appreciate the niftiness of his story.)

However, in a nod to the putative subject matter—i.e., Unicorns—I decided my story should be about rhinoceroses doing what that other famous single-horned creature was known for: namely, Defending Virtue.

After a while it had Albrecht Durer and the founding dynasty of Cambodia in it as well. Also, there are three virgin-saving rhinos in the story, but they're all the same rhino, and only one of them is alive.

I'm confusing you, aren't I? Good. Now you'll have to read it just to make sense of this introduction...

— ✳ —

Father Joao contemplates the box, a wooden crate taller than the priest himself and as long as two men lying down, lashed with ropes as if to keep its occupant prisoner. Something is hidden inside, something dead yet extraordinary. It is a Wonder, or so he has been told, but it is meant for another and much greater man. Joao must care for it, but he is not allowed to see it. Like Something Else he could name.

Father Joao is weary and sick and full of heretical thoughts.

Rain drums on the deck above his head. The ship pitches forward, descending into a trough between waves, and the ropes that hold the great box in place creak. After a week he is quite accustomed to the ship's drunken wallowing, and his stomach no longer crawls into his throat at every shudder, but for all of his traveling, he will never feel happy on the sea.

The ship lurches again and he steadies himself against the crate. Something pricks him. He sucks air between his teeth and lifts his hand so he can examine it in the faint candlelight. A thin wooden splinter has lodged in his wrist, a faint dark line running shallowly beneath the skin. A bead of blood trembles like mercury where it has entered. Joao tugs out the splinter and wipes the blood with his sleeve. Pressing to staunch the flow, he stares at the squat, shadowed box and wonders why his God has deserted him.

— ✳ —

"You are a pretty one, Marje. Why aren't you married?"

The girl blushes, but she is secretly irritated. Her masters, the Planckfelts, work her so hard that when does she find even a chance to wash her face, let alone look for a husband? Still, it is nice to be noticed, especially by such a distinguished man as the Artist.

He is famous, this man, and though from Marje's perspective he is very old—close to fifty, surely—he is handsome, long of face and merry-eyed, and still with all his curly hair. He also has extraordinarily large and capable-looking hands. Marje cannot help but stare at his hands, knowing that they have made pictures that hang on the walls of the greatest buildings in Christendom, that they have clasped the hands of other great men—the Artist is an intimate of archbishops and kings, and even the Holy Roman Emperor himself. And yet he is not proud or snobbish: when she serves him his beer, he smiles sweetly as he thanks her and squeezes her own small hand when he takes the tankard.

"Have you no special friend, then? Surely the young men have noticed a blossom as sweet as you?"

How can she explain? Marje is a healthy, strong girl, quick with a smile and as graceful as a busy servant can afford to be. She has straw-golden hair. (She hides it under her cap, but during the heat and bustle of a long day it begins to work its way free and to dangle in moist curls down the back of her neck.) If her small nose turns up at the end a little more than would be appropriate in a Florentine or Venetian beauty, well, this is not Italy after all, and she is a serving-wench, not a prospect for marriage into a noble family. Marje is quite as beautiful as she needs to be—and yes, as she hurries through the market on her mistress's errands, she has many admirers.

But she has little time for them. She is a careful girl, and her standards are unfortunately high. The men who would happily marry her have less poetry in their souls than mud on their clogs, and the wealthy and learned ones to whom her master Jobst Planckfelt plays host are not looking for a bride among the linens and crockery, and have no honorable interest in a girl with no money and a drunkard father.

"I am too busy, Sir," she says. "My lady keeps me very occupied caring for our household and guests. It is a difficult task, running a large house. I am sure your wife would agree with me."

The Artist's face darkens a little. Marje is sad to see the smile fade, but not unhappy to have made the point. These flirtatious men! Between the dullards and the rakes, it is hard for an honest girl to make her way. In any case, it never hurts to remind a married man that he is married, especially when his wife is staying in the same house. At the least, it may keep the flirting and pinching to a minimum, and thus save a girl like Marje from unfairly gaining the hatred of a jealous woman.

The Artist's wife, from what Marje has seen, might prove just such a woman. She is somewhat stern-mouthed, and does not dine with her husband, but instead demands to have her meals brought up to the room where she eats with only her maid for company. Each time Marje has served her, the Artist's wife has watched her with a disapproving eye, as if the mere existence of pretty girls affronted Godly womanhood. She has also been unstinting in her criticism of what she sees as Marje's carelessness. The Artist's wife makes remarks about the Planckfelts, too, suggesting that she is not entirely satisfied with their hospitality, and even complains about Antwerp itself, unfavorable comparisons between its weather and available diversions and those of Nuremberg, where she and the Artist keep their home.

Marje can guess why a cheerful man like this should prefer not to think of his wife when it is not absolutely necessary.

"Well," the Artist says at last, "I am certain you work very hard, but you must give some thought to the other wonders of our Lord's creation. Virtue is of course its own reward—but only to a point, after which it becomes Pride, and is as likely to be punished as rewarded. Shall I tell you a story?"

His smile has returned, and it is really a rather marvelous thing, Marje thinks. He looks twenty years younger and rather unfairly handsome.

"I have much to do, Sir. My lady wishes me to clear away the supper things and help Cook with the washing."

"Ah. Well, I would not interfere with your duties. When do you finish?"

"Finish?" She looks at his eyes and sees merriment there, and something else, something subtly, indefinably sad, which causes her to swallow her sharp reply. "About an hour after sunset."

"Good. Come to me then, and I will tell you a story about a girl something like you. And I will show you a marvel—something you have never seen before." He leans back in his chair. "Your master has been kind enough to lend me the spare room down here for my work—during the day, it gets the northern light, such as it has been of late. That is where I will be."

Marje hesitates. It is not respectable to meet him, surely. On the other hand, he is a famous and much-admired man. When her day's work is done, why should she (who, wife-like, has served him food and washed his charcoal-smudged shirts) not have a glimpse of the works which have gained him the patronage of great men all over Europe?

"I will...I may be too busy, Sir. But I thank you."

He grins, this time with all the innocent friendliness of a young boy. "You need not fear me, Marje. But do as you wish. If you can spare a moment, you know where to find me."

— ✳ —

She stands in front of the door for some time, working up her courage. After she knocks there is no answer for long moments. At last the door opens, revealing the darkened silhouette of the Artist.

"Marje. You honor me. Come in."

She passes through the door then stops, dumbfounded. The ground-floor room that she has dusted and cleaned so many times has changed out of all recognition, and she finds her fingers straying toward the cross at her throat, as though she were again a child in a dark house listening to her father's drunken rants about the Devil. The many candles and the single brazier of coals cast long shadows, and from every shadow faces peer. Some are exalted as though with inner joy, others frown or snarl, frozen in fear and despair and even hatred. She sees angels and devils and bearded men in antique costume. Marje feels that she has stepped into some kind of church, but the congregation has been drawn from every corner of the world's history.

The Artist gestures at the pictures. "I am afraid I have been rather caught up. Do not worry—I will not make more work for you. By the time I leave here, these will all be neatly packed away again."

Marje is not thinking of cleaning. She is amazed by the gallery of faces. If these are his drawings, the Artist is truly a man gifted by God. She cannot imagine even thinking of such things, let alone rendering them with such masterful skill, making each one perfect in every small detail. She pauses, still full of an almost religious awe, but caught by something familiar amid the gallery of monsters and saints.

"That is Grip! That is Master Planckfelt's dog!" She laughs in delight. It *is* Grip, without a doubt, captured in every bristle; she does not need to see the familiar collar with its heavy iron ring, but that is there, too.

The Artist nods. "I cannot go long without drawing, I fear, and each one of God's creatures offers something in the way of challenge. From the most familiar to the strangest." He is staring at her. Marje looks up from the picture of the dog to catch him at it, but there is something unusual in his inspection, something deeper than the admiring glances she usually encounters from men of the Artist's age, and it is she who blushes.

"Have I something on my face?" she asks, trying to make a joke of it.

"No, no." He reaches out for a candle. As he examines her he moves the light around her head in slow circles, so that for a moment she feels quite dizzy. "Will you sit for me?"

She looks around, but every stool and chair is covered by sheafs of drawings. "Where?"

The Artist laughs and gently wraps a large hand around her arm. Marje feels her skin turn to gooseflesh. "I mean, let me draw you. Your face is lovely and I have a commission for a Saint Barbara that I should finish before leaving the Low Countries."

She had thought the hand a precursor to other, less genteel intimacies (and she is not quite certain how she feels about that prospect) but instead he is steering her to the door. She passes a line drawing of the Garden of Eden which is like a window into another world, into an innocence Marje cannot afford. "I…you will draw me with my clothes on?"

Again that smile. Is it sad? "It is a bust—a head and shoulders. You may wear what you choose, so long as the line of your graceful neck is not obscured."

"I thought you were going to tell me a story."

"I shall, I promise. And show you a great marvel—I have not forgotten. But I will save them until you come back to sit for me. Perhaps we could begin tomorrow morning?"

"Oh, but my lady will…"

"I will speak to her. Fear not, pretty Marje. I can be most persuasive."

The door shuts behind her. After a moment, she realizes that the corridor is cold and she is shivering.

"Here. Now turn this way. I will soon give you something to look at."

Marje sits, her head at a slightly uncomfortable angle. She is astonished to discover herself with the morning off. Her mistress had not seemed happy about it, but clearly the Artist was not exaggerating his powers of persuasion. "May I blink my eyes, Sir?"

"As often as you need to. Later I will let you move a little from time to time so you do not get too sore. Once I have made my first sketch, it will be easy to set your pose again." Satisfied, he takes his hand away from her chin—Marje is suprised to discover how hard and rough his fingers are; can drawing alone cause it?—and straightens. He goes to one of his folios and pulls out another picture, which he props up on a chair before her. At first, blocked by his body, she cannot see it. After he has arranged it to his satisfaction, the Artist steps away.

"Great God!" she says, then immediately regrets her blasphemy. The image before her looks something like a pig, but it is covered in intricate armor and has a great spike growing upwards from its muzzle. "What is it? A demon?"

"No demon, but one of God's living creatures. It is called 'Rhinocerus', which is Latin for 'nose-horn'. He is huge, this fellow—bigger than a bull, I am told."

"You have not seen one? But did you not...?"

"I drew the picture, yes. But it was made from another artist's drawing—and the creature *he* drew was not even alive, but stuffed with straw and standing in the Pope's garden of wonders. No one in Europe, I think, has ever seen this monster alive, although some have said he is the model for the fabled unicorn. Our Rhinocerus is a very rare creature, you see, and lives only at the farthest ends of the world. This one came from a land called Cambodia, somewhere near Cathay."

"I should be terrified to meet him." Marje finds she is shivering again. The Artist is standing behind her, his fingers delicately touching the nape of her neck as he pulls up her hair and knots it atop her head.

"There. Now I can see the line cleanly. Yes, you might indeed be afraid if you met this fellow, young Marje. But you might be glad of it all the same. I promised you a tale, did I not?"

"About a girl, you said. Like me."

"Ah, yes. About a fair maiden. And a monster."

"A monster? Is that...that Nosehorn in this tale?"

She is still looking at the picture, intrigued by the complexity of the beast's scales, but even more by the almost mournful expression in its small eyes. By now she knows the Artist's voice well enough to hear him smiling as he speaks.

"The Nosehorn is indeed part of this tale. But you should never decide too soon which is the monster. Some of God's fairest creations bear foul seemings. And vice-versa, of course." She hears him rustling his paper, then the near-silent scraping of his pencil. "Yes, there is both Maiden and Monster in this tale..."

Her name is Red Flower—in full it is Delicate-Red-Flower-the-Color-of-Blood, but since her childhood only the priests who read the lists of blessings have used that name. Her father Jayavarman is a king, but not *the* king: the Universal Monarch, as all know, has been promised for generations but is still awaited. In the interim, her father has been content to eat well, enjoy his hunting and his elephants, and intercede daily with the *nak ta*—the ancestors—on his people's behalf, all in the comfortable belief that the Universal Monarch will probably not arrive during his lifetime.

In fact, it is his own lack of ambition that has made Red Flower's father a powerful man. Jayavarman knows that although he has no thought of declaring himself the *devaraja*, or god-king, others are not so modest. As the power of one of the other kings—for the land has many—rises, Jayavarman lends his own prestige (and, in a pinch, his war elephants) to one of the upstart's stronger rivals. When the proud one has been brought low, Red Flower's father withdraws his support from the victor, lest that one too should begin to harbor dreams of universal kingship. Jayavarman then returns to his round of feasting and hunting, and waits to see which other tall bamboo may next seek to steal the sun from its neighbors. By this practice his kingdom of Angkor, which nestles south of the Kulen hills, has maintained its independence, and even an eminence which outstrips many of its more aggressive rivals.

But Red Flower cares little about her plump, patient father's machinations. She is not yet fourteen, and by tradition isolated from the true workings of power. As a virgin and Jayavarman's youngest daughter, her purpose (as her father and his counselors see it) is to remain a pure and sealed repository for the royal blood. As her sisters were in their turn, Red Flower will be a gift to some young man Jayavarman favors, or whose own blood—and the family it represents—offers a connection which favors his careful strategies.

Red Flower, though, does not feel like a vessel. She is a young woman (just), and this night she feels herself as wild and unsettled as one of her father's hawks newly unhooded.

In truth, her sire's intricate and continuous strategies are somewhat to blame for her unrest. There are strangers outside the palace tonight, a ragtag army camped around the walls. They are fewer than Jayavarman's own force, badly armored, carrying no weapons more advanced than scythes and daggers, and they own no elephants at all, but there is something in their eyes which make even the king's most hardened veterans uneasy. The sentries along the wall do not allow their spears to dip, and they watch the strangers' campfires carefully, as though looking into sacred flames for some sign from the gods.

The leader of this tattered band is a young man named Kaundinya who has proclaimed himself king of a small region beyond the hills, and who has come to Red Flower's father hoping for support in a dispute with another chieftain. Red Flower understands little of what is under discussion, since she is not permitted to listen to the men's conversation, but she has seen her father's eyes during the three days of the visitors' stay and knows that he is troubled. No one thinks he will lend his aid— neither of the two quarreling parties are powerful enough to cause Jayavarman to support the other. But nevertheless, others beside Red Flower can see that something is causing the king unrest.

Red Flower is unsettled for quite different reasons. As excited as any of her slaves by gossip and novelty, she has twice slipped the clutches of her aged nurse to steal a look at the visitors. The first time, she turned up her nose at the peasant garb the strangers wear, as affronted by their raggedness as her maids had been. The second time, she saw Kaundinya himself.

He is barely twenty years old, this bandit chief, but as both Red Flower and her father have recognized (to different effect, however) there is something in his eyes, something cold and hard and knowing, that belies his age. He carries himself like a warrior, but more importantly, he carries himself like a true king, the flash of his eyes telling all who watch that if they have not yet had cause to bow down before him, they soon will. And he is handsome, too: on a man slightly less stern, his fine features and flowing black hair would be almost womanishly beautiful.

And while she peered out at him from behind a curtain, Kaundinya turned and saw Red Flower, and this is what she cannot forget. The heat of his gaze was like Siva's lightning leaping between Mount Mo-Tam and the sky. For a moment, she felt sure that his eyes, like a demon's, had caught at her soul and would steal it out of her body. Then her old nurse caught her and yanked her away, swatting at her ineffectually with swollen-jointed hands. All the way back to the women's wing the nurse shrilly criticized her wickedness and immodesty, but Red Flower, thinking of Kaundinya's stern mouth and impatient eyes, did not hear her.

And now the evening has fallen and the palace is quiet. The old woman is curled on a mat beside the bed, wheezing in her sleep and wrinkling her nose at some dream-affrontery. A warm wind rattles the bamboo and carries the smell of cardamom leaves through the palace like music. The monsoon season has ended, the moon and the jungle flowers alike are blooming, all the night is alive, alive. The king's youngest daughter practically trembles with sweet discontent.

She pads quietly past her snoring nurse and out into the corridor. It is only a few steps to the door that leads to the vast palace gardens. Red Flower wishes to feel the moon on her skin and the wind in her hair.

As she makes her way down into the darkened garden, she does not see the shadow-form that follows her, and does not hear it either, for it moves as silently as death...

— ✳ —

"And there I must stop." The Artist stands and stretches his back.

"But...but what happened? Was it the horned monster in the picture that followed her?"

"I have not finished, I have merely halted for the day. Your mistress is expecting you to go back to work, Marje. I will continue the story when you return to me tomorrow."

She hesitates, unwilling to let go of the morning's novelty, of her happiness at being admired and spoken to as an equal. "May I see what you have drawn?"

"No." His voice is perhaps harsher than he had wished. When he speaks again he uses a softer tone. "I will show you when I am finished, not before. Go along, you. Let an old man rest his fingers and his tongue."

He does not look old. The gray morning light streams through the window behind him, gleaming at the edges of his curly hair. He seems very tall.

Marje curtseys and leaves him, pulling the door closed behind her as quietly as she can. All day, as she sweeps out the house's dusty corners and hauls water from the well, she will think of the smell of spice trees and of a young man with cold, confident eyes.

Even on deck, wrapped in a heavy hooded cloak against the unseasonable squall, Father Joao is painfully aware of the dark, silent box in the hold. A present from King John to the newly elected Pope, it would be a valuable cargo simply as a significator of the deep, almost familial relationship between the Portuguese throne and the Holy See. But as a reminder of the wealth that Portugal can bring back to Mother Church from the New World and elsewhere (and as such to prompt the Holy Father toward favoring Portugal's expanding interests) its worth is incalculable. In Anno Domini 1492, all of the world seems in reach of Christendom's ships, and it is a world whose spoils the Pope will divide. The bishop who is the king's ambassador (and Father Joao's superior), the man who will present the pontiff with this splendid gift, is delighted with the honor bestowed upon him.

Thus, Father Joao is a soldier in a good cause, and with no greater responsibility than to make sure the Wonder arrives in good condition. Why then is he so unhappy?

It was the months spent with his family, he knows, after being so long abroad. Mother Church offers balm against the fear of age and death; seeing his parents so changed since he had last visited them, so feeble, was merely painful and did not remotely trouble his faith. But the spectacle of his brother Ruy as happy father, his laughing, tumbling brood about him, was for some reason more difficult to stomach. Father Joao has disputed with himself about this. His younger brother has children, and someday will have grandchildren to be the warmth of his old age, but Joao has dedicated his own life and chastity to the service of the Lord Jesus Christ, the greatest and most sacred of callings. Surely the brotherhood of his fellow priests is family enough?

But most insidious of all the things that cause him doubt, something that still troubles him after a week at sea, despite all his prayers and sleepless nights searching for God's peace, even despite the lashes of his own self-hatred, is the beauty of his brother's wife, Maria.

The mere witnessing of such a creature troubled chastity, but to live in her company for weeks was an almost impossible trial. Maria was dark-eyed and slender of waist despite the roundness of her limbs. She had thick black curly hair which (mocking all pins and ribbons) constantly worked itself free to hang luxuriously down her back and sway as she walked, hiding and accentuating at the same moment, like the veils of Salome.

Joao is no stranger to temptation. In his travels he has seen nearly every sort of woman God has made, young and old, dark-skinned and light. But all of them, even the greatest beauties, have been merely shadows against the light of his belief. Joao has always reminded himself that he observed only the outer garments of life, that it was the souls within that mattered. Seeing after those souls is his sacred task, and his virginity has been a kind of armor, warding off the demands of the flesh. He has always managed to comfort himself with this thought.

But living in the same house with Ruy and his young wife was different. To see Maria's slim fingers toying with his brother's beard, stroking that face so much like his own, or to watch her clutch one of their children against her sloping hip, forced Joao to wonder what possible value there could be in chastity.

At first her earthiness repelled him, and he welcomed that repulsion. A glimpse of her bare feet or the cleavage of her full breasts, and his own corrupted urge to stare at such things, made him rage inwardly. She was a woman, the repository of sin, the Devil's tool. She and each of her kind were at best happy destroyers of a man's innocence, at worst deadly traps that yawned, waiting to draw God's elect down into darkness.

But Joao lived with Ruy and Maria for too long, and began to lose his comprehension of evil. For his brother's wife was not a wanton, not a temptress or whore. She was a wife and mother, an honorable, pious woman raising her children in the faith, good to her husband and kind to his aging parents. If she found pleasure in the flesh God had given her, if she enjoyed her man's arms around her, or the sun on her ankles as she prepared her family's dinner in the tiny courtyard, how was that a sin?

With this question, Joao's armor had begun to come apart. If enjoyment of the body were not sinful, then how could denial of the body be somehow blessed? Could it be so much worse in God's eyes, his brother Ruy's life? If there were no sin in having a beautiful and loving wife to share your bed, in having children and a hearth, then why has Joao himself renounced these things? And if God made mankind fruitful, then commanded his most faithful servants not to partake of that fruitfulness, and in fact to despise it as a hindrance to holiness, then what kind of wise and loving God was He?

Father Joao has not slept well since leaving Lisbon, the ceaseless movement of the ocean mirroring his own unquiet soul. Everything seems in doubt here, everything suspended, the sea a place neither of God nor the Devil, but forever between the two. Even the sailors, who with their dangerous lives might seem most in need of God's protection, mistrust priests.

In the night, in his tiny cabin, Joao can hear the ropes that bind the crate stretching and squeaking, as though something inside it stirs restlessly.

His superior the bishop has been no help, and Joao's few attempts to seek the man's counsel have yielded only uncomprehending homilies. Unlike Father Joao, he is long past the age when the fleshly sins are the most tempting. If His Excellency's soul is in danger, Joao thinks with some irritation, it is from Pride: the bishop is puffed like a sleeping owl with the honor of his position—liaison between king and pope, bringer of a mighty gift, securer of the Church's blessing on Portugal's conquests across the heathen world.

If the bishop is the ambassador, Father Joao wonders, then what is he? An insomniac priest. A celibate tortured by his own flesh. A man who will accompany a great gift, but only as far as Italy's shores before he turns to go home again.

Now the rain is thumping on the deck overhead, and he can no longer hear noises in the hold. His head hurts, he is cold beneath his thin blanket and he is tired of thinking.

He is only a porter bearing a box of dead Wonder, Joao decides with a kind of cold satisfaction—a Wonder of which he himself is not even to be vouchsafed a glimpse.

— ✳︎ —

Marje has been looking at the Nosehorn so long that even when the Artist commands her to close her eyes she sees it still, printed against the darkness of her eyelids. She knows she will dream of it for months, the powerful body, the tiny, almost hidden eyes, the thrust of horn lifting from its snout.

"You said you would tell me more about the girl. The flower girl."

"So I shall, Marje. Let me only light another candle. There is less light today. I am like one of those savage peoples who worship the sky, always turning in search of the sun."

"Will it be finished soon?"

"Tale or picture?"

"Both." She needs to know. Yesterday and today have been a magical time, but she remembers magic from other stories and knows it does not last. She is sad her time at the center of the world is passing, but underneath everything she is a realistic girl. If it is to end today she can make her peace, but she needs to know.

"I do not think I will finish either this morning, unless I keep you long enough to make your mistress forget I am a guest and lose her temper. So we will have more work tomorrow. Now be quiet, girl. I am drawing your mouth."

— ✳︎ —

As she steps into the circle of moss-covered stones at the garden's center, something moves in the darkness beneath the trees. Red Flower turns her face away from the moon.

"Who is there?" Her voice is a low whisper. Even though she is the king's daughter, tonight she feels like a trespasser within her own gardens.

Thunder rumbles quietly in the distance. The monsoon is ended but the skies are still unsettled. He steps out of the trees, naked to the waist, moonlight gleaming on his muscle-knotted arms. "I am. And who is there? Ah, it's the old dragon's daughter."

She feels her breath catch in her throat. She is alone, in the dark. There is danger here. But there is also something in Kaundinya's gaze that keeps her fixed to the spot as he approaches.

"You should not be here," she says at last.

"What is your name? You came to spy on me the other day, didn't you?"

"I am..." She still finds it hard to speak. "I am Red Flower. My father will kill you if you do not go away."

"Perhaps. Perhaps not. Your father is afraid of me."

Her strange lethargy is at last dispelled by anger. "That is a lie! He is afraid of no one! He is a great king, not a bandit like you with your ragged men!"

Kaundinya laughs, genuinely amused, and Red Flower is suddenly unsure again. "Your father is a king, little girl, but he will never be Ultimate Monarch, never the *devaraja*. I will be, though, and he knows it. He is no fool. He sees what is inside me."

"You are mad." She takes a few steps back. "My father will destroy you."

"He would have done it when he first met me if he dared. But I have come to him in peace and am a guest in his house and he cannot touch me. Still, he will not give me his support. He thinks to send me away with empty hands while he considers how he might ruin me before my power grows too great."

The stranger abruptly strides forward and catches her arm, pulling her close until she can smell the betel nut on his breath. His eyes, mirroring the moon, seem very bright. "But perhaps I will not go away with empty hands after all. It seems the gods have brought you to me, alone and unguarded. I have learned to trust the gods—it is they who have promised me that I shall be king over all of *Kambuja-desa*."

Red Flower struggles, but he is very strong and she is only a slender young girl. Before she can call for her father's soldiers, he covers her mouth with his own and pinions her with his strong arms. His deep, sharp smell surrounds her and she feels herself weakening. The moon seems to disappear, as though it has fallen into shadow. It is a little like drowning, this surrender. Kaundinya frees one hand to hold her face, then slides that hand down her neck, sending shivers through her like ripples across a pond. Then his hand moves again, and, as his other hand gathers up her sari, it pushes roughly between her legs. Red Flower gasps and kicks, smashing her heel down on his bare foot.

Laughing and cursing at the same time, he loosens his grip. She pulls free and runs across the garden, but she has gone only a few steps before he leaps into pursuit.

She should scream, but for some reason she cannot. The blind fear of the hunted is upon her: all she can do is run like a deer, run like a rabbit, hunting for a dark hole and escape. He has done something to her with his touch and his cold eyes. A spell has enwrapped her.

She finds a gate in the encircling garden wall. Beyond is the temple, and on a hill above it the great dark shadow of the *Sivalingam,* the holy pillar reaching toward heaven. Past that is only jungle on one side, on the other open country and the watchfires of Kaundinya's army. Red Flower races toward the hill sacred to Siva, Lord of Lightnings.

The pillar is a finger pointing toward the moon. Thunder growls, closer now. She stumbles and falls to her knees, then begins crawling uphill, silently weeping. Something hisses like a serpent in the grass behind her, then a hand curls in her hair and yanks her back. She tumbles and lies at Kaundinya's feet, staring up. His eyes are wild, his mouth twisted with fury, but his voice, when it comes, is terrifyingly calm.

"You are the first of your father's possessions that I will take and use."

— ✳ —

"But you cannot stop there, Sir! That is terrible! What happened to the girl?"

The Artist is putting away his drawing materials, but without his usual care. He seems almost angry. Marje is afraid she has offended him in some way.

"I will finish the tale tomorrow. Only a little more work is needed on the drawing, but I am tired now."

She gets up, tugging the sleeves of her dress back over her shoulders. He opens the door and stands beside it, as though impatient for her to leave.

"I will not sleep tonight for worrying about the flower girl," she says, trying to make him smile. He closes his eyes for a moment, as though he too is thinking about Red Flower.

"I will miss you, Marje," he says when she is outside. Then he shuts the door.

— ✷ —

The storm-handled ship bobs on the water like a wooden cup. In his cabin, Father Joao glares into the darkness. Somewhere below, ropes creak like the damned distantly at play.

The thought of the box and its forbidden contents torments him. *Coward, doubter, near-eunuch, false priest*—with these names he also tortures himself. In the blackness before his eyes he sees visions of his brother's wife Maria, smiling, clothes undone, warm and rounded and hateful. Would she touch him with the heedless fondness with which she rubs Ruy's back, kisses his neck and ear? Could she understand that at this awful moment Joao would give his immortal soul for just such animal comfort? What would she think of him? What would any of those whose souls are in his care think of him?

He drags himself from the bed and stands on trembling legs, swaying as the ship sways. Far above, thunder fills the sky like the voices of God and Satan contesting. Joao pulls his cassock over his undershirt and fumbles for his flints. When the candle springs alight, the walls and roof of his small sanctuary press closer than he had remembered, threatening to squeeze him breathless.

Father Joao lurches toward the cargo hold, his head full of voices. As he climbs down a slippery ladder, he loses his footing and nearly falls. He waves his free arm for balance and the candle goes out. For a moment he struggles just to maintain his grip, wavering in empty darkness with unknown depths beneath him. At last he rights himself, but now he is without light. Somewhere above, the storm proclaims its power, mocking human enterprise. A part of him wonders what he is doing up, what he is doing in this of all places. Surely, that quiet voice suggests, he should at least go back to light his candle again. But that gentle voice is only one of many. Joao reaches down with his foot, finds the next rung, and continues his descent.

Even in utter blackness he knows his way. Every day of the voyage he has passed back and forth through this great empty space, like exiled Jonah. His hands encounter familiar things, his ears are full of the quiet complaining of the fettered crate. He knows his way.

He feels its presence even before his fingers touch it, and stops, blind and half-crazed. For a moment he is tempted to go down on his knees, but God can see even in darkness, and some last vestige of devout fear holds him back. Instead he lays his ear against the rough wood and listens, as a father might listen to the child growing in his wife's belly. Something is inside. It is still and dead, but somehow in Father Joao's mind it is full of terrible life.

He pulls at the box, desperate to open it, knowing even without sight that he is bloodying his fingers, but it is too well-constructed. He falls back at last, sobbing. The crate mocks him with its impenetrability. He lowers himself to the floor of the hold and crawls, searching for something that will serve where flesh has failed. Each time he strikes his head on an unseen impediment the muffled thunder seems to grow louder, as though something huge and secret is laughing at him.

At last he finds an iron rod, then feels his way back to the waiting box. He finds a crack beneath the lid and pushes the bar in, then throws his weight on it, pulling downward. It gives, but only slightly. Mouthing a prayer whose words even he does not know, Joao heaves at the bar again, struggling until more tears come to his eyes. Then, with a screeching of nails ripped from their holes, the lid lifts away and Joao falls to the floor.

The ship's hold suddenly fills with an odor he has never smelled, a strong scent of dry musk and mysterious spices. He staggers upright and leans over the box, drinking in this exhalation of pure Wonder. Slowly, half-reverent and half-terrified, he lowers his hands into the box.

A cloud of dense-packed straw is already rising from its confinement, crackling beneath his fingers, which feel acute as eyes. What waits for him? Punishment for his doubts? Or a shrouded Nothing, a final blow to shatter all faith?

For a moment he does not understand what he is feeling. It is so smooth and cold that for several heartbeats he is not certain he is touching anything at all. Then, as his hands slide down its gradually widening length, he knows it for what it is. A horn.

Swifter and swifter his fingers move, digging through the straw, following the horn's curve down to the snout, then the wide rough brow, the glass-hard eyes, the ears. The Wonder inside the box has but a single horn. The thing beneath Joao's fingers is dead, but there is no doubt that it once lived. It is real. Real! Father Joao hears a noise in the empty hold and realizes that he himself is making it. He is laughing.

God does not need to smite doubters, not when He can instead show them their folly with a loving jest. The Lord has proved to faithless Joao that divine love is no mere myth, and that He does not merely honor chastity, He defends it. All through this long nightmare voyage, Joao has been the unwitting guardian of Virtue's greatest protector.

Down on his knees now in the blind darkness, but with his head full of light, the priest gives thanks over and over.

— ✳ —

Kaundinya stands above her in the moon-thrown shadow of the pillar. He holds the delicate fabric of her sari in his hands. Already it has begun to part between his strong fingers.

Red Flower cannot awaken from this dream. The warm night is shelter no longer. Even the faint rumble of thunder has vanished, as though the gods themselves have turned their backs on her. She closes her eyes as one of Kaundinya's hands cups her face. As his mouth descends on hers, he lowers his knee between her thighs, spreading her. For a long moment, nothing happens. She hears the bandit youth take a long and surprisingly unsteady breath.

Red Flower opens her eyes. The pillar, the nearby temple, all seem oddly flat, as though they have been painted on cloth. At the base of the hill, only a few paces from where she sits tumbled on the grass, a huge pale form has appeared.

Kaundinya's eyes are opened wide in superstitious dread. He lets go of Red Flower's sari and lifts himself from her.

"Lord Siva," he says, and throws himself prostrate before the vast white beast. The rough skin of its back seems to give off as much light as the moon itself, and it turns its wide head to regard him, horn lowered like a spear, like the threat of lightning. Kaundinya speaks into the dirt. "Lord Siva, I am your slave."

Red Flower stares at the beast, then at her attacker, who is caught up in something like a slow fit, his muscles rippling and trembling, his face contorted. The nosehorn snorts once, then turns and lumbers away toward the distant trees, strangely silent. Red Flower cannot move. She cannot even shiver. The world has grown tracklessly large and she is but a single, small thing.

At last Kaundinya stands. His fine features are childish with shock, as though something large has picked him up by the neck and shaken him.

"The Lord of all the Gods has spoken to me," he whispers. He does not look at Red Flower, but at the place where the beast has vanished into the jungle. "I am not to dishonor you, but to marry you. I will be the *devaraja* and you will be my queen. This place, Angkor, will be the heart of my kingdom. Siva has told me this."

He extends a hand. Red Flower stares at it. He is offering to help her up. She struggles to her feet without assistance, holding the torn part of her gown together. Suddenly she is cold.

"You know your father will give you to me," he calls after her as she stumbles back toward the palace. "He recognizes what I am, what I will be. It is the only solution. He will see that."

She does not want to hear him, does not want to think about what he is saying. But she does, of course. She is not sure what has happened tonight, but she knows that he is speaking the truth.

Marje is silent for a long time after the Artist has finished. The grayness of the day outside the north-facing window is suddenly dreary.

"And is that it? She had to marry him?"

The Artist is concentrating deeply, squinting at the drawing-board. He does not reply immediately. "At least it was an honorable marriage," he says at last. "That is something better than rape, is it not?"

"But what happened to her afterward?"

"I am not entirely sure. It is only a story, after all. But I imagine she bore the bandit king many sons, so that when he died his line lived on. The man who told me the tale said that there were kings in that place for seven hundred years. The *rhinocerus* you see in that drawing was the last of a long line of sacred beasts, a symbol to the royal family. But the kings of Cambodia have left Angkor now, so perhaps it no longer means anything to them. In any case, they gave that one to the king of Portugal, and Portugal gave its stuffed body to the Pope after it died." The Artist shakes his head. "I am sorry I could not see it when it breathed and walked God's earth."

Marje stares at the picture of the Nosehorn, wondering at its strange journey. What would it think, this jungle titan whose ancestor was a heathen god, to find itself, or at least its image, propped on a chair in Antwerp?

The Artist stirs. "You may move now, Marje. I am finished."

She thinks she hears something of her own unhappiness in his voice. What does it mean? She gets up slowly, untwisting sore muscles, and walks to his side. She must lean against him to see the drawing properly; she feels his small, swift movement, almost a twitch, as she presses against his arm.

"Oh. It's...it's beautiful."

"As you are beautiful," he says softly.

The picture is Marje, but also not Marje. The girl before her has her eyes closed and wears a look of battered innocence. The long line of her neck is lovely but fragile.

"Saint Barbara was taken onto a mountain by her father and killed," the Artist says, gently tracing the neck of the false Marje, the more-than-Marje, with his finger. "Perhaps he was jealous of the love she had found in Jesus. She is the martyr who protects us from sudden death...and from lightning."

"Your gift is from God, Master Dürer." She is more than a little overwhelmed. "So are we finished now?"

Marje is still leaning against his arm, staring at the picture, her breasts touching his shoulder. When he does not reply, she glances up. The Artist is looking at her closely. From this close she can see the lines that web his face, but also the depth of his eyes, the bright, tragic eyes of a much younger man. "We must be," he says. "I have finished the drawing and told you the tale." His voice is carefully flat, but something moves beneath it, a kind of yearning.

For a moment she hesitates, feels herself tilting as though out of balance in a high place. Then, uncomfortable with his regard, her eyes stray to the picture of the mighty Nosehorn, which seems to watch them from its place on the chair, small eyes solemn beneath the rending horn. She takes a breath.

"Yes," she finally says, "you have and you have. And now there are many things I must do. Mistress will be very anxious at how I have let my work go. She will think I am trying to rise above my station."

The Artist reaches up and briefly squeezes her hand, then lifts himself from his chair and leads her toward the door.

"When I have made my print, I will send you a copy, pretty Marje."

"I would like that very much."

"I have enjoyed our time together. I wish there could be more."

She drops him a curtsey, and for a moment allows herself to smile. "God gives us but one life, Sir. We must preserve what He gives us and make of it what we can."

He nods, returning her smile, though his is more reserved, more pained.

"Very true. You are a wise girl."

The Artist shuts the door behind her.

The Happiest Dead Boy
in the World

Some years ago Robert Silverberg asked me if I wanted to contribute a story set in my Osten Ard fantasy world (*The Dragonbone Chair*, etc.) to an anthology he was editing, called Legends. I had always avoided revisiting settings I'd already created, feeling that life is too short to go back over the same ground, no matter what new stuff you might bring to it, but now I gave it a lot of thought (nobody, least of all me, turns down an invitation from Robert Silverberg without having a damn good reason.) And at last I decided that my personal prohibition didn't entirely make sense: you can revisit something without turning it into a soulless franchise. So I wrote a long Osten Ard story, titled "The Burning Man," for that anthology. (That story is one of the few I've written not included in this collection, because it's going to be in another collection someday—I hope before too long.)

So when Mr. Silverberg invited me to participate in a second *Legends* anthology, I said yes immediately, as long as I could do an Otherland story instead of Osten Ard, for my own sake as much as anything else.

For those who don't know the Otherland books—most of my regular readers seem either to love them or not to have read them at all—they take place in the near-future, and are probably the most complicated four-book story in the history of science fiction and fantasy. I mean really, the things make "Gravity's Rainbow" look like "Dick and Jane," at least in terms of keeping track of all the plotlines. (I do not pretend for an instant to write as well as Mr. Pynchon. But I am easier to interview.)

The Otherland books are more SF than F, since most of the tale takes place in virtual reality, in a universe made up of the world's most powerful and realistic simulated worlds, built specially for a bunch of unpleasant old rich people known as the Grail Brotherhood. A number of more or less ordinary people, including a very ill young man, Orlando Gardiner, and his online buddy Sam Fredericks, wind up being dragged into the mystery of the network and its deadly effect on children all over the world in the first volume, *City of Golden Shadow*.

And then it gets really, *really* complex.

However, I don't think you need to have read the Otherland books to understand and enjoy this story. For one thing, I doubt there will be many veteran readers of fantasy who won't understand what's amusing about Beezle Bug visiting Middle Earth, even if this is the first time they've encountered him. Also, even if you haven't had a chance to read the books yet, I think you'll enjoy meeting our protagonist, Orlando Gardiner, who has just about the most interesting job of any teenage boy in history...

Tharagorn the Ranger was deep in conversation with Elrond Half-elven in the quiet shadows of Rivendell's Hall of Fire. The man of the west had just returned from roaming through the world, and he and the elven lord had not spoken together in a long time. Things of moment were in their minds, not least of which a sudden rash of goblin raids near the Misty Mountains. Thus it was that the elven messenger, with the graceful diffidence of his kind, waited for some long moments in the doorway before either of them noticed him.

"A visitor is here who wishes to speak to Tharagorn," the elf replied to Elrond's question. "He seems to be a halfling."

"Yeah, that would be me." The voice was louder and, it had to be said, a bit less cultured than what was normally to be heard in the house of the great elven lord. The figure in the doorway was half the size of anyone else present, his feet covered in hair so thick and matted he appeared to be standing ankle-deep in the corpses of two small mountain goats. "Bongo Fluffernutter, at your service," he said with a sweeping bow. "Nice place you got here, Elrond. Love the old-world craftsmanship. Tharagorn, can you spare a second?"

"Oh, for God's sake, Beezle," the ranger said under his breath. "I am truly sorry," he told the master of the house. "Will you excuse me for a moment?"

"Of course." Elrond looked a little puzzled, although the simulation was adept at incorporating or simply ignoring anomalies. "Is it really a halfling? We have not seen such a one, I think, since Gandalf brought his friend Bilbo Baggins to us from the Shire some years ago."

"Yes, well, this...this is a different sort of hobbit." Tharagorn lowered his voice. "A less successful branch of the species, if you get my drift."

"Hey! I heard that!"

Elrond and the messenger withdrew, leaving Tharagorn, also known as Orlando Gardiner, alone in the high-raftered hall with his small, shabby visitor.

"Beezle, what the hell are you doing?"

"Don't blame me, boss, you're the one who said I couldn't show up here unless I was in character." He lifted a foot and admired it. "Whaddaya think? Nice pelt, huh?"

"Bongo Fluffernutter?"

"Isn't that the kind of name they all have? Jeez, I've only got so much room for Tolkien trivia, y'know."

Orlando stared at the pint-sized horror in front him. Whether it was a better fit with the simulation than Beezle Bug's normal, multi-legged, cartoonish appearance was open to debate, but there was no doubt he was looking at the world's ugliest hobbit. Orlando was beginning to suspect the software agent's sense of humor had moved on a bit beyond what was covered by the original warranty. Maybe he'd given Beezle a bit too much freedom over the years for self-programming off the net.

"I mean, really," Beezle said, "look at which pot's calling which kettle black, boss—Tharagorn? *Tharagorn?* Are you just waiting around here for the Return of The King or something?"

"Ha ha. Oh, you're one funny piece of code. I picked it because it sounds like 'Thargor'." Who had been, of course, Orlando's online avatar for most of his childhood, the brawny barbarian swordsman who had conquered so many gameworlds back in the old days, when Orlando Gardiner had still had a real world to return to at the end of the adventure. Not that he wasn't a little embarrassed by it all now. "Look, I wanted something easy to remember. Do you know how many names I have on this network?" He realized that he was justifying himself to an entity that had once been a birthday present, and not even the most expensive present he had received that year. "What was it you wanted, anyway?"

"Just to do my job, boss." Beezle actually sounded hurt. "I'm only serving as a furry-footed link to your busy social calendar. We already talked about dinner with your folks, so I know you remember that. You know you've got Fredericks scheduled in first, right?"

"Yeah. She's meeting me here."

"Oh, good, I'm sure that'll be fun for everyone. May I recommend the Hall of Endless Nostalgic Singing? Or perhaps the Silvery Giggling Lounge?"

"Your sarcasm is noted." It wasn't as though Orlando didn't harbor occasional less-than-reverent thoughts about the Tolkien world himself, but it was still the closest thing he had to a home, after all. Back in the beginning of his full-time life on the network, when Orlando had been overwhelmed by all that had happened to him, Middle Earth—and Rivendell in particular—had been a blessed haven for him, a familiar, much-loved place where he could relax and heal and come to terms with his responsibilities and even with the possibilities of immortality, a subject that surrounded him on every side in Elrond's ancient residence.

"By the way, tonight's also the first Friday of the month in Wodehouse World," Beezle went on. "Did you remember that too?"

"Oh, *fenfen.* No, I forgot. How long do I have?"

"Meeting's in about three hours."

"Thanks. I'll be there." But Beezle just stood, waiting expectantly, forcing Orlando to ask, "What is it now?"

"Well, if I have to stay in character and walk out of this overgrown bed and breakfast and all the way across the bridge just so I can leave the simulation, you could at least say, 'Fare thee well, Bongo Fluffernutter!' or something."

Orlando glowered. "You're joking."

"It's only polite."

"Fenfen." But Beezle showed no signs of leaving without it. "Chizz, then. Fare thee well, Bongo Fluffernutter."

"Don't forget, 'And may your toes grow ever more curly.'"

"Just get out of here."

"Okay. Fare thee well, also, Tharagorn, Cuddler of Elves."

It turned out Beezle could move quickly on those furry feet when he had to.

—⁂—

Sam Fredericks was almost an hour late, but that was all right: guests could get something to eat and drink at pretty much all hours in Rivendell if they didn't mind the limited menu. The people who had programmed this simworld years ago—a team from the Netherlands, as Orlando had discovered—had stuck to the original very carefully. There was no specific mention in the books of meat being served in Imladris, the elven name for Elrond's sumptuous house, so what the kitchen offered was pretty much limited to bread, honey, fruit, vegetables, and dairy products. Orlando, who had spent a lot of time in the Tolkien simulation during his early days living in the network, could remember more than a few times when he would have been willing to crawl to Mordor for some pepperoni.

When she showed up, she looked exactly the same as she had on her last visit, dressed in the manner of a male elf, her coffee-and-cream skin radiant, her frizzy hair a glorious confusion held only by a cloth band that made her look slightly piratical. She and Orlando hugged. Sam let go first.

"Something to eat?"

"I'm not really hungry," she said. "You go ahead if you want to."

"Sam, the food here won't fill you up, and I don't need to eat at all. It's just social." He led her onto one of the covered balconies instead. They could hear the river ringing in the valley below them, although the lanterns of Rivendell only illuminated the tops of the trees.

Sam slid onto a bench. Orlando sat down beside her and stretched his long legs. That was one of the holdovers from his illness that even he recognized: he was never going to be in a sick or crippled body again if he could avoid it. "So, you," he asked. "Are you okay?"

"I'm fine. How are you?"

"Oh, you know. Getting around, keeping an eye on things. This whole job has turned out a lot different than I expected. When I first agreed to be the sort of head park ranger, I thought I'd be, I don't know, stopping wars or something."

Sam smiled. "Like Superman?"

"Or God, yeah. I try not to limit my ambitions." He waited; Sam's laugh was a little late. "But since Sellars and Kunohara convinced all the others to let whole simiverse go free-range, I'm kind of more like an anthropologist or something." Patrick Sellars had brought together the group of people who had prevented the network from being used for its original purpose, which had been to give immortality within its confines to the Grail Brotherhood, a group of people as unpleasant as they were rich. Kunohara, a former minor member of the Grail who had changed sides, joined Sellars at the end in saving the network—and in essence, saving the lives of all the network's complex sims, as well as Orlando himself, who had been copied into the network before his physical death and now existed only as information. Sellars, too, had soon after left his own dying body behind to take up existence on the Otherland network, but unlike Orlando, his move had been voluntary.

"Anthropologist?" Sam prompted.

"Yeah, well, except for fixing obvious code errors, which don't happen much, I mostly make a lot of reports and keep an eye on the interesting, unexpected stuff. But since Sellars is gone now and Kunohara's so majorly busy, I kind of wonder who I'm making reports for."

"The rest of us, I guess. And other people who might study it someday." Sam shrugged. "Do you miss him? Sellars?"

"Yeah. I can't say we were utterly friends or anything. Not like you and me." He hoped to see her smile, but she only nodded. "He was just too…something. Old. Smart. But I liked him a lot once I got to know him. And he was the only person who lived here with me, Sam. I knew he wasn't going to be around forever—that he was tired, that he wanted to follow his information-people out into the great whatever. But I sort of thought we'd get to have him for few more years." He was playing it down, of course, for Sam's benefit. It had been even more devastating than he had expected when Sellars moved on: Orlando had felt deserted, bereft. After all, the crippled ex-pilot had been the only other person in the universe truly to understand the strangeness of knowing you were alive only on a network, that your real body was ashes now, that most of the people who had known you thought you were dead…and were more or less right.

Also, Sellars had been a kind person, and—either because or in despite of his own suffering—a good listener. He had been one of the only people who ever saw Orlando Gardiner cry. That had been back in the earliest days of living on the network, of course. Orlando didn't cry anymore. He didn't have the time for things like that.

Sam and Orlando sat on the Rivendell balcony another half an hour, talking about all manner of things, even sharing a few jokes, but Orlando continued to feel something awkward in his friend's behavior. It touched Orlando with something he had never expected to feel around Sam Fredericks; it took him long minutes to recognize it as fear. He was almost terrified by the idea that she might not want to be here with him, that their friendship had finally become no more than an obligation.

They had wandered back to the subject of the network. To his surprise, she seemed to think he was the one who needed cheering up. "It's still an amazing job you have—the ranger for a whole universe. All those worlds, your responsibility."

"Three hundred and ninety-eight at the moment, but a few others have just temporarily collapsed and they'll cycle back on again. That's like a quarter of what there used to be, but Sellars just switched a bunch of them off because they were too scanny, too violent or creepy or criminal."

"I know, Orlando. I was at that meeting, too."

"Are you sure you're okay, Sam? You seem…I don't know, sad." He looked her up and down. "And now that I think about it, you haven't changed sims in like a year's worth of visits."

"So? Jeez, Gardiner, you're the one who wants everyone to dress up all elfy-welfy here."

"I don't mean the clothes." He almost told her about Beezle's version of Rivendell chic, but he could not get past what was suddenly bothering him. "Sam, what's going on? Is there a reason you won't change your sim? You must have something more up-to-date you use for remotes and friendlines and all back home."

She shrugged—she was doing it a lot—but would not meet his eyes. "Yeah. But what does it matter? I thought you were my friend, Orlando. Is it really that important to see if…if my boobs have grown since the last time you saw me?"

He flinched. "You think that's why I want to see the real you?"

"No. I don't know. What's *your* problem?"

He swallowed down the anger, mostly because it scared him to be angry at her. There were times when it felt like his friendship with Salome Fredericks was the only thing that kept him connected to the world he had been forced to leave behind. His parents were different—

they were his parents, for God's sake, and always would be—and the other survivors of the Otherland network would always be his friends as well, but Sam…"Damn it, Fredericks, don't you get it? You're…you're part of me."

"Thanks a lot." Despite the mocking words, she looked more unhappy than angry. "All my life I wanted to be something important, but part of the great Orlando Gardiner? I never even hoped…!"

"That's not what I mean and you know it. Fenfen, I mean you're in my…okay, you're in my *heart*, even though that sounds utterly drooly. You're why I still feel like I'm a living person when, well, we both know I'm not."

Now she was the one to flinch, but some kind of wall still loomed between them. "What does that have to do with my sim? When you first met me, you thought I was a boy!"

"But this is different, Sam." He hesitated, then put his hand on her arm. The world's most powerful simulation engine made it feel just as it was supposed to feel, the warm skin on her wrist, the velvety folds of her sleeve over muscle and tendon and bone. "I know I'm never going to grow up, not in the normal way. I may not have a real body anymore, but that doesn't mean I expect everyone else to play with me forever here in the Peter Pan Playground. Look at me, Sam." He knew it was mostly guilt that kept her eyes on him, but just now he was willing to use whatever he had. "If you hide things from me, especially the normal stuff, because you think I can't take it—well, that's the worst thing I can think of. I was a cripple my whole life. Having progeria wasn't just knowing I was going to die young, it was having every single person who saw me for the first time look at me and then look away real fast, like I was some kind of horrible human car accident. Even the decent ones who tried to treat me like anyone else…well, let's just say it was obvious they were working at it. I don't want to be pitied ever again, Sam."

She looked miserable and ashamed. "I still don't understand, Orlando. What does that have to do with my sim?"

"You don't want me to see the way you look now, but it's not because you've got a zit or something and you're embarrassed. It's because you know you look different, that you're growing or changing or whatever. Tell me I'm wrong. Jeez, Fredericks, I've been living on this network almost three years, do you think I expect things not to change? It's not going to hurt me. But if you can't show me, then…well, it's like you don't trust our friendship. Like we can only be the kind of kid-buddies we used to be back in the Middle Country game."

She looked at him with something of the familiar Sam in her expression again, amused even though she was irritated. "Same old Gardiner. You still know everything." She took a long breath. "Okay, you want to see how I look now? Fine." For a moment her Rivendell-self froze as she reselected her appearance, the new information passing through the series of blind relays that kept the very private Otherland network isolated from the real-world net. Then, suddenly, like a hardcopy picture dropped onto the top of a stack, Sam's image changed. "Satisfied?"

"You don't look that different," he said, but it wasn't really true. She was an inch or two taller, but also more curved and womanly—she had wider hips that the elven breeches only emphasized. The Sam he had known had been a greyhound-slender athlete. She also had a length to her face that he hadn't seen before. She was really lovely, and not just because she was the Sam he loved. He also realized he hadn't told the truth about something else: seeing her suddenly a year older, seventeen instead of sixteen, *did* hurt. It hurt like hell. "Thanks."

"Oh, Orlando, I'm sorry. I'm being utterly jacked. It's not that, it's not any of that." She slumped on the bench, leaned forward until she could rest her elbows on her knees. She had stopped meeting his eye again. "It's just…I'm seeing somebody."

For a moment he didn't understand what she meant, thought she was still talking about sims and images. "Oh. Is it…serious?"

"I don't know. Yeah, I guess. We've been going around together for a couple of months."

Orlando took a breath. "Well, I hope it works out. Fenfen, Frederico, is that what's been bothering you all day? We've been past that jealousy stuff for a long time." In part, he had to admit, because Sam had made it clear from the beginning of their real friendship, after he knew she was a girl and she knew about his illness, that although she loved him as much as he loved her, it was never going to be the romantic kind. Which was just as well, he had decided, because what they had was going to last their whole life and not be messed up by sex.

He often wondered if real, living teenagers told themselves the same kind of pathetic lies he did.

"I don't know, it just...scares me. Sometimes I feel like..." She shook her head. "Like I'm not a very good friend for you. *To* you," she amended hurriedly. "I don't see you as often as I should. You must think I'm terrible."

He laughed, surprised. "It never even occurred to me. You know, Sam, no offense, but it's not like when you're not here I just sit around waiting for your next visit. Two days ago I was dodging arrows in Edo while a bunch of warlords tried to overthrow the Tokugawa shogunate. The week before I spent a few days with Captain Nemo exploring some undersea ruins."

"So...so you're okay? With everything? Not bored or...or lonely?"

He gave her arm another squeeze before letting go. The elves were singing again in the Hall of Fire, a meditation on the light of the Two Trees. The voices seemed almost to belong to the valley itself, to the night and the forest and the river singing together. "Bored? Not when I consider the alternatives. No, don't fret about me, Frederico—I always have places to go, things to do, and people to see. Why, I must be the happiest dead boy in the whole wide world."

It wasn't really so much that Sam was dating someone that was bothering him, he thought as he got ready to connect to his parents' house, or even that she'd kept it a secret for a while. In fact, now that he thought of it, he *still* didn't know if her new soulmate was male or female. Sam had always been funny that way, not wanting to talk about those sorts of things, irritated by questions, as if Orlando might think differently about her if she ever clarified her gender and sexual issues. No, it wasn't so much that she was dating someone, or even that she was growing up. He loved her, he really, truly did, and he wanted her to have a happy life no matter what. Instead, it was the sudden worry that he might not be growing up himself, as he had always assumed he was, however weird his situation. He felt a chill and wondered whether he was becoming irrelevant to everything, not just to Sam, whether despite the fact that years were passing for him in Make-Believe Land just as they did for her in the real world, his experiences here might not be the same as growing up at all.

Maybe you have to be real to do it. Maybe you have to do real things, make a fool of yourself at a party, trip and skin your knee, fall in love, or just...just...have a heartbeat. Maybe I'll never really change. I'll be like one of the sims—a sim of a fourteen year old kid. Forever. He pushed away the sickening thought. He had enough to deal with right now: tonight was Family Night, which was hard enough to get through at the best of times.

It didn't really seem fair, being dead and still having to go home for visits. Not that he didn't love Conrad and Vivien. In fact, it was because he loved them so much that it could be so difficult.

He took a deep breath, in a metaphorical sort of a way—he felt as if he was taking a deep breath, anyway—and as he did so, he remembered that his mother and father apparently had a surprise for him tonight. They had asked him to connect to a different location in the house for his visit instead of the wallscreen. *"Well, actually, it's really Conrad's surprise,"* his mother had explained. She had smiled, but she hadn't seemed entirely pleased with whatever it was going to be. Orlando had seen that expression before: she had worn it when Conrad had given him the bike for his eleventh birthday. Anyone, even Orlando himself, could have told his father that his bones were too brittle and his muscles too weak even to think of riding a bicycle, but Conrad Gardiner had insisted that his son should have every chance to be normal.

When Orlando had become more or less bedridden in the last year, they had finally got rid of it to make more room in the garage for medical equipment, spare filters and oxygen pods. He had never ridden it, of course.

As he made the connection, Orlando wondered why he couldn't just join them through the wallscreen, as usual. He liked doing that, because it felt no different than an ordinary kid-to-parents call, as though he were simply away at school in a different state instead of living in what was functionally a different universe.

Maybe Conrad swapped in the old screen for one of those deep-field things. He was talking a while back about investing in one of the solid-crystal ones.

The connection opened and he was looking at his parents, who looked back at him. His mother was teary-eyed, as she always was when they first saw each other. His father was beaming with what looked like pride. But there was also something unusual about the way they both appeared; it took him a moment to process what it was.

I'm looking through a different imager, he decided. *I guessed right—it's a new screen.* But if his parents had indeed bought a new unit, he suddenly realized, they had installed it in the dining room instead of the living room: he could see the old oak sideboard behind their heads, with the poster of the French can-can dancers next to it that had hung on the wall there for years.

"Hi. What's up—new screen?" Without thinking, he raised his hand to blow his mom a kiss as he always did—yes, it was embarrassing, but you had to do things differently when you couldn't actually touch—and something shadowy rushed toward him. Even after years without a real body, he could not help flinching a little. The new thing stopped and hung in his view in the same way a simulated hand would.

It *was* a hand, but not being simulated on his end. Instead, it seemed to be looming in front of his parent's screen and thus effectively hanging in front of his eyes, a weird-looking, smooth, maroon hand made of what appeared to be shiny plasteel. Half-forgetting his bodiless state, he reached out to touch it. The hand reached out too, extending away from his viewpoint, just as if it were his own hand, responding to his thoughts. Fascinated and troubled as he began to catch on, he tried to make the fingers wiggle as he would with one of his own simulated hands. The fingers wiggled. But these fingers weren't on one of his sims, and weren't even in the network—they were in Conrad and Vivien's dining room in the real world.

"What the hell is this?"

"Do you like it?" His father was nodding, the way he used to nod when someone was trying out his home-brewed beers, back when they had still had visitors.

Well, that's one thing, Orlando thought. *Now that I'm gone, at least they can have people over again.* "Like it? What *is* it? Some kind of robot arm attached to the new screen?"

"It's not a new screen, it's a whole body. So you can, you know, be here. Inside the house with us. Whenever you want."

Orlando had discovered the other arm. He flexed it, held the two hands up together, then looked down. The viewpoint swiveled, showed him the cylindrical, beet-colored torso, the jointed legs. "A…body?"

"I should have thought of it before," his father said. "I don't know why I didn't—your software agent used to have that little body with all the mechanical legs so it could crawl around the house, remember? I looked around until I found something that seemed like it would work. It's a remote figure they use for certain kinds of reconnaissance operations—I think it was built for Antartica originally, maybe military or something. I found a collector and bought it. I had to get different feet put on it—it sort of had hands at the end of the legs." He was clearly a little nervous: when he was nervous, he babbled. "Better for climbing and moving on ice or something. I'm surprised they weren't skis or tractor-treads or maybe…"

"Conrad," Vivien said, "that's enough. I don't want to hear about hands on legs. It's…disturbing." She darted a quick look at Orlando, who was more than a little stunned.

"What…what am I looking out of?"

"The face," his father said. "Well, it should be, but we'll have to change what you're putting out from your end. I didn't want to spoil the surprise, so right now there's a whole little Orlando standing there in the face-screen."

"I'm still trying to figure this out. You mean, I'm supposed to…move around in this?"

"Sure, go ahead!" Conrad was delighted by the question. "Walk! You can go anywhere in the house!"

"He doesn't have to if he doesn't want to," said his mother.

Orlando flexed his muscles, or performed the mental actions that flexed muscles in the real world and the better virtual worlds. The cartoon fingers reached out and gripped the tabletop. He put his feet under him and stood; the point of view rose, not altogether steadily. Now that he was listening for it, he could hear the faint wet hiss of fibromotors bunching and relaxing.

"Do you need some help?"

"No, Conrad. I'll be okay." He got up and took a few swaying steps, then stopped to look down at the feet—they were huge ovals, like

Mickey Mouse shoes. It was strange to be in a body as clumsy as this: his Otherland network bodies all responded exactly as though they were his own, and made him stronger, faster, and far more nimble than he had ever been in real life.

He hadn't been in the bathroom since his death. It was interesting, even strangely touching, to have movement around his old house restored to him, but he wasn't certain about any of this. He looked at his reflection in the mirror, the strange stick-figure shape of the thing. The screen in the faceplate showed Orlando's full-body sim, so that he looked like one of those giant Japanese robot-monsters with a human controller rattling around inside its head. He scaled his sim's output so that only the face appeared, and suddenly, even though it wasn't his real face, not by a long shot—no one including Orlando himself had seen that since his physical body had been cremated—it made the whole thing more real and also far more disturbing.

Is this what they want for me? This...thing? He knew that Conrad meant well, that his parents were only trying to find a way to make his continued presence in their lives more real, more physical, but he didn't know if he could stand to live for even short periods as this stalking, plasticized scarecrow.

He looked at the face he used with his parents, a teenage face appropriate to his age, made with help from various police forensic illustration nodes, scaled up from scans of his own skull and incorporating features from both his mother and his father. *Not even a real face to begin with. The face of the kid they should have had,* he thought. *Stuck on this thing, now, like a lollipop on a stick.*

Orlando did his best. He sat through dinner and tried to concentrate as his parents told him things about friends and relatives, about their jobs and the small annoyances of life in security-walled Crown Heights Community, but he felt even more like an alien than he usually did. The servo-muscles on the body were clumsy and the tactors less advanced than what he was used to: he knocked over his mother's glass twice and almost tipped the table over when he stood up at the end of the meal.

"I'm going to have to make it an early night," he said.

"Are you all right?" his mother asked. "You seem sort of down."

"I'm fine, I've just got a meeting to go to at the Drones Club."

"That's that 1920s English place you told us about?" Conrad asked. "That must be interesting. Didn't you say there was a war there?"

"Sort of." It was still hard to make his parents understand about John Dread, about the terrible destruction the killer had wrought in so many of the Otherland network worlds in the brief days he had ruled over the system as a kind of evil god. "The simulation is coming back, but we're letting things sort themselves out instead of just wiping out what's happened and starting the cycles over, so there's some pretty scanny stuff going on in some of them. Adaptations, almost like after a forest fire has changed an ecosystem. Very barky." He noticed their puzzled faces. "Barky? It means funny. The weird kind of funny."

"You know so much about these things," his mother said. "This complicated network. You've learned so much. And you've really worked hard to make something out of…" Vivien Fennis was about to say something like *your terrible situation*, but of course she was too much of an old hand for that, too smart and too kind to mess up this proud-mom moment she was giving him. "Out of your life in this new world. New universe, really. It's still so hard to believe or even understand."

"You have the makings of a first-class scientific education there," Conrad chimed in. "Even if it's not the accredited type. Life experience has to count for something, doesn't it? Maybe someday…"

"This all has to stay secret, Conrad—me, the Otherland network, everything. If it ever becomes public, there will be lawsuits for decades over who owns the network. It's worth gazillions—it'll be torn apart by the military looking for weapons-quality code, at the very least. You know that." Orlando tried to puncture his dad's fantasies gently, but they did have to be punctured: Conrad came up with hopeful, impractical plans every few months, and some of them made the maroon robot body seem positively normal. "Look, the chances are that I'm not ever going to live in the real world again. I'm sorry. I wish I could have had a grown-up life here and done all the things you guys wanted for me." He took a breath: he found himself getting angry and he didn't want to, but why did everyone keep projecting their ridiculous expectations and ideas onto him? He more or less figured on getting it from his parents, but Sam's lack of trust in him was still hurting. "Anyway, it doesn't matter. This is a lot better than being dead. Don't worry about me. Like you said, the network's a whole new universe and I'm the one who gets to explore it. I'm happy."

Happy or not, he was beginning to feel like he couldn't breathe. He did his best to be cheerful as he said his goodbyes, even allowing his mother and father to give the robot-body a hug, although it was a weird and uncomfortable experience, probably even for Conrad. As he sat the mechanical form down in a chair so it wouldn't fall over when he was no longer animating it, Orlando was finding it harder and harder to hide his ugly mood. Getting out of that horrible, whirring prison and back into the freedom of the network was like finally being allowed to take off a scratchily ill-fitting Christmas sweater after the aunt who gave it to him had finally gone home.

He had half an hour to kill before the meeting of the Worldwalkers Society. He wandered the streets of P. G. Wodehouse's London, thinking.

Before Dread, this simulation world had been a shiny little confection of unadulterated good cheer, a London where the poor were content to be that way and the unguilty rich could concentrate on important things, like eating a really good breakfast and avoiding dragonish aunts (who could pop up and spoil the aforementioned breakfast, not to mention zillions of other innocent pastimes, with amazing swiftness.) Now this particular London had become a much different place. Like some Socialist demagogue that even the most paranoid Tory could barely have imagined, John Dread had first enraged and then armed the city's working class—a group in short supply in Wodehouse, but not entirely absent. A horde consisting mostly of gardeners, butlers, chauffeurs, delivery men, maids, and cab drivers had stormed the haunts of the upper crust, besieging and attacking the rich in their mansions, Kensington flats, and clubs. Whole blocks had been put to the torch as some of Wodehouse's wild-eyed Socialists and anarchists, rumored but scarcely ever seen, turned out to be more than merely rumor, and a few turned out to be dab hands at arson as well. There had even been some massacres, public slaughters of the class enemies—the class of the victims depending on which side was top of form at that particular moment of the struggle—although because of the happy-go-lucky nature of the Wodehouse world, even Dread's malign influence had waned quickly once his direct supervision ended. Still, by the time Sellars and Kunohara had got round to shutting down the particulars of Dread's intervention, some weeks after Dread himself had been dethroned, the city had descended into a sort of weird twilight state, something that combined the ruination of post-Blitz London with the freewheeling lawlessness of its earlier Elizabethan incarnation and more than a touch of the fearful shadows that had clung to the 19th century city during the Jack the Ripper crimes.

Curzon Street was full of horses and wagons these days—very few cars had survived the Unpleasantness, as the reign of terror was referred to—and Orlando had to watch what was under his feet as he made his way to Hyde Park. The squatter camps that had appeared in the first few weeks of the upheaval had become more or less permanent settlements, and with the chill evening coming down, bonfires burned everywhere. It didn't do to walk too obliviously through the park—desperately cold and hungry people had long ago obliterated the park squirrels and the water-fowl of the Serpentine, and chopped down most of the beautiful old trees for fuel. Many wealthy folk who supposed that now the Unpleasantness had ended they could return to riding along Rotten Row had discovered that although horsemeat might come into the park on its own hooves as in the old days, the only way it was leaving again was inside someone's stomach.

However, if anyone could walk heedless of personal safety in Hyde Park these days, it was Orlando Gardiner, the system's bashful demigod, and the demigod had a lot to consider.

Is it just me? Conrad and Vivien mean well. Why is it so hard to humor them? After all, I'm their only kid and it's pretty obvious things aren't going to work out the way they hoped—no graduation, no girlfriends, no marriage, no grandkids... But no matter how he thought about it, he couldn't feel anything but resentful horror at the idea of wearing that remote body. Instead of making him feel more natural it did the opposite, made the distance between his new life and his old one more acute, as though the real world had become some kind of alien planet, a toxic environment he could only enter dressed in a clanking robot-suit. The fact that the real world had become exactly that for him, and had been that way for going on three years, didn't matter: as long as he only visited his folks by phone he could half-pretend he was just putting in a year in Africa with the UN Service Corps or something, but now Conrad's compulsion to fix things was going to put a serious crimp in Orlando's hard-earned denial.

It was the stuff with Sam, though, that really got to him. He didn't want to be someone that never grew up, never changed no matter what he experienced. That was worse than the suit—that was like being truly dead. He would be a sort of ghost.

A ghost in a dead universe. Nothing changing, not me, not these worlds.

He turned back across the park toward Dover Street and the club. Crews of young toughs were gathered around rubbish-bin bonfires, singing mocking serenades to their rivals. It sounded like they might be working up to a reading, as in a "read and write," local slang for a gangfight.

They're free range, he reminded himself. *None of my business. Happens all the time, anyway, and I couldn't be here to stop them all.*

He looked at the laughing young men in scarves and fingerless gloves and stolen top hats, dapper as Dickensian urchins. Some were openly sharpening knives and razors. In the simworld's more normal operation they would be prone to no worse mischief than flinging snowballs at unsuspecting vicars and fat uncles, but even this evidence of a certain flexibility of ambition allowed by the system didn't change Orlando's feelings. They might have adjusted to the high level of local chaos, but these hooligans were still essentially the same kind of minor characters they had been in the world's earlier incarnations. It was becoming obvious that for all Kunohara's and Sellars' florid early predictions, a certain depth of reality, a flare of unpredictability, had gone out of the Otherland network for good with the death of the operating system. What was left was still fabulously complex, but ultimately lifeless.

No wonder everyone keeps asking if I'm okay. It's not me that's the problem, it's this network. Nothing really changes, or if it does, it's just like ivy growing wild in someone's yard or something—the same kinds of changes over and over and over. It's not an evolving universe, it's a big, broken toy, and even if it's more complicated than anything anyone ever made before, it's still never going to be like living in the real world. It wasn't so much a lack of other people that was depressing him, he realized—the sims who inhabited the various worlds were astonishingly diverse and self-actualized, their inter-active programming so flexible and their canned histories so comprehen-sive that in most cases you could never get to know any of them well enough to see the gaps in their near-perfect mimicry of life. But Orlando *knew* they weren't real, and that was a very big part of the problem. He was also the most powerful person in this pocket universe now that Sellars was gone and Hideki Kunohara was so frequently absent, which added to the imbalance between himself and his cohabitants.

Yeah, that's it—that's who I am, he realized. I'm not Aragorn or the Lone Ranger, I really am Superman, like Sam said. I'm one of a kind in these worlds and I'm going to spend my life doing things for people who are lesser beings—who won't ever seem quite real to me. And that's a long time to do something, because I just might live forever.

For the first time since he had been reborn into the system, his potential immortality felt more like a burden than a gift.

The meeting was underway, but a few other latecomers were still wandering into the Bertram W. Wooster Memorial Salon—a chamber dedicated, Orlando had gathered, to a former Drones Club member who had been smothered to death by a mob of crazed railway porters during the Unpleasantness. Orlando took his Coca Cola and sat at the back of the room. His first requests for the beverage had baffled the club's bar staff, but the proprietor had stepped in and now a bottle of syrup and siphon of soda water was waiting for him whenever he dropped in.

That was only on meeting nights, of course—the Wodehouse simu-lation was not really his kind of world in the first place, and Orlando had never been interested in joining clubs even when he was alive, but the Society was different.

"Before we welcome tonight's speaker," the chairman was saying, "we have a few orders of business—messages sent by members who were not able to attend tonight, but who nevertheless have information of importance to share." The chairman, Sir Reginald de Limoux, was a handsome man in his middle thirties, hawk-nosed, lean, and tanned in a way that proclaimed him in this world as a laborer or an adventurer. He was clearly not a laborer. "The gateway between Chrysostom's Byzantium and Toyland is no longer safe. Toyland is still unstable, and some kind of military group has captured the shop where the portal operates and made it their headquarters. They are wooden soldiers, I am told, so unless you are a termite, it is suggested you avoid that gateway for now." A few of the club members laughed politely. "Visitors to Toyland can still use the forest gate, which is protected by factions more sympathetic to free travel. Now, still on the subject of gateways, we have a report of a new one discovered in Benin, at an oasis just outside the city..."

As de Limoux continued with the announcements, Orlando sipped his Coke and studied him, wondering how much of the chairman's source personality remained. He was one of the Jongleur-shadows, based on copies that had been made of Felix Jongleur, the Otherland network's original master, at a time when the ancient industrialist was planning to live forever within its circuits, a god ruling over many worlds. Jongleur had indeed achieved immortality of a sort (as had many of the network's other wealthy, powerful, and largely amoral founders from the Grail Brotherhood) but not in the way he or any of them had hoped.

Instead of serving the purpose for which they had been intended, these copies, meant to be the basis for what would be immortal information-based incarnations, had been warped and changed during the last mad days of the original operating system, then the copies had been allowed to scatter and disperse through the system. Nobody knew how many of them existed, or what they had become, since there was no foolproof way to track individual sims in the huge network. One of the reasons Orlando Gardiner, in his role as the network's conservator, had become involved with the Worldwalkers Society was so that he could keep tabs on these various Grail Brotherhood clones, many of which seemed drawn to the club by a compulsion that might have been subconscious—their hidden psychological DNA at work.

Orlando had been surprised at first that Kunohara and Sellars, the two men who best understood the Otherland system, had never even *tried* to remove these remnants of the network's original masters, but they had pointed out to him that even if all the shadow-copies could be found and identified, they were not automatically criminal themselves, any more than the children of a thief could be assumed to be inherently dishonest, and that even the least pleasant of the Grail Brotherhood originals were no worse than many other nasty sim personalities that were original inhabitants of some of the network worlds. It had been the Grail masters' personal wealth and power, and also their control over the network from the outside, that had made them dangerous. Inside the network these clones and imitations started over from scratch, some with admitted personality defects which cropped up in most incarnations, but others with a surprising capacity to become decent citizens. As he watched the Society's chairman at work, Orlando thought that this particular version of Jongleur, Sir Reginald de Limoux, seemed somewhere in the middle—sharp-tempered and obviously ambitious, but certainly no out-and-out villain.

The other legacy granted to the Grail shadows and a few similar beings that the old operating system had created—some based on Orlando's real friends and acquaintances, like the Englishman Paul Jonas—was that they alone of all the simulated souls on the network could travel with relative freedom between the network worlds, or even knew that there were worlds outside the simulation in which they lived. Unlike Orlando, most of these travelers did not understand what they were, or what kind of universe they lived in, but they did have a freedom of thought that set them apart from the rest of the sims. In fact, they were the closest thing to equals Orlando Gardiner had these days. Sitting around in the Drones Club bar after a Worldwalker meeting, listening to the humorous stories and impossible boasts of Society members, was the closest thing to the happiness he had once found in the adventurers' taverns of his old Middle Country game.

And, of course, even in their wildest stories, these walkers-of-worlds brought back gems of information which Orlando found very useful. He might be a ranger with godlike powers, but he still couldn't stamp out every untended campfire in four hundred different worlds.

When the chairman had finished his announcements, the featured speaker took the lectern and began to describe the findings from his most recent expedition. This gentleman seemed to have spent most of his time in Troy and Xanadu, two simworlds Orlando knew well, so he let his attention drift to other things. He became so caught up in wondering how to re-connect with Sam that he did not realize for several moments that someone who had harrumphed significantly several times behind him had given up on subtlety and was now tapping on his shoulder.

"Mr. Roland? Someone urgently wishes to speak with you." The tapper was the proprietor of the Drones Club, a tall, poker-faced fellow named Jeeves who, rumor suggested, had been in some kind of domestic service before the Unpleasantness but had risen very high, very quickly during those unstable times. "Did you hear me, Mr. Roland?"

Orlando had almost forgotten his local pseudonym. "Sorry, sorry. Someone to see me?" Could it be Beezle again, dressed for maximum embarrassment value in a cummerbund or pith helmet? But it was only when Orlando was in Rivendell, the closest thing to a refuge he had, that the agent wasn't allowed to contact him directly: it was hard to relax and enjoy the peaceful singing of the elves and the flickering of firelight when you were getting four or five calls an hour from a virtual bug with the raspy voice and abrupt manners of an old-school Brooklyn cabbie.

"Yes, a visitor, sir," said Jeeves, leaning close. "A young lady. Very attractive, if I may say so, but perhaps a bit…confused. I've taken the liberty of installing her in one of the unused lounges—some of the older members are less than open-minded about women in the club, even now. I do beg pardon for interrupting you—she said it couldn't wait, and it seemed from her conversation that it might be something with which you would wish to deal…discreetly."

Orlando looked at the man's somber mouth, his tall, intelligent brow. Jeeves was not supposed to know who the Worldwalkers really were—on the surface, they were only a stuffily ordinary club of travelers and adventurers who met at the Drones Club once a month—let alone have even an inkling of Orlando Gardiner's true nature, but he had always treated Orlando with extra care and a certain glint in the eye, as though he suspected him of being more than he appeared. Orlando in turn had often wondered whether the club's new owner weren't a

Worldwalker himself, albeit an undiscovered one. If so, he had found the perfect place to hide, right under the Society's nose. Orlando made a mental note to do some research on this Jeeves fellow when he had some spare time.

The Society members in the Wooster Salon had fallen into civilized but contentious discussion about a proposed new expedition. Orlando knew they would be batting it around for at least half an hour, and probably wouldn't finish the discussion this month. Expeditions took resources, and those Worldwalkers who were independently wealthy in one simworld could seldom move valuables or tangible resources from one simulation to another. In fact, the only really certain, completely portable capital was knowledge, and that was one of the reasons most Society members valued their membership above anything except their lives. Orlando hated to miss the rest of the meeting, but nothing was going to happen here tonight he couldn't pick up later, in the bar.

Jeeves led him to the doorway of the lounge before sliding away down the corridor, silent as a cat burglar. Orlando stepped into the snug room and almost knocked over a young woman dressed in a pale frock who was warming herself before the coal fire. It was only as he put out a hand to steady himself that he realized he was still carrying his Coca-Cola.

"Sorry," he said and balanced the glass on the narrow mantel. "My name is Roland. I'm told you were looking for me."

She was pretty, as Jeeves had suggested, in a wide-eyed, consumptive sort of way, the darkness of her curly hair and the blush on her cheek only emphasizing the almost translucent pallor of her skin. She returned his stare a little wildly, as though at any moment he might lunge at her—or, worse, laugh at her. "Perhaps I am mistaken," she said. "I was told…I understood the person I was seeking could be found here. The name Roland was given to me. I'm looking for Orlando Gardiner." She peered at him as though she might be nearsighted, or as though she were looking for a resemblance in a newly-met, very distant relative, then her face fell. "But you are not him. I have never seen you before"

He was astonished to hear his real name spoken aloud by a sim, and almost equally surprised to be told he was not himself, but hearing her voice confirmed what he had guessed when he had first seen her. This young woman was another Avialle Jongleur shadow, either one of the original copies of Felix Jongleur's dead daughter or a variant coined from those copies in the last days of the operating system. The original Avialle had been obsessively in love with the Englishman Paul Jonas, and most of the copies, certainly all those that had been made from the living Avialle after she met Jonas, had continued this infatuation. They had popped up in numerous guises during Jonas' amnesiac wanderings through the Otherland network, sometimes encouraging him, sometimes actively aiding him, other times brokenly pleading for his love or understanding.

But none of them had ever had much or anything to do with Orlando, and he had no idea why one should be seeking him now, especially under his real name.

"You say you haven't seen me before." He gestured for her to sit down—she seemed prepared to bolt like a rabbit at the slightest noise, and he was curious now. "I have to admit, I don't recognize you either. I do know someone named Orlando Gardiner, however, and I might be able to get a message to him. Can you tell me something of your problem?" The surroundings were beginning to get to him, he realized: he was starting to sound like one of this Wodehouse simworld's native characters.

"Oh. You...you know him?" She looked a little more hopeful, but it was a miserable sort of hope, as though she had been told that instead of torture she would be given a mercifully swift death. "Where can I find him?"

"You can give me a message. I promise he'll hear it."

She brought a hand to her mouth, hesitating. She was very pale, shaking a little, but Orlando could see now that there was a determination behind the doe-eyes that belied her outward appearance. *She's taken some risk to come here,* he thought. *She must want to get this message to me very badly.* "Very well," she said at last. "My shame could not be any greater. I will trust to your discretion, Mr. Roland. I will trust you to behave like a gentleman.

"Please tell Mr. Gardiner that I need to see him as soon as possible. I am in terrible straits. Terrible. If he does not come to me I do not know what I shall do." Her reserve suddenly fell apart; tears welled in her eyes. "I am desperate, Mr. Roland!"

"But why?" Orlando hunted vainly for a handkerchief, but she had already produced one of her own from her sleeve and was dabbing at her face. "I'm sorry, Miss…Mrs….I'm afraid I don't know your name. Look, I don't want to make things worse, but I really do have to know why you want to speak with him before I can pass along your message."

She looked at him, eyes still wet, and seemed to come to a decision. Her lip stopped trembling. "It is not such an unusual story in this wicked world of ours, Mr. Roland. My name is Livia Bard. I am an unmarried woman and I am with child. The child is Mr. Gardiner's."

Then, as though they had reached the climax of a particularly good magic trick, the young woman simply vanished into thin air.

Find one single woman in only four hundred or so different sim-worlds, each world with life-size geography, maybe a few million simulated citizens, and no central tracking system? Yeah, problem not. Piece of cake. He couldn't even amuse himself these days. "Beezle? Any word back on that Amazon place, that Lost World thing with the dinosaurs? What's it called?"

"Maple White Land, boss. Yeah, we got a confirmed sighting. It seems like another Avialle Jongleur shadow, awright, but she looks different and she's using a different name—Valda Jackson, something like that. Older, too, if our informant's right. And she don't act much like a pregnant lady, either. She leads expeditions into the interior and she drinks like a fish."

"Fenfen." He looked around the spacious room, frowning. The river was loudly musical outside and the air smelled of green things, but it wasn't as soothing as it usually was. He was beginning to find Rivendell less comfortable than it had been, and even though he now permitted Beezle to contact him inside the simulation without having to make an actual appearance, it seemed less and less like the best place for this kind of work. After all, he didn't want to turn the Last Homely House, the ideal of his childhood, into the permanently busy capitol of Orlando Gardiner Land. Maybe he needed to think about moving his base of operations. "Three months now and this woman might as well have been drezzed right out of the network code for all I can find out about her. Where is she?"

"It's just a search operation, boss. Like you always say, there ain't no central registry office. It takes time. But seems to me, time's one thing you definitely got plenty of."

"When I want philosophy, I'll buy a plug-in module. When you get hold of Sam, ask if we can meet somewhere different this time. Her choice."

"Your wish is my command, O master."

"It's really pretty, isn't it? I always liked Japanese teahouses and stuff."

Orlando wrinkled his nose. "I think that's the first time I ever heard you use the word 'pretty' except when you're on something like, 'That's a pretty stupid idea, Gardiner.'"

Sam Fredericks frowned a little, but her samurai sim turned it into a scowl that might have graced a Noh mask. "What's that supposed to mean? That I'm turning all girlie or something?"

"No, no." He was depressed, now. He had only had a few brief visits with Sam since the whole Livia Bard thing had started, and he had missed her, but they still seemed to be out of rhythm with each other. "I just didn't expect you to pick a place like this for us to meet."

"You're always talking about how much you like it." She looked out from the teahouse. Beyond the open panels of the wall and beyond the tiny, orderly garden of rocks and sand and small trees, the wooden roofs of the city stretched away on all sides. On the far side of the Nihon-Bashi, the stately wooden arch across the Sumida, Edo Castle loomed proudly.

"Well, I like the war part, although that's mostly over for this cycle— the shogun has pretty much settled in for good. The armor is *ho dzang*, too."

"Ho dzang! I haven't heard anyone say that for a long time." She saw the look on his face and went on with nervous haste, "Yeah, that armor is great, especially those helmets with the sticking-up things—makes your elves almost look dull. I'm not crazy about the music, though. I always thought it sounded like unhappy cats."

Orlando clapped his hands and sent away the geisha who had been quietly playing *Jiuta* on her shamisen. The only singing now was the hoarse chant of a water-seller that drifted up from the street below. "Better?"

"I guess." She looked at him carefully. "Sorry I've been so hard to get hold of. How's your noble quest?"

"Noble quest? Like the kind we used to have back in the Middle Country?" He fought off a moment of panic—did she think he hadn't changed at all? "You mean about the pregnant woman."

"Yes." She made herself smile. "And it is a noble quest, Orlando, because you're a noble quest kind of guy."

"Except that apparently I impregnated this poor girl and then deserted her. Not really the kind of thing people usually call noble."

Sam frowned, but this time because she was irritated with his flippancy. "But you didn't do it. Just because there's some evil clone version of you running around..."

"Maybe, but I don't think so. There's never been any other sign of another version of me, not even a hint. Believe me, I've had Beezle combing every record since we started up the network again. I'd know."

"I thought there wasn't any main archive or whatever."

"There isn't, but there's the informal one that Kunohara started when he and Sellars got the system running again, and most of the individual worlds have their own records that are part of the simulation. For instance, the Wodehouse place where I met this woman started out pretty much like the real early 20th Century London, so there are birth records and death records and telephone directories and everything. The data is a bit hinky sometimes because it's sort of a comedy world, but there certainly wasn't any mention of a Livia Bard in any of those."

"So you think she must come from somewhere else, right? She's one of those travelers, the ones that can cross from one world to another. I can't remember—were all the Jongleur girl's shadows like that?"

He shook his head, felt the topknot bob. "I don't know. They've always been the weirdest of all the shadows because the operating system hacked them around so much." He sat back, toying with his bowl of tea. It was easy to believe his mystery woman could think she was pregnant—many of the Avialle-shadows thought they were pregnant, because the original had been, at least for a little while. Orlando had gone back and forth through Sellars' history and Kunohara's margin notes trying to make sense of it, even though he'd heard some of the story from Paul Jonas' own mouth—it was a bizarre bit of this simiverse's history and hard to figure out.

"Orlando?"

"Sorry, Sam. I was thinking about something."

"I just wanted to ask you…are you absolutely sure that…that you didn't do it?"

"Do what…? Fenfen, Fredericks, you mean get her pregnant?" He felt his cheeks reddening in a most un-samurai manner.

Sam looked worried. "I didn't mean to embarrass you."

He shook his head, although he definitely was embarrassed. He had been a fourteen year old invalid when he died, a boy denied a normal childhood or adolescence. Gifted with a life after death, with health and vigor beyond anything he had ever known, not to mention an almost complete lack of adult supervision, he had of course experimented. At first the knowledge that his partners were in some ways no more real than what you could rent on the crudest kind of interactive pornodes hadn't bothered him, any more than the literal two-dimensionality of women in girlie magazines disturbed earlier generations, but the novelty had warn off fast, leaving him lonely and more than a little disgusted with the whole situation. Also, because he was uncomfortable with their origins, he had made a personal rule never to get involved with any of the Worldwalker Society's female members, so he found himself more or less unable to date anyone with actual free will.

Of course, love and sex weren't things he'd ever been very comfortable talking to Sam Fredericks about, anyway. "Let's just put it this way," he said at last. "If I had been in a situation where it could have happened, I'd remember. But, Sam, that doesn't even matter. This isn't a real person and it's not a real pregnancy—she's a construct!"

"Didn't all those What's-her-name Jongleur girls have a pregnancy thing, anyway? They all thought they were, or some of them did, or something?"

"Avialle Jongleur. Yes, and like I said, they aren't real pregnancies. But that's not the point. The question is, why does *this* one know my real name and why does she think it's my baby?"

Sam slowly nodded. "Yeah, that all barks pretty drastically. So what are you going to do?"

"I wish I knew. I've been looking for months, but she's just vanished. Beezle wants me to authorize a bunch of mini-Beezles so we can search the system more effectively—not just for this one woman, but any time we need to. It's not a bad idea, really, but I'm not sure I want to be the Napoleon of an army of bugs."

Sam Fredericks set down her tea and sat back. "You seem…I don't know, a little more cheerful than the last couple of times I saw you."

He shrugged. "I keep busy. I thought you were the one who was depressed."

"Scanmaster. I was probably locked off with you for some reason."

Orlando smiled. "Probably."

Sam stirred. "I brought you something. Can you import it into the network? It's on the top level of my system, labeled 'Orlando.'"

"You brought me something?"

"You don't think I'd forget your birthday, do you?"

He had half-forgotten, himself. "Actually, it's tomorrow." It was strange how little something like a birthday meant when you didn't go to school and you had hardly any friends—any normal friends, that is.

"I know that, but I won't see you tomorrow, will I?"

"Seventeen years old. I'm an old man, now." It wasn't funny, really—progeria, the disease that had ruined and eventually ended his previous life, was a condition that turned children into doddering ancients and then killed them, mostly before they had even reached their teenage years.

"Old man—hah! You're younger than me, so six that noise." A small, gift-wrapped package appeared on the low table. "Good, you found it. Open it."

He took off the lid and looked at the thing nestled on virtual cotton in the virtual box. "It's really nice, Sam."

"Happy birthday, Gardino. Don't just stare at it—it's a friendship bracelet, you idiot. You have to read what it says."

He turned the simple silver bracelet. The inscription said, *To Orlando from Sam. Friends Forever.* For a moment he didn't trust his voice. "Thanks."

"I know there are places you go where you can't wear it, but I spent a lot of time thinking, like, what can you get someone who can have anything in the whole world—rocket cars, a live pet dinosaur, you name it? All I've got to give you that you can't get in one of these worlds is me. We're utterly friends, Gardiner, and you remember that. Utterly. No matter what. As long as we both live."

Orlando was very grateful that this sim was too *bushi* to cry—the blushing had been bad enough. "Yeah," he said. "No matter what." He took a deep breath. "Hey, you want to go for a walk before you have to leave? I'll show you a little of the Tokaido—that's kind of the main road. It's the best place to sightsee. If we're lucky, a few of the daimyos will still be coming into town. They're the nobles, and they have to make a pil-grimage here twice a year. Some of them come in with thousands of retainers and soldiers, horses and flags and concubines and all that fen, a big parade. It's like Samurai Disneyland."

"You really know this place!"

"I keep busy."

"You left tonight open, didn't you?" Beezle asked as Orlando re-ani-mated his Rivendell sim. "Your parents have got plans."

"Oh, jeez, right, my birthday dinner. That means they'll want me to wear that *tchi seen* robot body. Conrad's probably hooked it up with an air-hose so I can blow out the candles on my cake." He resented tromping around in that thing so much that he had been avoiding seeing his parents because of it. Still, in just three visits he'd broken a table-leg and several vases, and pulled a door off its hinges by accident. The thing had very delicate hand-responses, but the rest of it was meant for slogging around in mine shafts or in the holds of sunken ships and was about as graceful as an elephant on roller skates. Orlando didn't want to hurt their feelings, and Conrad was so proud of his idea, but he just hated it.

It's not as if I didn't have enough to deal with. Just at the moment, two Society members were stuck in the House simulation in the middle of an armed uprising and unable to escape, there was a programming glitch or something like it causing mutations in the plant life of Bronte World so that Haworth Parsonage was under siege by carnivorous cacti, and he still had no idea of where Livia Bard might be, let alone any explanation for her weird accusation. *Yeah, I keep busy.*

"Any decision yet on letting me whip up some sub-agents, boss?"

"I'm still thinking about it."

"Well, don't hurt yourself—I hear that thinking stuff ain't for beginners. You ready to go to your folks? 'Cause you got an urgent message from that Elrond guy you gotta deal with first. He needs you downstairs right now."

"Jeez, it never stops. Make the connection to that locking toy robot at my parents', will you? After I finish downstairs I'll duck into a closet or something and go directly."

"Yeah, wouldn't want to screw up the continuity." It sounded suspiciously like sarcasm. "Don't worry, boss. I'm on it. Just go see Elrond."

He was halfway down the delicate wooden staircase between the small house that he called his home and the central buildings when the thought occurred to him, *Why the hell would Beezle be passing message for Elrond? Rivendell doesn't work that way.*

All questions were answered when he walked into the main hall and discovered his mother, father, and several score elves, dwarves, and assorted other Middle-Earthers waiting for him.

"Surprise!" most of them shouted. "Happy Birthday!"

Orlando stopped just inside the doorway, dumbfounded. The hall was strung with cloth-of-gold bunting. Candles burned everywhere, and huge trestle tables stood against the walls, covered with food and drink. His mother came up and threw her arms around him, kissed him and hugged him. When she leaned back she looked at him worriedly, but she was also flushed with excitement. "Is this okay? You said your network can deal with incongruities. This won't spoil anything, will it?"

"It's fine, Vivien. I'm just...well, surprised."

She was wearing elven costume, a long dress in shades of butter yellow and pale beige, and had piled her hair up on top of her head where it was held by diamond pins. "Do I look funny?" she asked. "That nice Arwen girl gave me these hair things. I think that's her name—I don't remember her from when I read the books, but it was a long time ago."

"That nice Arwen girl?" Orlando couldn't help smiling. "Yeah, you look great."

Conrad came up with a goblet in one hand. "Those dwarves like to drink, don't they? What do you think? Did we surprise you?"

Orlando could only nod, appalled and touched. The party already seemed in high gear. Someone put a cup of ale in his hands. Elrond came up and bowed to Orlando's parents. "Regards to you on this festive day, Tharagorn," the elf said. "You are always an ornament to our house."

To Orlando's horror, Vivien actually began to flirt with Elrond, but the master of the house accepted it with good humor. Even more fortunately, Conrad had already wandered off to look more closely at the ceiling joists—he was a hobbyist carpenter—so at least Orlando didn't have to worry about his father picking a jealous fight with an elven lord.

Arwen Undomiel, Elrond's daughter—the one his mother had referred to as a "nice girl"—was standing with her love, Aragorn, who was dressed in a tattered cloak and seemed to have come straight in off the road. The man whose name Orlando had more or less borrowed for his incarnation in this world left his betrothed's side long enough to come and clasp Orlando's hand. "Good wishes, cousin. We have not met in many a long year. I did not know anyone outside the halfling lands celebrated the day of their birth in this manner."

"Blame my parents."

"There is no blame. They are noble folk." Aragorn embraced him, then returned to Arwen's side, where her brothers Elladan and Elrohir now also stood, as travel-worn as Aragorn, as though they had all rode fast and far to be here. The elven princess raised her glass toward Orlando in a silent salute. He would have been flattered if he hadn't known it was all make-believe, just programming.

"I don't even want to know how you arranged this, Vivien," he said to his mother.

"Beezle helped." She pointed to a small, disreputable, and extremely hairy-footed figure on the far side of the room, who was busy out-drinking three dwarves from Dale. "He's almost human, isn't he?"

"Who *isn't?*" He hugged her again. "Thanks. I really didn't expect it."

Vivien was asking Elrond something domestic—he thought he heard her use the phrase "finding kitchen help"—when Orlando's attention was suddenly drawn to a pale shape moving through the throng at the center of the hall. For a moment he could only stare, wondering which Tolkien character this was, why she looked so familiar.

"Oh my God," he said. "It's *her!*"

He was across the room before Vivien finished asking him where he was going. He caught the woman in white as she stepped into Hall of Fire. The unsteady light of the flames made her seem a phantom, but if it was not Livia Bard herself who stood before him, it was her exact duplicate.

She looked up at his approach, startled and even a little frightened. "What do you want?"

He realized the look on his face might very well be something that would frighten anyone. After months of searching, to have her simply walk past him...! "Miss Bard. Livia. I've been looking for you."

She turned to face him and he had a second shock. Beneath the flowing white gown, she was very obviously several months pregnant. "Who are you?" She stared, then blinked. "Can it be? Are you truly him...?"

And then she disappeared again.

"Beezle!" he bellowed. "That was her! Right here, then she disappeared! Where did she go?"

"Couldn't tell you boss. Hang on, let me just roll Snori here off me, or whatever his name is, and I'll be right with you."

By the time his parents and his faithful software agent reached him, Orlando was down on his knees on the floor of the Hall of Fire, pounding on the boards in frustration. Conrad and Vivien suggested calling off the feast, but Orlando knew it was for them as much as himself, so he let himself be led back to the party. Still, despite all the diversions and distractions offered by Rivendell in holiday mode, he hardly noticed what was going on around him. As soon as he could decently manage it he made his excuses and headed for bed, pausing on his way up to his room to have a word with Beezle.

"Okay, you have my permission—I've run out of ideas. Put together your little army of sub-agents. But do me a favor and don't make them bugs, huh? I'm going to have to visit Kunohara, and I'll get enough of the things there to last me for years."

"Will do, boss."

Orlando went to bed. Bongo Fluffernutter stayed up late drinking with the dwarves from Dale. He showed them how it was possible to belch several whole stanzas of *The Lay of Queen Beruthiel*, and also that there was a point at which even dwarves should stop drinking.

Elves don't complain, but Elrond's folk had a terrible mess to deal with the next morning.

"Mr. Gardiner, it is always a pleasure to see you, but I hope you will be understanding." Kunohara gestured for him to sit on one of the chairs that looked out from the balcony across the expanse of forest-high grass and the undergrowth that loomed beyond it like a frozen tsunami wave. He was a small, trim man in a modern-style kimono who appeared to be in early middle-age, or at least his sim always looked that way, his black hair and beard both gray-flecked. "My time is very limited these days. A nephew of mine—barely out of adolescence, or so it seems—is leading a hostile takeover against me. They claim too much of the family company's money has been spent on what they call 'the amusements of the chairman.' Who would be me, and this simulation would be one of the amusements, except they do not know it still exists." He glowered. "A company built with my patents, and they think to take it away from me. I will crush them, of course, but it is sad for the family and irritating for me. It wastes a great deal of my resources."

Orlando nodded. "I appreciate you making time for me." He had never quite warmed to Hideki Kunohara, not having known him as well as some of his other companions had; there were ways in which Kunohara never made himself really available, even when he was sitting right in front of you, chatting in a seemingly amiable, open way. Orlando had always wondered what the man was really thinking, and because of that had never entirely trusted him, but with Sellars gone, Kunohara understood the system's underlying logic better than anyone alive.

If there is such a thing as logic involved, Orlando thought sourly.

"I've reviewed your messages," Kunohara said, then stopped suddenly to watch a striking black and orange butterfly the size of a small plane flit down into their field of view, almost touch the ground, then lift away again, wings flashing in the sunshine. "A heleconid," he announced. "*Numata*, it looks like. Nice to see them so near the station."

Hideki Kunohara's house was a recycled building far too large to make a satisfactory dwelling for anything less substantial than a king's household, or at least it would have been in the real world, where people were limited by various petty annoyances like the laws of physics, but size was not such an issue in a private node where travel could be instantaneous. The house had formerly been a scientific station that Kunohara had leased to governments and the biology departments of universities because all visitors to Kunohara's world found themselves smaller than most of the insects and other invertebrate fauna. It was a fascinating if occasionally terrifying perspective: the research station had been destroyed by soldier ants and all the human sims in it killed during the upheavals of the network. Kunohara's own house had also been ruined. The balcony on which he and Orlando sat now had originally been one of the raised viewing stations which ran the length of the southern face of the complex's main building; as they talked, Orlando could watch all kinds of monstrous animals feeding and being fed upon in the field sloping away below them, including birds the size of passenger jets tugging worms that seemed as long as subway trains out of the damp morning ground.

"Anyway, I've read your messages and I don't really have much to say, Mr. Gardiner. Have you considered the possibility she's someone from outside the network? A real person who discovered your name somewhere, or even someone who knows you and is playing a trick?"

"That would be worse than the mystery we have," said Orlando. "Because unless it was one of my friends, and I can't quite picture any of them thinking this was funny, it would mean that our security is compromised. This network is supposed to be a secret."

"We have a few people on the outside who actively help us maintain it as a distributed network."

"Yeah, but even those people don't know about *me*."

Kunohara nodded. "The possibility of this being the work of some outsider does not seem likely, I grant you."

"I think there must be a shadow-Orlando, although I've never seen one or heard even a hint of one before now."

"That raises questions, too, Mr. Gardiner. It is possible that a duplicate of you might exist, and also possible that it could have escaped our notice for almost three years—it is a big network after all. It is even possible that this duplicate uses your real name, still without attracting our attention. But there still remains one question that would have to be answered before we could accept this hypothesis as a valid theory."

"I know." Orlando squinted at a pair of what looked like flies chasing each other across the tops of the tree-tall grass, iridescent objects the size of taxis performing a midair *pas de deux* with their glassy wings sparking light. He wasn't nuts about bugs in the first place, let alone bugs that were a lot bigger than he was, but there were moments like this when he could almost understand Kunohara's world, if not Kunohara himself. "The problem with the shadow-Orlando theory is how Livia Bard knew *I* had something to do with Orlando Gardiner when she found me in the Wodehouse world—and how she found me again in the Tolkien world. How could she track me like that?"

"The copies derived from Felix Jongleur's daughter really are remarkable, as you know," said Kunohara. "Some of the Avialle-shadows seem able to move at will from one simulation to another. Others can travel between simulations, but only in the workaday manner that your Worldwalkers employ, using the gateways. And some of the Avialles do not seem to move out of their home simulations at all, although those versions usually end up holding some powerful or unusual position in their worlds."

"Yeah, like the one we met in the freezer in the cartoon Kitchen world. I guess the original Avialle—the real person—was utterly important to the old operating system, so maybe all her shadows are still kind of important to the system." Something tugged at him, an idea that would not quite form. "But why? I mean, we've got a whole different operating system now, right?"

"In part, but it's far more complicated than that." Kunohara clicked his tongue against his teeth. "As you no doubt remember, all the remnants of the old operating system—that poor tortured creature known as the Other—could not be removed from the network. That is one of the reasons we suspected that some of its attempts to create a kind of life, as it did once already with raw materials from Sellars' own experimentation, might have permeated the entire network—the "simiverse" as

Sellars named it—and changed it into another order of thing entirely. A sort of living, evolving entity."

"But it didn't turn out to be that way. That's what you're always saying."

"It's true, there's been no evidence of it. We've seen no other information creatures like the ones it grew before, which are now gone. Neither has there been any sign of the evolutionary process beginning again in some other manner—not a one. You can trust me on that, Mr. Gardiner—the permutations of life, and now of pseudo-life, are my passion, and I have looked long and hard for any evidence of it on the current network. It is a fantastically complex creation, but essentially it has become what any other network is—an unliving artifact. I'm afraid that with the death of the Other and the escape of all its information-creatures into space, the network is now effectively dead."

Orlando had more or less known this—after all, the flatness of things, the lack of real change, had been troubling him for months—but being told it in such a categorical manner by Kunohara was a bit like being punched in the stomach. "But the sims themselves reproduce within their simworlds. They have babies. The animals have little animals. Look at your bugs here—they lay eggs, don't they? Make little giant baby bugs?"

"Yes, but only within the matrix of the simulations. It is part of the program for the sims to *appear* to reproduce, but it is not true life, any more than it would be if you wrote a story in which someone gave birth. New life in this system is a construct. Look at your Avialle-shadows— some of them have perpetual pregnancies, as is probably the case with the one you are seeking. But that is not a real pregnancy; it is a programmed trait, like the color of a sim's hair or how fast it can run."

"But the last time I saw her, she looked really pregnant! None of the Avialle-shadows ever get to the point of showing their pregnancy. I read that in your own notes."

Kunohara shook his head. "Mr. Gardiner, you are a smart young man and a very fine conservator of the network worlds and I'm sure that wherever he now is, Patrick Sellars is proud that he chose you, but you are not a scientist—not yet, anyway. Do you know for certain that she really *did* have the belly of a woman several months pregnant, or are you basing this entirely on what you think you saw from a distance of several meters for a period of just a few seconds? The simulated people can be nearly as psychologically complex as real people. Perhaps she feels herself to be with child but her belly does not grow—it never will grow, but she does not know this—so she pads herself with a pillow or some similar object, out of anxiety, perhaps. No, Mr. Gardiner, my friend, when you or I can examine her and see that she truly does have an advancing pregnancy, then we can begin to wonder about how she differs from the other Avialle Jongleur shadows. Until that time, I urge you not to jump to conclusions."

Orlando didn't particularly like being lectured. "So you're saying that this whole weird mess is just another hysterical Avialle-clone who's stumbled on my name somehow—nothing more, nothing less."

"I am saying nothing about what it *is*, Mr. Gardiner, because I do not have enough information." Kunohara steepled his fingers and slowly shook his head. "I am sharing what I suspect, and also what I strongly doubt. People spent trillions of credits on this network to make things *appear* as real as possible, but please do not confuse appearance with reality, and especially do not mistake the appearance of reproduction and other symptoms of life, however sophisticated, with real reproduction and actual life. Life is a very stubborn phenomenon that uses an astonishing number of strategies to perpetuate itself. What this network does is mimic those processes for the benefit of its human users, to create a realistic environment—an experience not tremendously different from an amusement park ride. But the gap between the simulated thing and the actual process it imitates is vast indeed. Now, forgive me, but I have kept my lawyers waiting for half an hour."

Orlando thanked him, but Kunohara was already making his call and only nodded. Orlando left him talking to himself, or so it appeared, as he gazed out across his supersized domain. Flowers tall as redwoods creaked and swayed in the freshening breeze.

Beezle Bug was waiting for Orlando back in his bedroom at Rivendell. Out of the elven public eye and with the rules now relaxed, the agent wasn't even bothering to masquerade as a hobbit, but was back in his usual form, something that could have been a black dustmop with eyes, a cartoon spider, or even a particularly disturbing Rorschach ink blot. Today Beezle had enhanced these natural good looks with a floppy, horizontally-striped top hat. He grinned toothily and did a little hairy-legged dance as Orlando came in.

"You're in a good mood."

"You don't sound like you are, boss. Any luck with Kunohara?"

"Nothing that cleared anything up. I think he thinks I'm overreacting."

"Well, I know what will cheer you up. You can meet my crew."

"Your what? Oh, the sub-agents. Look, Beezle, I don't think I'm up to having a bunch of bugs crawl all over me…"

"No bugs—you already told me." The agent swept off his new hat and a horde of small shapes began to jump out of it. Within seconds they were filling the floor all around him. "I kind of swiped the idea from the Dr. Seuss world. Meet Little Cats A1 through A99, B1 through B99, C1 through C99…"

"I get the drift." Already Orlando was ankle deep in a lagoon of tiny, hatted cats. "I don't need to meet all, what, 2600 of them. I suppose I should count my blessings you didn't steal your idea out of *Hop On Pop*." He squinted at the little cats which were now clambering up the bedclothes and trampolining across his pillow. "How the hell are these things going to get the kind of information we need discreetly? They're not exactly inconspicuous, are they?"

"Boss, boss." If Beezle had a neck, he would have been shaking his head. Instead, he was doing a sort of hairy hula. "They're my subagents. You don't think I go out looking for information looking like this, do you? Looking like anything, for that matter? I'm gear—good gear. I just interface with the stuff directly at machine level, and so will they. I just thought the reports would be more fun this way."

"Great." Beezle was the second person in an hour—second thing, anyway—to tell him that he was making the mistake of judging matters by face value. The network was seductive that way—so much time and money spent to make the worlds seem like real places. Reminded, he looked at his virtual wrist (his Tharagorn wrist since he was in Rivendell) at the virtual friendship bracelet he now wore on it. It seemed like a real bracelet, but it wasn't; it hadn't ever been real, but it meant as much as or more than any actual pieces of shaped metal, because the friendship it represented *was* real.

*Chizz, hold on...*he thought. There was the core of an idea there, something that he needed to think about, but he was distracted as the living cat-carpet abruptly swirled up into a spinning cloud of miniature felines, then vanished back into Beezle's hat with a loud *pop*. "Hey, boss, I forgot to tell you. They need you back in that P. G. Wodehouse simulation—someone left a note in your box at the club."

"But the next meeting's not for weeks."

"Emergency get-together of the steering committee, and you're in the rotation."

"I don't have time. Send an excuse for me."

"Actually, you might want to go. They're trying to get rid of whatsisname, de Limoux, the chairman."

"What for?"

"Seems a couple of the women members are going to have babies and they say ol' Sir Reggie's the daddy."

"I had nothing to do with it!" Sir Reginald was almost white with anger. "With either of them! I scarcely even know Edwina Hayes, and I despise that Macapan woman. Everyone knows that."

Orlando himself only barely recognized the first name: Mrs. Hayes was a quiet, colorless woman who seemed to owe her sim existence to some early equipment tests by one of the Grail Project's female engineers. The second was a shadow of Ymona Dedoblanco, a gorgon who had been the only woman in the Grail Brotherhood's inner circle. The real woman could fairly be termed a monster, but Maisie Macapan merely seemed to incorporate some of her less murderous, albeit still irritating, faults, namely self-absorption almost to the point of megalomania. Like her template, she also had a full measure of ambition, which was why she and the Jongleur-shadow, Sir Reginald, often found themselves at cross-purposes.

"Why aren't the two women here?" Orlando asked. "Shouldn't de Limoux should have a chance to confront his accusers?"

"Bless you, Roland, you are an honorable man," said Sir Reginald. "Yes, where are they? Why this star-chamber inquisition, based on accusations that are ridiculous on their face? Everyone knows I am a happily married man, with a wife and family in Third Republic Paris."

"Happily married men may stray," suggested a mustached traveler named Renzi whom Orlando suspected of being the shadow of another of the network's early engineers, or possibly even a much-degraded version of his friend Paul Jonas.

"But not with the Macapan!" De Limoux seemed more offended by that idea than by the accusation itself. "I would sooner throw myself into a cage with a hungry lioness."

"The women are both unwell, Mr. Roland," Renzi explained to Orlando. "And their stories, it must be admitted, are a bit confusing. But they both swear that their charges are accurate, and although Miss Macapan is known to bear Sir Reginald some ill feeling, Mrs. Hayes does not seem like the type to invent such a thing."

"Unless the Macapan bitch bribed her," snarled de Limoux. "She would do anything to steal the chairmanship away."

"If she could bribe one, she could bribe two," Orlando said. "If she's only trying to ruin your reputation, Sir Reginald, it seems strange she should make herself one of the victims, since everyone knows she has a grudge or two against you."

"Surely you are not suggesting you believe this twaddle, Mr. Roland?"

"I'm not saying I believe or disbelieve anything, Sir Reginald. I don't have enough information. I'm just thinking out loud."

After that he let the others talk while the idea began to form. Even in its earliest shape, it was a very strange one.

— ✳ —

Orlando had the travel records of the Worldwalkers Society members in hard copy form—leather-bound books handwritten in ink, in keeping with the simulation—spread all over the wooden table that served as his desk in Rivendell. A year earlier, Orlando himself had covertly lobbied for and helped to push through the particular Society rule that mandated all members keep diaries of their travels and make them available in the Society library inside the Drones Club, and just now he was glad that he'd done it.

Orlando had noticed something very interesting about de Limoux and his two accusers and had constructed a small chart to try to make sense out of their comings and goings. He had just confirmed his suspicion and was staring at the chart, chewing the end of his pencil in something like astonishment, when he heard his agent speaking in his ear.

"*Boss?*"

"Let me guess, Beezle. You've got some news for me. There's another pregnancy at the Society and another denial of responsibility."

After a moment's pause, the agent said: "*Hey, that's pretty good, boss. How did you know about the Society thing?*"

"I'm just starting to get a few ideas."

"*Do you want to know who's involved?*"

"If the ideas I'm starting to get are right, it doesn't really matter. Let me go back to what I'm doing, Beezle. I'll let you know when I need you, and I'll probably need you soon."

"*Boss?*"

"Beezle, I'm really trying to concentrate here. Thanks for bringing me the information, now get lost, okay?"

"*It's important, Boss.*"

Orlando sighed. "What is it?"

"*Well, it's about Little Cats N42 and N45—two of my sub-agents, remember? I think you might want to see about getting them a little treat—a year's supply of fish heads or something.*"

"Fish heads...? Beezle, you are making me crazy. What the hell are you talking about?"

"*Just as a reward, maybe. Because they found your girlfriend.*"

"They..." He sat up. "Are you sure?"

"*Avialle-shadow, dark, curly hair, visibly pregnant. Yeah, pretty much.*"

"Fish heads for everyone. No, give 'em the whole fish! Where?"

"*Living in an apartment in Old Chicago, of all places. We don't think she's been there long. I've sent you the address, but it's easy to find. It's over a club on 37th Street at Giles.*"

"I'm there."

And he was, a subvocalized command taking him to the heart of the simworld more swiftly and certainly than any magic carpet. Sometimes it was okay being a sort of god.

37th Street was loud and lively. There were no Al-Capone-type gangsters in sight, which was what Orlando usually associated with Old Chicago, but the sidewalks were crowded with quite a lot of ordinary people of a wide array of skin-colors. Everybody seemed to be dressed up to go somewhere important, all the men in ties and the women in dresses. The apartment was above a club called Toothy's Free-For-All, which had a buzzing neon mouth grinning above the door. A half-dozen black men in handsome, big-shouldered suits stood underneath the overhang, smoking and talking and looking up at the overcast sky, and coincidentally blocking the apartment building's stairway next to the club's front door. Orlando wondered if the men might be gangsters. He wasn't even sure if they *had* African-American gangsters back in those days, but he didn't want to waste time on trouble. Unfortunately, he was wearing his only prepared sim for the Chicago world, which was inarguably Caucasian and, although reasonably tall and strong, meant more to be inconspicuous than to scare people into leaving him alone. But the men in front of the doorway seemed much more interested in the cigarette they were sharing, and hardly looked at him as he angled through and started up the narrow staircase.

"Looks like Missy got a gentleman caller," one said to Orlando's retreating back.

"He ain't the first caller for that little girl," said another and the men laughed quietly.

The corridor smelled faintly of mildew, and the hall carpets were so dark with years of dirt that Orlando couldn't make out the pattern, although he was pretty sure there was one. He knocked on the door with the number on it that Beezle had given him.

She opened it on the chain. Her eyes widened. She let him in, but almost as if she were sleepwalking: she was clearly frightened and confused. She wore a quilted, pale blue housecoat and her hair was unbound, spilling over her shoulders.

"Who are you?" she asked.

If she was confused, he was even more so. "Who are *you*?" But he knew who she was, she was an Avialle Jongleur shadow—the dark curly hair, the big eyes, and especially the voice had removed all doubt. And, as Beezle had noticed, she was quite visibly pregnant. The problem was, she wasn't *his* Avialle Jongleur shadow, and the differences weren't subtle. Other than a similarity in the hair and eyes, this was a completely different woman.

"My...my name is Violet Jergens." She seemed on the verge of tears. "What do you want? You look familiar."

He had no other ideas, so he went for broke. "I'm Orlando Gardiner."

For a moment her face almost seemed to light up, a child's Christmas-morning face of wonder and joy, then her smile faltered and was replaced by bafflement and anxiety once more. "I've...I've dreamed of the day Orlando would come back to me, when we would be a family. But I've never seen you before." She backed away, raising her hands. "Please, whoever you are, don't hurt me."

Orlando shook his head. He had been working on a theory that seemed very promising, but now he was confused again. "I'm sorry. I mean you no harm." Perhaps his original idea could still make sense. He decided to ask her the same question he would have put to Livia Bard. "Just tell me one thing. What does Orlando Gardiner look like?"

The question seemed to anger her, but after a moment her face changed. "I...it has been such a hard time for me, lately. It is all...I would..."

"You don't remember, do you?"

She was crying now. "I haven't been well."

He saw a chance to add another piece of information. "You're going to have to trust me now. May I...may I feel your stomach?"

"What?"

"I swear I won't harm you or the baby, Miss Jergens. Please. I promise I'll be gentle."

She didn't assent, but she did not back away as he moved closer. He slowly extended his hand and put it on the curve of her belly where it made her housecoat swell like a wind-filled sail. The bump was firm and, as far as he could tell, warmly alive.

He was not at all surprised this time when Violet Jergens abruptly disappeared from her own apartment like a soap bubble popping. He did not bother looking for her on 37th Street or anywhere else. He didn't need to find her, he was beginning to feel certain, because the chances were he'd be seeing her again, and others just like her.

Kunohara, he thought, *you owe me an apology.*

— ✳ —

"I don't get it," Sam said. "So now *another* of those Avialles thinks you're the father of her child?" She was talking to him on the phone because she was in the middle of finals and couldn't leave her studying very long. It was kind of nice, Orlando decided, just talking face to face from different places. It was a bit like being back in the real world, except Sam Fredericks was in West Virginia and he, at the moment, was in Atlantis, or rather hovering above its watery grave, tidying up a wave-motion problem before the city rose out of the ocean and started its cycle again. "What's going on?"

"I went back to see Kunohara. We think we've finally got the whole thing figured out." He couldn't help adding: "I figured it out myself, mostly, but he agrees, and he came up with the one part I couldn't wrap my head around. It was the Worldwalkers Society pregnancies that tipped me off—there's about a half-dozen of them now, by the way. I haven't figured out yet how to straighten out that part of the mess. They're all utterly scanned about it: accusations, denials, meetings falling apart and people threatening legal action. And the thing is, just like with me and the Avialle shadows, everybody's right."

"Hang on." Sam put her book down. "I've been in, like, a death-struggle with colligative properties all day for my chemistry final, but this is worse. What do you mean, everybody's right? You said you never saw her before, let alone played bumper cars with her."

Orlando shook his head. "I hadn't and I didn't. Or with the other one, and there'll almost certainly be more. And the Society chairman de Limoux didn't suddenly get sweet on his arch-enemy Maisie Macapan and give her the gift of motherhood, either—except he did, in a way."

"That's it—you've gone way far scanbark, Gardiner. You are barking all the way to the moon and back, then taking a little side trip to Bark Island. I have no idea what you're talking about."

"Kunohara got me thinking about it first. He was telling me off about mistaking appearance for reality, and he said something like, "Never underestimate how many strategies Life will use to perpetuate itself, Mr. Gardiner," in that kind of irritating way he has. Well, it irritates me, anyway. And that made me think about how this network has always been so complex. The Other, the original operating system, actually bred life from information viruses and antiviruses. And it made imitation children, based on real children. They may not have been alive, but they weren't just normal sims, either."

"Not it, *him*. The Other was a person, Orlando, despite all the horrible things the Grail people did to him. But he's gone now."

"Yeah, but the system was built around his brain, so his original impulses have an effect on everything about the network. And especially—and this is where I started to get my idea—his influence is utterly strong in the shadow-people, all those copies that he made and then released into the system."

"Like your Society folks, the ones who can travel from world to world through the gateways. And the Avialle-shadows."

"Who don't need gateways, although they can use them. In fact, other than me, the Avialle shadows are the only sims who can travel freely throughout the network. That makes them the most advanced of all the copies, really, even if a lot of them are a bit mental. So, me and the Avialle shadows are pretty much the most advanced things in the network. Are you starting to get the picture yet?"

Sam frowned. "Don't be all Professor Mysterioso. I was up practically all night last night studying *Chemistry: The Central Science* and I have a drastic headache."

"Well, I've been up several nights in a row studying biology, so who's zoomin' now?"

"Just explain."

"How about if I said that instead of 'most advanced', you could also call me and the Avialle-shadows the fittest creatures on the network. As in 'survival of the fittest'?"

"You mean it's like an evolution thing?"

"Yeah, in a sense, it's beginning to look that way. Somehow, even without the original operating system, this network still has a tendency toward...well, if not actually being alive, then to lifelike behavior. It wants to reproduce. In fact, now that the original brain of the network is gone, it may be more like a true organism. It's just trying things and if some of them work, it will continue. See, in some ways the people in the network, at least those like me and the society people who are more or less alive, we really *are* people. We think, we feel, we make plans. But to the network, we're more like cells in a single organism—or maybe like individuals, but in a hive culture. The network is the hive, and we're the drones and workers and all that. That's the example that Kunohara kept using, anyway. He's utterly excited about all this, by the way, even though it means he was wrong about the network being dead."

"He would like it, if it's got hives in it. But I still don't get this, Orlando. Are you saying that the system wanted you and the Avialle-shadows to reproduce together? But you'd never seen each other and she's already pregnant. That doesn't make sense."

"It does if you remember what Kunohara said, that we shouldn't confuse appearance and reality, that Life has lots of strategies. Just because we look like humans and the women appear to be pregnant in the ordinary, human way doesn't really mean it has to be anything like the same process. Think about flowers. They reproduce too, but sometimes the genetic information comes from two plants that are miles apart—they certainly don't ever see each other. But when humans or us humanoid sims think they're pregnant, the natural assumption is that it happened the old-fashioned way." He frowned. "Unlike normal human reproduction, I have to say the network's model is a little lacking in the motivations department—you know, the *we-do-it-because-it's-fun* stuff."

"Slow down, Sherlock. So the system is just...throwing together genetic material from you and other people in the system to make new people? But you don't *have* any genetic material." She suddenly looked horrified. "I'm sorry, Orlando, I didn't mean..."

"Don't worry, I've been thinking about this stuff for days. This game is weird and different and even a dead guy like me can play. See, it's not genetic material in the normal sense, it's what Kunohara calls the network's codification of us—the blueprints used for us virtual copies, which is the closest to genes we're going to have. It's just found a way to mix them up." Sam still looked worried, so he smiled. "As far as throwing the stuff together—yes, more or less, but not so random. A good reproductive system usually has some component of winners-get-to-mate in it. That's why my material showed up first, and it was paired with an Avialle-shadow—the fittest parents, remember?—and why more than one of the Avialles is pregnant by me. We have the most mobility, and in my case I have the most power—I'm not sure the network really factors that in, though—so my material...I'm going to need a new word, 'material' just doesn't do it...my *information* is the most attractive. There's only one me, but there are more than a few Avialle-shadows, and they'll tend to select for my information if they can get it."

"How? Does the network just...impregnate them with it?"

"No. This is another weird touch. I began to get a hint of it with the Society members. Two women got pregnant, and the Jongleur-shadow said he didn't do it. After my own experience, I wondered if he might not be telling the truth. So I went through the travel diaries of the three people involved and found out they almost hadn't ever been in the same worlds at the same time, let alone shacked up. In fact, they were only near each other during Worldwalkers meetings in the Wodehouse version of London, and the Jongleur-shadow had traveled back to his own home world right afterward, which meant there wasn't much chance for a regular, old-fashioned simulated conception and pregnancy. But they all *had* traveled through a lot of the same gateways between the network worlds, de Limoux first—he's the man—and then the women."

"Gateways? You mean it was the gateways?"

"We think so, yeah. Like the way bees brush up against pollen and then take it to another flower, or even the way some fish or insects sort of go to the same spot to deposit sperm and eggs, but they don't have to be there at the same time. The system is making male information—from people like me and de Limoux—reproductively active in some way, and then receptive females can pick it up as they pass through the gateways. In fact, me and Kunohara are going to have to turn down the success rate of the connections or the Society women are going to be pregnant all the time."

Sam was now waggling her hands in the way she did when she was having problems. "You mean you're going to let it happen? But...but what kind of babies are these women going to *have*? This is far scanny,

Orlando! I mean, if these pregnancies are like fish or insects or something, maybe they'll have...uck!...*swarms* of babies." For the second time in a few minutes, she looked stricken. "Will they even look like human children?"

"We think so. Even if the methodology is more like a hive or something, the network seems to be using a lot of human-type models for the actual pregnancies—it was programmed to simulate things like that already, remember. They seem to be moving along at the right rate, and the doctors in Wodehouse World who've checked the Society women only hear one baby heartbeat per mother. Also, there's a couple of other clues that kind of suggest they'll be human babies—or as close to it as the system can manage, considering that they're not working with real humans as parents, but copies, some of them pretty imperfect. One is that it seems like a lot of trouble to use the human sims within the system as information-donors—parents—if you're going to change the information a whole bunch afterward. It's easier just to use the human models of parents and children that are already built in, see? But the other reason is the answer to one of the questions that was bothering me even after I started to figure all this out. I couldn't get it, but Kunohara did."

"Go ahead. I'm just trying to swallow all this." Sam really did look as though she had been thumped on the head. "Dozens of women lining up all over the network to have your babies, Gardiner. You must be living on Aren't I Special Street."

"It'd be a lot more flattering if it was happening the old-fashioned way. Anyway, while we were putting this all together, I told Kunohara that two questions were still burning up my brain. One was why the Avialle-shadows knew my name even though we'd never actually met. Kunohara figures that's another proof we'll have human-type babies. Higher mammals, especially humans, have long childhoods, and they need lots of parental care. It was in the interest of the network's reproductive strategy to give both donors a chance of bonding together to raise the children, so the females get implanted with not just the male genetic information, but also the knowledge of who the father is and an ability to locate him, even if they don't really know how the pregnancy itself happened. That's how the Society women knew de Limoux was the daddy, and how the Avialle-shadows know they're carrying my children—I guess I have to call them that, even if I didn't really have anything to do with it."

"But that doesn't make sense, Orlando. I mean it does in a sort of way, but if the network really wants you to be involved with these children like a father, why would the mothers keep disappearing every time you hooked up with them?"

"See? Even after hours of rubbing your poor, sore brain against honors chemistry, Frederico, you're still smarter than you think you are. That was exactly my other question. Kunohara figured that one out, too. It's kind of embarrassing, really."

"Chizz. Do tell."

"Well, among higher mammals, especially the ones like us that need both parents, there's usually an elaborate courtship strategy that helps to bind the father to the mother and the coming offspring. Since there isn't anything remotely like courtship before the pregnancy in the network's reproductive strategy…well, the system came up with a substitute. Kind of courtship *after* the pregnancy. Like a mating dance, or—what did Kunohara call it, bees do it? A nuptial flight."

"Huh?"

"It only works really well for the Avialle-shadows because they can travel instantaneously—just vanish—but some of the Society women have also dropped out and disappeared in more conventional ways. *Post*-nuptial flight. This woman named Maisie Macapan has taken off for Imperial Rome, for instance. All this running-away is supposed to keep the father interested. He chases after them, right?" He shook his head. "Boy, did it work on me."

This was the hardest bit, and Orlando knew he was stalling. He thought about the last thing Sam had said before they disconnected.

"I guess it's good," she'd told him, "because you look utterly excited and interested. I was really beginning to worry about you—you seemed so depressed for a while. But what does it mean? How are you going to deal with being a father to all these babies, if that's how it really turns out? What are you going to do, Orlando?"

And the truth was, he didn't know—in fact, there were still hundreds of questions to be answered. How had the system arrived at this point, seemingly all at once? Had it been trying things out in some evolutionary laboratory-world hidden in the folds of the network? Was it conscious, as the old operating system had been, or was it simply working out old tendencies left over from the original system? Or was it actually moving toward a new kind of consciousness—would Orlando and the other sims eventually become cells in some greater living thing? Some of the questions were downright scary. The elation of solving the mystery hadn't entirely faded, but he knew the reality of this wasn't going to be anywhere near as simple as explaining it to people. Not that explaining it was ever going to be easy—especially the explanation he was about to give, which was why he was stalling.

If there are dozens of children just from me, I can't be a full-time father, obviously. We may have to turn the process off after this first group, at least as far as my own information—otherwise, what if the network plans to keep doing this all the time, generation after generation? Like I'm the queen bee, the king bee, whatever, and it's going to make thousands of kids with me as a parent? He had some time to think about that, at least, to discuss the problem with Kunohara, since there were a limited number of potential mothers and the pregnancies seemed to be lasting as long as in the real world. The entomologist was in rapture over all these new developments, and was hurrying to settle his court case so that he could throw himself into investigating the new paradigm.

Easy for him—his information isn't copied into the system. He's not going to be a dad to dozens of kids, to have all that responsibility. But if there was ever anyone in a position to protect his children, it was Orlando Gardiner, network ranger. After all, like they used to say about the sheriffs in the Wild West, *I'm all the law there is this side of reality.*

God, I don't know. I'll figure it out. I've got friends. It'll be weird, but I'm dead and I'm on my way to visit my folks, so how much weirder can things get? It'll be an adventure.

He couldn't get over it. *I'm going to be a father! Me!* It was terrifying and exciting. What would the children be like? What would happen to the network as this first generation grew and then reproduced themselves, creating ever more complex patterns of inheritance? No one in the history of humanity had ever experienced anything like this. *Unknown country. It's all unknown country ahead.*

"I'm going now, Beezle," he announced. "I don't want to be interrupted unless the universe as we know it is actually collapsing, okay? Take messages."

"No problem, boss. I'll just hang out here in imaginary space and play with the cats."

Orlando summoned up the connection for his parents' house. This time he would even be willing to wear that horrid plasteel scarecrow. After all their work arranging that surreal and touching birthday party at Rivendell, he felt he owed Conrad and Vivien a little something. Even more importantly, he wanted them in a good mood when he told them that against all logic, they were apparently going to be grandparents after all.

Maybe forty or fifty times.

Rite

Just a piece, although more personal than you'd think at first. I wrote it, if I remember truly, when a friend's son turned fifteen and we were talking about the lack of rituals in our society for young men. I read it to my son when he was seven or eight and his only question was, "I don't get it—were there spiders or something?"

But he will get it someday. I've cursed him with the worrying-genes.

There was a boy whose father had died. He did not know the way of things, so he went to his grandfather and asked him: "When will I become a man?"

"Are you afraid of the dark?" the old man asked him. The boy nodded, more than a little shamefaced. "So," the grandfather said. "When you are no longer frightened of the darkness, come and tell me."

A year went by, and one day the boy came up the path to his grandfather's house.

"My mother was frightened last night because there was a strange noise outside the house," the boy said proudly. "I told her not to be foolish, that there was nothing out there to harm her."

The old man looked at him. "So you are no longer afraid of the dark?"

The boy started to speak, then hung his head. "I am still afraid." He went away again.

Another year passed. One day, the boy made his way back up the path. "Look, Grandfather," he said. "I am as tall as you now, and I am getting very strong—Mother said so. I can lift up the sack of flour that only Father used to lift, and put it in the store-room."

The old man nodded. "You are indeed almost grown."

"And if the things that are in the dark tried to get me or Mother, thieves or ghosts or monsters—why, I'd fight them! I can fight anything, because now I'm as strong as Father was."

"So you are no longer afraid of the darkness?" his grandfather asked.

The boy made his hands into fists and stared angrily, but at last he opened his hands again. "I am still afraid." He said good-bye very quietly and went back down the path.

Another year passed, and part of a second, before the boy returned. "I have been away," he told his grandfather. "I worked for a farmer outside the big town to the west, and made friends with some fellows who studied at the school there." His grandfather nodded, but said nothing. "And I have realized," the boy went on soberly, "that I was young and stupid before. Night is only the other half of day, and without shadow there can be no light. So darkness is a part of everything, and nothing to be feared."

The old man nodded. "Those are good things to know."

The boy's face turned bitter. "But I am still afraid of the dark." He went away.

Yet one more year turned, and the boy at last climbed the pathway to his grandfather's house again. "I have met a girl," he told the old man, grinning at the thought of her. "She is beautiful, and clever—and she thinks I am beautiful and clever too!"

His grandfather smiled.

"I want to marry her," the boy said. "And have a house, and a garden, and someday we will make children. But if I have those things, they can be taken away from me. Houses can burn, gardens dry and go to seed, and children—they could be stolen from their cribs by animals, or grow up and run away, or take sick and die." He looked down at the ground unhappily, then shook his head. "Still, that is what she and I will do, because we love each other." He turned back to the old man. "But Grandfather, I think now that I will always be afraid of the dark."

The old man took his hand and kissed him. "My blessings, Grandson" he said. "Now you are a man."